ALSO BY RONALD H. BALSON

A Place to Hide
An Affair of Spies
Defending Britta Stein
Eli's Promise
Karolina's Twins
The Girl from Berlin
The Trust
Saving Sophie
Once We Were Brothers

THE RIGHTEOUS

THE RIGHTEOUS

Ronald H. Balson

ST. MARTIN'S PRESS
NEW YORK

This is a work of fiction. All of the characters, organizations, and events portrayed in this novel are either products of the author's imagination or are used fictitiously.

First published in the United States by St. Martin's Press, an imprint of St. Martin's Publishing Group

EU Representative: Macmillan Publishers Ireland Ltd, 1st Floor, The Liffey Trust Centre, 117–126 Sheriff Street Upper, Dublin 1, DO1 YC43

THE RIGHTEOUS. Copyright © 2025 by Ronald H. Balson. All rights reserved. Printed in the United States of America. For information, address St. Martin's Publishing Group, 120 Broadway, New York, NY 10271.

www.stmartins.com

The Library of Congress Cataloging-in-Publication Data is available upon request.

ISBN 978-1-250-37308-3 (hardcover)
ISBN 978-1-250-37309-0 (ebook)

The publisher of this book does not authorize the use or reproduction of any part of this book in any manner for the purpose of training artificial intelligence technologies or systems. The publisher of this book expressly reserves this book from the Text and Data Mining exception in accordance with Article 4(3) of the European Union Digital Single Market Directive 2019/790.

Our books may be purchased in bulk for specialty retail/wholesale, literacy, corporate/premium, educational, and subscription box use. Please contact MacmillanSpecialMarkets@macmillan.com.

First Edition: 2025

10 9 8 7 6 5 4 3 2 1

THE RIGHTEOUS

6 September 1943

Fate has willed us apart . . . Yet the same fate has also willed that during the years of our people's greatest misery, your mother is fulfilling a great mission in order to ease this terrible suffering. If I survive this difficult period, I think I will be able to say that I have not lived in vain. In this spirit you must bear this separation. The suffering of the People of Israel stands above any personal pain.

—Gisi Fleischmann in Slovakia,
to her daughter Aliza (Lizi), in *Eretz Israel*

CHAPTER ONE

JULIA POWERS GAZED out of the DC-3 window at the Michigan landscape below and breathed a sigh of relief. The US Army plane would soon circle over Romulus, just west of Detroit, and Julia's impossible journey would come to an end. She knew that her mother and father would be there to greet her; she had alerted them by telephone. It would be a joyous occasion, so unlike six years ago when twenty-three-year-old Julia left Detroit with her then-boyfriend, Spencer. He was in a band, and they had dates in Europe. She could still see the tears in her mother's eyes when she kissed her goodbye. Her father had refused to come to the train station. "What a waste of a University of Michigan college degree," he'd said.

After seven weeks on their European tour, Julia lost interest in Spencer. The band members were an unsavory bunch, ill-mannered, and unsociable, not to mention their offensive hygiene. In two of the cities, they didn't even have a hotel room, and they stayed all night at a bar. Add to that: Spencer was unfaithful. Julia left the tour in Amsterdam.

Often referred to as "the Venice of the North," Amsterdam had four times as many bridges as Venice, 1,700 of them, spanning 165 canals. Julia immediately fell in love with its charm. Although her father offered to bring her home, no small undertaking, Julia decided to stay. She rented a small apartment, took a class in conversational Dutch, and was fortunate to land a job as a receptionist at the US consulate. That was 1937.

As the years passed, she was promoted up the ladder from receptionist/clerk to foreign service officer. She worked directly with Consul General

Frank Lee. Being bright and personable, it was easy for Julia to blend into Amsterdam's social scene. With her blond hair pulled back, her big brown eyes that twinkled, and her captivating smile, it didn't take long before Julia found herself involved again, this time with Willem, whose family owned a hotel in downtown Amsterdam. The two of them took advantage of the joys that Amsterdam had to offer, and Willem even had a boat. Life couldn't have been more agreeable. She formed several close friendships at the consulate, including Melissa Mitchell and Theodore "Teddy" Hartigan, who worked in different roles: Melissa in secretarial and Teddy as administrative assistant to Consul General Lee.

She wasn't oblivious to the tense situation in the neighboring countries. Hitler's racial tirades caused a turmoil in Germany, but that was in another country, and Julia did not intend to go there. The Netherlands' eastern border was Germany's western border, but the city of Berlin was hundreds of miles away and so was the German army. Julia had been in Europe less than a year when, in March 1938, Hitler moved on Austria. Was he finished, as he said he was, or would he take his army somewhere else?

The press releases from the US State Department were generally silent about Hitler and Germany. His cruel measures to isolate and harm Jewish people barely made official reports. As news of Nazi oppression became better known in Holland, mostly from reporters, it was hard for Julia to understand how it served US interests to bury the news back home. Her communications with friends and family revealed how little they knew about the German persecution in Europe. But Julia knew. She heard about it every day at the consulate. Immigration was her job.

The consulate was beset with applications from hundreds, if not thousands, of German refugees. After managing to escape from Germany and cross the border into Holland, the families would line up at the consulate for days on end and wait for their turn to apply for their US visas. The stories they told about their lives under the Nazi occupation were frightening, and the cause of many sleepless nights. As the refugees desperately pleaded for visas, Julia, Teddy, and the consulate staff found that their hands were tied. The State Department, following US immigration policy, applied restrictive quotas and turned almost all of them away. There were only so many visas available, a fraction of the number requested, and they quickly reached their limit. Yearly visa quotas for each European country had been set by Congress years before. The formulas were incomprehensible. The number of visas available for applicants from any given country was directly related to that country's percentage of the United States' population, all as of the year 1890. America had been founded and was largely populated by people from Great Britain and Ireland, and thus, the number of visas available for applicants from those countries was very generous. But other countries had a relatively small number of immigrants relative to the larger population. Julia quickly learned that US visas available for refugees from Germany, Poland, Austria, and Hungary reached their limit in the first few weeks of each year.

As the days and weeks passed, Julia witnessed the tensions increase for Jewish residents throughout Europe, even in Holland, which was considered neutral and safe. In January 1939, in a speech at the Reichstag, Hitler stated that an outbreak of war would mean the end of European Jewry, and it didn't escape Julia that he used the term *European*, not just *German* Jewry. Then, in September 1939, Germany turned to the east and invaded Poland. Because they had mutual defense pacts with Poland, England and France declared war on Germany. Julia worried that the war put Holland in danger of attack, but Willem assured her that Holland had not agreed to be a member of any defense pact. It was a neutral country. It had been that way during the First World War, and it was that way now. Germany had no reason to invade the Netherlands, and she would be safe. Besides, Julia worked for the US State Department. Employees of the consulate had diplomatic immunity.

No matter the assurance of neutrality, the devil came to Holland less than a year later, in June 1940. Within a matter of weeks, Nazi soldiers had conquered the entire country. Queen Wilhelmina and her cabinet escaped to England, and the Netherlands surrendered. Hitler appointed

Arthur Seyss-Inquart, an evil, soulless monster, to rule Holland as Reichskommissar. It didn't take long for him to commence enforcement of Hitler's racial laws against Holland's Jews.

In 1940, the US was not yet a declared enemy, and the State Department ordered the consulate to stay open in Amsterdam, but the issuance of immigration visas ceased. Living in Holland exposed Julia to the harsh conditions the German dictator inflicted on the Jewish citizens. Julia was not Jewish, and the restrictions didn't apply directly to her, but she wasn't unfeeling either. She had Jewish friends. She had a heart.

In the fall of 1941, the situation grew dire; it wouldn't be long before the consulate would close. Even before America declared war against the Axis powers, Consul General Lee was told to shut down the Amsterdam consulate. The American staff members were all given passage back in an army plane, the last and final way out of Holland. Julia and Teddy Hartigan were not on that plane. Teddy had married a Dutch woman who didn't qualify for a visa, and Julia had Willem. But for Julia, her romantic feelings once again had led her into a relationship that soon fizzled out.

Since Julia and Teddy were to be the last US consulate employees left in the Netherlands, and because they were knowledgeable about US politics, and because they were adept in operating the consulate's radio communication equipment, Frank Lee offered them a dangerous job. They could live in Amsterdam as undercover intelligence agents with the OSS, the Office of Strategic Services. They would be given a safe house and a reasonably sufficient salary.

In that role, over the next eighteen months, Julia and Teddy supplied invaluable information to the OSS, and also to England's MI6. It was the most dangerous, stress-filled time of Julia's life, but rewarding. She and Teddy both became involved in trying to rescue the lives of Jewish families who otherwise would have been arrested and transported to death camps. In 1943, the Nazis ordered the arrest and transport of every single Jew, not only in the Netherlands but in other occupied countries as well. Julia and Teddy met and joined with some extraordinary individuals who had dedicated their lives to making a difference. Julia was proud to have played a part in the rescue of hundreds, if not thousands, of

Dutch Jews, including almost a thousand babies and toddlers rescued from the Amsterdam nursery known as "the crèche."

By the summer of 1943, other than the ones who had managed to escape or find a hiding place, the entire Jewish population of the Netherlands had been arrested and deported to concentration camps. Over one hundred thousand Dutch Jews. Hitler and Seyss-Inquart smugly declared that the Netherlands was now *Judenfrei*. The SS then sharpened its claws and went on a hunt to find those who had assisted the Jews.

Julia spent her days and nights working for the OSS underground and trying to stay alive. By late fall, pictures of Julia and Teddy had been circulated and posted in police stations, SS offices, and other public places. It was only a matter of time.

Julia, along with Teddy, his wife, Sara, and their two adopted Jewish children were hiding in the home of Sara's parents in a wooded area outside Utrecht when they learned of a miraculous escape opportunity. With the SS closing in, they came into contact with a British undercover agent who had plans to pilot a rebuilt Fokker G.1, painted to resemble a German Luftwaffe Messerschmitt, across the North Sea into England. The hopes were that the Nazis would be fooled into believing the plane was one of their own and not shoot it down.

The disguise worked. Julia, Teddy, and his new family climbed into the Fokker and took off for England. Julia witnessed several SS soldiers wave to them as they flew overhead. The Fokker crossed the Holland coast and landed safely at an RAF airfield in Bradwell Bay, England. From there, they were shuttled to London. After several days assisting OSS and MI6, Undersecretary Sumner Welles arranged to fly them from London to Washington, DC, in a military aircraft.

Though Julia was physically and mentally exhausted, and though she wanted nothing more than to go home to her family in Detroit and collapse, she was forced to undergo three weeks of State Department debriefing in Washington. Who were her contacts? How many Wehrmacht divisions were stationed in northern Holland? What was the strength of the Nazi force on the Belgium border? What were their North Sea defenses? What SS transmissions had she intercepted regarding troop movements? It seemed odd to Julia that none of the State Department questions concerned the welfare of European citizens.

On her last night in Washington, she and Teddy were honored with a celebratory dinner, where they were each awarded a Distinguished Service Medal from Sumner Welles. It was enclosed in a frame with a certificate that read, "In Defense of Liberty." During the dinner, Undersecretary Welles took Julia and Teddy aside. The war was far from over, he said, and they had no obligation to continue their service for OSS, but they did have invaluable experience and the US would always benefit from their service. Welles understood Julia's desire to go home to her family and her familiar surroundings, but should she decide to come back, there would always be a place for her in the State Department, and he would make sure it was on this side of the Atlantic. Julia smiled warmly, took his hand, and said goodbye. She was confident it was a final handshake. She was wrong.

CHAPTER TWO

JULIA'S PLANE BEGAN its descent into the Wayne County Airport on the outskirts of Detroit, and she smiled. After a few bumps, the DC-3's propellors came to a stop, and Julia's mother and father ran out onto the tarmac to greet their daughter. Julia was home.

The ride into Detroit was a passage from one world to another. Julia was back in the land of her childhood, eons away from the insanities of war. They turned the corner onto Stuyvesant Street in the Dexter-Linwood neighborhood, and her heart skipped a beat. There stood her house, a four-bedroom, brick-and-stone Tudor with sloped roofs and a portico entrance, like so many other houses on her block. There were no canals, no bridges, no Nazi orders pasted on lampposts. There was space between the houses, green grass to play on, and sidewalks to ride a bike. She could even take a walk to Dexter Avenue for an ice cream cone without fear of being searched. If she turned the corner, she might see one of her friends. So unlike Amsterdam, where she never knew what lurked around the corner. It could very well be the Gestapo.

America was at war, and it was far away, but there were constant reminders on the radio, in magazines, and in the newspapers. It wasn't as though she could forget about the war—it had taken its toll—but the media kept it right in the front of her consciousness, all day and through the night. Her parents, Ruth and Todd, had so many questions, but Julia begged them to please wait and give her time to adjust. Maybe for a little while.

When she first arrived home, she walked around her house touching things, a couch or a table. Her mom had done some decorating in her absence, but Julia's room was just how she'd left it. Five years had passed not knowing whether they would ever see Julia again, but Ruth had kept Julia's room spick-and-span. Julia's dresses were where she'd hung them, her personal things were where she'd put them. Her U of M yearbook sat on her bedstand. It was more than Julia could handle. She lay on her bed, buried her face in her pillow, and cried. Before long, she was fast asleep.

Ruth's knock on the door brought Julia back to reality. She had been floating in a kaleidoscope of memories. First, she was urgently sending coded messages to OSS from the second floor of the Amsterdam safe house. Then she was running from the crèche, holding a little child in each of her arms. Then there were the gunshots, the rapid rat-a-tat, and the shouts to halt in German. She was shaking, and Ruth walked in to calm her. "It's all right," Ruth said, rubbing Julia's back. "You're *here* now. You're not *there* anymore."

At dinner, Julia asked if any of her friends had inquired about her. "Oh, all the time," Ruth said. "Carolann came by with her young daughter the other day. Cutest thing. She was pushing her in a stroller. We've had such a nice fall, you know." Julia smiled and asked if Carolann still lived in the neighborhood. "Of course," Ruth said. "Where else would she live?"

Ruth continued, "I saw Geena the other day. She has two darling children now, and they both look just like their mother. Carbon copy. Same dark, curly hair. Same dimples on their cheeks. Geena and her husband, Roger, bought a house on Ohio Street, near Six Mile Road. He works at the Ford plant."

Julia's eyes glazed over. How much of her life had she missed? Why did she ever leave? But then, she had served her country. She had saved lives. A lot of lives. She had made a difference, and she had a medal and plaque to prove it. She told her mom that she couldn't wait to see them all, and then she thought about Theresa. Julia and Theresa were the best of friends and classmates at Michigan. "Have you heard anything about Theresa?" she asked. "I've been thinking about her a lot. She comes from Hungary."

Ruth nodded. She reached into Julia's desk drawer and took out a piece of paper with Theresa's phone number. "She's still in Ann Arbor. She told me to give this to you when I got the chance." Ruth hung her head a bit. "She's not in a good way these days. She hasn't heard from her folks in a long time, and she's worried sick. They're Jewish, you know."

Julia nodded. "I do know. I'll call her right away."

THE NEXT WEEKEND, the two best friends met for lunch. They hugged, they cried, they shook their heads at the insanity of it all. "What have you heard about your family?" Julia finally said. "I remember meeting your mom and dad in Ann Arbor each year between 1933 and 1935. They were so nice. Are they okay?"

Theresa's jaw quivered. "I think so, but I don't know for sure. I wish I knew. My brother, my sister, my whole family." She paused. "I haven't talked to them in well over a year. As far as I know, they have phone service, but it's only local. So they can't call me, and we don't get any mail from people in enemy nations."

"Are they still in Budapest?"

"God, I hope so, but I don't even know that for sure."

"I'm sorry. There are a lot of Jews in Hungary, aren't there?"

Theresa nodded. "About eight hundred fifty thousand—one of the largest Jewish populations in Europe. I don't have to tell you these are dangerous times for Jewish families in Europe, although I still believe that Jews remain safe in Hungary. That's what they told me the last time we spoke. I haven't read anything to the contrary, but here in America, we don't get any news about Hungary."

"I'm sorry, I know you're worried. That's understandable."

"My father had a mild heart attack four years ago, but he seems to have recovered. The rest of my family—my brother, my sister, even my mother—were all healthy the last time we talked. And my Uncle Morris, my Aunt Pearl, my cousins, it's a pretty close family. Every day, I pray that they're all safe, but when I read what's going on in the rest of Europe, it tears my heart out."

"I just returned from the Netherlands," Julia said with tightened lips and a sad shake of her head. "Pray it doesn't ever come to that in Hungary."

"For a long time, we didn't get any news about what was happening to Jews in Europe," Theresa said. "I think it was suppressed. Then I read a story about Holland in the *New York Post*. I read that beginning last summer, the Nazis arrested all of the Jews and took them out of Amsterdam in trains, but the article didn't say where they were taken or what happened. That's as far as the story went."

"Well, the story is true, you can believe it. I was an eyewitness. The SS went through the city, collected as many Jews as they could find, stored them in the community theater building, and then shipped them out in boxcars. We were told it was to Westerbork, a camp in northern Holland, but Westerbork turned out to be just a transit camp on the way to somewhere else. I don't know where they ended up afterward. The rumors of prison camps are pretty awful. Anyway, that was about the time we left. Pray that scenario never happens in Hungary."

"God forbid," Theresa said. "The last I heard, while we still had long-distance phone service, the Hungarian government wasn't doing anything to physically restrain or mistreat our people. There were no mass arrests, no deportations, no murders. Even though Hungary is militarily aligned with Germany, they don't copy the Nazi racial laws. I'm not going to say that there are no prejudices. When I talked to my dad, he said that Hungary enacted some laws that restricted Jews in certain professions. For example, he said that only twenty percent of a certain workforce was allowed to be Jewish, and Jews can't enroll in certain schools. Jews are unwelcome in certain neighborhoods, that sort of thing, but nothing like the pogroms Jews faced in Poland and other places. The Budapest Jewish community is strong. What worries me the most is what's happening in the countries around Hungary. Germany has taken over so many countries." She counted them off on her fingers. "Austria, Slovakia, Romania, Croatia. So, how long can we keep the Nazis from occupying Hungary as well? Germany hasn't sent any troops into Hungary, as far as I know."

"They're on the same side," Julia said. "They're allies. Why would Hitler invade an ally?"

Theresa shrugged. "You tell me. Why does Hitler do anything? Yes, they are allies on the battlefield, just like they were twenty years ago. Hungary is a member of the Axis powers, but we're not made of the same cloth as Germany. Miklós Horthy, Hungary's regent, has thus far refused to impose Nazi oppression on Jews. He has never ordered innocent Jews to be put onto trains or sent off to camps, if you can imagine such a thing." She shrugged. "As far as I know. At least that's the way it was a couple years ago."

"I don't have to imagine, Theresa," Julia said. "I saw it all taking place in Holland during the last several months. It was the most inhuman thing I've ever seen. Children, toddlers, even little babies, led by armed soldiers and put into those boxcars to be sent off to a camp. Can you even conceive of someone so heartless as to sentence an innocent baby to a prison camp where it will probably die?" Her voice froze.

Julia tried to take a minute to compose herself. She took a few deep breaths. Her jaw quivered. Visions flashed in her mind, and for a moment, she was staring down the street in occupied Amsterdam. *When will these visions go away?* she thought. *When will I get over the shakes?*

Julia finally said, "We fought it, Theresa. We knew we couldn't win, but we fought as hard as we could to save as many Jews as we could, especially the children, but it wasn't nearly enough. We knew that we had to find places where Jewish families could hide from the SS, or else they would be captured and sent to die. That's what underground rescuers did. We searched for basements, attics, barns, toolsheds, you name it. We split up families when we had to. You couldn't put a family of five into someone's attic. Parents gave up their little children, Theresa. It was so sad. They gave us their children to be placed with a non-Jewish family who was willing to adopt them. Otherwise, those little children would have been killed. We found good, loving Christian parents who would take in an extra child, or even two. Or maybe three. We did whatever we could until the babies were all gone: adopted or taken away. All those little Jewish babies." Julia's voice caught again in her throat, and the words were blocked. She blotted her tears. It was too soon.

"I'm so sorry, Julia. I didn't want to bring it all up. Your mother told me what a hero you were, and I'm so proud to have you as my friend. What baffles me is why people in Nazi countries go along with it. Why do they turn their heads? Why do they look the other way? Don't they have a conscience? A heart?"

"They don't all turn their heads, not all of them, but you're right—Hitler's racism wouldn't go anywhere if people didn't support it. They buy into it. They chant Nazi slogans. Hitler speaks to cheering crowds."

"As far as I know, that doesn't happen in Hungary," Theresa said. "I hope and believe that Hungarian people will stand up for their countrymen. All of their countrymen. So far, Jews are safe there."

"Well, I hope you're right, but don't be too complacent. It was safe for Jews in Amsterdam too until 1940, when Hitler invaded and appointed Seyss-Inquart as his governor. Almost immediately, he imposed rules and regulations that had the effect of limiting Jewish freedom, and the non-Jewish majority just looked the other way. They went along with it. Maybe they were afraid, maybe they didn't give a damn. There were signs in restaurant windows, 'No Jews Allowed.' Small steps at first, then bigger. Soon the Jews were separated and forced to live in small cities, where they could be rounded up and sent away. If you talk to the average non-Jewish Dutch citizen, and I did, he would respond by saying there was nothing he could do. He was only one man against the power of the Nazis. And maybe a lot of the Dutch felt that way, but there were plenty of people who felt otherwise, good people, and they stood up. Just keep praying that Hungarians stand up too."

Theresa agreed. "I have to believe that Hungarians are different. Judaism is a recognized religion there. Jews are well integrated and economically prosperous. They own over half of Budapest. Anyway, I'd hate to think that such a nightmare could ever come to Hungary. I love Hungary, and Budapest is such a lovely city. I'd love to take you there someday, when all this madness is over, and show you around. I know you'd fall in love with it."

"You didn't go home to Budapest after we graduated, did you? There wasn't any war going on then. It was safe in 1938, wasn't it?"

Theresa shook her head. "It depended on where you lived. It was safe in Hungary, but not across the river in Austria. That's where the Anschluss took place in March 1938. But I didn't stay at Michigan because I was afraid to go home. I stayed so that I could go to graduate school and get my master's degree. I always wanted to be a teacher. European history, of course."

"Of course."

Theresa nodded. "Just last week, I became an associate professor at the U of M." She paused and said, "There was a ceremony, and it was a wonderful day, but it all took place under a cloud, if you know what I mean. My parents couldn't attend, and there's no doubt they would have come if they could. It broke my heart; they were the reason that I received my diploma in the first place. My father was the guiding force. He sent me to the University of Michigan to study history. He loves history too. He used to read history stories to me at bedtime when I was a little child. Edited, of course. Just the good parts."

"I'm sorry for you, Theresa. I know they would have been here. After this horrible war is over, I'm sure they'll come to the ceremony when you are promoted to full professor. I remember your mom and dad so well. Your father is a doctor, isn't he?"

Theresa nodded. "A surgeon, but he doesn't practice full-time anymore. He has slowed down quite a bit. Now he's in an advisory position. He's called in to help on difficult cases, and he's on the board of a well-known Budapest hospital, Semmelweis University Hospital." She sat back and gazed up. "I'd give anything just to hear from them, Julia, just to know that they're all right. I want to know what's going on with my older brother, Sammy, and my younger sister, Becca." Theresa paused as a few tears rolled down her cheek. She bit her lip. "I can't help it, Julia, I'm so damned worried."

Julia gently placed her arm around Theresa. "You have a right to be worried, Theresa. I would be too. But I'm thinking of something; maybe there's a way for me to help you get information about your family," Julia said with raised eyebrows. "My friend Teddy is still in Washington working for the State Department. They have contacts all over the world. Maybe he can find out what's happening to the Hungarian Jewish community or maybe even learn something about your family. Write down their names and addresses, and I'll give Teddy a call."

"That would be wonderful," Theresa said. "I would really appreciate it." She took a sip of her drink and said, "Let's change the subject. What is Julia Powers going to do with herself now that she's back home?"

Julia tipped her head to one side as she shrugged, what her friends referred to as Julia's tilted shrug. "I don't know," she said. "My father owns a clothing store, and with the holidays approaching, I know he can use the extra help. That's probably what I'll do for a while. You know, technically I'm still an officer in the State Department." She smiled with a twinkle in her eyes. "I have special skills."

Theresa laughed. "So I've heard. Are you thinking about getting back into it anytime soon?"

Julia grimaced. "I don't think so. Undersecretary Sumner Welles told me I was welcome to come back, but I don't know what he had in mind. Maybe something in Washington, something to do with transmitting coded messages and monitoring the OSS wires. That's what I was doing in Amsterdam. But I'm not ready to go back. The whole thing has taken its toll on me, and I can't see myself jumping back into it. Not right away." Julia looked out in the direction of the university quadrangle. "Do you ever hear anything from our campus buddies?"

"Sometimes," Theresa said. "Mostly the ones who live around here. Walter is a councilman. Glynnis runs a boutique in Midtown."

"Ha!" Julia said. "That figures. Do you ever hear from Rudy?"

"Hmm." Theresa grinned. "Raoul Wallenberg. I should have figured that you'd ask about him. You two were a number at one time. You knew he was enrolled in Michigan's school of architecture, didn't you?"

"Of course I knew. He graduated with honors, and he won the American Institute of Architects silver medal. It's only awarded to the student with the highest scholastic standing in the architecture school. Professor Slusser said Rudy was one of the brightest students he had ever taught in thirty years at the University of Michigan. Rudy was brilliant."

"And good-looking?" Theresa said with a grin. "Wasn't he that too?"

Julia's hand covered her mouth. "That's for sure, but after graduation, he left town, and we lost touch."

Theresa raised her eyebrows. "I think I know the reason. It was called Spencer, the bass player."

Julia exhaled. "What a mistake he was. When Rudy graduated, it was still in the winter term, and I had a semester to go. He went back to Sweden; I was in Ann Arbor. Rudy was over there and I was here, and I had to go out with someone. Anyway, Rudy and I stopped communicating."

Theresa struggled to keep a straight face. "Too busy with the Spencer band?"

"Stop it."

"Well, I kept up with Rudy, even if you didn't. We corresponded for a while," said Theresa. "When he returned to Stockholm, he found out that Sweden wouldn't recognize his Michigan architecture degree, and they wouldn't give him a license to practice. They would have required him to go back to school in Stockholm and take a lot more courses before he could be licensed."

"That's too bad."

"Right. He didn't want to do it; he was sick of school. You know he was a free-spirited kind of guy."

"You don't have to tell me," Julia said with a smile. "Sometimes we would dream about going on trips to romantic places all over the world. We were going to go to Hawaii someday."

"Well, I don't know how romantic it was, but Rudy left Stockholm and went to South Africa. He was there for about six months, and then he went to Palestine. He sent me postcards from Jerusalem. He said, 'Theresa, you should join me. This place is fabulous. There are some great Jewish sites for you to see.'"

"That sounds so much like Rudy, like it was a piece of cake to jump on a ship and take it halfway around the world to Jerusalem."

Theresa smiled with a faraway look in her eyes. "I know, but it sounded like a really good idea. Anyway, after Palestine, he returned to Stockholm and worked as an apprentice for a Jewish banker from Holland.

The banker was a friend of his grandfather Gustav, who suddenly died shortly thereafter. A real tragedy."

Julia had a pained expression. "Poor Rudy. You know, his real father died before he was even born. He was practically raised by his grandfather. Grandpa Gustav was a prominent Swede, and he mentored Rudy all his life. I was sure Rudy was going to be successful. But then in my last semester, I got sidetracked. Rudy was gone, and I met Spencer, and . . ."

"I know. Out of sight, out of mind."

"I'm afraid that's true, but I was twenty-two years old, and Spencer was in a band, and he was fun." Julia hesitated. "At least he was for a while."

"Well, after Grandpa Gustav died, Rudy wandered around Stockholm, took a couple of jobs that didn't work out well, and was really down on himself," Theresa said. "He would write me a letter every now and then that sounded glum. Then his Uncle Jacob Wallenberg, a very successful industrialist, took Rudy under his wing. Jacob set Rudy up with another successful man named Kálmán Lauer. Mr. Lauer owns an export-import firm, and Rudy is now trading between Sweden and countries in central Europe. And that's all the Rudy news I've got."

"He's working in central Europe? In 1943? You mean like Germany, Slovakia, Austria, even Hungary? He's there? You have to be kidding me. He could be killed."

Theresa shrugged with a tip of her head to the side, which made Julia laugh. Julia pointed and said, "Aha." A tilted shrug. "You've got it down pat."

"Guilty," said Theresa. "Rudy is traveling through central Europe, almost all of which is controlled by Nazi Germany, but he's under the protection of the Swedish government. He has diplomatic immunity, which is recognized by Germany and all of its satellite countries."

Julia sat back. "What a life, and to think I could have been part of it."

The afternoon crowd was starting to filter in, and the two friends were getting looks from the hostess.

"I think she wants our table," Julia said. She rose and placed a few bills on the table. "I'll give Teddy a call and see if I can learn anything about Budapest."

CHAPTER THREE

"THIS IS THEODORE Hartigan," said the voice on the phone.

"Well, I sure hope so, because that's who I called. This is Julia."

"Ah, Julie, what a surprise. I mean what a *pleasant* surprise. I thought you would stay away from anything governmental and lie low, at least for a while."

"True. That's the plan. We'll see how well it works. I called the State Department looking for you, and they told me that you had been transferred to the Treasury Department. I thought they were kidding. You said you were staying in Washington to work for Sumner Welles and Frank Lee in State."

"I was," Teddy said. "Sumner believed my talents were best applied working for Treasury in a division called Foreign Funds Control. It's a long story. Anyway, it's great to hear from you. Sara and I both miss you. How are things in Detroit?"

"Weird. I don't think I'm as resilient as you are. Amsterdam was rough. What they did to all those people. It's hard for me to put it all out of my mind. I hear voices in my head. Last night, I dreamed I saw Walter Suskind walking twenty or so little toddlers down the sidewalk behind a Nazi guard. When he arrived at the crèche, Sara's sister was there to let them in."

"Ooh, that's hard. Do you get those dreams very often?"

"All the time. Don't you? It's difficult for me to adjust to being at home."

"Then don't adjust. Come on back, and let's keep fighting them together. We could use your help."

"Well, not right now," Julia said. "I need to step away."

"I understand, please believe me. When we arrived from Europe, my plan was to take a few weeks off, maybe go to the shore and relax, but I couldn't do it. Like you, I couldn't unwind. So, I decided not to try. I can't just sit back and watch those Nazi bastards kill innocent civilians, even babies, and do nothing. It has been revealed here that Reinhard Heydrich and Adolf Eichmann met in secret almost two years ago at a suburb of Berlin called Wannsee, and devised a plan for the sole purpose of murdering all of Europe's Jews. All, can you believe it? One hundred percent. Eleven million innocent human beings. *Judenfrei*, they called it. Why? Would it help them on the battlefield? No. Would it help them win the war? Hell no. Hitler has some sick hatred of people that worship God as Jews. Like those Nazis even know what the Jewish religion is about. Did they read the Torah? They don't worship anything except Hitler."

Julia heard the rage in Teddy's voice and understood why he remained in Washington. "We were the witnesses," she said. "We saw what they did in Holland."

"That's why I decided to stay and do whatever I could until we put them all back under ground where they belong."

"Bravo," Julia said. "You and I share the same feelings, but I need some time. Sometimes I dream about returning to Amsterdam and saving all those little babies, but they're not there anymore, are they?"

"Thankfully, some are," Teddy said. "The ones that are with new homes, and you of all people know that. They're just not in the crèche anymore. The crèche is history."

"Sadly, so is Henriëtte Pimentel. It's such a shame, but tell me, how are Sara, Katy, and Danny? I bet they're happy to be in America."

"They are," Teddy answered. "The children are adjusting, but I wouldn't be surprised if they carried a scar. They had it rough. Sara is worried about her parents and her sister back in Utrecht. She hasn't heard a word since we left. I tried to contact Saul the other day on the shortwave, but I had no success."

"He's a resourceful man, Teddy, and I have faith in him. He'll get through it if anyone can. What does the Treasury Department have you doing in Washington? Are you counting cash?"

"Right. I'm looking for free samples. Actually, I'm working with a section using Treasury funds to aid refugees and civilian victims," Teddy said. "My group is focusing on Jewish refugees in Romania and France. The group is a real cross section of government, industry, and mainstream society, and we're getting bigger every day."

"Isn't Romania a member of the Axis powers? And isn't France under Nazi control? Aren't they our enemies now? How can the Treasury Department fund those areas?"

"It's complicated," Teddy said. "We're not raising money to fund the country. It's for the victims, the refugees. I admit I don't know that much about Romania. It's in southeastern Europe, in the Balkans, on the Black Sea. From what I hear, conditions are awful there. Their leader, Ion Antonescu, is as hateful as Hitler. They are two of a kind. We intercepted a message earlier this year where Hitler promised Antonescu that after the war, the Germanic and Latin races would rule the world in a partnership."

"Horrible thought. Now it's the world, not just Europe."

"There are over a half million Jews in Romania, so you can appreciate the scope of our problem. Many are escaping into Hungary."

"How does the Treasury Department provide aid to Jewish refugees in Europe?"

"We have to work around the system," answered Teddy. "Funds are earmarked here in Treasury to aid refugees. That wasn't being done at the State Department. There wasn't any money channeled to aid refugees. That's why Sumner took me out of State and placed me here at Treasury. He knows my history; he calls me a rescuer. He knows all about what we did in Holland to help people. Hell, he knows all about what *you* did, Julia, rescuing children and then sending out intelligence briefs to OSS. He asked me about you when he transferred me here. He wanted to know if you were coming with me. Regretfully, I said no, but I'm sure he'd put you with our group if you changed your mind."

"Don't tempt me, Teddy. You're killing me."

"Sorry. Sumner knows our history, and he also knows that there are those in the State Department who don't have any desire to help refugees, especially Jews."

"Oh, come on."

"It's true, and that's why he transferred me here to work with a man named John Pehle. He's a Yale lawyer who came over to Treasury last summer. He can tell you stories about certain State Department officers who are trying to suppress the news of Nazi atrocities. Can you believe that? Suppress! They don't want anyone to know."

"I can't believe that," Julia said. "Why would any State Department officer suppress the truth? Which officers? Who is doing that? If they doubt that the atrocities are really happening, just have them talk to me. I'll set them straight."

"I know you would, but I can't reveal their names. They're pretty high up. You can appreciate why I shouldn't even be discussing this over the phone. I've already said too much. This stuff is highly confidential."

"Can you tell me what your Foreign Funds Control group is doing now?"

"Well, not really. Again, it's confidential. Generally speaking, we're funding escape routes. Some go west from Romania into Hungary, or north into Ukraine or Russia. There are passages to Palestine if you can get to the coast, maybe through Turkey. It's dangerous, and we need to hire people on the ground. We need boats, we need trucks. Unfortunately, the bulk of the money necessary for our work is being held up in Congress by those certain people who I can't mention on the phone."

"Is it the same ones who are trying to suppress information about atrocities? Is it the America First people, or the anti-immigration people, or the antisemites? One of those? The same ones who tried to block America from entering the war at all? I remember them well."

"You got it," said Teddy.

"So it's hard to help the people who need it, the refugees?"

"It's tough. There are other ways, other agencies for helping refugees. Organizations like the JDC, the American Jewish Joint Distribution

Committee, also known as JOINT. It raises money through charitable donations, mostly through religious organizations. The JDC was formed thirty years ago to help Palestinian refugees. Now it provides money and food for refugees in wartime Europe, who are mostly Jewish."

"Does the JDC have offices in Europe?"

"No, it used to, but since the war started, they are not allowed to have offices in German-controlled countries."

"What about your group, Foreign Funds Control?"

"There is a lot of positive momentum in our group too, and pretty soon, you're going to hear a lot about us."

"What do you mean *pretty soon*?"

"Soon, that's all I can say. John has been working on this project for weeks. Come work for us; you'll find out everything you want to know."

"Sounds like the Teddy I know," Julia said. "Let me think about it. Speaking of southeast Europe, I have a very close friend here in Detroit, Theresa Weissbach. She's Hungarian. Her family is very prominent in Budapest, and they sent her to study at the University of Michigan ten years ago. When I was down there, she and I became close friends. After graduation, like so many others, she decided to stay. She's even teaching at the university. I've met her mom and dad a couple of times and they are really nice people, but unfortunately, they're back in Budapest. She hasn't heard from them in a long time."

"Are they Jewish?"

"They are. Do you know anything about the Jewish families in Budapest?"

"I don't know anything specifically," Teddy said. "I just know that there is a very large Jewish community in Hungary, getting larger every day, maybe close to nine hundred thousand. I haven't heard any reports of mass arrests or killings in Hungary, but like I just told you, that news would be buried at the State Department. I'm not really the one to ask. It's possible that there are other staffers who have better information. Even though Hungary is a member of the Axis powers and a military ally of Germany, I understood that Hungary's leader is not a solid Nazi.

He doesn't treat Jewish citizens like we saw in the Netherlands." Teddy paused. "Can you believe what we're saying? How callous it has all become? In modern times, in 1943, we question whether a ruler is either making plans or not making plans to murder all the Jews in his country."

"When we were in Amsterdam," Julia said, "the Jewish population was one hundred seventy thousand. It was the first city in Europe where Jews were free from persecution and where they enjoyed enough religious liberty that it was referred to as the 'Jerusalem of the North.' We found it hard to believe that Germany could or would try to capture or kill a community that large. We were wrong. Except for those who were able to find hiding places, the Nazis succeeded in eradicating them in only a matter of months. That's the terrifying part; they can do it *in a matter of months.*"

"Think about the bigger picture, Julia; when this war started, there were eleven million Jews in Europe, and unless he's stopped, Hitler will kill them all. It's insane, and that's why I'm here in Washington."

"I'm proud of you," Julia said. "You're the man for the job. Soon the US Army will defeat Germany and do away with Hitler. We have to believe that."

"I wish it were soon, but to be realistic, Germany's defeat is pretty far off. There are no US or Allied forces on the European continent. Not even close. You were with me last March when we were following the army's Africa Corps on our shortwave."

Julia grimaced. "I remember. They were defeated by Rommel at the Kasserine Pass."

"True, but they did regroup under General Patton and defeated the Germans in Tunisia. Now they are landing on the island of Sicily. That's progress. Italy is next. Sadly, that's a long way from landing in Germany or protecting your friend's family in Hungary."

"Do you think you could ask around? Their name is Weissbach. He's a doctor in a big hospital in Budapest."

"Happy to do it. Let me talk to someone who knows about Budapest and I'll get back to you. In the meantime, there is a chair right next to mine, and it has your name on it. Isn't that a coincidence? No one can fill it like you can."

"I appreciate your kind thoughts, but I don't think I'm up to it right now. Maybe in a little while."

CHAPTER FOUR

JULIA WAS BUSY gift-wrapping a sweater for a customer in her father's store when she was informed that there was a telephone call for her. She stepped into the back room and lifted the receiver. "This is Marcus Hertzl," the caller said. "I'm a friend of Teddy Hartigan. I work with him here at Treasury. He asked me to call you because I know a thing or two about Hungary. Your mom gave me this phone number."

"Thank you so very much for calling, Marcus. Do you have a few minutes?"

"Sure. Teddy told me all about you, and I am in awe of your heroic work in the Netherlands."

"No more so than Teddy," Julia said. "He was the real hero. Anyway, I called him because I have a very close friend at the University of Michigan, a Hungarian girl named Theresa Weissbach. She and I were friends in college. I would see her parents when they came to drop her off or pick her up in Ann Arbor. I saw Theresa just the other day. She teaches history at the university. She's an associate professor."

"Congratulations to her. That's a prestigious posting."

"Yes, she's very smart. Anyway, she is extremely worried about her family back in Budapest. She hasn't been able to reach them in a long time, and she doesn't know what is going on. It's the middle of Nazi Europe, and there isn't any news coming out of Hungary."

"That's understandable," Marcus said. "Long-distance calls to or from Budapest are nonexistent. As you know from experience, news of the Nazi atrocities gets buried here in the State Department. There's really no way for ordinary folks to know what's happening or to communicate with families back in Hungary."

"Well, what makes it even more concerning for Theresa is that she and her family are Jewish," Julia replied. "I hope you can understand."

"I certainly can. I am Jewish as well."

"Can you tell me what is happening to the Jewish community in Budapest? Theresa knows how things were when she left for college, but she's been gone for ten years. Are they mistreating Jews? Are they being persecuted? Theresa said that she heard that some laws were passed in 1938 putting restrictions on Jews, but she doesn't know to what extent. She believes that Miklós Horthy is not sending Jews to concentration camps or—"

"All right, all right, hold on," Marcus said. "Let's back up. She told you about Miklós Horthy, the admiral without a boat, the regent without a king?"

"Yes, the admiral. She said that he was the regent and the head of Hungary, that Hungary was a member of the Axis powers, but Horthy wasn't the same kind of wicked person as Hitler. He was not antisemitic."

"Hmm," Marcus said. "Well, she's not entirely correct. He's not a fan of Jews, because he's envious of their success and privileges in Hungary. He says they own everything. He is quoted as saying, 'I have considered it intolerable that here in Hungary everything, every factory, bank, large fortune, business, theater, press, commerce, et cetera should be in Jewish hands, and that the Jew should be the image reflected of Hungary, especially abroad.'"

"Well, that sure sounds antisemitic."

"True, but despite his covetous attitude, the steps he's taken against the community are comparatively minor. He certainly hasn't taken any of their property or imprisoned them. He's far more anti-Communist than he is antisemitic. In fact, in recent conversations, Horthy has been heard to be critical of Hitler and his Nazi policies. He's trying to create a distance between Germany and Hungary."

"He doesn't follow Hitler's orders?"

"He is a regent and an Axis member, and Hitler is the head of Europe, so he doesn't have a lot of choice. However, Hitler hasn't made social or religious demands on Horthy. Most of the orders are military. Two years ago, Hungary was compelled to contribute troops to Germany's attack on Russia because Hungary was a member of the Axis powers and because Hitler demanded it. Hungary contributed two hundred thousand men to the Russian Front. So far, the military campaign has turned out to be a disaster. During the Battle of Stalingrad, the Hungarian Second Army suffered terrible losses. Russia's advance through the Don River hit the Hungarian troops directly. Last January, during the Battle of Voronezh, Russia was advancing, crushing the Second Army, and the Hungarians were trying to retreat when Hitler sent orders to Horthy demanding that the Hungarian troops 'stand and fight to the death.' The troops were undermanned, ill equipped, lacking in anti-tank weapons, and facing another brutal Soviet winter. So, they ignored Hitler's orders and retreated to Hungary. Many were taken prisoner by the Red Army. Of the casualties, Hungary lost one hundred forty thousand men. That was a turning point for Horthy, who began to back away from Hitler."

"What did he do to back away?" asked Julia.

"This is confidential. Horthy's prime minister, Miklós Kállay, reached out to the Allies. He tried to initiate peace negotiations with both the United States and Great Britain. We have also received intelligence reports that Horthy has offered to enter into a peace treaty with Russia."

"That would be wonderful news," Julia said. "I'm sure that Theresa will be overjoyed to learn that Hungary is pulling away from Germany. She is so worried about her family and her Jewish community. The fact that they are still safe and unharmed, and that Horthy and his prime minister are turning away from Hitler and his murderous ways, is such good news."

"Not so fast. You're jumping to conclusions. It hasn't happened yet, and considering Hitler's power, it is not likely to happen. The fact is, he could take over Hungary in the bat of an eyelid if he wanted to. But so far, the community is safe and unharmed."

"So, as far as you know, Jews aren't being harmed or sent to prison camps?" Julia asked. "Is that so?"

"That's right, they're not, and I don't think Horthy would ever choose to do that. Nevertheless, tell your friend to keep her fingers crossed that Hitler doesn't decide that Hungary is not loyal enough and he moves to conquer it."

"One more thing," Julia said. "Theresa's father is Dr. Benjamin Weissbach."

"I don't think I know him."

"He's a surgeon, and he is on the board of a well-known hospital in Budapest." Julia looked at her notes. "It's called Semmelweis University Hospital."

"That's well-known, all right. Dr. Ignaz Semmelweis founded the hospital. It's definitely one of the best hospitals in Budapest. Maybe even all of Europe. Dr. Semmelweis is a legend."

"Does he still work there?"

"Ha! If he does, he'd be one hundred twenty years old."

As soon as Julia hung up the phone, she called Theresa. Most of what Marcus said was calming to Theresa. Marcus's impression of Horthy and Kállay as antisemitic was troubling, but she had heard that before. Julia agreed to call again if she received more information about Theresa's family.

CHAPTER FIVE

THE FOLLOWING SATURDAY, Julia decided to drive down to Ann Arbor and have lunch with Theresa. She had already called and told her about the conversation with Marcus and that he was going to keep his ears open for more information about Budapest. Julia didn't have any further news, but she needed something to do. The boredom was driving her crazy. Besides, it was a sunny day in December, no snow in the forecast, and the ride was easy. Julia took a wicker basket filled with sandwiches her mother had made.

Theresa's second-floor apartment was decorated with travel posters of Hungary: winding rivers, castles, mountains, vineyards. It looked delightful. Theresa herself had a European flair; there was something about her. She was tall, her posture was straight, her shoulders were square, and her waist was thin. Her dark hair was held back in a bun. Her speech had a tinge of a Hungarian accent that added a bit of mystery to her bearing. She brought out a bottle of wine and set it on the table.

Julia smiled. "I could sure use a bit of that," she said. "I had a rough night."

"Again?" Theresa said with a concerned look. She knew her friend well enough that her "rough night" meant she didn't sleep at all. "What was it this time?" Theresa said. "Were you fleeing SS guards back in Amsterdam?"

Julia shook her head. "I don't know where I was. It was in Europe somewhere. I think it might have been Hungary, although I have no idea what Hungary looks like. It was the same old story: trying to lead people away from the Nazis."

"You should get some help."

Julia nodded. "I know. Maybe when the war is all over, it will go away. Maybe one day, I'll pick up a paper and read that Hitler has surrendered and that the Jewish communities are all rejoicing."

"Try dreaming that instead; you'll sleep better at night."

Julia smiled. "I spoke with Teddy again yesterday. I can't seem to stay away. I don't have any further news," Julia said regretfully. "He said he would report back to me if he learns anything."

"I appreciate your effort," Theresa said. "I look for information myself, but it's all secondhand. The foreign students that I come across here at school are generally from Western Europe. As you may imagine, their stories are terrible, but they don't seem to know anything about Eastern Europe."

"I spent five years in Holland," Julia mused, "and I heard more stories than you can believe. Most of them were from families applying for US visas at the Amsterdam consulate. The applicants were generally from Western European countries—Denmark, Belgium, Luxembourg, and Germany. They would tell us about the horrible conditions they endured, and they would beg for a visa. They would absolutely be entitled to one but for the fact that our hands were tied by the congressional quotas set on each country. Teddy tells me the restrictive quotas are the result of those in Congress and the State Department who don't want any foreign immigrants. But of all the stories I heard, I don't remember any from Hungary. Really, other than what Marcus told me, I don't know very much about Hungary. To tell you the truth, I don't even know where Hungary is. I mean, I know it's in Europe, but if you showed me a map, I couldn't point it out. Isn't that embarrassing?"

"No, you probably didn't hear much about refugees in Hungary, because it was so far from Amsterdam. I doubt that Hungarian refugees would have been able to travel all the way across Europe to apply for a visa in Amsterdam. I'm sure you and Teddy had a lot on your hands trying to get visas for Dutch Jews and, later on, trying to save them from deportation."

"True. Even if Hungarian Jews had made it to Holland, it probably wouldn't have done them any good to apply for a visa," Julia said. "Though there are almost a million Jews in Hungary, the yearly quota for visas to the US is set at 869. That's all. If you came from Great Britain or Northern Ireland, there were 65,721 visas available. Sounds crazy, but try to explain that to applicants. That's what we were dealing with in the Amsterdam consulate."

"That is crazy, but the main reason you didn't interview many Hungarian Jews is that there weren't that many Jews fleeing Hungary. It has been comparatively safe for Jews. The community is strong, they are financially well off, and there has been a vibrant Jewish community there for centuries. Unless Miklós Horthy decided to turn his back on a million successful people, they wouldn't have tried to move somewhere else."

"Marcus told me about Miklós Horthy. He is the admiral, right?"

Theresa started to laugh. "The admiral without a ship or a navy. Hungary has this magnificent history, going back fifteen hundred years, filled with emperors and empresses, kings and queens, and now we have Miklós Horthy, the admiral."

"How did that happen? Was he elected?"

"By the people? No," said Theresa firmly. "He was appointed by the National Assembly. In 1919, when the Great War ended, it was clear that the victorious Allies would not accept a return of Blessed Charles, Charles IV, the fifty-sixth king of Hungary. He led Hungary into war, and the Allies wouldn't allow him to rule again. Admiral Horthy was a soldier. He fought bravely in the Great War and he was very popular, so the National Assembly appointed him as regent of the king in 1920."

"Why was Hungary allied with Germany in the Great War?"

"They were allies because they had a defense pact. As you know, countries make treaties to defend each other in the event of a military attack, and many are drawn into wars because of their defense pacts. Hungary was part of the Austro-Hungarian Empire, and we had a mutual defense pact with Austria. Serbia had mutual defense pacts with Russia, who had a defense pact with France. France had a pact with England, and so on, and so on. The Austro-Hungarian Empire was allied with Germany, and they fought on the battlefield together. Thus, the Great World War."

"I understand."

"That doesn't mean that Horthy is a friend of Hitler. Hitler started the Second World War by invading Poland in 1939. Hungary found itself caught in the middle. It was physically positioned between Russia on the right and Germany on the left. Which side should it join? Horthy has always been a vehement anti-Communist, and he doesn't like Russia at all, so he joined with Germany. But Horthy is not made out of the same cloth as Hitler. At least not so far."

Julia smiled. "My friend the history teacher."

Theresa took a bow. "Your history teacher knows about the past pretty well, but not the present, and that's what upsets me so. I've been in the dark about my homeland for well over a year."

"I'm sure that Teddy and Marcus will keep their ears open, but they told me as much as they know. They think your people are safe back in Hungary," Julia said. "At least for now."

Theresa reached out and grabbed Julia's arm. "I haven't told anyone, but I have had some disturbing nightmares lately. I fall asleep, I have these terrible dreams, I wake up shaking, and then I can't fall back asleep."

"Oh, that's awful. What do you dream about that keeps you up like that?"

Theresa shook her head. "Just terrible dreams. They're scary."

"About what? Is it about your family?"

Theresa nodded. "They are being attacked. They're running for their lives. Sometimes they're captured and put in railroad boxcars. Isn't that bizarre?"

"Terri, those are scary dreams, all right, but they aren't bizarre. That kind of thing really happened, and for all I know, it is still really happening to people overseas."

Theresa nodded. "I know. I haven't heard anything to make me believe that my parents are actually in danger, but the dreams come to me at night like someone is sending me a message. And I want to talk to my parents to make sure they are safe, but I can't. I've got a bad feeling, Julie. A real bad feeling."

Julia reached over and held her best friend tightly while she wept. "Dreams don't make it so, Terri," Julia said gently. "That's just your imagination talking."

"I know, but I have been wondering, would it be possible for me to talk directly to either Mr. Hartigan or Mr. Hertzl?" Theresa said with hope in her eyes. "Maybe I can find out some information about the Jewish community in Budapest. If you could arrange it, I'd jump on a train tomorrow."

"I don't think that Mr. Hertzl will have the answers you seek, but I'll give Teddy a call. Maybe there are other people that Teddy knows who are more familiar with Hungary."

"We're on winter break at the university now," Theresa said. "If someone with information would meet with me, this would be a good time to go. Any day in the next three weeks would work for me. Do you think you could get me an appointment?"

"THIS IS THEODORE Hartigan."

"It's me again," Julia said.

"Julie! It's always good to hear your voice. What can I do for you?"

"My friend Theresa is on winter break, and she wants to come to Washington and talk to you or Marcus, or anyone who has knowledge about what's happening in Hungary. Her family is in Budapest, and she hasn't heard from them in a long time. Terri could also be a valuable asset for you and the Foreign Funds Control group if you want to know about Hungary. She is very bright and extremely knowledgeable. You wouldn't believe how much Hungarian history she knows, and her family is very well connected. You and Marcus could learn a lot from her. It might benefit all concerned."

"Then I have two questions," Teddy said. "First question concerns security. What sort of recommendation can she supply?"

"She's been working at the University of Michigan for five years as a respected member of their faculty. I'm sure that people who know her would vouch for her. How about the head of the History Department or maybe an officer of the university?"

"Any of those would work. Can you get such an endorsement?"

"Probably not. She's just an associate professor, but I've known her for ten years, and I trust her. Isn't that good enough?"

"It is for me," Teddy said. "See if she can get a recommendation from someone at the university, and I'll do my best to make it happen. Second question: Are you going to come to Washington with her?"

There was a pause on the line while Julia pondered the question. Thoughts swirled around in her head. She searched to find the right words, the ones that had been gnawing at her for days on end. Though she was safe and secure with her family in Detroit, and though she promised herself that she would never return to the insanity of the world war, she never really left it. It had occupied her mind during her waking hours and given her the shivers at night. She stared at her telephone, tapped her fingers on the table, and squeezed the handset with all her might. What should she say to Teddy? Should she open up the floodgate? While she pondered her response, it slipped right out. "Teddy, I'll be happy to accompany Terri, but if I do come back to Washington, it's only as Terri's friend. I'm willing to help her in any way I can, if you think I would add value to the discussion."

That was the Julia he knew. "You're damn right you'd add to the discussion. There are a lot of folks here who respect you very much. Undersecretary Welles is one of them—he told me so. When he transferred me over to Treasury, he asked me about you. He wondered if you were going to transfer as well. He was very impressed with the work you did for OSS back in Amsterdam."

"That's nice to hear. Tell me something: Why did Sumner transfer you out of the State Department? Why didn't he want to keep you there?"

"There are reasons. I can't really talk about them on the telephone. I'll tell you when I see you in person. But I can tell you this: It was a great move for me. Amazing things are about to explode here at the Treasury Department, and believe me, you want to be a part of it. It's a chance to make a difference, just the kind of thing that you were made for."

Julia sighed. "I'll give it some thought. We'll talk about it when I come to Washington with Terri. Can you give us an appointment?"

"The only appointment you ever need with me is to ring the doorbell. If Theresa can bring something, even a letter of recommendation from a fellow teacher at Michigan, bring it with you."

"Are you available in two weeks? We could come on January 9."

"It's a date. Wait until I tell Sara. Won't she be excited!"

CHAPTER SIX

JULIA'S MOTHER DROPPED her off at Michigan Central Station on the morning of January 8, 1944. "Have a safe trip," she said. "Call me when you get to the hotel tonight. How long do you think you'll be gone?" Julia loved her mother's concern, but she answered truthfully, "I really don't know how long we'll be there. It depends on who we get to talk to. We're trying to find out about Theresa's family. Teddy thinks that we can find information through the people he knows at the Treasury Department, which sounds odd to me, but if they can't help us, maybe Undersecretary Welles would know someone who would talk to us at the State Department."

Julia met Theresa at the gate, and the two boarded the B&O Limited for Washington, DC. Their plan was to check into a hotel near the Treasury Department, get a good night's sleep, and show up bright and early the next morning.

"I really appreciate how you set this meeting up," Theresa said. "I know that you promised yourself you wouldn't get involved again, and here you are jumping back into the fray. You know that Teddy is going to try his hardest to talk you back into the State Department. Or maybe now it's the Treasury Department. What made you change your mind?"

"I didn't change my mind. I'm only helping out a friend. I'm not re-enlisting."

"Well, your friend is very grateful. I just didn't think I was making any progress trying to get information over the phone. Did Teddy tell you why he was now with the Treasury Department?"

"Not really. He said that Undersecretary of State Sumner Welles transferred him there when he returned to Washington, but he didn't give me a good reason. He said he couldn't talk about it over the phone—it was confidential. He told me that Sumner used all the magic words—'Make a difference,' 'Something exciting is going to happen,' 'You want to be a part of it'—and it piqued his interest."

Theresa looked at Julia, smiled, and said, "Those magic words piqued yours too. Admit it. You're two of a kind."

"Maybe. To get him to meet with you, I went out on a limb, Terri. I stretched the truth. I told Teddy that you were very smart and knowledgeable." Julia grinned.

"Very funny," said Theresa. "Maybe I can repay the compliment. I'll tell him you are very wise and perceptive where men are concerned."

"Oh, now that's cruel. Besides, Teddy knows all about that. He knew Willem in Amsterdam. Truthfully, I did tell him that your family was influential and well connected. I told him that you can be a valuable source of information about Hungary."

Theresa nodded. "I think that's fair. Before his heart attack, my father was a top surgeon at Semmelweis University Hospital, working crazy hours every day. Now he has slowed down, but I still think he's connected in some way. He and my uncle are both on the board at the Great Synagogue. He knows everyone. If something is going on in the Jewish community, he'll know about it. In our community, word travels fast. They're a bunch of gabbers. My brother, Samuel, works in administration at the Budapest Telephone Company. Word travels fast there too, ha ha."

Julia had an inquisitive look on her face.

"How come your brother didn't follow in your father's footsteps and become a doctor? How in the world did he end up at the telephone company?"

"It was because of Joel Brand. He was Sammy's friend. Joel was kind of a free-spirited sort, and his family is very wealthy. His father owns the Budapest Telephone Company. When Joel was nineteen, he went to stay with his uncle in New York. Then he became a vagabond. He went all over the US doing odd jobs, working in restaurants as a dishwasher, working in a copper mine. He had some friends who were in Comintern, the Communists. He joined with them and went sailing around the world—Hawaii, the Philippines, South America, China, and Japan. He would send Sammy postcards and make him very jealous."

"But your brother stayed in Budapest?"

"My father put his foot down. Sammy had to finish school and get his degree. Joel went back to Budapest in 1934. As you well know, I was a sophomore at Michigan. Joel managed to get Sammy a job at his father's telephone company in an administrative position. Meanwhile, Joel became very involved in Jewish affairs, which suited his father just fine. He became a vice president of the Budapest Palestine Office, which organized Jewish immigration to Palestine, and he sat on the governing body of the Jewish National Fund. Apparently, thousands of Jews have immigrated to Palestine through his efforts. He and his wife, Hansi, opened a knitwear and glove factory ten years ago on Rósza Street in Budapest, and they have been making a fortune. They employ a hundred people. Whatever he touches turns to gold."

Julia leaned back, stared out of the train window, and watched the countryside roll by. From time to time, she would shake her head in a troubled way. After a moment, she said, "Where am I going, Terri? What am I doing? I told myself I wasn't going to do this again."

"You're where you should be," Theresa said with an understanding smile. "Relax. We're just going to talk to people about Hungary."

"But when I do things like this, I get myself into trouble. You know what I mean. I don't know who I am anymore. When I was in Holland, it was fraught with danger, but I felt alive. I felt like I had a purpose, like I was making a difference."

"You were, and you have a medal to prove it."

"I don't have that feeling anymore, Terri. I don't know what my purpose is or what I'm supposed to be doing. I can't just stay home and work in my father's clothing store anymore, but what should I do? I feel useless."

"Give yourself a break; you're unwinding. It will all come to you. You once told me you had special skills, remember? Well, we're going to Washington, where there is a market for those skills. Let's talk to your friend Teddy. Maybe he can suggest something? Maybe you can work with him?"

"Counting cash in the Treasury Department?"

"Oh, cut it out. You know he's not doing that. He told you he was working on trying to save Jewish refugees in Romania and France. If you joined him, you'd be making a difference again, but this time, you'd be doing it from relative safety. There wouldn't be Gestapo around the corner. You could use your special skills."

Julia nodded. "I know you're right. We'll talk to Teddy."

CHAPTER SEVEN

JULIA AND THERESA took a taxi to the west entrance of the Treasury Building at 1500 Pennsylvania Avenue NW. To their right was the White House. Before them stood an immense building, built out of the same white granite as the White House, the largest building that either one had ever seen. A tall bronze statue of Alexander Hamilton greeted them as they walked to the entrance. They informed the receptionist that they had an appointment with Theodore Hartigan, and she asked them to have a seat. A few minutes later, an ebullient Teddy walked into the hall with a bounce to his step.

"Julie, Julie, how I've missed you," he said, giving her a big hug that lifted her off the floor. "We've gone from seeing each other and working together all day, every day, to not seeing each other at all. Both Sara and I have missed you a lot." He turned to Theresa and held out his hand. "You must be Theresa Weissbach. It's nice to meet you, Miss Weissbach."

"Just Terri," she said, "and I'm delighted to meet you as well. Needless to say, Julia has told me quite a bit about you." Theresa reached into her purse and pulled out a few letters that were addressed "To whom it may concern." She handed them to Teddy. "These are signed commendations from the dean of the History Department, the faculty dean, and my rabbi. It was all I could gather on short notice. I hope they give you some confidence in my trustworthiness."

Teddy gave her a warm smile. "I'm sure they will do just fine. When I mentioned to Mr. Pehle that you were coming, Terri, and that you would be bringing a letter of recommendation, he gave me an interesting response.

He said he was more interested in learning what you could bring to the discussions about Hungary. He was confident that any friend of Julia's would be a trustworthy person."

"Does Mr. Pehle have information about the Jewish population in Hungary?" Julia said.

"I'm sure he knows something," Teddy answered. "He knows a lot about each of the European Jewish communities."

Julia smiled and elbowed Theresa. "I told you. It sounds like Mr. Pehle is the one who could answer your questions." Then she turned back to Teddy and said, "It just seems curious to me that an officer of the US Treasury Department has foreign refugees as his principal concern. That should be the province of the State Department, don't you think?"

"Hmph," groaned Teddy. "Do I think? Yes. Is it happening? No."

They started walking down the hallway, and a group of men and women in business suits rushed by them. They carried folders in their hands and were engaged in animated conversations. Julia raised her eyebrows in awe.

"Welcome back to Washington, Julie," Teddy said. "Are you jealous you're not part of the scene? Have you been thinking about reentering the intelligence world?"

Julia started to shake her head, but Theresa interrupted. "Tell him the truth, Julie; it's on your mind all the time. Teddy—if I may call you that—she thinks about it all day and night. She mentioned to me that upon her return from the Netherlands, she spoke with Undersecretary of State Sumner Welles, and he offered to find a place for her. She assumed it was at the State Department. Am I right, Julie?"

Julia paused, then nodded.

"That's good to hear," Teddy said, "but I'm sure that the position Sumner was talking about would not have been at the State Department. He would have placed you here with me at Treasury. Knowing you like I do, I don't think you would want to be at State right now. That is not where your interests lie. You'd be much better off here."

"I don't understand why you say that," Julia said. "Why wouldn't I want to go back to State? That's where I was able to do good work. We saved lives, Teddy—you know that's true."

"Don't get me wrong," Teddy said. "If you want to do intelligence work for OSS and MI5, then State is for you. That is our intelligence arm. But if you want to focus on refugees and saving lives, then you want to be here. There are opportunities here at Treasury for continuing the kind of humanitarian work that we did in Holland."

Julia wrinkled her forehead. "I don't get it. Why do you say that? Aren't they doing humanitarian work at State? Aren't they rescuing refugees?"

Teddy looked around at the busy hall and quietly said, "Let's not talk about that out here. Let's go back to my office, and we'll talk in private."

TEDDY ARRANGED SOME chairs around his desk, had a secretary bring in coffee, and shut the door.

"Your comment back there surprised me," Julia said. "I was good at what I was doing for the State Department in Amsterdam. You know that. We helped rescue Jewish families, thousands of them. We found homes for little babies, hundreds of them. I have a medal to prove it. And so do you. So why wouldn't I want to return to State—that is, if I wanted to return at all?"

"At all, Miss Woman of Mystery? I thought the same things when I was placed here at Treasury, but State is the wrong place for us, unless you want to do intelligence work. If you want to be a spy, that would be the place for you. But I know you better than that. Your heart was in saving the lives of innocent families. If you want to keep rescuing refugees, you're much better off here at Treasury. They're not doing that at State. If you asked Sumner, he would tell you the same thing, and he'd place you right here with me."

Julia stared at Teddy with a questioning look. "Why? You haven't answered my question. Why the Treasury Department and not at the State Department? That doesn't make sense to me. The State Department is the arm of government that helps refugees. Our consulates issue the visas in foreign countries."

Teddy looked first at Theresa and then back at Julia. "How many visas did you issue to desperate refugees when you were in Amsterdam, Julie?"

Julia shook her head. "The quotas were filled; there were no visas to issue. All we could do was place people on the waiting lists."

"And why was that, Julie? Those Jewish refugees were in desperate straits. If they didn't find a way out of Europe, they feared they were going to die. Yet Congress set immigration limits. There are Democrats, and there are Republicans. There are liberals, and there are conservatives. They don't always agree. Sometimes they serve different masters. The position on immigration by a government agency at any given time depends on the powerful politicians in charge." Teddy shrugged. "Maybe Theresa doesn't understand how American politics works."

Julia tightened her lips. "Terri is an award-winning history professor who understands politics just fine. If you can tell me, you can tell Terri. Which politicians are influencing the State Department to limit immigration?"

Teddy shrugged. "I suppose it's not as classified as I think. If you can read the newspapers and put two and two together, it's not much of a secret. You will come to understand that at this time there is no arm of the State Department designed to aid refugees."

"I can't believe that," Julia said. "That is the function of the State Department."

"It is certainly one of them," answered Teddy, "but that doesn't mean it's an operating function of our State Department today. Quite the opposite. I grew up in Washington with very conservative people. You know that, Julie."

"I remember the photograph of you, your dad, and Senator Gerald Nye. He was very conservative. He was an isolationist. He wanted nothing to do with citizens of foreign countries. He didn't want them coming here, and he didn't want his money going there."

"That is exactly correct," Teddy said, "and he still doesn't. There was a time he offered me a job, and I almost took it. Little did I know."

Julia smiled. "You told me about that. Your girlfriend Betsy wanted you to take his offer, live in DC, and marry her. She did not want you to go overseas with the State Department."

"That's true, but I'm glad I did. The conservative arm of Congress was very powerful in the thirties, and it still is. They were against getting involved in foreign matters, and they were anti-immigration. One of the loudest spokesmen was Breckinridge Long. He was credited with writing Woodrow Wilson's electioneering slogan, which was 'He kept us out of war.' That political stance helped Wilson win the presidency in 1916. Of course, he wasn't able to keep us out of war. The US went to war a year later. Breckinridge Long ran for the Senate twice, but he was roundly defeated each time. He was very wealthy, and he contributed large amounts to President Roosevelt's campaign. He knew FDR from the navy, but they were very different people. When FDR was elected, Long got appointed to the dream job he always wanted: He was the ambassador to Benito Mussolini's Italy."

"Why is this relevant? Why would I care about Breckinridge Long?" Julia said. "I certainly don't care about Fascist Benito Mussolini. So what if Long is a wealthy ultraconservative who kisses ass? How does that affect the State Department and refugees?"

"Be patient, young Julia. I'm giving you a chronology. While in Italy, Long was close to Mussolini, and Long was quoted saying that Italian Fascism was 'the most interesting experiment in government to come above the horizon since the formulation of our Constitution.'"

"He said that?"

"Yes, he did. He believed in authoritarian government. He also read Hitler's *Mein Kampf*, and he said, 'It is eloquent in opposition to Jewry and to Jews as exponents of Communism & chaos. My estimate of Hitler as a man rises with the reading of his book.'"

"He praises Hitler and Mussolini, and he works for the State Department?"

Teddy nodded. "Long never retracted either of those statements. Still hasn't. You ask me why Long matters? Because when he came back from Fascist Italy, he was appointed as assistant secretary of state in 1939 and held that post for three years, until 1942, long enough to shape policy. In that position, he tried as hard as he could to keep immigrants out of the United States."

Julia was getting angry. "Teddy," she said, "you and I both know how hard it was to help people get visas, and that was our job with the State Department, but Congress set strict limits."

"I agree, but Congress was motivated by extremely conservative advisors. As assistant secretary of state, Long advised Congress to delay and effectively stop the number of immigrants coming into the United States. He said we could do this by simply advising our consuls to put every obstacle in their way and to require additional evidence to be produced that would 'postpone and postpone and postpone the granting of the visas.' Those were his words."

Now tears were in Julia's eyes. "Those poor people stood in line outside the Amsterdam consulate for days and days. They were so needy. They were trying to escape before being sent away to die. We tried so hard, but our hands were tied because of people like Long? All the strict quotas, all the documents they required of those poor refugees, the horrible delays, it was always a struggle we couldn't overcome. What a callous man."

"Just two months ago, in November, the House was considering establishing a separate agency to assist with the rescue of Jewish refugees, and guess who gave top secret testimony to that very House committee?"

"It was Long, wasn't it?"

"That's right, and we have a copy of his testimony. To this very day, the House hasn't formed that agency." Teddy held up his index finger. "But a change is coming, Julie, and it's top secret. Do we all agree to keep this confidential?"

Both Julia and Theresa nodded.

"Right now, as we speak, there is a report being prepared. It will reveal that certain individuals in the State Department are purposefully standing in the way of aid to refugees. I'm sure you can guess the name of one of them. This report will blow the whistle."

"Wow," said Julia. "Who is writing this report, and when will it be released?"

Teddy held his index finger to his lips. "Soon," he said. "Very soon, but you should know the report will come from Treasury. I've seen portions. If you want my opinion, it's earthshaking."

"Can you tell us what the report will recommend?" Theresa said.

"I can't. I haven't read the final copy, and I've already said more than I should. Keep it under your bonnet. With any luck, John Pehle will be coming here this afternoon. I want you to meet him. He's a remarkable man. So damn smart. Maybe he will open up to you, but don't pressure him. Please don't volunteer that you know anything about this upcoming report. Deal?"

Julia and Theresa nodded enthusiastically. "Deal!"

"All right, then," Teddy said. "Let's catch a ride back to the house. Sara's making something special for lunch."

"Where are you staying?" Julia asked.

"We're staying at my dad's in Silver Spring. It's a big house, the one I grew up in. Imagine his surprise when I showed up last November with Sara, Katy, and Danny in tow. He and my mom wouldn't hear about our moving to an apartment. Especially now. He's crazy about the kids."

THE MOMENT JULIA walked in the Hartigans' front door, little Katy ran into her arms, yelling, "Julie, Julie!" It had been months since Katy had last seen her. The six-year-old had witnessed the Nazi cruelties and inhumanities visited upon the Jewish community in Amsterdam. Sara first met Katy when an older woman brought her to the front lawn of the crèche nursery school. The woman, believed to be the child's relative, didn't say a word, but kissed Katy, turned, and walked away. One might think it was a thoughtless abandonment, but it saved little Katy's life. Sara's sister, who was working at the crèche that day, took Katy into the school. When it became obvious that no one was coming for her, they had a decision to make. Either find an orphanage or find an angel. Sara was the angel. She took little Katy under her wing and then adopted her. It wasn't long after that, during the Nazis' campaign to take all the Jews out of the Netherlands and send them away to a concentration camp, that Julia and Teddy joined others trying to find hiding places for the children. During the ensuing months, when Teddy and Julia were working as intelligence agents for the State Department, all five of them lived together in the OSS safe house.

"How are your children doing in Washington?" Julia asked.

"They're doing very well," Sara said. "The Hartigans are such a loving family. We found a Jewish nursery school, and the kids are fitting right in. We've all been very lucky."

"My dad considers himself the luckiest one of all," Teddy said. "It's funny how long-held attitudes can change overnight with the addition of grandchildren. When I left home, my father was a very conservative, right-wing gentleman. He belonged to a wealthy country club, and his friends were all just like him. They were good people, but they were America Firsters. They wanted no part of Europe or its constant wars. Despite what the Statue of Liberty says, they were not pro-immigration."

Teddy turned to Theresa. "It was my dad who got me my first job with the State Department. I worked in the basement doing research. Then a golden opportunity arose. They needed an officer at the US consulate in the Netherlands. My dad recommended me, and I was appointed. Supposedly, it was a temporary stepping stone designed to further my government career. I met Julie on my very first day in Amsterdam."

Julia smiled and nodded. "I showed him to his apartment above the Heineken sign."

Teddy continued, "When the Nazis took over the Netherlands in 1940, the consulate remained open for business, but my dad saw the writing on the wall. He begged me to come home, but by then, it was too late. I told him that I couldn't, and I told him why. Still, he told me that I would always be welcome. When we showed up at his door last November, he opened his arms to Sara and the kids as wide as he could, like he had known them all their lives. The fact that they are Jewish didn't matter to him at all. I've never seen him happier."

"That's lovely," Theresa said. Turning to Sara, she said, "I understand that your family is still back in the Netherlands. In Utrecht. Do you hear from them at all?"

Sara shook her head. "Either the shortwave is broken, or . . . I hate to consider the alternatives. But I have faith in my dad. I know he'll survive." Sara placed her hand gently on Theresa's arm. "And so will yours. They'll all be okay."

Just then, the door opened, and Broderick Hartigan walked into the house. "Grandpa, Grandpa!" yelled Katy and Danny and they ran to him. He picked up one in each arm. A smile broke out from ear to ear, and it was contagious. Everyone in the room mirrored his smile.

CHAPTER EIGHT

FOLLOWING LUNCH, BRODERICK arranged for a car to take Julia, Theresa, and Teddy back to the Treasury Building for their afternoon meeting with John Pehle. They waited in Teddy's office, hoping that John wouldn't be late and he'd be able to give them a little time. Theresa hoped he would have some of the answers she was seeking.

"Wait until you meet him," Teddy said. "He's a terrific guy, and he's not much older than we are. In his mid-thirties, I think. He went to Creighton and Yale Law School. He smokes a calabash pipe, and he looks like the pictures of Sherlock Holmes in the books." He nodded in Julia's direction and said, "And he's very good looking, but he's spoken for. Sorry, Julie."

"He's a Midwesterner?" Julia said.

Teddy nodded. "Omaha. He's very close friends with the secretary of the treasury, Henry Morgenthau. The secretary appointed John and a couple of his colleagues to head up a division they call Foreign Funds Control, the unit that I am working in right now. The group is trying to tap into Treasury funds and send money to refugee organizations in European countries where the Jewish population is fighting for its life. There is presently no US agency that is doing that. There are several small charitable organizations that are funding relief efforts, but nothing on a large scale. In fact, John will tell you that our government hasn't taken any official position on the plight of the refugees. You would think that would be the business of the State Department, but they refuse to do anything to aid Jewish refugees. That's why John is here at Treasury and not at State."

"As long as there are influential men like Breckinridge Long, aren't your hands tied as well?" Julia asked.

"Oh, you'd be surprised. I'm so excited to hear about the report that John and Joe DuBois are writing. Sometimes reports can change people's minds."

AT THREE O'CLOCK, Teddy's office intercom buzzed, and he was told that John Pehle was now in his office on the third floor, and he would have a short time to visit with them.

"A short time?" Theresa said. "I came all this way for a short interview?"

Teddy shrugged. "He is very busy with the report and all. I suppose we are lucky that he has any time for us."

Pehle rose from his seat as Julia, Theresa, and Teddy entered the room. Pehle reached out his hand to Julia and said, "It is my pleasure to meet you, Miss Powers. You are an American hero. I've never met someone who has been awarded a Distinguished Service Medal."

Teddy cleared his throat. John nodded and smiled. "Except, of course, for Theodore."

"I appreciate the kind words, Mr. Pehle," Julia said, "and I'd like to introduce my good friend Theresa Weissbach."

"Yes, of course, the university professor who wishes to learn about her family back in Hungary. How do you do, Professor Weissbach?"

"I am fine, thank you, Mr. Pehle. The reason I requested a meeting with you is because I have no information about my family. I haven't heard about the health or welfare of my family or the folks in my community in well over a year. My family lives in Budapest, and as of my last communication, they were unharmed, but conditions change so rapidly. I have had absolutely no information since then."

Pehle nodded with a solemn face.

"My father is a noted surgeon at Semmelweis University Hospital,"

Theresa continued. "My uncle and my father are both on the board of directors of the largest synagogue in Hungary." She took a breath. "I have several cousins and friends who are also well connected and gainfully employed in what was once a prosperous and successful Jewish community. I have no reason to believe that they are in harm's way, except that they border Germany and that Hungary sits in the middle of a continent controlled by Nazi oppressors."

"Hmm," John said. "That's very disconcerting, isn't it?"

Theresa nodded. "The last I heard, there were no roundups, transports, or mass murders taking place in Hungary. I am hoping that you have current information and can confirm that the situation hasn't deteriorated."

Pehle pulled on his lip and gave a quick nod. "I'm afraid I don't have much current information. As far as I know, the situation is unchanged. At this time, we don't have very reliable contacts in Hungary. We hope that's going to change. Right now, the borders are tightly controlled, the communication lines are down, and they are in the center of Eastern Europe, surrounded by German-occupied countries. If the State Department has more information, they are not sharing. From time to time, we receive reports through MI5 or a Soviet contact we have, but they lack detail and are unverified. Off and on, over the past couple of years, discriminatory laws have been enacted limiting Jewish privileges, but basic freedoms still exist. The Jewish community in Budapest is large, strong, and financially influential. I have no reason to believe that the Jewish people are in imminent danger. We know that is quite different from the Jewish population in Romania and France, and that is where our committee is focusing our efforts. Of those on my committee, I don't believe that anyone is intimately familiar with Budapest or Hungary."

"I am familiar with Hungary," Theresa said, "and I would like to assist your committee in some way. I am happy to evaluate a report and fill in any missing information where applicable. I am glad to offer whatever assistance I can provide."

Pehle raised his eyebrows. "I appreciate your offer, Professor. What is your availability over the next few weeks?"

"I have a class in European history starting on January 20, but I have a research assistant who can fill in for me, if necessary."

"As you may know, my committee is currently working on a study, and we intend to report our results to the president. In large part, it concerns the Jewish communities throughout Europe, and Hungary is a significant part of that population. We are aware that right now Hungary has the largest Jewish community in all of Europe. By far."

"Almost a million," Theresa said. "That makes it vulnerable, doesn't it, Mr. Pehle?"

"It certainly does, but no adverse steps have been taken so far, which seems strange to us. Since the Wannsee Declaration, the Nazis have pledged to make Europe free of all Jews. That places Hungary in the crosshairs. As far as we can figure, Hungary has been a loyal ally of Germany's. They have fought together on the battlefield. Hungary has lost over two hundred thousand soldiers in Germany's war against the Soviet Union. For that reason, we believe, Berlin has not pressured Hungary's president to do anything to its Jewish citizens."

"That would be Admiral Horthy," Theresa said. "He doesn't like being told what to do by other countries. While most have bowed down to Berlin, Horthy has not. I think he stands alone in not following Hitler's racial orders."

Pehle shrugged. "Hungary's neighbors have each enacted Hitler's racial orders. Hungary is an exception, but we don't know whether Horthy has ever received a direct order from Berlin regarding Jews. If he does, will he honor it, and will the racial situation stay the same? There are signs it may not."

"I spoke with Marcus Hertzl on the telephone recently," Julia said. "He said he was a member of your group."

"He is, and I know that he spoke with you. Marcus is gathering information on Romania and France."

"He had some recent information about Hungary as well, but limited,"

Julia said. "He told me that Horthy replaced his prime minister because he was becoming subservient to Germany. So, Horthy replaced him with Miklós Kállay. Kállay agreed to support the Axis armies against Russia, but he is determined to keep Nazi racial policies out of Hungary."

"That's true, but the war with Russia is going badly for Germany and the Axis countries, including Hungary. Because of that, Kállay sent a secret message to Washington indicating a willingness to open peace negotiations."

"He was willing to strike a peace accord with the US and the Allies?" asked Theresa in a surprised tone.

"That's what we heard, but given the current posture of our State Department, when they received Kállay's peace feeler, it went nowhere. It was disregarded. Thrown away."

"That seems unbelievable. Why wouldn't the State Department follow up on those peace feelers?"

"Why does our State Department do anything? I don't know. A larger problem now exists for Hungary. We don't know whether Berlin has discovered that Kállay made those contacts. On the one hand, Hitler wants to keep Hungary on his side, so thus far he has refrained from issuing demands on Horthy, including orders to the Hungarian Jewish community. On the other, Berlin doesn't trust Kállay or Horthy. Hitler could change his mind and move on Hungary at his will. Can you imagine the upheaval in trying to round up and transport one million Jews to some detention camp?"

"We've seen it," Julia said, "albeit on a smaller scale."

Pehle stood, a sign that the meeting was over. "I'm sorry to cut this short," he said, "but I have given you all I know about Hungary, and I have to run. As you may know, I am working on a project."

Teddy stepped forward. "I know about the project, John. Are you speaking of the report that you and Joe are preparing?"

"Yes. We're almost done. We hope to have it finished, maybe even tomorrow."

A smile broke out on Teddy's face, and he said, "Tomorrow's the day? Delivery day? I can't wait."

Pehle gave a sharp nod. "Hell or high water. Joe will bring it here tomorrow morning, and we will give it a final edit. You're welcome to review it with us. No one knows European refugees any better. We have a meeting to present it to the secretary in the afternoon. Like you said, 'Special delivery!'"

"God bless it," said Teddy. "I'll be here."

CHAPTER NINE

WHEN THE MEETING with John Pehle concluded, Teddy took Julia and Theresa to the Oak Tree, a restaurant and cocktail bar not too far away on Jefferson Drive. They arrived just ahead of the early-evening crowd and were shown to a booth. Teddy ordered a round of beers and some appetizers. He still had a confident smile on his face.

Julia, on the other hand, was not smiling. Something big was going on, and she was being kept in the dark. "All right, Teddy, what's this report all about? 'Tomorrow's the day,'" she said mimicking Teddy's voice. "'Hell or high water.' 'Special delivery.' C'mon, Teddy, it's me, Julia. What in the world are you talking about? What report is being delivered? And who is Joe?"

"Joe is Josiah DuBois, an attorney here at Treasury, and he is the one drafting the report. Believe me, Julia, it's huge," Teddy said.

"And I don't have a right to know about it? Didn't we put our lives on the line together in Amsterdam? Weren't we soldiers in arms in a combat zone?"

Theresa assumed that Teddy's reluctance to discuss the secret report was due to her presence. She was an outsider. She stood up to leave. "I'm going to go and take a walk," she said. "You two can discuss the matter in private."

"Oh no, you stay right where you are," Julia said. "You and I have no secrets. Whatever Teddy has to say, he can say it in front of you."

Teddy took a deep breath, glanced to either side, and leaned forward so the conversation stayed right at the table. "Do either of you know about an organization called the World Jewish Congress? Because it all started there."

Julia shook her head, but Theresa nodded. "My uncle mentioned something about a World Jewish Congress organized in Switzerland," Theresa said, "but I don't know much more than that. I was in college at the time."

"Your uncle was right," Teddy said. "It was formed in 1936 in Switzerland by Nahum Goldman and Rabbi Stephen Wise."

That caught Theresa's attention, and her eyebrows raised. "Rabbi Wise?"

"That's right."

"I know about him; in fact, I've met him. He was born in Budapest, but now he lives in New York. His father and grandparents were rabbis in Hungary. They're well known. Rabbi Wise was one of the first advocates of the movement we call Progressive Judaism. My father, who is on the board at Dohány Street Synagogue, and used to be the president, knows him very well. He is the one who introduced me."

"So Rabbi Wise is a Progressive Jew?" asked Teddy.

"Very much so. Very modern. And very outspoken. Apparently, Rabbi Wise gave a controversial sermon eight or nine years ago. It has become well known among progressive, or reform, rabbis. I've seen a copy."

"Do you remember that sermon?" Julia said.

"Not word for word, but my uncle was right—it was controversial. The sermon was titled 'Jesus the Jew.'"

Teddy gave a low whistle. "That could be controversial."

Theresa continued, "I don't think it was meant to be. It was progressive, that's for sure, but not demeaning or insulting in any way. It didn't criticize Christian religions. Rabbi Wise's sermon praised Jesus as being a great moral and ethical teacher, a Jew of whom we should be proud because of his ethical teachings. There is no doubt that Jesus was born a Jew."

"Then what's wrong with calling him Jesus the Jew?" Julia said.

"Well, I can understand the controversy," Teddy said. "It goes against traditional teachings. Especially for Christians who believe Jesus is God, not just an ethical teacher. Jewish liturgy doesn't mention Jesus. So, no matter what church or temple Rabbi Wise spoke to, it would rub some people the wrong way. When was that sermon given?"

"About the time Rabbi Wise was a delegate to the Democratic National Convention, where he gave the invocation," Theresa said. "My father knows him well. Like I said, he's famous, influential, but also controversial. Why did you bring up Rabbi Wise?"

"Because he was a founder of the World Jewish Congress in Switzerland," Teddy said. "The organization stayed in Zurich for a few years and then moved to Paris. When the Nazis started to ramp up their antisemitic campaign, the WJC began to lobby French and Allied governments on behalf of Jewish refugees fleeing Germany and Austria. He also urged US Jewish organizations to lobby Congress to loosen the immigration quotas for Jewish refugees."

"We're very familiar with the plight of fleeing refugees, and the harsh immigration quotas," Julia said. "That was our job at the State Department in Amsterdam from 1938 till 1941."

"The aims of the WJC are set forth in its charter," Teddy added. "It is to mobilize the Jewish people and the democratic forces against the Nazi onslaught, and to fight for equal political and economic rights everywhere. That was conveyed to the State Department by Rabbi Wise."

"We were with the State Department," Julia said, "but I never heard about Rabbi Wise, or his address, or the WJC."

"That's not surprising, is it?" Teddy answered. "No doubt it was buried away by the State Department. In 1940, General Charles de Gaulle, the leader of the French government in exile, got Wise's message and pledged to the WJC that all measures taken by the Vichy regime against the Jews would be repudiated upon France's liberation. In late 1941 and early 1942, diplomats and journalists started to receive scattered reports about mass murders of Jews in Nazi-occupied Poland and Russia, but the news was difficult to confirm. In June 1942, the WJC held a press conference in London with a member of the Polish government in exile, where they stated that an estimated one million Jews had already been murdered by the Germans."

"That's not hard to believe," Julia said. "We heard the reports when we were in Amsterdam. We met many Polish refugees."

"Working here at Treasury these last few months has opened my eyes," Teddy said. "No one outside of Germany knew the details of the Nazis' plans to commit mass murder or the Wannsee Declaration until the Riegner telegram. Allied intelligence agents had collected information about the Einsatzgruppen."

"I never heard of them," said Julia and Theresa together.

"Neither did I until recently. They were German SS mobile killing squads that ultimately murdered over one million Jews on the Eastern Front between June 1941 and June 1943. On September 12, 1941, British intelligence agents informed Prime Minister Winston Churchill, and Soviet officials publicly acknowledged it in January 1942. Gerhart M. Riegner, a representative of the World Jewish Congress, sent a cable to British and American diplomatic contacts telling them about it in August 1942. That cable went straight to the State Department."

"And I suppose the news was buried away?" said Julia. "That is so hard to believe."

"It is, isn't it? Treasury Secretary Morgenthau told me that he saw a copy. The Riegner telegram informed the Allies for the first time about the Nazi plans for the Final Solution—that is, to kill every single Jew on the continent. Riegner asked the State Department if it would also pass the message on to Rabbi Wise at the WJC, but true to form, the State Department officials did not pass it along to Wise or anyone else."

"What did the State Department do after it received the telegram? That's the important question," said Theresa.

"I just told you, the answer is nothing," said Teddy. "The State Department considered it 'a wild rumor, fueled by Jewish anxieties.' It was only three months later, on November 25, 1942, that the WJC was allowed to release that news to the world, and by then, the number of Jews murdered had already reached two million."

"It's hard to believe that the State Department would suppress that information," Julia said. "Why would they do that? Why wouldn't they want the world to know? There are good people in the State Department. We knew plenty of them. What about Sumner Welles?"

Teddy nodded. "He's a good man. Do you remember that it was Undersecretary Welles who appointed me to the position of consular officer and sent me to Amsterdam in 1938? When you and I escaped Holland last fall, it was Welles who steered me away from going back to State and sent me here to Treasury. At the time, I didn't know why. Now I do. In January 1943, at the same time you and I were passing along intelligence reports to State, telling them what was happening in the Netherlands, Rabbi Wise cabled the American embassy in Switzerland asking for more information on the Nazi murders so that it could be made public. A month later, a State Department official sent a cable basically ordering the diplomats in Switzerland not to make such information public. For the first six months of 1943, while you and I were scrambling to find places for Dutch families to hide and for good, honest people to take in a little toddler or two, or a baby, there were several cables to and from State discussing proposals to fund refugee rescues, but they never made it happen. Finally, last July, State approached Treasury to discuss releasing funds for refugees, and Treasury promptly approved. Did it happen? No. Because of certain individuals whose names you already know, the State Department continued to delay the funding."

"You mean like Breckinridge Long?"

Teddy nodded. "That's right. It was the assistant secretary of state, Breckinridge Long. When Henry Morgenthau found out what had happened, he decided to take the matter into his own hands. Maybe because he's the only Jew in the president's cabinet, I don't know, but he wanted to make a difference. He appointed John Pehle and Joe DuBois to write a report that would accurately and thoroughly detail the history of how our government had done absolutely nothing to help Jewish refugees."

"Good for them," Theresa said. "That takes courage, but that's a powerful accusation to make."

"It's true! Time after time, State buried away information or just refused to help. The final catalyst for the report was an incident involving seventy thousand Jews whose evacuation from Romania could have been bought with a $170,000 bribe. The Foreign Funds Control unit of the Treasury Department authorized the payment of the funds. Both the president and Secretary of State Cordell Hull supported it. That was five months ago. The payment has still not been funded."

"If both Cordell Hull and the president supported paying the ransom, and it is still stalled in Congress, what makes you think that the DuBois Treasury report is going to make any difference?" Julia said. "There are too many Breckinridge Longs in this country, and they don't want taxpayer money going overseas, and, I'm sorry to say, they don't want it going to Jewish refugees either. How do we change their minds?"

"We're never going to change the minds of the hard-liners, but we can change the course of affairs with a powerful report. The president can create an official government agency with his executive power and authority to help Jewish and European refugees. That's the plan," Teddy replied. "If we show it to the president, and he believes strongly in it, he can make it happen."

"Is it finished?" Theresa asked.

"I guess we'll find out tomorrow. Like I said, 'Tomorrow's the day.' 'Special delivery.'"

"As I understand American politics," Theresa said, "President Roosevelt would have to create it by an executive order, not through Congress, or it would be stalled. Isn't that true?"

"That's true," Teddy said, nodding in her direction. "Theresa knows her politics."

Julia smiled. "Professor Weissbach."

"Can I come to the meeting, or is it too confidential?" Theresa asked.

"It is super confidential," Teddy said, "but come over here with Julia tomorrow morning, bright and early, and I'll do my darndest to get you in."

CHAPTER TEN

THE NEXT MORNING, January 13, 1944, Julia and Theresa showed up at Teddy's office. "I just checked with John, and we are full speed ahead," Teddy announced. "Joe is expected to be here about nine o'clock, and we will review the report as a group. I am told it is a bombshell. Eighteen pages long. You are still a member of the State Department, Julia, so you have authority to be there."

"Did you mention Theresa?" Julia asked. "She could be a positive addition to the group. She's not only a history professor who knows political science, but she's Hungarian."

Teddy's expression changed to apologetic. "I did, but they only said they would consider it. I don't know what Joe or John is going to say. Maybe they would want to keep the report confidential from someone who is not with the government or even a US citizen."

"I have a permanent visa," Theresa said. "As of two years ago."

"I'm sorry," Teddy said. "I didn't know. I just didn't feel the time was right. This is such a dynamite report and it's so top secret, but maybe I could ask them when they arrive."

Julia put her hands on her hips. "Well, don't get your shorts in a bundle," she said. She was peeved. "I'll just ask them myself."

Teddy started to speak when the intercom buzzed. "Mr. Hartigan," the secretary announced, "Mr. Josiah DuBois, Mr. John Pehle, and Treasury General Counsel Randolph Paul have arrived. They are gathered in the third-floor conference room, and they request your presence."

Theresa looked at Teddy and said, "I'd better wait here."

"Absolutely not," said Julia. "John Pehle already knows and respects you. I'm sure they'll welcome your input."

Pehle, DuBois, and Paul were all seated around the conference table. A stack of typewritten reports sat in the middle of the table. It was Paul who spoke first. He looked at Julia and Theresa and said, "I don't think I know either of you. My name is Randolph Paul."

Teddy stepped forward. "This is Julia Powers, a member of the State Department, who served with me in Amsterdam. She is also a Distinguished Service Medal recipient." Julia shook hands with the group. She started to introduce Theresa, but Teddy held his hand in front of her and said, "Allow me. The other woman here is Miss Theresa Weissbach, a Hungarian citizen. She is also a permanent US resident. She is a professor of history at the University of Michigan, and she has a wealth of knowledge about Hungary. She's well acquainted with important people in Europe, including Rabbi Wise." The group nodded and smiled. Teddy continued, "Julia and Theresa are here to contribute in any way they can to the content of the report. They understand that the report is classified at the highest level, and they will not speak of it outside these chambers without your prior consent."

The introduction was well received, and Paul, Pehle, and DuBois motioned for Julia and Theresa to be seated. "We welcome your input," John said.

Joe placed a copy of the report in front of each of the attendees, except he was short one copy. Julia offered to share hers with Theresa. It seemed odd to Julia that a report of this magnitude should be presented on loosely clipped typewritten pages. The title page read, *Report to the Secretary on the Acquiescence of This Government in the Murder of the Jews.*

Theresa was shocked. She covered her mouth with her hand and had to bend over to read the title twice. *"Acquiescence?"* she said incredulously. "That means 'consent without objection,' does it not? Do we have proof that the US acquiesced in the murders?"

"Not in writing," DuBois replied, "but in their actions, or inactions,

I should say. If you are an official agency of the government and have knowledge of refugee murders that are about to take place and you do nothing, then you are acquiescing!"

Paul tightened his lips. "You know that we are going to present this to President Roosevelt. We may have to smooth out the title a bit, but there is no doubt that the report lays blame on the State Department for doing nothing."

Joe DuBois then invited everyone to go through the report and make notations in the margins. If there were any questions, additions, or corrections, they would discuss them.

Julia and Theresa opened the report to the first page. It began with the following statement: "*One of the greatest crimes in history, the slaughter of the Jewish people in Europe, is continuing unabated.*" Julia and Theresa looked at each other. The opening passage was tragic, but true.

The report pulled no punches in blaming the United States government for what it termed acquiescence. "*This government has for a long time maintained that its policy is to work out programs to save those Jews of Europe who could be saved.*" The report continued in the first person with DuBois's own words: "*I am convinced on the basis of the information available to me that certain individuals in our State Department, which is charged with carrying out this policy, have been guilty not only of gross procrastination and willful failure to act but even of willful attempts to prevent actions from being taken to rescue Jews from Hitler.*"

"Shocking!" said Julia. Theresa's jaw was quivering. This was to be an official government document. There was no beating around the bush about who bore the responsibility.

"*Unless remedial steps of a drastic nature are taken and taken immediately, I am certain that no effective action will be taken by this government to prevent the complete extermination of the Jews in German-controlled Europe and that this government will have to share for all time the responsibility for this extermination.*"

Over the next several pages, the report went on to list the numerous failures of the State Department: failure to cooperate with private organizations, failure to fund refugee efforts, and failure to use government machinery to rescue Jews. In fact, it did the contrary.

"The most glaring example of the use of the machinery of this government to actually prevent the rescue of Jews is the administrative restrictions that have been placed upon the granting of visas to the United States."

Julia nodded. "We have seen it, and we have lived it," she said.

For those individuals who lent their support and tried to do the right thing, the report did not hesitate to praise them. It named individuals like Congressman Emanuel Celler of New York, who opposed isolationists and called the immigration policy "cold and cruel." Like Congressman Samuel Dickstein, who held hearings on the Child Refugee Bill, whose purpose was to save "German Jews from annihilation." But their efforts often fell on deaf ears.

Page after page, the report listed failures and inactions and, worse, acts by certain American political leaders to prevent Jewish rescue. The first section of the report focused on one such situation when the State Department failed to act upon warnings from the World Jewish Congress. It was titled "World Jewish Congress Proposal to Evacuate Thousands of Jews from Romania and France." It went on to describe the five-month-delayed response, between March 13, 1943, and December 15, 1943, placing the delay squarely on the shoulders of Breckinridge Long, assistant secretary of state.

The second section was titled "Suppression of Facts Regarding Hitler's Extermination of Jews," and it named those who delayed or changed the wording on cables and reports to omit the damning information from being known, once again including Breckinridge Long.

At the end of the report, Julia and Theresa read the final paragraph: *"If men of the temperament and philosophy of Long continue in control of administration of immigration, we might as well take down the plaque from the Statue of Liberty and black out 'the lamp beside the golden door.'"*

The group sat in silence trying to digest the accusations. Some grammatical errors were corrected, one word was exchanged for another, and the report's title was changed, eliminating the term *acquiescence*.

"What happens now?" Julia asked.

"That's up to Secretary Morgenthau," Pehle answered. "He'll review the contents, and if he approves of them, and I'm quite sure he will, then he'll set an appointment with the president and deliver it. The rest is up to FDR."

"There are a number of things the president can do," DuBois said, "but we are hoping he will set up a separate agency of government to oversee the refugee problem and provide assistance in whatever way we can."

"Does that mean sending people into Europe?" Theresa said.

"I don't know if that's possible at this time," Pehle responded. "We have no forces there; the borders are all closed. Perhaps smuggling people in with false identities—is that what you're saying? What would they do once they're in?"

Theresa shrugged. "Maybe channel funds to the refugees in some way? Maybe food or medicine? I would be willing to go over there and do that."

"Terri, are you nuts?" Julia said. "Then you would become a refugee yourself."

"That is a noble proposition, Terri," said Teddy, "but you can't go over there now. There is no way for you to enter the country, no place to stay, and Julia is right, you'd become a target yourself. You could best serve your family by assisting from this side of the Atlantic. Besides, we're getting way ahead of ourselves. We don't know what FDR is going to do when he sees the report. I'm sure that Secretary Morgenthau will meet with the president very soon."

THREE DAYS LATER, Treasury Secretary Henry Morgenthau, the ranking Jewish official in the president's inner circle, met with FDR at the White House. The report, which was now titled *Personal Report to the President*, had been cleaned up and some of the damning language was more restrained. Even so, it was still a forceful, accusatory document. After the meeting, Secretary Morgenthau returned to Treasury to report that he was confident that no time would be wasted in effectuating the report.

And he was right. Within a week, on January 22, 1944, the president signed Executive Order 9417 establishing the government agency known as the War Refugee Board. The order was printed on a single page and signed by the president, granting sweeping and powerful authority to the board.

Order 9417 began with the following preamble:

Whereas it is the policy of this Government to take all measures within its power to rescue the victims of enemy oppression who are in imminent danger of death and otherwise to afford such victims all possible relief and assistance consistent with the successful prosecution of the war;

Now, Therefore, by virtue of the authority vested in me by the Constitution and the statutes of the United States, as President of the United States and as Commander in Chief of the Army and Navy, and in order to effectuate with all possible speed the rescue and relief of such victims of enemy oppression, it is hereby ordered as follows:

The order went on to list the responsibilities and powers of the board, which would answer to no one but the president. The board was to take *"all effective measures for (a) the rescue, transportation, maintenance, and relief of the victims of enemy oppression, and (b) the establishment of havens of temporary refuge for such victims."*

So that there would be no mystery about the cooperation of the State Department, the order was explicit. *"The State Department shall appoint special attachés with diplomatic status, on the recommendation of the Board, to be stationed abroad in places where it is likely that assistance can be rendered to war refugees. Additionally, the State Department, the War Department and the Treasury Department are authorized to accept the services or contributions of any private persons, private organizations, State agencies, or agencies of foreign governments in carrying out the purposes of this Order."*

The order provided that the board would appoint an executive director and concluded by stating, *"The Board shall be directly responsible to the President in carrying out the policy of this Government, as stated in the Preamble, and the Board shall report to him at frequent intervals concerning the steps taken for the rescue and relief of war refugees."*

"YOU SEE," SAID Theresa, "the order said, 'The War Department and the Treasury Department are authorized to accept the services or contributions of *any private persons.*' Well, I am a private person. I want to contribute. There has to be a way."

Teddy answered, "You're right and we will find a way, but here in America, not in Hungary. This order is a first of its kind and everything that we have wished for. No longer will humanitarian proposals die at the State Department."

Teddy was right. Never before had a US agency been created for the sole purpose of aiding "victims of enemy oppression" regardless of their citizenship, nationality, or religion. In its charter, the War Refugee Board (WRB) would be responsible for devising and carrying out programs for the rescue and relief of victims of Nazi persecution. American diplomats worldwide were instructed to enforce all WRB policies. The original members of the board were Secretary of State Cordell Hull, Secretary of the Treasury Henry Morgenthau, and Secretary of War Henry Stimson. The president allotted $1 million in federal funds for administrative purposes, but virtually all other funding for the board's work would have to come from private sources. John Pehle was appointed as executive director of the WRB.

Teddy, Julia, and Theresa knew they would be part of the effort, in whatever way they could contribute.

CHAPTER ELEVEN

BEFORE LEAVING WASHINGTON to return to Michigan, Theresa had a second meeting with John Pehle. Teddy was able to arrange it, even though John was enormously busy with his new appointment as head of the WRB. He said that Theresa could have five minutes. She reminded John that no one in Foreign Funds Control was intimately familiar with Hungary, especially regarding the Jewish population, but she and her family were well connected. Even though it was not possible for her to go to Budapest and help her family, she could serve their interest by assisting the WRB. She practically begged.

Three weeks later, Julia and Theresa were contacted at their respective homes in Michigan. An organizational meeting of the War Refugee Board was scheduled to take place at the Treasury Building, and Director John Pehle invited each of them to attend. Julia immediately called Theresa. "Did you get a letter? Did you know that John was going to ask us to the organizational meeting?"

"I had a hunch," Theresa answered. "After the president issued his executive order and before we left Washington, I had that meeting with John. I specifically asked him if I could be involved in matters concerning Hungary. I asked if the board could use me in some way. I'm dying to help, and please understand, my family is at risk. My father is a respected man, but he's not in the best of health. To continue as a leader in his community, he might need someone's help. Like mine. And if there is a crisis, he's not in a condition to defend himself or my mom. You know

I want to go there and help them if it's at all possible. If the conditions deteriorate, I need to get them out of Hungary."

"I know they already rejected your offer to go to Hungary," Julia said, "but you could still be a very valuable asset to the WRB."

"John said he was sure that the WRB could use me in some way, but he repeated that he didn't think it was possible for me to go there in person at this time. There are no easy ways of crossing the border and no way to conceal my identity once I'm in the country. I would be identified as a Jew—my birth records would show it. If I were to make it into Budapest, I would be at risk along with the rest of my people. But I would have gone if he would have let me."

"You are a brave girl."

"John told me that the board was aware of Hungary's political situation," Theresa said. "He knew that Regent Horthy had appointed a new prime minister, Miklós Kállay, and he was less enthusiastic about Germany. Kállay thought it was insane to wage a murderous campaign against the Jews who posed no threat, but he could not be considered a supporter of the Jewish community. I told John that I heard that Kállay had secretly sent messages to the State Department expressing a willingness to negotiate a peace agreement. John responded that State did receive those messages, but they disregarded them, buried them away, and nothing came of it. Then I asked him if State had received any messages directly from the Jewish community? Were there any messages from the head rabbi, from bankers, from Jewish businessmen, from my father? He shook his head. 'It's difficult to get messages in or out of Budapest,' he said, 'and often, if we do, we don't know who to contact. We have to rely on information from those who have traveled through Hungary more recently.' From what he had heard, things were quiet for the Budapest Jewish community at the present time."

"Wait a minute," Julia said. "How did someone travel through Hungary *more recently*?"

"I asked John the same question," Theresa said, "and he answered that there were people who had diplomatic immunity. I said I didn't understand, and he answered, 'Diplomats from countries that are neutral, or friendly to Germany or other Axis countries, can travel throughout Europe freely. For example, if you can show credentials that prove you are a citizen of a neutral country, like Switzerland or Sweden, you can travel and conduct your business throughout Europe and enjoy protection from local prosecution.

"I seized upon that issue. I asked John if a person would have to be a politician or an elected or appointed diplomat from a neutral country, and he said no. He said, 'Switzerland can grant immunity if a person is conducting business that benefits Switzerland or its citizens. It could be anyone. Switzerland might issue an official stamped letter showing that the carrier is under the protection of the Swiss government, and that would convey diplomatic immunity to the traveler.'"

"And the Nazis would honor that?" Julia asked.

"John said they're supposed to, and up to now, they have. Germany has reciprocal immunity for its citizens, and they do business all over Europe. I wanted to pursue this further and find out if I could get a diplomatic pass and go to Hungary and check on my family, but John looked at his watch and said he had to leave. Maybe he was just tired of my questions. Before he left, I offered to do whatever I could to help the WRB. He said that there was a good chance that information on Hungary might still be filed away with the State Department. The hope is that it will be located and transferred to the WRB in the new spirit of cooperation. He asked me if I'd be willing to go through some of the State Department reports, when and as they are delivered to the WRB. Of course, I said yes."

"Can you do that from your apartment in Ann Arbor?" Julia asked.

"No. He wants me to return to Washington. I took a leave from the U of M history department, which was very understanding. What about you, Julia?"

"I'm sitting on the fence. I spoke with John as well and beyond attending the organizational meeting, I offered to help in any way I could. He said he would contact me. I'm still waiting for the phone to ring."

"What are you doing in Detroit?"

"Nothing," Julia said. "Wasting away in the Motor City."

"Good. Pack your stuff. Come with me, and we can stay together in

DC. Until they find something for you, you can examine documents with me."

JULIA WAS FOLDING her clothes and packing them into her suitcase when her mother entered the room. "I wish you weren't going," she said to Julia. "You just got home."

"I know, but I might be able to help out for a little while in Washington. Wouldn't you want me to do that?"

Her mother looked at her sheepishly. "Truthfully speaking, no, I wouldn't. I missed you so badly, and I keep thinking that I almost lost you. The world is so dangerous. You did your part; now stay here and find something interesting to do."

"I'm only going to Washington, Mom; I'm not going to the Netherlands," Julia replied. "Theresa and I are staying in a room near Dupont Circle. The government is paying for it. We're going to review documents for the War Refugee Board. We even get a salary. They expect to receive information from the State Department, and they need people to sort through it. I'm not going anywhere near Europe."

Her mother gave her a challenging look. "Promise?"

The taxi honked, and Julia leaned over to give her mother a kiss. "That's the plan. There are meetings set up starting tomorrow." She took her suitcase and headed out the door.

Her mother watched her go with a doleful expression. "You didn't say *promise*."

THERESA AND JULIA entered the Treasury Building and were directed to the conference room where twenty or so other people were gathering. At nine AM, John Pehle walked in with Josiah DuBois. "Thank you all for coming so nice and early," John said. "We are still assembling information, much of which has been in boxes in a State Department storage room, and we have been going through them and organizing them by country. Those who have a background in France or who are fluent in French will be given documents concerning France. A slightly larger group will be given papers concerning Romania. Other groups will focus on Russia, Austria, Hungary, Bulgaria, or Poland, and we will place everyone in rooms where you can spread out the papers and examine them." John gestured to the conference table, where separate piles of documents were arranged by country with a label on top. "You will each find your names next to a stack of documents. Some are letters, some are cables, some will be important, and some will not. Go through them the best you can, make your notes, and pull out the ones that are of obvious importance. No matter how deeply engrossed you are in your analysis, I'd like you all back here in the conference room at five PM."

John continued with his instructions. "When you return this afternoon, you will all hear our exciting plans for the operation of the WRB. Our purpose is stated in our title; we are going to do everything we can to aid in the rescue of European refugees. To that end, we have been reaching out to talented and influential persons who have means of assisting us in our rescue efforts. You will meet the first of those individuals this afternoon."

There was a buzz in response to John's announcement. "I wonder who it will be?" was the chatter. Everyone wanted to know how this person would help in WRB's refugee efforts. *Can he physically evacuate a community of refugees? We don't have an army anywhere near Europe. We have no soldiers on the continent. All Europe is Hitler's playground. How do we effectuate a rescue?* But John waved them all off. "Later," he said. "Right now, let's split into our groups and start sorting the messages."

Julia and Theresa were given a stack of papers labeled *Hungary/ Transylvania* and directed to a small meeting room. Many of the papers were handwritten, sometimes in Hungarian, sometimes in German, and some appeared to be intraoffice notes in English. Theresa was a big help. Aside from her fluency in Hungarian and English, she had studied German in high school. She'd also brought a Hungarian dictionary. They decided to organize the documents by subject matter: government, communications with Germany, military, immigration, human relations, and those documents specifically concerning Jewish matters.

Many were hard to read or even harder to understand. The great majority concerned complaints to the State Department that the allotment of visas for Hungary was insufficient or that the limited number of permissions to enter the US was unfair. "They're right," Theresa said. "Hungary has a population of about nine million people, ten percent of whom are Jewish, and the State Department limits the visa quota to 869 per year."

"You're preaching to the choir," said Julia. "I dealt with those complaints for five years in Amsterdam. It's in the hands of Congress, and they're not about to change the quotas. Some things never change. But let me ask you about something different. I've seen documents that mention the Nyilaskeresztes Párt and its leader, Ferenc Szálasi. They're scary. What do you know about them?"

Theresa shook her head. "Nothing. *Nyilaskeresztes Párt* means the 'Arrow Cross Party.' I'm not familiar with them. From what I can piece together," she said, holding up a few pieces of paper, "it's a new political party in Hungary, started in 1937. Their literature is anti-capitalist, anti-Communist, and definitely antisemitic. They are critical of Miklós Horthy in a nasty way, but they are not critical of Germany or the Nazis. In fact, they quote Hitler and his goals."

Julia shrugged. "Probably just some fringe outfit."

"I wouldn't be so sure. This paper claims that they received twenty-five percent of the 1939 Hungarian national vote. If they did, it was four years ago," Theresa said. "If Horthy is still in power today and holding his own, this Arrow Cross gang hasn't made much inroad. Hungary is still free from Nazi rule."

AS FIVE PM approached, Julia and Theresa gathered up their papers and headed to the conference room. "If they ask us what new things we have learned, it hasn't been much," Theresa said. "Nothing new except for the Arrow Cross bunch. We didn't see anything about unrest in Budapest. There isn't anything we've read concerning mass arrests, or deportations, or anything like that. Everything seems stable. I have been looking for signs of danger, but Budapest seems relatively predictable for the Jewish community."

When the WRB group reassembled in the third-floor conference room, John Pehle stood at the front with a good-looking man who nodded and smiled at the members as they passed. Many stopped on their way in to say hello. He appeared to be about forty and was well dressed, with thick, curly hair, dark eyebrows, and an engaging Hollywood smile.

Theresa elbowed Julia. "Watch yourself," she said. "This man could be trouble."

"I like that kind of trouble," Julia answered. Then it was their turn to stop and say hello to John and his guest.

"Allow me to introduce Ira Hirschmann," John said to the two of them. "He is a most interesting man, as you will soon learn. Ira, this is Theresa Weissbach and Julia Powers. Miss Weissbach is Hungarian and a history professor at the University of Michigan."

Hirschman held out his hand to greet her. "Very impressive," he said.

"It's nice to meet you," Theresa said. "My friend Julia is also from Michigan. She just finished serving the State Department in the Netherlands and was awarded the Distinguished Service Medal."

Ira shook her hand. "Congratulations," he said. "I'm pleased to meet you as well."

John added, "Theresa's family is quite prominent in Budapest, and she hasn't heard from them in a long time. She is most concerned about their welfare. They're Jewish."

Ira nodded. "Of course, I understand. I was in Budapest recently," he said. "I don't know a family named Weissbach, but things seemed relatively calm for the Jewish community in Budapest. I wouldn't say *safe*, because no place is safe for Jews in Europe, but to my knowledge, no displacements or mass arrests are taking place. Of all the countries surrounding Germany, Jews seem the securest in Hungary. That's why Jewish refugees from surrounding countries are migrating to Hungary if they get the chance. Romania, Bulgaria, Ukraine all have refugees fleeing to Hungary."

"If I may ask," Theresa said, "those refugees that are traveling into

Hungary, how do they do it? You were there recently. How did you travel safely in that area? How does someone who wants to travel into Hungary, let's say for a visit and return home, go about doing that? I desperately want to see my parents. It's been a long time, and I'm worried about them. How could I do that safely?"

Ira grimaced. "Safely? That's a hard question. For someone in your particular position, a Jewish person, I would strongly recommend against it. It's far too dangerous."

"But you can come and go without risking your life. You've done it."

"I have, that's true, but it's a long story. Maybe someday we'll talk about it."

Then the line moved up, and John and Ira greeted the next group. Theresa and Julia took their seats.

"That was pretty personal," Julia said.

"I'm desperate. I'm sorry if I was rude, but I need to get back to my family. Don't you remember when John announced that he would introduce us to a talented and influential person who has the means of assisting the WRB in rescue efforts? If that is Ira, and if he can travel to and from Hungary, maybe I can too. I'm talented and influential. Sort of."

Julia rolled her eyes. "Talented, yes. Influential, in what way? Are you a diplomat? You're being foolish."

"I am not. If Ira is only the first of several, maybe the next one could tell me. The WRB may bring in someone who does have an answer, and I will keep asking until I get one. Maybe I can go to Budapest with Ira when he returns?"

JOHN TAPPED ON the podium, cleared his throat, and said, "Welcome back, everyone. I think you all know Josiah DuBois and Randolph Paul, two of the men who helped us form the WRB," and he motioned to them sitting in the first row. "It is my honor to introduce you all now to our very special guest, Ira Hirschmann. Mr. Hirschmann is the board's first overseas representative. The first of several, we hope."

Theresa elbowed Julia. "See? The first of several."

John continued his announcement. "Mr. Hirschmann is going to Ankara, Turkey, where he will be stationed."

With that statement, Theresa put her hand on her forehead and exhaled. "Ankara. Just my luck," she said.

John continued, "Mr. Hirschmann will develop WRB programs for the rescue, transportation, maintenance, and relief of Jews and other persecuted minorities in Europe. Turkey is a neutral country, and its citizens are not under control of the Third Reich. Ira has been working to use Turkey as a gateway to British-occupied Palestine. To the extent possible, and providing they can escape into Turkey, Jewish refugees will be sent south from Ankara to Palestine."

Everyone clapped. Ira smiled and nodded.

"Ira has considerable experience in Western and Central Europe," John continued. "In 1938, he attended the Evian Conference as an observer for the United States government. Later, he went to Austria, where he helped several hundred refugees leave the country. Many of you may know Ira from his many other successful endeavors. He was a vice president of Saks Fifth Avenue and a marketing director for Bloomingdale's. He is a lover of classical music. Ira started experimental television and an FM radio station. That FM station became New York's WABF, which broadcasts live classical-music concerts. Finally, Ira is a political associate of Mayor Fiorello La Guardia.

"Last year, Jewish rescue organizations asked Ira to check out the possibility of bringing Jews from Romania, Bulgaria, and Hungary to safety in Palestine via Turkey. As I mentioned, Ira is leaving this week for Ankara on behalf of the War Refugee Board. He and the American ambassador to Turkey have managed to convince the Turkish authorities to allow refugees to land in Turkey. They promised to ensure better living conditions for thousands of Jewish refugees who manage to make their way to Turkey from war-torn Europe."

John smiled, stepped to the side, and held out his arm in Ira's direction. "Ira Hirschmann, everyone," John said, and clapped. "Let's hear it for WRB's man in Turkey!"

John's introduction was met with a standing ovation. Drinks and hors d'oeuvres were served by uniformed waiters. While people mingled, Teddy walked over and joined Julia and Theresa.

"Oh, you came at the right time," Julia said. "Drinks are served."

"I've been here for a while," Teddy responded. "I had a nice chat with Ira. He is a remarkable man. You have to ask yourself why a wealthy, comfortable man would put his life on the line, halfway around the world, to save Jewish families in Europe from being slaughtered by the Nazis. He could be killed as well."

"If you have to ask that question, you wouldn't understand the answer," Julia said. "It's because he can."

"Did you happen to speak to Ira about Hungary?" Theresa asked. "When I asked him about the Hungarian Jewish community, he told me that it was 'calm,' but then he added, 'I wouldn't say safe.' What does that tell you?"

"I'm not sure," Teddy answered. "It sounds like he's telling you that Hitler is unpredictable, but we all know that. Ira told me that the majority of Hungarian Jews hear reports from refugees, but they discount them because nothing major is happening in Hungary. They predict that such horrors will never happen in Hungary. They have faith in Horthy."

"That's foolish," Julia said. "Who is going to stop Germany from crossing the Hungarian border if Hitler wants to? The Nazi hatred of Jews is a sickness. It starts at the top and flows right down to the SS squadron leaders. I witnessed it. I saw it in their eyes. I watched them take little children and load them onto trains without a second thought, knowing they would be murdered upon arrival. The Nazis expressed no emotion whatsoever."

Teddy nodded and said, "I saw it too, but Ira said the Hungarians are confident in Horthy. He's kept the Nazis away so far."

CHAPTER TWELVE

WHILE REVIEWING THE State Department documents, Theresa searched diligently for any news concerning the Budapest Jewish community. Nothing significant had surfaced thus far, but one afternoon, John Pehle came to see her.

"I've received some disturbing news about Hungary," said John. "I'm sorry to say the situation is getting dicey. I want you to hear it from someone you trust, not just from the rumor mill."

Theresa's face flushed. Her jaw trembled. "What do you mean by that?"

"It seems that the complacency enjoyed by the Hungarian citizens might be threatened. Though Hungary is a country in a state of war, the Hungarian people have been relatively unaffected. Their way of life hasn't materially changed. That is true for the Jewish population as well. Oh, it's true, young Jewish men have been drafted as soldiers and laborers, and the economy is strained with less goods and materials, but the relationship with Germany has been stable. That may be changing."

"Hungary and Germany are allies," Theresa said. "Hitler has kept his hands off Hungary for the last five years, since the war started. Why would that relationship change? What has happened?"

John held up a hand. "Hold on. I didn't say that it had changed; I said it *may* be changing. There are rumors, unconfirmed, and no one knows for sure, but Prime Minister Kállay has apparently sent another round of peace feelers to Germany's enemies. He's done that before, but it was always kept a secret from Germany. This time, there is cause to believe that Germany has learned about it. The question is, why would Kállay turn his back on Germany and reach out to its enemies? Is Hungary's loyalty now in question? If so, how does that affect German-Hungarian relations?"

"Maybe Kállay reached out because Hungary is tired of fighting Germany's war," Theresa suggested. "Germany caused Hungary to send hundreds of thousands of soldiers to the Russian Front as an Axis member, and one hundred thousand never came back. From what we hear, Germany is not doing well on the Russian Front."

"They're not. There is no doubt of that, but think about this," John said. "Hitler has up to now let Horthy and Kállay run their country without his interference. That is extremely rare in that part of the world. Now, if Hitler hears that peace feelers are floating, Hungary's loyalty might be in question. Anyway, that is what we hear, and that is what I mean by the relationship is dicey. You and Julia have been examining the State Department's records on Hungary, right? Did you see anything that would confirm that peace feelers were received by the US from Hungary?"

Theresa shook her head. "We haven't seen any peace feelers. If they were sent, then the State Department destroyed them."

"Well, there are a lot of ifs here. If peace feelers were actually sent, if Hitler does learn about them, then he will have to weigh his options. Would such a message really pose a threat to Germany? Probably not. How could a peace feeler, sent to the US, thousands of miles away, make any difference? What can the US do for Hungary? Probably nothing. There are no Allied troops anywhere on the continent. On the other hand, Hitler might conclude that Kállay and Horthy are no longer trustworthy, and he may want a change in Hungary's leadership, and he may send his troops to occupy the country. Anyway, keep your eyes open while you are reviewing the documents."

"Of course. Although it doesn't make a lot of sense to me," Theresa said. "What does Hitler have to gain by occupying an ally? That's irrational."

"Hitler is not rational," John said flatly. "If he reads such a message and becomes furious, like he frequently does, he will send his troops into Hungary without a second thought. They would immediately occupy Hungary and make it a puppet state."

"That's a horrible thought," Theresa said, "because the first thing he'd do is implement his racial laws, right? He'd send his squads to arrest all the Jews wherever they could be found. That's what he did in the Netherlands and Poland and Belgium and Austria—"

"All right, all right." John held his hand up. "We know. Just keep your eyes open for further information you might come across in your review."

"If you want accurate information, why doesn't the WRB send someone into Budapest to find out and report back?" Theresa said. "Like me?"

"Easier said than done. The WRB is planning on sending its agents wherever they are needed. That is the WRB's reason for being. It's in the charter, to aid refugees wherever they may be. But it takes time; it doesn't happen overnight."

Theresa stuck out her chin. "Send *me*. I'll report back. I know who to talk to. My family has contacts. I'll find out what is going on."

"I appreciate the offer, but not at this time. For one thing, we already have a contact in Budapest. He's not exactly a WRB agent, but he is someone we can talk to in confidence. His name is Carl Lutz. Do you know him?"

"I'm not familiar with the name. It doesn't sound Hungarian. Is he Hungarian? Has he always lived in Budapest?"

John shook his head. "No and no. Carl is Swiss. He is the vice consul in Switzerland's embassy in Budapest. As you know, Switzerland is a neutral country, and it represents the interests of other foreign countries that do not have diplomatic relations with the host country. The US previously had diplomatic relations with Hungary but has broken them off since the war. The Swiss embassy in Budapest is a go-between for governments that do not have embassies or consulates in Hungary but want to interact. Switzerland is the representative of fourteen countries in Hungary. Much of our Hungarian information comes through Carl."

Theresa's expression conveyed a bit of uncertainty. "Is Mr. Lutz Jewish? If not, I would wonder whether his reports contain accurate information about the Jewish community. You know, the kind of information someone like *me* could provide," Theresa said with a smile. "But if he is the only source of our information from Hungary, I would question how thorough it is. He's not Hungarian, he didn't grow up there, he's not Jewish, and he doesn't have roots or family ties there. How deep can he dig for information? Is it only on the surface or does it go deeper?"

"I see your point, Theresa, and that's very astute," said John. "I'm sure you have contacts in the Hungarian community that Carl does not have, but he's been there for two years and he's an experienced diplomat. Moreover, he is a Swiss diplomat, safe from German or Hungarian arrest. This is not his first posting. I have confidence in him, and once you meet him, you will too."

"I respect your confidence and your evaluation of Mr. Lutz. I suppose because he's a Swiss diplomat he can come and go as he pleases, and everyone will regard him as untouchable?"

John nodded. "That's correct, and Carl knows how to use it. Give him a chance and you'll feel the same way I do. He is a very intelligent, college-educated man. In fact, he graduated from George Washington University. I met him when he was here in Washington. Carl was appointed chancellor at the Swiss consulate in Philadelphia. Then he was with the Swiss consulate in St. Louis, which was where he met his wife, Gertrud, a remarkable woman. Then they were transferred to British Palestine, where Carl served as a diplomatic representative of several nations, including Germany. While there, Carl and Gertrud worked to aid both Jewish and non-Jewish refugees from Germany who had found their way to Palestine. The stories that Carl told me about what he and Gertrud did for women, children, and elderly people in Palestine are beyond belief. Now Carl has been appointed to the prestigious post of Swiss vice consul at the embassy in Budapest. That is where he and Gertrud are now."

"He is a contact, not a WRB agent? Is that correct?"

John nodded. "Yes, Theresa, you are correct. Carl is a Swiss diplomat. He runs the embassy. If he were a representative of a US agency, he would lose his immunity. So he is a contact, not a WRB agent. He exchanges information. He performs the same function on behalf of other countries that do not have diplomatic relations with the host country."

"Then let me ask this," Theresa said. "Did Kállay's peace feeler to the

US go through Carl? Otherwise, how would they get to Washington? Did he pass it on to the State Department?"

"Who knows? Could be," John said, "but that would be confidential. I wouldn't have that information. Carl does provide information to us about Hungary, and Budapest in particular. It may not be as deep as the information that you could supply, but it is valuable. Up to now, the Jewish community isn't clamoring to be rescued. Things have been quiet there. My worry is that things could change. Quite abruptly."

"Things may be quiet, but that doesn't mean that citizens can come and go as they please. You said so yourself," Theresa said. "The families are basically trapped. My parents are basically trapped in a country run by a despot, who is admittedly antisemitic. Do you deny that?"

"No, I don't, though there are degrees of antisemitism. Horthy does not seem troublesome to the Jewish community right now."

"If a refugee needs help, or a community of refugees needs help, who can they turn to? Who speaks on behalf of my community? Who would stand up for them? I hope those are the questions the WRB is asking when it considers appointing agents."

John smiled. "You are a tough number, Miss Weissbach. You have the heart of a diplomat. Or a lion."

"I want to be that WRB agent."

"I know you do. Look, the WRB is just getting its feet on the ground, and at this time, we're beginning to make inroads throughout Europe. We're establishing contacts in places where there are refugees. Carl Lutz is such a contact."

"And he may be a very good one, but between you and me, our goals may not always be the same." Theresa placed a hand on John's shoulder. "I have a suggestion. Listen to me before you say no. I know the people, the culture, and the history. My information would be intelligent and sound, and I could look for ways to aid refugees. Isn't that our business? Appoint me as a WRB representative in Budapest."

John quickly shook his head. "I'll take it under consideration when the time is right. It's not something I can do today. We don't have an organization there. There is no office, there is no equipment, there is no staff. The WRB cannot just send an innocent civilian, even one as astute as you, Theresa, into a hostile country where she might be a target. You're Jewish, you're Hungarian, and you have no claim to diplomatic immunity. You could be captured and tortured for information. If Hitler attacks, as he might do any day, you would find yourself in the same boat as the rest of the Jewish refugees. I can't let you go. Hold off for the time being. There is a good chance that Carl will be in Washington next week. He may have answers or suggestions for us."

LATER THAT EVENING, Theresa met Julia and Teddy for dinner. She recounted the afternoon's discussion with John Pehle. "He said things were dicey, unsettled, disturbing," Theresa said. "If you read between the lines, it means that Germany is on the verge of a takeover. It may just be a rumor, but John seems to think that it is a possibility."

"Here we go again," Julia said. "I've seen it. I've lived through it. If the Nazis overrun Hungary, they'll appoint a monster like Seyss-Inquart to run the country, just like in the Netherlands. And I hate to say it, but you know what he will do, don't you? He will try to make Hungary *Judenfrei*. They did that in Holland. They herded all the Jews into ghettos, put them onto trains, and sent them to concentration camps. I agree with Theresa that the leaders of the Jewish community should be alerted to prepare for the worst. They need to plan whatever measures they can to protect their people."

"Take it easy, Julia," Teddy said. "The sky hasn't fallen yet. These are just possibilities. And now you have the WRB."

"There are no WRB agents stationed there, none who have the experience to assist the people in such a situation," Theresa said. "John gave me a positive description of Carl Lutz that does convey some confidence. When I told John that I was the right woman to be appointed as a WRB agent, he spoke glowingly about Carl, his intelligence, and his dedication. Maybe Carl is the right man for the job."

"What job? That is the question. He is not a WRB agent," Julia said. "Where do his loyalties lie?"

"This is all foolish talk," Teddy said, "and it's not getting us anywhere. There are almost a million Jews spread all throughout Hungary. How is one person or twenty people going to outmaneuver the Nazis and their troops? I know you have contacts, Theresa, but we have no way of getting into Budapest. We have no credentials, no diplomatic immunity. According to John, we would just be sitting ducks, sacrificing ourselves as two more victims. To make any difference at all in the face of a Nazi occupation, you need experienced people, you need rescue squads, you need credentials, and you need an organization. That is a job for the WRB, and as we sit here, I have no idea how or if John will make that happen."

Julia nodded. "As much as I would like to go, John is right. In the Netherlands, we had hundreds of people working together to rescue Dutch Jews, and there were one hundred fifty thousand of them, not a million. That effort had to be well organized, and even with all our joint efforts, we were only able to save a percentage, and I was lucky to have escaped Amsterdam alive."

"John told me that Carl Lutz is coming here to Washington next week and we will be able to talk to him," Theresa said. "I'm sure he will have current information about Hungary; he's been there for two years. He's with the Swiss embassy. He has the credentials; he can go anywhere he pleases. John also told me that Lutz and his wife have done outstanding humanitarian work in Palestine. Let's listen with an open mind. Maybe something will come of the meeting."

"You know what just occurred to me?" Julia said with a bright smile. "Do you know who else spends time in Hungary and who has diplomatic immunity? Raoul Wallenberg. Swedes can come and go wherever they want if they bring their Swedish credentials. Rudy travels all throughout Europe as a sales representative. For all I know, Rudy may be in Hungary right now on business. Maybe Carl knows him. I wonder if Carl can put me in touch with him."

"Oh, wouldn't you like that?" said Theresa with a grin.

"I would, indeed," Julia said with a smile. "Rudy is a good, honest man, and he works for Kálmán Lauer, who is Jewish. He might be just the person that the WRB needs in Hungary."

"Do we know where Rudy is or how to get in touch with him? Do we know where Kálmán Lauer is? Just because they do business in Hungary doesn't mean they are reachable or that they would agree to be contacts for WRB." Theresa shrugged. "I don't know how that helps us at this particular time."

"Don't be a doubter, Terri. I'm sure he would be a great contact. Let's try to find him."

CHAPTER THIRTEEN

A FEW DAYS later, as Theresa and Julia were about to break for lunch, they received a telephone call from John Pehle. "The Swiss vice consul, Carl Lutz, has arrived from Hungary," he said, "and he is meeting with the WRB this afternoon at two o'clock. It is not open to the public, only to the board, and the fact that Mr. Lutz is in Washington for a meeting is itself confidential."

"Only to the board?" Theresa groaned. "You told me that I would be able to talk with him when he came. I'm disappointed."

"Well, don't be. While Carl and I were talking, I brought up the issue of contacts within the Budapest Jewish community. Did he have them, did he need them? Carl bemoaned the fact that he didn't have deep contacts in that community, at least not any that he could trust. He would like a contact who would trust him and could make the leaders feel more at ease."

Theresa jumped up. "That's me! I could be that contact. I could provide introductions to the head rabbi, to the business leaders, to my father. They would all trust me. They know my family."

"I mentioned you to Carl," John said, "and he asked if he might meet with you prior to this afternoon's board meeting. He's at the Swiss embassy. If you can make it, I'd advise you to come right away."

"What about Julia?"

"We only spoke about you. This afternoon's meeting with the WRB is very private. I don't know how many people are aware that Carl is even in the US. He has a few high-level diplomatic meetings, and then he is returning to Budapest. If you can, come over here as soon as possible. You would have a few minutes with Carl before the others arrive."

"On my way," she said, and set down the phone.

WHEN SHE ARRIVED at the embassy, Theresa was shown into an office where Carl and John were seated. Carl looked to be in his middle to late forties. He was thin and nicely dressed in a suit and tie, and he wore frameless glasses. His dark hair was combed to the side. Most importantly to Theresa, he wore a welcoming smile.

"Carl," John said, "allow me to introduce you to Professor Theresa Weissbach. She is the one I have been telling you about."

Carl nodded and extended his hand. "Very nice to meet you, Professor Weissbach. John tells me that you have been imploring him to be appointed as a WRB agent in Budapest. Is that right?"

John smiled. "*Imploring* is a gentle term to describe Theresa's gift of persuasion. *Persistent* is more like it. She is understandably worried about her family. She hasn't heard from them in a long time. The news that comes out of Hungary these days is by rumor only, and it is disturbing."

Carl agreed. "Long-distance communications are limited, if they are available at all. We have them at the embassy, but the average man has only local service."

"Do you happen to know my parents," Theresa said, "Benjamin and Greta Weissbach? Until recently, my father was a top surgeon at Semmelweis University Hospital. He is on the board of directors. He is also on the board of directors of the Great Synagogue on Dohány Street, the largest synagogue in all of Europe. But I haven't heard a word in so long. I am worried sick about them."

"I've heard his name mentioned," Carl said, "and I wish I had better news about your community. I'm afraid it's all very unsettling. A big part of my problem is that I lack access into your community on a personal level. As a Swiss diplomat, my job is to cultivate relationships with all prongs of Hungarian society, not only the Hungarian government but also influential leaders in the community, including religious leaders and even German officials stationed in Budapest. I can tell you that while the Jewish people are physically unharmed, they are not free from discrimination. There are numerous laws restricting their freedom. That is why I have assisted some in contacting representatives of British-occupied Palestine."

"Before his appointment in Budapest, Carl was at the Swiss consulate in Jaffa in British Palestine," John interjected. "And for a brief time, he served at the Swiss embassy in Berlin."

"He was at Berlin in the midst of the war?"

John nodded. "Germany respects Carl and also Switzerland's neutrality. Carl was in Jaffa in 1939 when the war started. Germany was one of the countries that asked Switzerland to represent its interest in British Palestine, especially with regard to German citizens."

Theresa shook her head as if to clear the cobwebs. "This is all confusing to me. Germany is at war with Great Britain, yet Germany has interests in British Palestine that it wants protected?"

"That's right," John said. "German people have economic interests throughout the Middle East. The Swiss embassy represented them in dealings with British Palestine. During this time, thousands of German refugees made their way out of Germany and down to Palestine. Carl witnessed their plight and learned their stories. The first thing he did was take down the German consulate's swastika and replace it with the flag of Switzerland. He even looked after German prisoners of war held in Jaffa, for which the German state praised him."

Theresa's eyes opened wide. "He can do that? He can arrange for Jewish citizens to immigrate to Palestine? Were there many who took advantage of that and emigrated?"

John nodded. "Thousands. Isn't that right, Carl?"

Carl shrugged modestly and then nodded.

"If it was necessary for all those children to leave Hungary," Theresa said, "then the conditions must have deteriorated badly after I left in 1933. Is that correct?"

"As you know, 1933 was a pivotal year, not only for Germany but for all of Europe," Carl answered. "That was the year that Adolf Hitler was appointed as German chancellor and took power. Since then, there have been many laws directed against minorities, not just Jews, and not only in Germany, but in the countries that Germany now controls."

"Germany doesn't control Hungary," Theresa argued, "at least as far as I'm aware."

"And we hope it never will," said Carl, "yet through the social and political biases held by Germany and the Axis countries, antisemitism in Hungary has increased. The Hungarian government has passed laws restricting Jewish freedom, making it difficult for Jews to hold a license or earn a living, limiting Jewish freedom to travel or even to own property. These days, Jews are prevented from leaving the country. I'm sure I'm not telling you anything you don't already know."

"I don't know all that," Theresa said. "I've lost touch with my people. Tell me, if Jews are prevented from traveling outside the country, how did the thousands of Jewish children immigrate to Palestine?"

"Many of them were protected by the government of Switzerland. They were covered by Swiss letters of protection. It allowed safe travel to and from Swiss areas."

"Why would the Nazis honor that? They don't have to. If they felt like it, they could take over Switzerland tomorrow."

"The Germans are not at war with Switzerland, and in many respects, the neutrality serves German interests. Germany recognizes Switzerland and its sovereign immunity. I was allowed to come to Berlin as a Swiss emissary, and I lived in Germany for a year. Because of my credentials, I was free from Germany's abuse and its restrictive laws."

"Let me ask you a question, if I may," Theresa said. "If I had one of those letters you mentioned, could I travel to Budapest, spend time there, check on my family, and then leave and return to America?"

"Conceivably," Carl said. "It would not be easy to travel there, and you have no Swiss business, but it is likely that your letter of protection would still be honored."

"And I wouldn't be arrested or restricted because I am Jewish?"

"Again, conceivably. You might be stopped at the border and asked for your identification, and they might ask you what your business is. And it is possible that your religious affiliation might be revealed, but the letter is supposed to allow for safe passage."

"So, I could travel to Budapest and see my family without fear of arrest or punishment if I had one of those letters?"

"Hmm. Nothing is free from risk these days. A Swiss letter of protection indicates that your business is in Switzerland's interest. It should ensure your safety, but we are in a world of human beings. Some understand and follow the law and its regulations, and some do not. Swiss letters are official. They are numbered. Some are issued to travel away from Hungary to a safe location, like Turkey or Palestine, but their most common use is for businessmen from friendly or neutral nations to conduct their business within the Axis countries. There is a lot of money to be made by going into Germany or Austria on business. They come and go, protected from local restrictions."

"Wouldn't my providing you with information about the Budapest Jewish community help you to cultivate relationships? You said that a letter of protection would have to be in Switzerland's interest. I could be your assistant, right?"

"Theoretically, but even if you possessed such a letter, Miss Weissbach, how do you plan on safely traveling into Budapest and back again?"

"I don't know that part yet. How do you safely travel there and back?" Theresa asked with a shrug. "I'm not afraid. If my family can face the dangers, so can I. If you can issue a letter to me, I'll find a way."

Carl looked over at John and said, "Is she always this unrestrained?"

"This and much more," John said.

Carl's expression turned serious. He spoke softly. "What I am about to tell you is very private," he said. "Keep in mind I am not recommending that you come to Hungary as my assistant. Hungary right now is a very dangerous place to be. It is teetering, and that is the principal reason I have come here to Washington. Things could escalate quickly in Hungary, and the government may struggle to maintain its stability. It is not the place to go these days. If there is a weakness of leadership . . ."

"Then Hitler would fill the void? Is that what you're saying?" Theresa added nervously. "He would send his troops and conquer Hungary, even though it is an ally?"

"I'm afraid we believe that to be correct."

"Does this have anything to do with Minister Kállay's peace feeler?" Theresa asked.

Carl turned to John. "How does this woman know about that?"

"She knows," John answered. "Apparently, Kállay's messages are no longer a secret."

"That's right," Theresa said. "We heard that they were sent to the State Department and to Great Britain. Maybe to Russia as well. What do you think Hitler will do when he considers that? If he determines that Horthy and Kállay are no longer loyal, will he replace them? Will he require Hungary to hold another election, just like Hungary was forced to do at the end of the First World War, but this time under Hitler's rules?"

"It wouldn't be an election," John said, "it would be an appointment. If Germany overtakes and occupies Hungary, it would appoint a ruler. Kállay's message is a turning point. Hitler cannot allow a peace agreement between Hungary and Russia. Germany is already retreating on the Russian Front. If Hungary aligns with Russia, then Germany has a stronger enemy on its southern border."

"But right now, they are allies," Theresa said, "and it makes no sense for them to battle each other."

"I'm afraid that logic may not hold," said Carl knowingly. "Even though an alliance or a peace agreement has yet to be formed between Hungary and Russia, or between Hungary and Great Britain or the United States or any other member of the Allied forces, we find it extremely likely that Germany will decide to take over Hungary in the very near future. It may be purely defensive, but the result would be the same."

"Very near future?" said John. "What do you know that we don't know?"

"We both know that the Kállay peace feelers, as they are called, have been delivered to Washington. The State Department has yet to act."

"And it won't. Kállay's messages have been discarded," John said. "That offer has been sent before. Six months ago, I think. Nothing came of it."

"Ah, but Moscow received the peace feeler and did not discard it," Carl said. "There are diplomatic discussions taking place. They may come to nothing, or maybe they will be kept on hold. Or they result in a military partnership. But the fact that Kállay has reached out to Berlin's closest and most powerful enemy is enough."

"What do you mean, it's enough?"

Carl hesitated, looked to one side, then to the other, and said in a quiet tone, "Germany is mobilizing forces right now, mostly along its southwest border. Tanks and armored vehicles are being moved there. Troop strength is being increased."

"And you know this for a fact?"

"We have sources deep in the Reichstag. I am confident that the information is correct. That is the real reason why I have come here to talk to both the Pentagon and to the WRB."

Theresa's hand shot up and covered her mouth. Finally, she said, "If Germany moves into Hungary, they will commence plans to make Hungary *Judenfrei*, won't they? And it will happen right away, won't it?"

Carl lowered his eyes.

"Won't it?" Theresa repeated, raising her voice. "They will make plans to arrest, transfer, and murder nine hundred thousand innocent people in cold blood, won't they? Won't they?" Theresa repeated, her voice becoming shriller and her tears beginning to cover her cheeks. "And who will stand between them and this ghastly scenario?"

Carl and John stood silent. Their lips were clenched.

"We can't allow this to happen," Theresa insisted. "We can't let them commit mass murder." She looked at Pehle. "Now that the US knows about it, why can't we stop them? Good people must stand up."

"Theresa, we must face reality," John answered. "Germany is in control of Europe. There are no Allied forces anywhere on the continent. If Hitler decides to institute another Poland, there will be nothing in his way, and it would be hell to stop him."

"Julia told me what she witnessed when she was assigned to Holland," Theresa said. "How the SS collected all the innocent Jewish families, their children, even the babies, and shipped them by train to concentration camps to die. But there were other people who think like we do, and they chose to stand up. In the face of the Nazi plan to murder the nation's Jews, some people did stand up,"

Theresa continued boldly, "The Nazis didn't get all of Holland's Jews, did they? Julia and Teddy and Sara, along with all the others, formed rescue squads and saved tens of thousands of innocent Dutch. Those who were saved went into hiding, and they're still there, alive in the Netherlands, waiting until Germany is finally smashed. And it will be. You know it will be. Evil may win a battle, but it never wins the war."

Carl held up his hand. "Theresa, we don't know for certain that Germany will invade Hungary," he said. "It may be massing its forces, but it hasn't moved. As of today, Hungary and Germany are still allies, and Hitler hasn't invaded."

"But you said you have information from your contact in the Reichstag," Theresa said. "We shouldn't wait. What good does waiting do? We must do something. We must make plans. Over nine hundred thousand Jewish lives depend on it!"

Carl lowered his eyes. "There were over three million Jews in Poland when this war started, and it was a much larger and stronger country than Hungary. Nothing stopped the Nazis from their *Judenfrei* murders. We don't know how many they murdered, but there aren't many left to save."

"But she's right. It doesn't mean that we give up," John said. "That's why we have a War Refugee Board. The president supports us. The American people support us. We are well funded. Theresa is on the right track when she says that good people will stand up against tyranny. Our forces are on the southern tip of Europe. They are moving up the Italian peninsula. Mussolini is gone. Russia is moving in from the east. Until Hitler and his henchmen are defeated, we must do all we can to rescue the civilians. That is the purpose of the War Refugee Board."

Theresa raised a finger. "Mr. Lutz, you said that the Germans strictly abided by laws and rules enacted by countries that were not their enemies. For example, they respected safe conduct passes issued by Switzerland and other neutral countries. Isn't that right?"

Carl nodded. "That's true. A citizen with a Swiss letter of protection should be able to travel anywhere without fear of arrest."

"Why couldn't we protect the Jewish community by issuing and distributing safe conduct letters? Pass them out to all nine hundred thousand?"

Carl shook his head. "That is not possible. All nine hundred thousand could not possibly be on Switzerland's business. Official stamped, embossed letters are personal to the holder. They are issued to a specifically named person. They are not issued to a city or a community. Can you imagine the manpower needed to write out nine hundred thousand personal letters of protection? Even a few thousand letters? It couldn't be done."

"What if you had extra help?" said Theresa.

Carl smiled. "We would need an army, but we could always use an extra hand at the embassy. A little while ago, you said you have deep contacts in Budapest. Isn't that right?"

"I do, and my family does. Many, many contacts."

"What if I were to accept your offer," Carl said, "and you were to supply a contact for me when I go back to Budapest, maybe an elder from the synagogue?"

"I can do better than that. I can supply myself. I could be your contact to the Jewish community in Hungary."

Carl stood silent. Should he take her offer? Finally, he said, "What if you were to come and work with me for a given period of time? I am not suggesting that you come solely to write safe conduct letters for nine hundred thousand people but that you act as a go-between with the Jewish community. You could help get the word out. There might be something they could do or steps they could take to defend themselves."

Theresa smiled. "I would be happy to accompany you back to Budapest and be your assistant. I can help you interface with the leaders of the community like Rabbi Levy and my father. I can help you pass out letters of protection when necessary. But at some point, if things get bad enough, we have to help people escape from Hungary. Should it become necessary, I will need the assistance of the Swiss embassy to get my family safely out of Hungary."

Carl nodded. "We would do whatever we could, not just for your parents but for the entire Jewish population. You could introduce me to leaders in the Jewish community and help me cultivate a closer relationship. In some instances, it may be possible to issue multiple letters of protection. We're on the same side here."

"If I understand you correctly, Mr. Lutz, am I to travel with you when you return to Budapest?" Theresa glanced at John, who nodded his approval. "If so, I'm ready, and I gratefully accept," she said.

"Wonderful," Carl said. "I'll get to work on your papers. Get your things together. We'll be leaving in a couple of days."

"One more thing," Theresa added. "A few minutes ago, I mentioned my friend Julia Powers, the woman who was assigned to the US consulate in Amsterdam. She and I are very close friends. We are staying together in Washington. It would be rude just to walk out without talking to her. May I disclose our agreement to her? She would respect the confidentiality. She's very trustworthy. She received a medal for the services she performed rescuing people in the Netherlands. She is presently volunteering for the War Refugee Board."

"I'm sure it would be all right to discuss this with her."

CHAPTER FOURTEEN

"WHERE HAVE YOU been all day?" Julia said as Theresa entered the apartment. "The last I heard, you were going to a meeting with John Pehle."

"Oh, I did," Theresa answered with a confident smile. She pulled up a chair and sat across from Julia at the kitchen table. "Carl Lutz was there. He's the Swiss vice consul in Budapest, and he was willing to talk to John and me about Hungary."

"Was he able to answer your questions? Is it true that things are quiet in Budapest? Did you ask him about the safety of the Jewish community? Did he set your mind at ease?"

Theresa leaned forward. "Julia, you won't believe this. I'm going there. I'm going to travel to Budapest in two days. Carl is taking me! I'm going to be his assistant, and I'll be able to find out the answers for myself. I'll be able to meet with my parents, my sister, my brother, and my aunts and uncles. It'll be a great reunion."

Julia's eyes opened as big as quarters. "You're right, I don't believe you. Hungary is halfway around the world, an ally of Germany and an enemy of the United States. People are begging to get out of there. Why would you do that? I know you want to see your parents, but you'd be putting your life on the line."

Theresa gave Julia a tilted shrug. "Maybe, but I don't think so. I will be Carl's administrative assistant, an intermediary between the Swiss embassy and the Budapest Jewish community. You know, a go-between."

"You'll have an ID that will keep you safe?"

She nodded. "Carl says the Hungarian officials, even the Germans themselves, will honor the independence of Swiss government officials, and even those people who have been given a Swiss letter of protection. I will also have a Swiss ID."

Julia shook her head in disbelief. "How did all this come about?"

"John called me this morning, remember? I went to a meeting with him and Carl Lutz. It was just the three of us, and everything we said was strictly confidential."

Julia sat back and raised her palms. "Then don't say anything more."

"No, it's okay. He knows we are very close and that we're staying together, and he gave me permission to discuss it with you. But what I'm going to tell you is absolutely top secret."

Julia took her finger and ran it across her lips like a zipper.

"First, Carl advised me that as of now, the situation hasn't changed for Hungarian Jews. There are no mass arrests and no cruel pogroms punishing them."

Julia was confused. "So, if they're all right and not under any threats, why are you going into enemy territory?"

Theresa leaned forward. "Remember, this is totally confidential. Carl said that the real reason he had come to Washington was to meet with our military leaders at the Pentagon and with John Pehle at the War Refugee Board. Carl is convinced that Hitler is prepared to invade Hungary."

"What? Why? Hungary is part of his Axis group. They fight side by side on the battlefield."

"Apparently, that relationship is on shaky ground. Up to now, there have never been any reasons for Germany to doubt Hungary's loyalty. But recently, Hitler found out that Prime Minister Kállay sent secret messages to a few of Germany's enemies asking to form an alliance."

"The State Department said that nothing ever came of Kállay's so-called peace feelers that were sent some months ago," Julia said. "Besides, even if Kállay could offer such an alliance, Germany would not be threatened by Hungary. Maybe this is all just a rumor."

Theresa shook her head. She spoke in a whisper, mimicking Carl Lutz. "It's not just a rumor, and we know it for a fact. Switzerland has a contact deep inside the Reichstag. Carl feels very strongly that Germany may pull the trigger and move into Hungary within a short time."

"Then you can't go to Hungary," Julia said. "That would be insanity. The Nazis could conquer Hungary within a matter of days. Germany will install its leaders, and Hungary will become a puppet state with a monster like Seyss-Inquart pulling the strings. It would be a carbon copy of what they did in the Netherlands. I lived through that, Terri. It's far too horrible. You absolutely cannot go to Hungary!"

"I have to, Julia. I can't just sit here and not know anything about my parents, especially if there's a chance to help them escape. I want to do whatever I can to protect them. If the Germans move in, I need to get my parents out and move them to a safe place like Palestine. I have Carl's assurance that he will help me do that. If I go with Carl, a Swiss officer, then I will be protected, at least to some degree. Please don't criticize me. You'd do the same thing if it was your parents."

"I understand, and I don't fault you," Julia said. "I told Teddy I would meet him for lunch today. I was just about to leave when you walked in. Why don't you join us? Maybe Teddy can share some thoughts and offer some suggestions."

Theresa winced. "I don't think so. He'll just try to convince me not to go. Teddy will take your side, and then it will be two against one. I really don't want to argue. I want to go home, pack my bags, and go with Carl to help my parents."

"No arguments," Julia said. "The arguments are over. Just lunch."

"WHAT A NICE surprise," said Teddy as Julia and Theresa walked into the Capital Grill. "I'm glad you could come along, Terri."

"I am too," Theresa said. "It's been a busy and stressful morning."

"So I heard," Teddy said with a smile. "Are you packing?"

"You heard?"

"I just talked to John. I guess you're about to take a trip."

Julia's mouth hung open.

Theresa closed her eyes in exasperation. "I thought it was a secret. Strictly confidential."

"Well, I didn't tell anyone," Teddy said apologetically. "It's not like I called *The New York Times*."

"What did you say when you heard I was going?" Theresa asked.

"I said, 'Lucky her. I wish I could go.'"

"Seriously?" said Julia. "You said that knowing there would be an invasion?"

"I didn't know anything about an invasion. Now I do, and I still wish I were going to Budapest with Theresa and Carl." He smiled. "This is going to be the Netherlands, part two. There are innocent people there that are going to need a lot of help, the kind of help we provided last year. I guess it's in my blood."

"You're both crazy," Julia said. "What can you two possibly do to provide help? We both witnessed it, Teddy. We've experienced it. We fought against it. If Theresa goes back to Budapest, she'll put herself right in the middle of the Jewish community, and she'll be a target. I don't want my best friend to do that."

Tears were running down Theresa's cheeks. "I love you so much for saying that, and I know it's because you care, but I have to go back. You and Teddy did things in the Netherlands to save lives, and I know you don't regret it. You told me that tens of thousands of Hollanders were saved. My family and all the people I knew and loved growing up are in harm's way. You didn't run away when you were in Holland. When they closed the Amsterdam consulate and everyone went home to be safe and sound, you stayed behind because you cared about the people. You wanted to do what you could to save them."

Julia reached over and gripped Theresa's wrist. "But I wasn't alone, Terri. There were many others who had my back. There were groups of people, rescue organizations, and we all worked together to save as many as we could. We forged documents, hid families, and drove laundry trucks with hidden children, and families adopted babies who would have otherwise been killed. Even at that, we were only able to save a percentage. When the rescue efforts ended and there were no more Jews in

Holland, Teddy and I and other volunteers became targets. Our faces were posted on walls and telephone poles. Teddy and I were fortunate; we escaped with our lives. But we were able to do that because we had each other. We weren't alone. Tell her, Teddy. What can Terri do if she's alone in Budapest?"

"I don't know that she'll be alone; she'll be an assistant to the Swiss consul," answered Teddy. "But I do agree that if people don't band together and do whatever has to be done, like we did in Holland, then Jews will die. Julia, you just said that the rescuers in Holland were only able to save a percentage, but that percentage wasn't insignificant. Tens of thousands were saved, and they are alive today. A thousand babies who would have died will now live to grow up in families that love them."

Theresa nodded. "I know you are worried about my being alone, but Carl said I could go to Budapest with him, so I won't be alone. I will be working at the Swiss embassy. I will have credentials. I will be protected by diplomatic immunity. Maybe I'll help to distribute Swiss letters of protection, or help people to immigrate to Turkey or Palestine, or . . . I don't know. But I will help my family and my community in any way I can."

Julia's head sagged. She was losing this battle. "And when you go out into the city to help your family, who protects you? Who has your back? Carl is a diplomatic officer. He may or not be in Budapest at the time. Face it, Terri—you have no experience in matters like this," Julia said. "What plans would you make to help your family? Survival is a skill, an art, and you have no training. After the US consulate closed in December 1941, Teddy and I lived on the run for two years. Sometimes we hid in a safe house, sometimes with Sara's parents in the woods. We found ways of joining with secret rescue groups. We learned techniques. Ultimately, we were lucky. We escaped. But none of that would have happened if we didn't have each other. I was never alone, that's the key." Julia shook her head. "I can't let you do this alone. What kind of friend would I be if I let you go into Budapest by yourself? I'll go with you."

"I'm afraid Julie is talking sense," Teddy said. "She and I survived in Holland for two years and managed to escape because we had each other's back. You don't know what the Swiss embassy will be doing, if they'll cover for you when you are trying to rescue your people, or even if the Nazis will continue to respect Switzerland's diplomatic immunity. Julie and I were able to accomplish some wonderful deeds because we did it together and because we had the support of others in the Amsterdam community."

"I love you both for saying that," Theresa said, "but Julie can't come with me. I leave in two days, and Julie doesn't have any credentials. I'm a Hungarian citizen, and I will be a Swiss official, but Julie doesn't have anything."

"Let me talk to Carl," Teddy said. "I'd like to know his thoughts on you needing a backup or whether it's possible for Julie to have a Swiss ID too. He might agree, but he may not approve of Julie going along. Julie, you certainly don't want to go unless Carl approves."

Julia nodded. "I agree. I wouldn't go if Carl didn't want me to, although I don't know why he would object. Try to talk to him as soon as possible, Teddy. We don't have much time."

CHAPTER FIFTEEN

IT WAS THREE o'clock the next afternoon when Teddy walked into the room at the Treasury Department where Julia and Theresa were examining documents related to Theresa's assignment. He took a folder and placed it on the table. "Here we are. One set for Miss Julia Powers, and one set for Miss Theresa Weissbach. I was thinking about joining you on the trip, but I had to decline."

Theresa was surprised. "You were thinking about going to Hungary? Why?"

"For the same reasons that Julie expressed yesterday," he answered. "Julie felt that it was too dangerous for you to go alone. You're a history professor, not a soldier, and not an intelligence agent. When it comes time to transmit private messages on the wireless, or meet with partisans, or walk among the enemy, you'd be a rookie. Julie and I aren't exactly Mata Hari, but . . ."

"That's not funny," Theresa said. "Mata Hari was a German spy in World War I, and she was executed. And I don't like being called a rookie."

"I apologize," Teddy said. "I didn't mean anything by it. Carl is worried about you, justifiably, but your familiarity with Budapest's Jewish community is useful to him. He can keep an eye on you when you're in the embassy. On the other hand, you're not useful to him, Julie. You've never been to Hungary. He can't promise to watch out for you."

"I don't need a babysitter," Julia said. "I'm a seasoned intelligence agent, remember? I can use the wireless, the two-way, and I know Morse code."

Teddy held his hand up like a stop sign. "I told Carl those very things.

I told him how valuable you were in the field. I told him how many lives you saved, how well you performed for the OSS. I suggested that you would help protect Terri."

Julia had her hands on her hips. "And what did Ambassador Lutz say to that?"

"He's a vice consul, not an ambassador," Teddy interjected, "but he still had a doubtful look in his eyes, and he looked at me and said, 'I don't think so.' Then I asked him if it would change his mind if I went along and kept an eye on both of you. I told him we were a great team. I still don't think he was convinced, but when I said we were very close to Undersecretary Sumner Welles and other State Department officers, he changed his mind. Not that he was intimidated; he just thought that our connections might be useful. He agreed to let me go, but then I woke up. I apologized and said, 'What am I thinking? I have two children at home, and Sara's pregnant. I can't go; I have to decline. But Theresa needs a backup, and Julia is just as valuable as I am. And she's volunteered to go.' I said I would closely monitor your progress from Washington."

"I appreciate what you've done," Julia said. "Of course, I know about your two kids, but I didn't know about Sara. How far along is she?"

"Seven months."

"Congratulations!"

"I can't leave her."

"No, you can't, and we wouldn't let you. Terri and I do not have husbands or children. We're going."

"Actually, Sara encouraged me to go. She's worried about you, Julie. She still considers you her best friend, just like you were in Holland. Sara's worried about you going to Budapest, and she thinks that I could take care of you. If it weren't for the kids, she'd be going too. But in the end, I had to decline."

Julia walked over and gave Teddy a hug. "You're a sweetheart," she said. "I gotta leave now."

"Where are you going?"

"I'm going to Garfinckel's Department Store. I have some serious shopping to do before I leave, but first I have to call my mother, and that's going to be tough. She is not going to take this well. She was so relieved to see me when I returned from Amsterdam. She said over and over that her prayers had been answered. I don't want to hurt her feelings. So, how do I tell her that I intend to fly back to Europe, into Hungary, an ally of Hitler's?"

"You don't," Theresa said. "You don't have to go. Your mother is here, and she needs you. I have to go because my mother is not safe. She's in danger. That's the difference. You stay here, Julie. I can manage on my own. I have Carl's protection."

Julia shook her head. "He won't always be there. He has responsibilities that take him other places. He has duties that take precedence over babysitting Theresa Weissbach, but I don't. I will watch your back. You'll need help over there. It's too tough on your own. Ask Teddy, he'll tell you."

Teddy nodded. "She has a point. It won't be easy, especially if you are depending on Carl. He's a nice guy, but he's very busy."

"I never thought it would be easy, but Terri needs a companion. I just hope my mother understands. I'll do the best I can to assure her of my safety. Hopefully, we won't be gone that long. If Terri can see her family and be assured of their safety, then we'll come back. If she isn't safe, then we need to help them emigrate. Either way, I shouldn't be gone that long."

CHAPTER SIXTEEN

THE SWISSAIR DC-2 sat on the tarmac at Washington National Airport. The top half of the sleek twin-engine plane was painted pearl white, and the belly was a brilliant silver. *Swiss Air Lines* was written on the fuselage. The plane's vertical stabilizer displayed Switzerland's national emblem: a red square with a white cross in the center. The plane was completing its fueling and final check. The boarding stairs had been wheeled out to the passenger door. The Swissair attendant waved to her coworker at the gate and the five passengers proceeded onto the tarmac—Carl Lutz, two Swiss staff members, Julia, and Theresa.

"Wow, this is a first for me," Theresa said. "I've never flown. When I came to the United States, I took a train to Lisbon, a ship to New York, and a train to Detroit. Altogether, it took me almost a week."

"I flew," said Julia. "In secret, in the dead of night, from the woods of Utrecht to England in a plane disguised to resemble a German Fokker. From there, Teddy and I flew to Washington in a US Army plane. With four stops along the way, the flight took thirty hours. It seemed like a hundred and thirty hours."

"I understand we will be making stops along the way," Theresa said. "We fly to Barcelona and from there to Bern, with stops in between. Thankfully, at each of the stops, we are allowed to get off the plane. I think we are going to stay in Bern for a couple of days before going on to Budapest."

"Why Bern?" Julia asked.

"It's the capital of Switzerland, and Carl has a meeting with his superiors," Theresa replied. "The Swiss Federal Department of Defense is located there, and they manage all the Swiss consuls, including the one in Budapest. Carl reserved rooms for us at the Hotel Schweizerhof in Bern. He said we'd like it."

After the plane was in the air, Carl walked back to Theresa and Julia. "How is everybody this morning?" he said cheerfully. "Smooth takeoff, wasn't it? Are we ready for the long ride?"

"Ready as ever," said Theresa. "I am so anxious to see my family. Teddy told me that we are flying from Washington to Barcelona, Spain. That seems odd to me. Isn't Barcelona south of Switzerland and even Hungary? Why do we land there?"

"True, it is south. It's not the most direct route to Bern, but we want to get there alive, and it's the safest way. There is no war going on there. If you flew straight to England, across Nazi-occupied France and then Germany itself, you'd stand a good chance that some Nazi air patrol or some trigger-happy Luftwaffe squad leader would order the plane to be grounded. Or maybe he'd shoot at us. Barcelona is out of the way, but it's a lot more peaceful. And it is also a Swissair hub. Swissair has a terminal and a hangar in Barcelona. It's a short flight from there to Bern."

"Okay then, how do we get from Bern to Budapest?" Julia asked.

"An hour-and-a-half plane ride," answered Carl. "Another puddle jump. You could take the train, but it would be ten hours, and you'd go through border checks at Germany, Austria, and again at Hungary. It makes more sense to fly."

Theresa thanked him for the information, and he returned to his seat. She reached into a bag she was carrying. "Since we are going to be on this plane for such a long time," she said to Julia, "I bought you a book." She handed her a book titled *Hungarian Phrase Book and Dictionary*. Theresa smiled. "We have so many hours between here and Budapest, you should know some simple phrases by the time we arrive. Otherwise, how are you going to talk to my mother and father?"

"That's a great idea," said Julia. "It will be my fourth language. I had to learn Dutch and German when I was in Amsterdam, so thank you very much for the book."

"You're welcome," Theresa said, "but you should say, *Nagyon szépen köszönjük*, which means, 'Thank you very much.'"

"Oh my goodness," Julia said. "If I'm going to say that, I have a lot of practicing to do."

"True, but remember, I am a teacher. So, *kezdjük el*."

"Huh?"

"That means, 'Let's get started.'"

THIRTY-SEVEN HOURS AFTER takeoff, the group landed in Bern. It was morning when they checked into their rooms at the Hotel Schweizerhof. The rooms were impressive, as Julia and Theresa expected they would be. The view overlooked the Swiss Parliament building and afforded spectacular views of the Alps. They agreed to take a couple of hours to rest and freshen up before meeting for lunch at the Brasserie.

That afternoon, Carl took them to the Federal Department of Defense, where they met with two senior officers, Rolf Weiss and Martin Steuben. Carl informed them that Martin was coming with them to Budapest. He was Carl's first administrative assistant at the embassy. After being introduced, Julia and Theresa thanked the Swiss government officials for agreeing to provide official Swiss identification cards.

"We are greatly indebted to you for agreeing to hire us as assistants," Theresa said. "As you may already know, my family is in Budapest, along with most of the people I knew growing up, and we couldn't visit them without your help. We understand that Hungary, and even Germany, will respect and honor the diplomatic immunity afforded to Swiss officers and their assistants."

"Hmm," Rolf, the elder officer, muttered, then added, "at least for the time being." Rolf had white hair and a full white beard, which led Theresa to believe he was in his seventies or maybe even older. He spoke slowly, deliberately, with much distinction. His demeanor demanded respect.

Theresa replied, "I'm sorry, sir, but what did you mean when you said, 'For the time being'?"

"No immunity is certain where Adolf Hitler is concerned, Miss

Weissbach. I understand that you have been informed by Vice Consul Lutz that there is a strong possibility that Hitler may decide to take over Hungary. Is that not so?"

"We've heard that," she said, "even though Hungary has always been Germany's ally. Carl told us that troops and materials have been moved into southern Germany."

"That is correct," said Martin, a fine-looking young officer in a dark blue uniform. "They are stationed just north of Munich. Maybe half a million men or more."

"Half a million?"

Martin nodded. "We believe that would be sufficient to commence an attack on Hungary. Larger numbers would follow for occupation purposes."

"You must think we are crazy to be traveling into Hungary at this time," Julia said.

"To be fair, the thought had occurred to me," Rolf answered, "but your reasons are your business."

"Aiding wartime refugees seems to be our principal business at this time," Theresa added. "Although the populace is reported to be safe, Hitler is known for making rash changes at the drop of a hat."

Rolf nodded. "Just so. I must tell you that we are also troubled that Hitler may have his ambitious eyes on Switzerland as well as Hungary."

"Switzerland?" Theresa said. "What would lead you to worry about Switzerland? I thought the führer respects Swiss neutrality and independence."

"Hmph," Rolf muttered again. "Respect? He barely understands the word, if he knows it at all. For some time now, we have been privy to intelligence reports from a source deep within the Reichstag. He confirms that Hitler detests Switzerland and that he intends to conquer us at some point. Military plans were formulated three years ago."

"I never heard that," said Theresa, "and I have been examining US State Department cables for some time. None of them refer to such a thing. Switzerland poses no threat to Germany. Germany has always honored Swiss neutrality, and don't they do business together?"

"Indeed," Rolf said. "Hitler talks out of both sides of his mouth. He was quoted saying, 'We will respect the inviolability and neutrality of Switzerland,' but then, eighteen months later, he was overheard talking to Benito Mussolini in Florence. Hitler said, 'Switzerland possesses the most disgusting and miserable people and political system. The Swiss are the mortal enemies of the new Germany.'"

"Is that because Switzerland is a democracy and Nazi Germany an autocracy?" said Theresa, in her professor demeanor.

"You are right," Martin said. "I know the person who overheard Hitler say that in Italy. Hitler mentioned Switzerland with a sour look on his face, and then he spit on the ground. A year later, Hitler was quoted as saying that Switzerland is a pimple on the face of Europe, and as a state, it no longer has a right to exist."

"Do you think that Germany is preparing to invade Switzerland at the same time he attacks Hungary?"

"Invasion plans have long been prepared," Rolf said. "Immediately after Germany defeated France in 1940, Germany started drawing up plans for the invasion of Switzerland. The German Twelfth Army submitted its fourth draft, now called Operation Tannenbaum. We are fortunate to possess a copy. With eleven German divisions and fifteen more Italian divisions entering from the south, the Axis plans are to invade Switzerland with somewhere between three hundred thousand and five hundred thousand men."

"That is the same number of men that are presently camped north of Munich," Julia observed.

"What is Switzerland doing to prepare in the face of this threat?" asked Theresa.

"That is restricted information," cautioned Rolf. "We prepare, as would any sensible Department of Defense. We have defensive strategies, and we are well supplied with advanced weaponry. We can mobilize quickly, if necessary."

Julia looked at Carl and raised her eyebrows. "Against a Nazi blitzkrieg?"

Martin leaned forward and proudly said, "We know the mountains; they do not. We are a nation of sharpshooters; they are not. We have righteousness on our side, and they most certainly do not. And we can mobilize to more than four hundred thousand overnight."

Rolf held up his hand. "Ah, but this is not a subject for our discussion today. We are here to discuss Hungary and your mission. Is that not so?"

"It is, and I apologize for being out of line," Theresa said.

"You have no need to apologize," said Rolf. "It is reasonable for you to seek a clear understanding of the entire situation, especially if your mission depends on the validity of Swiss letters of protection. Given the fact that it is 1944, and no offensive measures have been taken against Switzerland, one might wonder why we consider a German threat to be viable at this time. Tell them, Martin."

Martin nodded. "If you are familiar with the National Socialist manifesto, it is clear that it is Hitler's intention to unify all of Europe under a single banner. *All of Europe* would obviously include Switzerland. The first goal of their twenty-five-point National Socialist program states, 'We demand the unification of all Germans into Greater Germany on the basis of the people's right to self-determination.' *Greater Germany* has no set boundaries. It is wherever Germans can be found. Hitler considers it to be everywhere. *All Germans* probably means anyone of German heritage. There are German-speaking people who reside in Switzerland, so many of them that it places us within Hitler's single banner."

Martin continued, "German unification is Hitler's excuse for sending troops into an innocent country. He wants more territory to rule. It was his excuse for the Austrian Anschluss and for attacking the Czechoslovak Sudetenland. In 1939, and even before that, Hitler claimed that he was reuniting Germans from the Free City of Danzig, and that was his justification for attacking Poland. Hitler has been quoted as saying, 'One day, we will group ourselves around a single banner, and whosoever shall wish to separate us, we will exterminate!'"

Theresa cleared her throat and decided to change the subject if she could. "We came all this way to help my people in Hungary. Now we understand that Germany may be in a position to invade Hungary. They have moved troops and machinery in that direction. I would assume that

Hitler is responding to Regent Horthy and Minister Kallas, and their recent cables. He may consider them to be disloyal."

"That is a wise and informed assumption," remarked Rolf. "Let me ask you a question, Professor, if I may. Where are the two of you planning to set up your command post?"

Julia and Theresa looked at each other. "Well, we hadn't thought that through. We are going as Carl Lutz's administrative assistants. We hope that we will have office space in the Swiss embassy. Carl also mentioned that he would help us find an apartment. We have faith in Carl."

Rolf shut his eyes and shook his head. "He didn't mention that to me."

Theresa responded, "My father and his associates are important people with strong economic interests all over Budapest. If necessary, they could have a place for us. I'm sure there is an empty apartment somewhere. In an emergency, we could bunk with my parents. I haven't heard from them in over a year. I sure hope it will be all right."

Rolf looked at Carl and said, "The embassy does have extra apartments, does it not?"

Carl nodded. "Of course. Extra apartments and extra offices. We presently occupy the space vacated by the US embassy on Castle Hill. I'm sure we have accommodations for our two travelers."

"That is very kind," Theresa said. "Julia has come with me at great personal risk because she believes in aiding oppressed people."

"Swiss letters of protection should keep her safe from arrest by the Germans or the Hungarians on this trip," Carl said.

"That is very much appreciated," Theresa said, "but in the unlikely circumstance that Hitler were to invade Switzerland, what would become of all the letters of protection? Would Hitler honor them?"

Martin looked over his shoulder at Rolf. The two exchanged a silent message, and Martin turned to Theresa. "In such a case, Miss Weissbach, your guess is as good as mine. If we became enemies, I wouldn't count on Germany honoring anything we did."

Rolf pursed his lips. "For what it's worth, Professor Weissbach, allow me to offer my advice. Vice Consul Lutz has informed us about your mission to support and aid your family and the broader Jewish community in Budapest. You are worried about them, as well you should be. Carl has been trying to aid Jewish families for some time. Some of the Jewish refugees did escape carrying Swiss letters of protection. That was so even though the cantons of Switzerland may have no record of the issuance of letters to such persons." Rolf smiled and nodded in Carl's direction. "Alas, that is not a requirement. Carl has authority to issue them. My advice to you is simple: To plausibly aid the Jewish community, you are going to need more support. Qualified, experienced, and well-organized support. Especially if Germany moves on Hungary."

"That is why Julia has come with me," Theresa said. "She is experienced in aiding refugees. Our friend Teddy is also behind us, working from the War Refugee Board in Washington. They are very supportive."

Rolf smiled. "You may need more. A lot more. You need people with knowledge in such matters. Politically influential people. Carl is one such person, but he can only do so much. You need to find more Carl Lutzes, if you understand what I am saying."

"There are others," Theresa said. "Those who the WRB has come in contact with. I'm thinking of Ira Hirschmann, and Rabbi Wise of the World Jewish Congress."

Rolf beamed. "Now you have the idea. Dedicated, courageous people are essential to your mission. If one man can save a hundred lives, two can save five times that many, three can save a thousand times, and so on. It is a logical progression. Find and employ those collaborators; that should be your mission."

CHAPTER SEVENTEEN

LIMOUSINES WERE WAITING when the Swiss airplane landed at the Budapest airfield. It was midmorning, the sun was bright, and the countryside was a verdant green, even though it was early March. The ride to the city was peaceful. There were no signs of violence or of the bloody world war that was going on east of Hungary in Russia. As they approached the Buda side of the Danube River, Castle Hill came into view. It was a fairyland, something out of a children's book. Castles, towers, statues, all rich in diverse architectural styles and time periods, some reaching back to the 1200s. On the south end of the hill, the Buda Castle reigned supreme.

Theresa pointed at the large domed structure. "Look over there," she said. "That is the Royal Palace. King Charles lived there until he was deposed at the end of World War I. Now it is the home of Regent Miklós Horthy."

"You mean we're going to live next to Regent Horthy?" Julia asked.

"Not next door," Carl answered. "His residence is blocked off and heavily guarded. Your rooms are in the building at the base of the hill, next to the National Assembly, where the Swiss embassy is located."

"Look!" Julia exclaimed, pointing. "There is the statue of Prince Eugene of Savoy on his horse, just like you described it to me. Where are the King Matthias and Ilonka statues?"

Theresa smiled. "In the western courtyard on the other side. You have a good memory."

"I feel like I've been here before," Julia said, craning her neck to see in every direction. "Thanks to you, Terri, I've already seen these buildings in my mind."

The limousine stopped at a large granite office building bearing the address *Szabadsag tér 12*. One of Carl's assistants came out to meet the car and motioned for Julia and Theresa to accompany him. "Paul will show you to your rooms," Carl said.

The tall, heavyset man put their suitcases on a cart and motioned for Julia and Theresa to follow. When he had reached the rooms, Paul said, "Mr. Lutz requests that you meet with him in two hours in his office, room 217."

Each room was like a small studio apartment, with a desk and a sofa bed. There was a kitchenette and a full bathroom. The picture on Julia's wall above the couch was a watercolor painting of the San Francisco Bay Bridge, a sure sign that her room had been a US consulate apartment before it was vacated. Julia felt right at home. She put her things away, rested for a while, and then went to meet up with the others in room 217.

Theresa was the first to address the group. "Before you say anything, Carl, I want you to know how grateful I am. You have accomplished the impossible. You enabled me to return to Budapest in the midst of a terrible war to visit my family, and if necessary, to help them emigrate. I left in 1934, almost ten years ago, when my community was peaceful and prosperous. In the ensuing years, the world has witnessed the German aggression in Europe and its unjustifiable treatment of millions of innocent Jewish families. Hungary's leadership must be praised for not following Germany's racial orders. As far as I am told, Regent Horthy has not persecuted this country's Jews. But now we may have reason to fear. We heard that Hitler has massed his military troops not far from Hungary's border. I also understand that you, on occasion, have arranged for innocent families, Jewish and non-Jewish, to leave Hungary and find safety in other countries. I hope to be able to do the same thing for my family, should that be necessary. Now that I am here and working for the Swiss embassy, I want you to feel free to use me in whatever capacity you wish."

Carl smiled. "Your assistance will be most welcome, Theresa. Your experience and knowledge of Hungary are priceless, not to mention the connections that you and your family have with Budapest society. You can go places that I cannot. Together, we can form a headquarters for passing information and if necessary to manage rescue operations."

"Thank you," she said, "and if you do not mind, I would like to use your telephone to call my parents. I tried from the US without success, and I haven't spoken to them in a year."

Carl nodded and gestured to the phone sitting on the desk. "It's all yours."

Theresa quickly walked over, picked up the phone, took a deep breath, and dialed. After a moment, she shook her head. "It's ringing—that's a good sign—but there is no answer. I'll just have to walk over there and surprise them in person. I pray that they are all right."

"And I'll go with you," Julia said.

"There is another matter to discuss," Julia said. "John Pehle is expecting me to relay information to the WRB each day, if possible. I haven't spoken to him since we left Washington five days ago. I'd like to bring him up to date, especially with Rolf's comments that Germany may have its sights on Switzerland. I don't know if the WRB, or even the State Department, is aware of that information. Does the embassy have access to any long-distance communication equipment?"

"Of course," Carl said. "The embassy has a Hallicrafters SCR-299, if you're familiar with it. It has a range of two thousand miles, more than enough to reach England. From there, US Army communication officers stationed in England will be able to transmit messages on the subsea cable. Are either of you up to date on US codes?"

"I am," Julia said. "I used that equipment to contact OSS and England's MI5 when I was in Amsterdam."

"Very well. Our communication room is in the basement. You will find the transmitter down there. If you have any trouble, Charles will assist you. Just let him know when you need access. I would like it if you were present this evening at a get-acquainted meeting. Try to be in my office at eight o'clock. You can meet Charles at that time."

"Well," Theresa said, "I'd like to see my parents. Are we ready to go to their house?"

"Just a minute," Julia said. "If your father doesn't have a working telephone, how are you supposed to stay in contact with Carl and the embassy?"

"Good point," said Carl. "Julia is an American citizen and a staff member of the US State Department. Theresa is a US permanent resident and a professor at a noted US university. You are in an enemy Axis country. The two of you would make valuable hostages. The embassy has a private phone number that is monitored at all times. Feel free to use your parents' phone or a public pay phone if you need to contact us. Remember, each of you is carrying a Swiss letter of protection. Don't lose it. And be careful."

Julia and Theresa were walking to the door when Carl added, "What are you doing about currency? Even a public pay phone costs money. How do you get a cup of coffee? If you didn't bring Hungarian currency, what will you do?"

"I still have some checks from my account at the bank here in Budapest. Can't I write a check?"

Carl slowly shook his head. "The answer is no, for any number of reasons, including that you may not have any money left in the account. Several accounts have been frozen or depleted. I assume you haven't used the account for the past ten years. So, don't write a check." He reached into his desk and pulled out some currency. "We'll charge it against the WRB. If the Treasury Department can't repay it, we're in trouble," he said with a smile.

THERESA AND JULIA left Castle Hill and headed out into the neighborhoods of Budapest. It was March 14, the weather was pleasant, and the sky was clear. There was a smile on Theresa's face and a bounce in her step. "It feels like I never left," Theresa said. "Everything looks just the same. If I turned the corner and walked that way, I'd be back at my high school."

Julia nodded. She understood. "When I first returned to Detroit after serving in Amsterdam, I felt the same way. I was home where I belonged, but the feeling didn't last. The neighborhood hadn't changed, it all looked the same, but I had changed. Six years had passed with nothing to show for it. All of my friends had moved on with the rest of their lives. They had husbands and children and jobs. I had nothing. I didn't belong."

Theresa brushed away the remark. "Nonsense. You were a hero. You received a Distinguished Service Medal from the State Department and a lot of memories."

Julia shook her head. "But you have a postgraduate degree and a professorship. Most importantly, you have a future waiting for you in Ann Arbor. What do I have? I ran off with a stupid bass player."

"Give yourself a break, Julia. You've been serving your country at great risk to yourself, and you're still doing it. Even more importantly, you've been serving humanity. What about the hundreds of Dutch children you rescued? There are thousands and thousands of American soldiers who come home after their years of service. Are they supposed to say the same thing? That they wasted their time, that they don't belong anymore and they have nothing to show for their service? Are they supposed to feel shame? I hope you don't feel that way. Like the returning soldiers, you should say, 'I proudly served my country.' Our country should honor that service, and I think it does."

They turned the corner, and Theresa's face lit up. "Look," she said, "Ruszwurm Pastry Shop."

"I remember you telling me about it," Julia said. "They have creamy hot chocolate and Esterházy tortes."

"Exactly. Let's stop in," said Theresa. "We'll get a bag of tortes to take to my mom. She loves them."

As they approached the clerk, Julia said, "*Szia,*" and the clerk smiled, nodded, and said *szia* in return. Julia elbowed Theresa and waited for a compliment.

"Very good," Theresa said. "You just told her hello, and she said hi to you. Well done."

Julia cleared her throat and said, "*Orvendek,*" and the clerk nodded. Theresa ordered the tortes, smiled, and said, "You just told her it was a pleasure to meet her. Nicely done."

The clerk handed the bag of tortes to Theresa, along with a few words in Hungarian, but Julia did not understand all of them. Theresa smiled and paid for the tortes.

"*Koszonom a cipodet,*" Julia called out to the clerk as they turned to leave, but this time, the clerk wrinkled her forehead as if to say, "What?"

Theresa laughed. "What do you think you just said to her?"

Julia responded, "I said, 'Thank you for the pastries.'"

Theresa laughed again. "Not exactly. You should have said, '*Koszonom a sutemenyeket.*'"

"Uh-oh. What did I actually say?" Julia asked.

"You said, 'Thank you for the front door.'"

Julia grimaced. "I think I'll let you do the talking when we get to your parents' house."

"Keep studying," Theresa said. "You're doing well."

CHAPTER EIGHTEEN

"THIS IS IT," Theresa said in front of a classic two-story brownstone home. A street sign read *Harmat Utca*.

Julia was puzzled. "Harmat Utca?"

Theresa smiled. "It means 'Dew Street.' Don't ask me why." They stood there for a moment. Theresa finally said, "I'm nervous. Maybe this isn't our house anymore. I don't see my father's car." She walked up to the door and put her hand around the doorknob. "It's locked," she said. "I've never known them to lock the door."

"Times are different," Julia said. "Why don't you just knock?"

"It seems weird, knocking on my own door. What if my parents moved? I left ten years ago. There was no war back then. How would I know who lives here now?"

"Like this," Julia said as she reached out and rang the doorbell.

After a moment, they heard a woman's voice. *"Ki az?"*

Theresa immediately shouted, *"En vagyok az, Anya! A lanyod, Theresa!"*

The door was opened by a woman, tall and thin like her daughter, but with gray hair. Their facial features were remarkably similar, but Anya's jaw was trembling, and her breaths were short, like gasps. "Terri, Terri," she said hysterically as she threw her arms around her daughter. Julia also broke into tears. Theresa reached over, put her arm around Julia, and pulled her into a three-way hug. *"Anya,"* she said, gesturing at Julia, *"ö Julia."*

Her mother stepped back and said, *"Emlekszem rad, Julia."*

"She says she remembers you," Theresa said. Her mother showed them into the living room, searched her memory for the correct words, and finally said, "I meet you at Michigan, Julia. When we come with Terri."

Julia was surprised. "You speak English so well, Mrs. Weissbach."

"She taught herself when I went away to school," Theresa said.

"Remarkable."

"She asks that you either call her *Anya*, which means 'Mother,' or by her given name, Greta."

Theresa asked where her father was. Was he working at the hospital?

Greta shook her head and answered that he was not working full-time. Only for special cases. "He has been very active at the synagogue lately, and right now, he is in a meeting there. He says it is an important meeting." When Theresa asked what the meeting was about, Greta admitted she did not know. It was a hush-hush meeting—that was all she knew. Greta tapped her finger on her lips.

"I almost forgot," Julia said, and she handed the bag of tortes to Greta, who responded with a string of *koszonom*s, which Julia knew meant "Thank you very much."

"I love these," Greta said as she stepped into the kitchen to brew a pot of coffee. A few minutes later, she set a table and invited them to be seated. "Such a surprise," she said. "I did not expect to see you here in Budapest. Not these days. Not since the war started in 1941."

"We had special permission," Theresa said. "But the real reason I'm here is that I begged and begged to come see you, and the right people heard me and brought me to Budapest. To you, Anya. I've been so worried about you and Apa and Sammy and Becca. It is so dangerous these days."

Greta answered with a smile, saying, "No, no, Terri, we're not in danger. Budapest is safe. You just walked along the streets, didn't you? Were they dangerous? You didn't see armies and guns. It's been very quiet for the last three years even though we are in a state of war with England and Russia."

"And the United States," added Julia.

"You're not following why I'm so concerned, Anya," said Theresa. "It's because you are Jewish, our family is Jewish, and that's why you are in danger. Hungary is the last Jewish community left in Europe. Hitler has decimated all the others, and if he has his way . . . well. It doesn't matter. I came here because I want you to think about moving somewhere safe until the danger is gone."

Greta shook her head. "Oh, Terri, you are so sweet. But this is the only home we've ever known. I know that our government has, from time to time, issued unfair rules against Jews, but religious prejudice is nothing new. The Bible tells you that Jews have faced prejudice for thousands of years. But you grew up here, you know Budapest; it is home to a lovely Jewish community, no matter what the Hungarian leaders may think about us from time to time. I really don't know anything about Jewish communities in other European countries. We don't get that news. I assume there may be prejudice in other countries too. Maybe it's like us, maybe it is worse."

"I'm not talking about simple prejudice, Anya. Obviously, the truth is being withheld from the Hungarian Jewish community. The Budapesti have no access to the outside world, and they don't know what is going on. You don't even have a working telephone."

"I have a telephone. It had better work—your brother is an administrator for the Budapest Telephone Company. Two years ago, they blocked international calls for security reasons. That is why you couldn't call us." Greta shrugged. "Look, the first half of my life, we didn't have phones at all, and we got along just fine. When the war is over, the telephones will work again just fine. Sweetheart, I don't want to think about leaving Hungary. Where would I go? The Nazis aren't here, and there is no reason for them to come here. Hungary is on the same side as Germany. They don't want to fight us."

"Anya, we think they may come here anyway. They have gone into other countries that are on their side. They wouldn't have to fight; they would just walk in and take over the government without a fight. Then they will appoint people to run our country. That's what they do. They've done that elsewhere. And when they do, they pass terrible laws and pogroms designed to punish the Jews. That is the reason I came here. Of course I wanted so badly to see you, but also to tell you that it may be necessary to leave Hungary before it gets bad."

"Oh, I don't know," Greta murmured. "What would your father say?"

"We'll see." Theresa checked her watch. "When will Apa be home?"

Greta shrugged. "He left for synagogue early this morning, and I don't know when he will come home. I don't know if he is still at synagogue or if he has gone someplace else."

"Can you call him at the synagogue? Can you tell him that we are here and we want to talk to him? Don't say we want you to leave Hungary or anything like that. Don't talk about the war or the Nazis. Just say we're here, we love him, and we want to talk."

"He doesn't like it if I interrupt him at synagogue. He is a very important leader there. He was the president for several years before his heart attack, and he is still well respected. The congregants all look up to him."

"Then I'll call him," Theresa said. "He won't get mad at his little girl."

Greta gave the telephone number to Theresa, who made the call. "This is Theresa Weissbach," she said to the man who answered the phone. "Is it possible to speak to my father, Mr. Benjamin Weissbach?"

"I'm sorry," the man said, "but he is in an important meeting with Rabbi Levy, and the assistant rabbi, and members of the board of directors. He would not like it if I disturbed him."

"How long will the meeting last?"

"There is no way to know, Miss Weissbach. I would not expect your father to return home until very late tonight. Like I said, it's very, very important."

"Well, this call is just as important, maybe more so. So, if you don't mind, please put him on the phone. Otherwise, I will come over to the synagogue. I want to speak to my father, meeting or no meeting."

The man breathed a sigh of surrender followed by a series of grumbles. "All right. Just wait, and I will see if he will talk."

"FOR GOD'S SAKE, Greta," Benjamin Weissbach said, "what is so damn important that you would disrupt my meeting? You know better than to call me out of a meeting."

"It's not Greta," Theresa said firmly. "It's Terri. Your daughter. And I came to Budapest to see you!"

"Gottenyu! Theresa, how were you able to call long distance to Budapest? What is the emergency? Are you ill?"

"I didn't call long distance, Apa. I just said I'm here at home, our home, and I'm fine. I came a long way to see you and Anya."

"Why did you come here from Michigan, where you were safe? How did you even get here? Wait! Don't answer. No more talking on the phone! The lines are not secure. Whatever we have to say should be said only in person."

"That's why I called. When can I see you?"

"We will break around four o'clock for dinner. Can you come over to the synagogue at that time?"

"No. Anya is making dinner. I'd rather see you both together, anyway. Then I can answer all your questions. And I have questions."

"Ah, I can't leave right now. Today's meeting is crucial. I cannot tell you the reasons on the telephone. Please, come to the synagogue after break. We can talk for a while then."

WHILE THEY WAITED until it was time to leave for the synagogue, the conversation turned to Theresa's brother, Samuel, and her sister, Rebecca. After all, it was Theresa's intention to rescue all of them and take them all out of Hungary. "What is Samuel doing these days?" Theresa asked.

"A few years ago, he took a job with his friend Joel Brand at Joel's father's company. He owns the Budapest Telephone Company," Greta said.

"Mr. Brand owns the telephone company? That's interesting. Sammy works for the phone company and my mother isn't able to call her daughter in Michigan."

"We've been through all that," Greta said. "There is nothing Sammy can do about that. It's a security measure. If Sammy could get my international phone service turned on, he would. When they lift the ban, we will be the first in line to get service. But if you want to know about your brother's life, he is doing well. He is a manager at the company. He makes good money. And he has a girlfriend." Greta nodded with a smile. "They live in an apartment together, even though I don't approve. They're not married."

Julia smiled. That's exactly what her mother would say.

"What is his girlfriend's name?" Theresa asked. "What is she like? It's been ten years, and now my brother is living with a woman and I don't know about it or even who she is. How time does fly."

"Her name is Alana," Greta said. "She's very pretty and very quiet. At least she is around me. Sammy is crazy about her."

"And Becca?" Theresa asked. "The last time I saw her, she said she wanted to grow up and be a nurse. Did she follow a career in nursing?"

"Very much so. She is a nurse at Semmelweis University Hospital in the surgery department."

Theresa hung her head with a touch of sadness. "My brother is an executive at the Budapest Telephone Company, and he has a girlfriend I have never met. My little sister is a nurse at a prestigious hospital, and the last time I saw her, she was only fourteen years old. Where did the time go? Shame on me for missing out on the lives of my family. I didn't even visit."

"Don't do that, Terri," her mother said. "Stop punishing yourself. You've worked hard and made a nice career for yourself at Michigan, and for the last five years, it has been impossible for you to visit."

"I know. It's that stinkin' war; that's the reason why I am here. But I'll tell you about it later. I have missed so much, and I want to make sure that the Weissbachs are out of harm's way."

"I do not feel in harm's way," Greta said. "It's been the same for us since the war started. Nothing's changed. We live our lives from day to day. Oh, we know there are shortages, and there are regulations, but our lives are stable."

"Anya, it doesn't matter what you feel; you don't know the details. Hungary is in danger, take my word for it. I can tell you more about it when I get a chance. I just want you to protect yourself. Maybe that means leaving Hungary."

"I'm not leaving without my husband," Greta said, "and you would have to convince him. That won't be easy. He refuses to even talk about the war. If I ask him anything about the war or our safety, he just tells me not to worry about it."

"Anya, he wouldn't tell you about the dangers because he wouldn't want you to worry. It's his job to protect you. But we should all have a conversation about whether it make sense to leave. Plans would have to be made. It can't happen overnight. Visas, protection letters, travel arrangements, destinations—all those details have to be planned, and that takes a lot of time. We should begin those discussions before it is too late."

"I have an idea. Let me make a nice dinner and invite the family. You and Julia will come too. If the time is right, and if the others don't object, you can have your conversation. Don't be forceful. Maybe say that you think it might be wise to leave Budapest for a little while, until the danger passes. Then give them a chance to express their opinions. Talk nicely, please, and don't make a fuss. I don't want hollering at my table. Are you willing to do it on that basis?"

"That is a wonderful suggestion, Anya. I don't think we are scheduled for something tomorrow night. I can check when I get back to the embassy this evening. I'll call you."

Greta smiled. "Your father is always in a good mood when his stomach is full. You can tell him your thoughts, but remember, he is the man of the house. He will make the decision."

Julia and Theresa nodded to each other.

"What about Sammy and Becca?" Theresa said. "Will they come to dinner?"

"I will call them. Leave it to me. Unless work says no, they will be here. Are you going to see Apa at Dohány this afternoon? Tell him that Greta said he needs to be home for dinner tomorrow night; he shouldn't make any of his meetings for tomorrow."

BY AGREEMENT, THE remainder of the afternoon was spent with talk about the community and the friends that Theresa grew up with, not the war or plans to leave. When it was time to go, Theresa stopped at the door, gave her mother a big hug and a kiss, and said, "It has been so wonderful to see you, Anya. I can't tell you how much I've missed you. I look forward to having dinner with the family tomorrow."

"Your visit is a blessing," said Greta. "I hope it never comes to leaving Budapest, but if we decide that would make sense, I will listen to what you have to say."

Theresa nodded, and the girls left the house.

CHAPTER NINETEEN

THE DOHÁNY STREET Synagogue, often referred to as the Great Synagogue, was an architectural masterpiece. It was built in the 1850s as the second-largest synagogue in the world. Twin towers 140 feet high, with onion-shaped domes and rich stone cuttings containing the Star of David, framed the arched entrance. The entire structure resembled a palace, built out of cream-colored bricks, almost 300 feet long and 80 feet wide. Atop the pointed roof were two stone tablets engraved with the Ten Commandments. Tablet-shaped windows, spaced around the building, contained designs and biblical figures. A large, round, Byzantine stained glass window brought to mind Moorish Andalusia, leading many to mistake the building for a mosque. Yet it was clearly a Jewish temple with dozens of Jewish references. Above the entrance gate was an inscription from Exodus reading: "And let them make Me a sanctuary that I may dwell among them."

As they approached the Great Synagogue, Julia stopped and stared in awe. It was even immenser than Theresa's stories had led her to imagine. They walked through the gate and into the synagogue, where they met a man who was organizing prayer books. He asked if he could help them, and Theresa told him it was important that she speak to her father, Benjamin Weissbach. She knew that he was in a meeting with the rabbi, but he was aware that she was coming, and he was expecting her. A few minutes later, Benjamin Weissbach walked into the large sanctuary. When he saw Theresa, he quickened his pace. He wrapped his big arms around her and lifted her off the floor.

"Terri, Terri, Terri, I have missed you so badly. I am so happy you came home, but you visit at a troubling time."

"I understand, but don't think I'm being foolish. I'm more aware of the situation than you realize."

"Terri, hundreds of questions are circling my brain, and they all want answers," Benjamin said, "questions like when, how, and why? Why now? It's not that I don't want to see you, but you chose to come home in the middle of the war. You walked into a lion's den."

Theresa's father then said hello to Julia. He said it was nice to see her again, and kindly asked that she call him Apa or Benjamin, not Mr. Weissbach. He was a little taller than Theresa, but stocky. The hair visible under his black fedora was salt-and-pepper colored, which matched his beard and bushy eyebrows. A slight tremble in his hands testified to his age, which Theresa had informed Julia was sixty-six years. He led them into an office and shut the door.

"Okay, my daughter, to say that I am shocked beyond belief would be an understatement. So, let me have the whole story. What are you doing here? I know you two didn't come here on an all-inclusive Danube River cruise."

Theresa translated the discussion for Julia, who chuckled and said, "Very funny, Apa."

"You want the whole story?" Theresa said. "You don't have enough time. The bottom line is that we came all the way from America to make sure that you and Anya and the rest of our family would be safe, and if necessary, to take you all out of Hungary, as far away as possible, as soon as possible. This must be done before the Nazis enter the country and take control. You are not safe here."

Benjamin raised his eyebrows and nodded.

Theresa continued, "Anya told me that the Jews of Budapest feel safe, that they are economically sound and not worried about the Germans."

Benjamin nodded again. "That's right."

Theresa continued, "To date, the Germans have allowed Regent Horthy and his group to run the country without interference."

"That is correct," he said. "The Germans are not our enemies. They have no reason to interfere in our internal business. We don't interfere with theirs. It's mutual."

Theresa sighed. She said in her most professorial tone, "Apa, you and the rest of the Jewish community are apparently unaware of what the Germans have done to Jews in neighboring countries that they have conquered. That's understandable, because that knowledge has been withheld from you. But the Germans' history is predictive. It will reveal what they are planning to do in Hungary in the near future. As far as the Jewish community is concerned, the Nazis must be regarded as enemies. Enemies who are prepared to kill."

Benjamin stroked his beard and muttered, "Mm-mmm."

Theresa shook her head. Either he wasn't listening or he chose not to believe that such a fate was possible for Hungarian Jews. "Apa, listen to me; I'm serious. If the Nazis conquer and occupy Hungary—and smart minds think that they will—then they will devastate the Jewish community, every last one. Hitler will exterminate the Jews; that is his mantra."

Benjamin sat still, like an owl on the roof, slowly nodding at the words. It was as though Theresa were speaking another language.

"Apa, Theresa is right," Julia said, and Theresa translated. "I have been present in other European countries that were conquered by the Nazis, and I have witnessed what they did. I have seen their savagery once they occupy a country. Murderous cruelty follows them wherever they go, and we believe they are coming here to Hungary very soon."

Theresa added, "We know this is so, because we have information that five hundred thousand German troops are stationed just north of Munich, not far from Hungary's northwest border."

Benjamin held his hand up for her to stop. "We know that too, Terri. We're not as oblivious as you think. Maybe the common man is unaware, but leadership is not. We have sources. We know what the Nazis did in Poland. How do we know? Because thousands of Jews escaped Warsaw and Kraków and Lvov and made it across the border into Hungary. We have heard their stories. But all of that doesn't mean that the Germans intend to do the same thing in Hungary. Germany was at war with Poland. They were enemies. Hungary is not at war with Germany. We are strong, and we are Germany's military ally. At Germany's request, Hungary sent a hundred thousand Hungarian soldiers to back up the German army in the fight at Stalingrad. Many of them were Jews. Does Hitler want those Hungarian troops to be his enemy and turn against him, or does he need them to help defend Germany against Russia? I think you know the answer."

Theresa took a deep breath and shook her head. "Why would Hitler move all those troops close to Hungary's border if not to use them against us? There is no reason for the troops to be there if Hungary is still Germany's ally."

"That is correct, but Hungary is still Germany's partner. Nothing has changed. Hungary is a member of the Axis powers. Those troops may be stationed there because Russia is getting closer and may attack us. The war with Russia has not been going well. That may be the reason."

"We have heard a very disturbing rumor, Apa, which is confidential and not to be revealed to anyone at this time," Theresa said. "Will you keep it confidential?"

"Of course."

Theresa continued, "According to our information, Prime Minister Kállay has delivered messages to three of Germany's enemies—Russia, England, and the US—expressing a willingness to enter into a separate peace treaty. We don't know if Hitler has uncovered the same information, but if he has, it is reasonable to conclude that he no longer trusts Horthy or Kállay. And that is our conclusion why five hundred thousand German troops have been stationed on Hungary's border."

"We have not heard that rumor," Benjamin said, "and maybe because it is only a rumor. To my way of thinking, if the rumor was true, it would be a smart move on Kállay's part. Nobody knows who is going to win this war. Kállay is covering all the bases. May I ask you, where do you get your information?"

"From US intelligence," Julia answered. "From the War Refugee Board. It was through their efforts that we were able to travel here. That so-called rumor of Hitler's intention to attack Hungary is why Theresa begged the board to let her come here. She came to rescue you and your family, if the rumors are true."

"The WRB is a newly formed government agency," Theresa said, "just enacted and signed into being by the president. It is designed to do exactly what its name expresses: to rescue refugees caught up in World War II."

Julia put her arm around Theresa's shoulders. "Theresa is valuable to the WRB because she gives them what they need and what they didn't have: access to the Budapest Jewish community. You, Mr. Weissbach, are a significant part of that access. If there is an attack, mass emigration will be necessary to escape Germany's racial attacks. We want you to be among those who escape."

"How does the WRB plan on accomplishing this mass escape? Does it have an army?"

"A military army? No. It has an army of volunteers," Julia said proudly. "We have connections to people, powerful people who are pledged to aid refugees. It doesn't take tanks and guns. Sometimes even a small rescue squad can lead a group to safety, as we did in Holland. These well-connected people have access to diplomatic letters of protection, but I would ask that you hold that information in confidence at the present time. The identity of these people is a secret."

"Are they Swiss letters of protection?" Benjamin asked.

Julia took a deep breath. He knew more than she gave him credit for. "Our letters are Swiss. May I ask where *you* get your information?"

"Nothing as formal as the WRB," Benjamin answered, "but we have people strategically placed throughout Hungary and even in the Hungarian government. Who did the WRB appoint as its representative in Hungary?"

"You might say that it's us," Theresa answered, "but that's not entirely true. We don't have permission to reveal his identity at this time."

Benjamin raised his eyebrows. "I'm proud that you're honoring his confidence." He walked over and put his arm around Theresa. "And I am so proud of you, my Theresa. A professor and a trusted member of the US War Refugee Board. You have accomplished so much at such a young age. You have always been brave, and you have always been a leader. The reason that I asked you about the WRB representative is that I would like to meet with him. That way, we can pool our efforts and realize both of our goals. We should be working together. We can save a lot more lives that way."

"Apa, that is exactly the WRB's intention. They told Julia and me to come here and use our connections to interact with the Jewish community, to make it possible to rescue them from a German takeover."

"It's not a certainty, but give your father a little credit. What do you think we were discussing at the synagogue when you arrived today? There is a split of opinion among our people. Some take the position that the situation is calm right now and that is the way it will stay. You don't want to kick a sleeping dog. They argue that the Hungarian Jewish community has been safe and prosperous during wars for the last eight years, so why shouldn't it continue? But the other half dissents and believes that we should plan for the worst. That means prepare to escape while it's still possible."

"Which half are you in, Apa?"

"I'm on the side of caution. I can't just think about myself. I must think about your mother, your brother, and your sister. I must think about our synagogue and our people. It's a big decision. Right now, we are still debating, but as of this morning, we are still safe. There is no present danger."

"You are a realist, Mr. Weissbach," Julia said. "Isn't it obvious that Hitler is making plans to invade? Why else would he take five hundred thousand troops out of the front lines and place them on our border if he wasn't going to use them?"

"I suppose you could argue if he was really going to attack Hungary, he would need a lot more than half a million," Theresa said. "Hungary has a strong military with almost that many. Hitler doesn't go into a fair fight. He would want a large troop advantage."

Benjamin nodded. "Very astute, my daughter. That was part of the argument this morning. The ones who don't want to make waves said that very thing. If he was going to attack, he wouldn't station only five hundred thousand troops and only in one place. And it is true that Hitler has his half million troops north of Munich, we know that for a fact, but that is not the whole story. There is much more that you don't know."

"What do you mean?" Julia asked. "What don't we know?"

"Hitler can call upon troops from Axis partners. Remember, Hungary is surrounded by Axis countries. We have information that there are two divisions of Austrian soldiers now stationed close to our western border. There are three hundred thousand Croatian troops massing on our southern border, and three Serbian divisions stationed to the southwest. Add to that one division of Slovak troops lying north of our border. That combination of Axis soldiers totals in excess of one million, and they are surrounding Hungary, able to attack at Hitler's command."

Julia had a shocked look on her face. "Carl didn't tell us that. Either he doesn't know about it, or maybe your information is flawed?"

Benjamin shook his head. "It's not flawed. Our sources are reliable. Still, I would like to talk to Carl. I assume you are talking about Carl Lutz, the Swiss diplomat? Can you arrange it?"

"I think so," Theresa said. "We will be meeting with him tonight. I will try to get an appointment for tomorrow."

"Excellent. You know, I always thought my daughter was the brains of the family, and now I know it's true. Meet with Carl tonight, and call me here at the Dohány synagogue. I'll be here for several more hours. This meeting will take all day and probably go into tomorrow as well. Anytime you put fifty Jews in a meeting, you end up with three hundred opinions." He looked at his calendar. "I'll make sure the meeting ends before sundown tomorrow. If you can, try to set the meeting with Carl for tomorrow, March 15, late afternoon or night."

"Okay," Theresa said, "I'll do that, March 15, but beware."

"What?"

"Shakespeare, Apa. 'Beware the ides of March.' It didn't work out well for Julius Caesar."

CHAPTER TWENTY

IT WAS LATE in the afternoon when Julia and Theresa left the Great Synagogue on Dohány Street and headed back toward Castle Hill. They had placed a call to Carl before leaving to alert him that they had discovered important information that should be discussed. They asked if they should go over right away, or wait until their eight o'clock meeting. Carl regretted that he had already set appointments for the rest of the afternoon, but he was available for a private discussion after the eight o'clock meeting.

Theresa thanked him, hung up, and turned to Julia. "Eight PM Hungary time," she mused. "That would be two PM. Washington time. We are six hours ahead. Does that sound right?"

Julia shrugged. "We've been traveling so much that I get confused. It's six o'clock now in Budapest, which means it's noon in Washington, which means it's lunchtime. Why don't we stop for something to eat? I'm hungry."

"There used to be a good Hungarian restaurant on Mester Street. Want to give it a try?"

Julia shrugged. "Why not?"

The restaurant was crowded, but after a few minutes, they were seated and given menus. Julia took out her dictionary and tried to make sense of the entries printed in script. Finally, she said, "What's good?"

Theresa pointed her finger at a listing for *Csirke Paprikas*.

"Is that chicken paprikash?" Julia asked. "If so, I'll take it."

"Good. I'm going to have the goulash. They're famous for that here."

Midway through the meal, a young man entered the restaurant. He walked with a profound limp, leaning on a single crutch under his right armpit. It was obvious that his right leg had been severely compromised. His pant leg was tied just below the knee. As he made his way across the room, he stopped, stared at Theresa, and finally said, "Theresa Weissbach? Terri, is that you?"

A light went on in Theresa's memory and she replied, "Leon? Leon Gorstein? Oh my goodness. It's been so long." She turned to Julia and said, "Julia, this is Leon Gorstein, an old friend of mine. We went to secondary school together."

"And we went out on a couple of dates. Did you forget?" Leon said.

Theresa laughed. "No, of course not. We were just about to order dessert, but you are welcome to join us here. Have a seat."

Leon looked around the room. "I don't see Frederick yet, so I can sit for a minute or two." Julia rose from her seat and pulled back a chair for Leon.

"What are you two well-dressed women doing in Budapest today?" he asked. "The last I knew, you were going to go to college in the US. That was a long time ago. I guess that didn't work out."

"Yes, it did. I went to the University of Michigan and obtained a master's degree in history. I'm an associate professor there now. That is where I met Julia."

Leon looked at Julia and smiled. "Was Theresa wild in college?" he asked, biting his lower lip. "She could be a little sassy when she wanted to. She was fun when we were in secondary school. Terri and I went to a couple of social dances together. She could sure cut a rug, so they say." Then Leon paused. "I could too, back then." He patted his leg. "Not anymore."

"What happened to your leg?" Theresa asked. "Is it a war injury?"

Leon sadly nodded. "I was in the Hungarian Second, and we were deployed into southwestern Russia to fight at the battle of Stalingrad. We got our asses kicked. Germany was losing badly with its troops, so they called for us to come in to bail them out. I was hurt at the Battle of Voronezh, an important bridgehead over the Don River." He closed his eyes and shook his head. "We never had a chance. We were retreating, and I caught a leg full of shrapnel." He shrugged. "I fared better than some. We lost thousands."

"I am so sorry," said Julia. "I hate this war."

"Everybody hates war," Leon said, "except the generals who never fight. So tell me, was Terri a social whirlwind in college?"

Julia waited for Theresa to translate and then answered in broken Hungarian. "No. Theresa not wild. She was excellent student. Very brainy."

Leon looked at Theresa quizzically. "Your friend isn't fluent in Hungarian?"

Julia understood that question and answered it herself. "No. I speak English."

That answer didn't sit well with Leon. "What are you doing here?" Leon asked.

"She came with me," Theresa said. "I wanted to visit my family, and she came with me. She's enjoying her trip to the city."

"You brought her here in the middle of the bloody war, when she is an enemy of our country and isn't welcome here? Why would you invite her? How did she even get into our country? We're supposed to keep enemies out. Did you sneak her in, or did she sneak in with the Russians?"

"That's rude, Leon. You can apologize to her or you can leave our table."

"It ain't *your* table. It's the restaurant's table. Why should I apologize to an enemy sitting at *my* table in *my* country? Not a chance in hell. And I'll leave when I'm good and ready. Do you see this leg? I got this fighting for my country, not by playing footsy with the enemy. What is she doing here? Is she a spy?"

Theresa stood, placed a few bills on the table, and said, "Let's go, Julia."

Leon raised his voice. "She is, isn't she? She's a goddamned spy. Someone stop her." He faced the back of the room and yelled, "This woman is an enemy spy! She's from the US and she's got no business here in Hungary! She's a spy!" Leon kept up his rant, and he shouted for someone to call the police.

The restaurant was in tumult as Julia and Theresa stood to leave. All eyes were on them as they went through the front door and headed down the street. Their steps were quick, but not quick enough. A uniformed

Hungarian officer caught up with them and told them to stop. "What did you do back there?" he said. "That wounded soldier said you were an enemy spy."

"We didn't do anything, and we're not spies," Theresa said. "The soldier is a disturbed man."

"Let's see your identification," the officer said.

"For what reason?" Theresa said. "We have done nothing wrong."

He held his hand out. "Papers. Now!"

Julia stepped forward, standing between the officer and Theresa. Trying her best to recall some correct phrases from the Hungarian phrase book, she stuck out her chest and said in a firm voice, "You have no right to detain us. We are administrative officers of Switzerland. We are here on official Swiss business. We are under the protection of the Swiss government at all times."

The officer smiled. "Right. And I suppose your official Swiss business is eating goulash. Let me see your papers, or I am taking you to jail, little miss Swiss girl."

Julia didn't understand what he said. She looked to Theresa for instructions, who translated the officer's words.

"Little miss Swiss girl?" Julia said. "Is that what you called me? You are insulting an officer of Switzerland."

The statement caused the officer to furrow his forehead and stare. He stuck out his hand and repeated his demand for papers.

Theresa shut her eyes and shook her head in exasperation. "You messed up some of the words," she said. She translated for the officer and then said to Julia, "Take out your letter of protection."

Julia just stood there with her hands on her hips.

"Will you please show him your letter of protection, Julia? He's not kidding." Theresa held hers out for him to see.

Julia reached into her purse and carefully withdrew her letter of protection. The officer stuck out his hand and beckoned with his index finger for her to hand it to him, but Julia didn't want to. She didn't trust him. "Oh no," she said. "I was told never to surrender it." Theresa translated as rapidly as she could, but Julia was firm and continued to shake her head. "I'm not handing my letter over to anyone. I'll hold it up for you to read. That should be sufficient." Theresa, in an apologetic expression, translated for the officer.

By now, the officer was equally exasperated. He nodded his agreement. Julia held her letter in front of her stomach, and the officer bent over at the waist to read it as best he could. He made some notes in a little pad, looked up, and said, "Where are you staying while in Budapest. Miss Weissbach?"

Theresa responded for her. "We're staying at the Swiss embassy. Szabadsag tér 12. Do you want to call the Swiss consul and verify?"

"That won't be necessary," the officer said. "You and your stubborn friend are free to go."

AN HOUR LATER, Theresa and Julia met with Carl Lutz and Martin Steuben in room 217. They related the afternoon's conversation with Theresa's father, and his belief that Hungary was surrounded by Axis troops from Germany, Croatia, Slovakia, Serbia, and Austria, although they were stationary. No forward or aggressive movements had been reported.

"We were already aware of some of your father's information," Carl said. "It was reported to us by a member of the Aid and Rescue Committee. We're still trying to verify that information, but we have no reason to doubt its accuracy."

"I'm not familiar with a group known as the Aid and Rescue Committee," Theresa said. "Is it part of the World Jewish Congress?"

Carl shook his head. "No, it's totally different, though they have similar goals. It's not connected with any government. It was formed by certain private individuals here to help refugees in Hungary and the surrounding areas."

"We had those in Holland," Julia said. "They were underground rescue groups. I worked with them. They saved thousands of Dutch Jews. That was in 1942 and '43."

"Then you have the idea. That's the function of the Aid and Rescue Committee."

"I asked about the World Jewish Congress," Theresa said. "I've met Rabbi Wise. Are you familiar with the WJC? Are they active in Hungary?"

"Not in Hungary, not at this time, but I do know about the World Jewish Conference. In fact, I was there in Geneva in 1936 when they held their first conclave. I was representing the Swiss government. There were hundreds of delegates from over thirty countries, including many from the United States, but there were no Germans! I remember Rabbi Wise criticizing German Jews for ignoring the WJC and not attending. The WJC's expressed goal was Jewish unity and the strengthening of Jewish political influence in order to assure the survival of the Jewish people, but it was no surprise to me that German Jews did not participate. It was before the war, but it was three years into Hitler's reign, and he was already screaming insults against the Jews. Had German Jews gone to the conference, they would have been marked as opponents of the Reich. The whole point of the conference was to show unity and togetherness in defense of Jewish rights. There was even talk at that time of creating a Jewish state."

"I understand," Julia said. "It would have been too dangerous for German Jews to attend even back then."

"Probably, but you initially asked me about the Aid and Rescue Committee, not the WJC," Carl said. "The Aid and Rescue Committee, known as *Va'ada* for short, was formed not too long ago by Ottó Komoly and his assistant Rezso Kasztner, sometimes called Israel Kasztner. Both of them are very important men for you to know."

Theresa broke in, "My father knows Ottó Komoly well. Mr. Komoly is a prominent man in Budapest. Everyone admires him. In fact, he commands the respect of Jewish leaders, Christian leaders, government officials, you name it. My father is on a first-name basis with Mr. Komoly. His daughter, Esther Komoly, and I were friends in school. They are members of our synagogue."

Carl agreed. "You're right, Theresa, he is a very important and well-respected man. In the First World War, Ottó was a captain in the Austro-Hungarian Army, and he was a hero. The Komolys are Zionists. Ottó's father, David Komoly, was the founder of the Zionist movement in Hungary, and Ottó Komoly is now the chairman of the Hungary Zionist Federation."

"I remember Esther telling me that her family was going to move to Palestine, but her father changed his mind, and the family stayed in Budapest," Theresa commented. "Esther said he did that so he could help his community. I don't know Esther's father that well, but they have a beautiful house in Budapest, and they are financially comfortable."

"I am meeting with Ottó tomorrow," Carl said. "If you want me to mention it, I can tell him that you are here as a representative of the WRB. The WRB may be in a position to provide money or equipment to the Aid and Rescue Committee. I'm sure they would welcome any help the WRB could supply. Anyway, going back to the beginning, it was a member of the Aid and Rescue Committee that first told us about the three hundred thousand Croatian troops on Hungary's southern border."

"And the Austrian soldiers too?"

Carl nodded. "While we do not have precise numbers of Austrian soldiers under German command, we know that some are stationed near Hungary's border. We have no reason to doubt your father's estimate of Serbian and Slovak troop strength. The important question is why? Why does Germany need troops to surround its partner Hungary?"

"It could just be a show of strength," Martin said.

"True, but for what reason?" asked Carl. "Has there been a demand made upon Hungary that we don't know about? Did Hitler order them to accept terms or face attack? We do not know of any such threat. What does Regent Horthy have to say about these troops standing on his borders? Does he provide an explanation?"

Martin shrugged. "He hasn't said anything that we know of. Horthy is at the opera with his wife tonight. Either he is totally unaware of the troops, or he knows of them and is not concerned."

"My father may know more about this than we do," Theresa said. "He is the one who alerted me to the standing armies. He told me he would like to meet with you. He has meetings all during the day, so he has suggested tomorrow night at the synagogue. That won't make my mother happy—she has invited the family for dinner tomorrow—but I'm sure she would understand. My father's business has interrupted many dinners. I think you should meet with him because he has connections to many of Budapest's important families, and other resources we talked about when we were in Bern. My father has solid relationships with both the Jewish business community and the financial community. And as I said, he knows Ottó Komoly. If anyone can help you reach the leaders of the Jewish community, it is my father."

"Well said," Carl replied. "There is no doubt that your father would be very helpful. However, I can't meet tomorrow night, and that should make your mother happy. I already have plans. I could meet on March 18. Would your father be available?"

Just then the intercom buzzed. "There is a call for you, Mr. Lutz. It's Roberts. He would like to talk to you right away. He says it's urgent."

"Put him through," Carl said. As he listened to the call, Carl nodded and made eye contact with each of the people in the room. This was obviously a troublesome call that concerned the group. "When did this happen?" Carl said into the phone. "Did he make any threats or demands? What about the troops? Are they moving?"

Carl hung up the phone and faced the others. "We just received word that Regent Miklós Horthy was interrupted at the opera this evening by the German minister. He was handed a letter from Adolf Hitler, and Horthy immediately left the opera. A little while later, he was seen at the train station carrying a suitcase. He boarded a train for Salzburg."

Martin said, "Hitler has a palace near Salzburg, at Klessheim, where he has met leaders from other countries. He met Italy's Mussolini, Romania's Antonescu, and Croatia's Pavelić there at his palace. Those were high-level meetings with Germany's allies. That makes me think that a meeting with Horthy at the palace is a good sign. Why entertain someone you were going to threaten with a show of force? He could threaten Horthy with a phone call or a written demand carried by his minister. I think it is a show of camaraderie, one to bolster their alliance. Did Roberts say anything about the troops or other threats?"

Carl shook his head. "He didn't know of any. There was no mention of the troops surrounding Hungary. He did say that Horthy seemed to be in a good mood, so that would tend to confirm your opinion of camaraderie."

"So, Horthy is pulled out of an opera for an emergency trip to Salzburg at the invitation of the führer, a total surprise, and we are to consider that as friendly?" Julia said.

Martin shrugged.

Theresa responded, "I'll repeat what I told my father: 'Beware the ides of March.' It's not a joke."

Carl looked at his watch. "I don't know how much more we can learn today. It's late. Let's check in during the day tomorrow."

CHAPTER TWENTY-ONE

AT JULIA'S SUGGESTION, the two Michigan alums decided to go to a neighborhood bar for lunch. After all, it was March 17, Saint Patrick's Day, and a beer sounded good. As they were getting ready to leave their apartment in the Swiss embassy building, they saw Martin Steuben.

"Where are you two lovely ladies headed?" he said.

"We're going out to find a pub. It's Saint Paddy's Day, you know. Any suggestions?"

"Vernon's Kocsma. They have a great selection of beers, including Irish beers, and the food ain't bad either. It's about six blocks from here."

"Have you eaten lunch?" Julia asked. "Would you care to join us?"

THE THREE WERE seated in a booth in the crowded pub. Julia bemoaned the lack of genuine Irish food on the menu, but settled for *sütőkolbász és hurka*, which was a plate of roasted sausages with mustard and vegetables. "Close enough," she said.

Theresa ordered *rántott hús*, or schnitzel, which was a traditional breaded veal cutlet, served with potato noodles. Martin had the closest thing he could find to fish and chips, *hal krumpli*. Of the greatest importance, the waitress brought them three steins of Guinness draft.

"How long have you been working with Carl Lutz?" Theresa asked. "He is a terrific guy."

Martin concurred. "He's the best. I met him in 1935. I was a young man with the Swiss foreign service, and I was assigned to the Swiss consulate in Jaffa. Carl was appointed as chancellor of the consulate."

Julia looked confused. "Where is Jaffa?"

"It's the major port city in what is now called British Mandatory Palestine. Over the past ten years, there has been a large influx of European refugees. At the consulate, we tried to serve a broad mixture of refugees, immigrants, and permanent residents. That included twenty-five hundred German residents, along with eighty thousand Jewish refugees who fled Nazi Germany."

"We saw the same thing in Amsterdam, but not that many," Julia said. "Thousands of Jews were fleeing Nazi Germany, and there were also German emigrants who weren't Jewish but wanted to get out of Germany anyway. They wanted to live in Amsterdam. It's a pretty nice place." Julia paused, then added, "Or it was. We listened to their stories, and they were rough."

"So did we," Martin said. "It was during the mid-thirties that Carl became immersed in the cause of the persecuted Jews. He has been a strong advocate ever since. When war broke out in 1939, Germany asked Switzerland to represent its interests in Mandatory Palestine. Carl Lutz was assigned this task, which he was glad to undertake, because he would be honest and fair. I was his assistant, and it was a damn hard assignment. How do you balance the two conflicting interests between German residents who chose to live in Palestine and German refugees who were fleeing their German persecutors? We finished our tour of duty in Jaffa in 1941, and we were transferred to the Swiss office in Berlin, but only for six weeks. That was at the request of the Yugoslavian government. We were transferred to other offices, and just a few months ago, we were transferred to Budapest."

"Lucky for us," Theresa said. "All that packing and moving must have been a lot of work for you and Carl."

"Carl left most of that to Gertrud, his wife. If you haven't met her, you should. She's a lovely lady and a good manager."

After another round of Guinness, Theresa said, "Did you notice the number of men walking around in uniform this morning? They all appear to be Germans."

Julia didn't seem alarmed. "They weren't in formation. It was just groups of soldiers walking casually down the street. That's not so unusual, is it? They were probably looking to get a beer, just like us."

"Many of them look like officers," Theresa said.

"I don't find that unusual either," Julia said. "We've seen German soldiers walking down the streets in Budapest before. After all, they are Hungary's allies. What do you think, Martin?"

Martin shook his head. "Theresa's right; it is unusual. These Germans weren't wearing army uniforms, Julia. They were wearing Waffen SS uniforms. Those men are the military branch of the Schutzstaffel, the secret police. They're dangerous. The question is, why are there so many more walking around in Budapest now?"

"Do you think it has something to do with the troops that are gathered on Hungary's borders?"

"I hope not, but I'm not discounting it."

Julia looked at her watch. It was one PM, which meant it was seven AM in Washington. "We should return to the embassy," she said. "I have to call John Pehle first thing in the morning, Washington time. I promised to keep him informed, and it has been a couple of days since we last spoke."

"Okay," Theresa said, "but don't forget Anya is making a big family dinner. As far as I know, everyone is coming."

"Then we should invite Martin," Julia said. "Are you doing anything for dinner tonight, Martin?"

Martin smiled. "I thank you for thinking of me, but I have a meeting scheduled tonight. I would have to decline."

"Well, maybe next time," Julia said.

CHAPTER TWENTY-TWO

IT WAS EVENING and the sun was setting, leaving a palette of colors in the sky over the Hungarian hills. Theresa and Julia arrived at the Weissbach home, and Theresa smiled as she put her hand on the doorknob. It wasn't locked. Just to be polite, she knocked anyway. Greta came to the door. She wore an apron with embroidered figures of children. Rich aromas emanated from the kitchen.

"Mmmmm," said Julia and Theresa together.

"Is everyone here?" Theresa asked.

"Everyone but your father," Greta answered. "I believe he is still at the synagogue. He told us to start without him, and he would be here as soon as he could."

"I'm sorry that he's delayed," Theresa said, "but I know what they're discussing, and there are no easy answers."

Suddenly, there was an excited shout. "Terri? Terri, is that you?" yelled a voice from the living room. "Is that my brilliant big sister? Is that the Wolverine from Michigan?" A moment later, Becca Weissbach ran into the hallway and into Theresa's arms.

With her arm around her sister, Theresa said, "Becca, this is my close friend Julia, and to corrupt a little Yiddish, she's a Michigunah too."

Becca laughed and reached over to shake Julia's hand. "Did you meet my sister at the University of Michigan?"

"I did. We were classmates and very good friends."

Then Becca leaned over and whispered, "Sammy and his new girlfriend are in the living room. And she is a looker."

"Oh, really?" Theresa said as they walked into the room to see for themselves.

A tall, handsome young man who clearly carried the Weissbach genes rose off the couch and came over to exchange hugs with his younger sister.

"I have missed you," Theresa said.

"Me too," he answered. He gestured to his right to a strikingly beautiful blond woman who had been sitting quietly next to him. "And this is my friend Alana."

"So nice to meet you, Alana," Theresa said, and gesturing to Julia, she said, "Sammy, Alana, I want you to meet my best friend, Julia Powers. If it weren't for Julia, I wouldn't be in Budapest at all. She knew all the right strings to pull, she put it all together."

Greta excused herself for a minute to check on the dinner. The young folks sat in the living room, getting acquainted and catching up on what had happened over the past ten years. They were all proud of Theresa for achieving the rank of assistant professor of history, but Becca waved it off, saying, "I don't think that's so unusual. All she did in Budapest was study."

"Oh, you're one to talk. You're four years younger and you are already a registered nurse at Semmelweis University Hospital. In what department?"

Becca shyly answered, "Cardiac surgery. I am registered in the surgical department."

As they sat there exchanging stories, Theresa inhaled deeply through her nose and shut her eyes. "My God, what magic does Anya have brewing up in that kitchen?" She stood and walked into the kitchen, followed by Julia.

"Anya, Anya, what hidden treasures do you have in your pots and pans? The smells are intoxicating."

Greta walked to the stove and lifted the lid off a large pot. "That is my hen soup with *galuska* dumplings," Anya said with pride.

Julia leaned over to look into the pot and saw small potatoes, large carrots, a large bulb of kohlrabi, and dumplings in the bubbling soup. "What's in the dumplings?" she asked.

Greta answered with a shrug, "Just the usual. Farina wheat, peppercorns, butter, eggs, seasoning, and, of course, schmaltze." She dipped a ladle into the soup and offered it to Julia.

"Mmm, heavenly," Julia said.

Greta moved to the next pot, lifted the lid, and said, "Main course. Anya's goulash with chopped meat."

Becca stepped forward and said, "Come on, Anya, don't keep me in suspense. What's for dessert?"

A cloth was laid over a dish on the counter. Greta lifted it and Theresa shrieked, "*Aranyagoluska!*"

Greta nodded. "It's been a long time since I made this dish, but this is a special occasion."

Theresa turned to Julia and said, "It's my very favorite dessert since I was a little girl. It's a Hungarian dish, very popular in the Jewish community, but no one can make it like Anya. It's pull-apart cake. It's coated with cinnamon and crunchy nuts. Everyone digs in, takes an individual piece of dough, and pulls it out."

"That sounds delightful," Julia said, "but I suppose we have to wait until dessert to get our share?"

"I'm afraid so," Theresa said. "Rules are rules."

Julia looked at Becca, who stood still, like something was amiss. Her eyes scanned the kitchen for something. Theresa knew. Greta knew.

"Oh, I know what Becca's thinking," Greta said. "She's thinking, *You made Theresa's favorite. What about my favorite?*" Anya shrugged. "I must have forgotten. Isn't that a shame."

"Aww," said Becca.

Greta tipped her head toward the other counter and said, "But maybe, just maybe, if you looked at the plate sitting over there . . ."

Becca came alive in anticipation. She could feel it coming. "Is that what I think it is?" she said.

Greta lifted the cover to reveal a plateful of crescent-shaped rolled cookies. Becca shrieked, "Bubby's cinnamon rugelach!"

* * *

THE SERVING DISHES were carried to the table, everyone took their seats, and Sammy led them all in a prayer thanking Almighty God for his blessings.

Julia cleared her throat. "If I may say a word or two, please. I want to thank you all, especially you, Anya, for inviting me to share this wonderful evening. It's not only that I'm thankful for attending such a lovely family dinner, which I am certain will be delicious, but it's the privilege of being allowed to experience Budapest's rich Jewish culture. To the extent that I am here and able to help support that culture is a privilege for which I am deeply grateful."

"We are the ones who are grateful," Theresa said softly. "For you, for Carl, for John, for the entire WRB, and for all those who stand courageously against the forces of evil. Our community represents centuries of Hungarian Jewish life, rich in tradition and love. It's why our people don't want to relocate somewhere else. Our roots are here."

AFTER DINNER, AFTER the last crumb of rugelach had been scooped up and the coffeepot was empty, the conversation turned to present endeavors. Julia, being the newest and most mysterious guest, went first. She told her story, from following a bass player to Amsterdam, to being part of a rescue operation, to escaping from the Utrecht woods in a reconstructed airplane painted to resemble a Nazi Fokker. "I returned home, and I really had nothing to do. The war was still happening, and I felt like I should be there. Truth is, I was bored. Then my college friend Theresa needed my help, so here I am in Europe again." Julia turned to Sammy and said, "I understand that you are working for the Budapest Telephone Company."

"That's right. I got the job through my friend Joel Brand. Do any of you remember him? He used to come to Budapest quite a bit when he was a teenager. The Brand family lived in Germany, but his father's business was here in Budapest. His father founded the Budapest Telephone Company years ago, and the family would come here often, but their home was in Erfurt, Germany, at least it was until ten years ago."

"I know Joel," Theresa said. "I remember you telling me that he got married and finally settled down. He and his wife, Hansi, bought a knitwear and glove factory in Budapest that became very successful. You told me that his factory employs a hundred people."

"Correct. He got married in 1935 while you were at Michigan. Joel and Hansi belonged to a group that was making plans to move to a kibbutz in Palestine. That was their dream, but before he could leave, his mother and his sisters were forced to flee Erfurt to escape the Nazis, and they moved to Budapest. Joel and Hansi had to forgo their kibbutz plans, and they stayed in Budapest to support the family. That was three years ago, and then, in 1941, Hansi's sister and brother-in-law . . . oh well, that's another long story."

"Tell us," Julia said. "If it's about Joel Brand, I want to know. He leads an exciting life. I understand he has some involvement with a rescue organization."

"Joel has a history of rescuing people, so when it came to his wife's relatives, he didn't shy away," Sammy said. "They lived in Poland, then immigrated somewhere else, and ended up in Slovakia. You know what happened there? Four years ago, Jews were facing mass executions after Germany overran the country. Tens of thousands of Jews were fleeing and many came to Hungary."

"And they all settled here?" asked Julia.

"No. Many did, but Horthy and the Hungarian government would only accept a portion of those immigrating Jews, and eighteen thousand would-be immigrants, including Hansi's relatives, were sent to Ukraine. That ended up being a terrible mistake. Ukraine was under German control, and killings followed. To get Hansi's family out of Ukraine, Joel bribed officials with a lot of his money. He got Hansi's family out of Ukraine and brought them back into Hungary. He also helped many other refugees. Rescue efforts became Joel's focus, and he was very creative. To save other refugees, Joel joined a Zionist group with Israel Kasztner. Then they joined Ottó Komoly at the Aid and Rescue Committee, and he has been active there ever since."

"I will never understand the German hatred of the Jewish religion," said Becca. "There is nothing in our religion that preaches hate against Germans or people of different religions. We are not taught to hate them. Two days ago, a German SS Gruppenführer, a very high-ranking officer, lay on our operating table close to death, as close as one could get. The German officer came to our hospital, a hospital founded by Ignaz Semmelweis, a Jewish surgeon, a hundred years ago. Why did the German soldier come to Semmelweis? Because we are the best. Our surgical teams are the most advanced, and his surgery was technically difficult. He would have died at some other hospital that wasn't similarly proficient. The surgery team took six hours, and it was successful. He will live. No one stopped to ask what religion he belonged to. All of us knew that as a high-ranking member of the SS, he wasn't Jewish, and that, as a Nazi captain, he would have no love for the Jews. Yet we did what we were trained to do. That's the irony."

Then it was Theresa's turn. "Why am I here?" she said. "I was comfortable in Ann Arbor and moving up the career ladder. I missed you all, of course, but I came here because I had an opportunity. Naturally, I was worried half to death about you. I hadn't talked to you in a year, I didn't know what was happening. It was always my mission to take my family out of here to a place of safety."

"I know that is your mission," Sammy said, "and I can't speak for the rest of the family, but I'm really not ready to leave. Alana doesn't want to leave either."

"No one wants to leave," Julia said, "but given the choice between immigrating to a safe country like Turkey or being arrested and deported to a Nazi concentration camp, the answer is simple. It is one of survival."

"That may have been the case in other countries, like Poland or Holland, but Hungary is different," argued Sammy. "The Jewish side of Budapest society is strong and wealthy. Germans respect us. Horthy respects us. That is why there have been no deportations in the three years of the war. Hungary is Germany's ally."

Suddenly, the door opened and Theresa's father, Benjamin Weissbach, entered. He looked tired. Theresa thought that the weight of the recent stress had aged him. His back, formerly upright, now showed a curvature, and his shoulders, formerly strong and square, now tended to slope. There were bags under his eyes. Theresa went to him immediately and helped him to the chair at the head of the table. Greta darted into the kitchen to fix a plate for him.

"Apa, are you okay?" Theresa said.

A slight shrug was his answer. "It has been a stressful day and night," he said softly.

"Was it a stormy meeting at the synagogue?"

He nodded slowly. "It wasn't stormy because we were fighting among ourselves. It was because of the dreadful news we received and the uncertainty of how to respond." He shook his head. "There are no answers."

Greta placed dinner in front of him and kissed him gently on his forehead.

"What was the news?" Sammy said. "It can't have been that bad."

Benjamin shook his head and waved his hand back and forth, a sign that he didn't want to discuss it.

"Well, let me ask this," Sammy said. "Was it a matter that concerned only the synagogue, or did it concern all of Budapest?"

"Tell me, son, what is the difference? Does an impending disaster in Budapest not also affect our synagogue? Have you not seen the German soldiers on our streets?" he said. Everyone agreed. "Their numbers are increasing by the hour. They have come to stay."

"How do you know that?" Sammy asked. "Is that just a rumor Rabbi Levy has started?"

"I wish that were so. The soldiers march in and go where they want, all without any opposition. None whatsoever. No one has even asked them to leave. They cross the border as if there is no border. There are no Hungarian forces stationed at the border to stop them. It was reported at the meeting that the Nazis have taken control of the police station, the train station, the bus station, the city hall, even the newspaper. There is no shooting. There are no arrests, at least not yet. It has been a quiet takeover, but it has been thorough. There is no doubt that they are now in charge of Hungary."

"Why are we letting them do that?" Sammy said. "What about our defense department? We have a strong army. What are they doing?"

"The commander of our army is the regent, Miklós Horthy, and he is out of town. Absent his authority, there is no one who can order or command our army to do anything about the influx of German soldiers. Regent Horthy is in absentia. Now there is no doubt why Horthy has been called to meet with Hitler in the palace outside of Salzburg. He has been there for three days, enough time for the German army to occupy our country."

Theresa rose and walked across the room. She picked up the telephone. "I want to contact Carl," she said. "I want to inform him of what you have seen, and he might have information to share with us." She dialed and waited. Then she shook her head. "It's dead."

"I'd better get down to the office," Sammy said. "There is no reason for service to be down."

"We need to get back to the embassy," Julia said. "Carl is bound to have answers, and if anyone has ideas on what we should do, it would be Carl."

"Apa, maybe you should come with us," Theresa said. "You are Budapest's conscience. You speak for the people. You know the responsible people in every facet of Budapest society. Carl has mentioned to us that he intended to use you as a valuable resource."

"I can't leave your mother," he replied.

"Nonsense," Greta said defiantly with her hands on her hips. "I'm safe. What do they want with an old lady like me? You go with your daughter to meet with the Swiss ambassador. If you are in a position to help your country, you need to go."

Alana, who had been mostly silent throughout the evening, said, "I'll stay with Anya. She'll be all right. Theresa is right. You should go, Mr. Weissbach."

CHAPTER TWENTY-THREE

JULIA AND THERESA sat patiently in room 217 at the Swiss embassy while Benjamin paced the floor. They were told by an administrative staffer that Mr. Lutz was busy in a meeting at the moment but that he expected to be free to talk to them shortly. "If it isn't too inconvenient," she said, "he asks that you have a seat and make yourselves comfortable, and he will be here as soon as he can." That was ninety minutes earlier.

IT WAS ALMOST eleven o'clock when Carl finally arrived at the meeting. Expressing his apologies, he said, "I'm sorry that I made you wait so long. Just when I thought we had all the latest bulletins, another messenger showed up with further news."

"This is my father, Benjamin Weissbach," Theresa said. "I asked him to come along because you and I have spoken about him and his connections to the Budapest Jewish community. You mentioned that he would also be a valuable asset to the WRB."

"Without question," Carl answered. "Thank you so much for coming, Mr. Weissbach. I am honored to meet you. I know you are very busy."

Benjamin smiled. "Thank you, Mr. Lutz," he said. "Very kind of you. But I came along to offer whatever assistance I can on behalf of my people. Like you, I was in a meeting most of the day at the Great Synagogue. The congregants are deeply concerned about what appears to be an invasion of German troops on our streets. To us, a military invasion makes absolutely no sense. We are not at war with Germany. As far as we know, the two countries are still allies. They fought, and still fight, side by side on the Russian Front. So we ask, what are these German troops doing here?"

"Carl," Theresa interjected, "may I add that my father told us earlier today that the Germans are now in the bus stations, the train station, the post office, on Castle Hill, and who knows where else? As far as we know, they have been peaceful, so far. Has Germany made any demands of Hungary that you know of? Have there been arrests? What is the response of our government leaders to this incursion?"

"I am not aware of any response from the Hungarian government," Carl said. "Not officially. German soldiers have taken positions throughout Hungary, not just in Budapest. There have been no demands of the Hungarian government that we know about." Carl paused. There was a solemn look on his face. "If I were a member of the Budapest Jewish community, I would be very concerned, but it is possible that the influx of German troops may be a preventative measure. They may be here in case the meeting in Salzburg doesn't go well."

"Hungary has not threatened Germany in any way, has it?" Theresa asked.

"Unfortunately, that is not entirely true," Carl answered. "While it's true that there haven't been any direct threats, Prime Minister Kállay secretly sent messages to the United States, Great Britain, and even Canada, offering to enter into a mutual peace agreement. Such a move would replace a military ally with a secret enemy on Germany's border. While a similar message was initially sent weeks ago, it was recently repeated. As far as we know, none of the recipients have agreed to form such an alliance. While Kállay's correspondence was supposed to be secret, Hitler found out about it and considered it a betrayal. Previously, he considered Hungary to be a loyal ally without question. Now, he must ask, is it colluding with the enemy?"

"We heard that Hitler called Regent Horthy to meet with him at his palace outside of Salzburg, am I right?" asked Julia. "Did he call him there for an explanation? Did Kállay act at Horthy's direction? Was Hitler seeking Horthy's assurance of loyalty, or was it Hitler's plan to take

Horthy out of the picture altogether while his army moves into Hungary? And if Horthy is guilty of telling Kállay to send the peace feelers, why would he voluntarily go to Hitler?"

"You ask pointed questions, Julia," said Carl. "Very perceptive. Your question, that of removing Horthy from Hungary while German troops move into the country, might be the real reason. Despite that, Horthy sent word this morning that he is coming back to Budapest tomorrow. He is leaving Hitler's palace and returning to his office. Apparently, he is not under arrest. Now, we ask ourselves, has Horthy made a deal with Hitler? Will Horthy tell his army to stand down in the face of a Nazi invasion? Will his return change anything on the ground here in Budapest? Or is Hitler satisfied that Hungary is loyal, and will he recall his soldiers? Your guess is as good as mine. Either way, right now Hungary is effectively under German control."

"If Hitler's troops are here to stay in Hungary, will they be enforcing Germany's laws? Is Budapest destined to become another Amsterdam?" Julia posed. "Another Warsaw? Another Vienna? If the German army will be enforcing Germany's laws, then what about the Jewish people? Will Germany be implementing its racial laws? Will the Jews now be arrested and deported to prisons? If that is your expectation, shouldn't we be making preparations for evacuation? Shouldn't we be forming secret rescue groups like we did in Holland? We can't just sit back and do nothing in the face of a slaughter. We witnessed over sixty thousand Jews captured and taken out of Holland to prison camps, we believe to be murdered. That was almost half of the Jewish population in the Netherlands. There are almost a million Jews in Hungary. Can you even conceive of such a slaughter?"

"There are over nine hundred thousand Jews here," Benjamin said, "and that very issue is exactly what we were debating at the synagogue."

"And what was your consensus?" Carl inquired.

"Your question assumes that a sanctuary full of Jews is capable of agreeing on a single premise, let alone a single theory. We did not reach a consensus. Some wanted to leave Hungary, and no doubt they will try. Some believed that the prominence of Jewish manufacturing, commercial enterprises, and financial markets would keep the social structure intact. Horthy would be a fool to permit such a slaughter, they say. His economy would fall apart. Why ruin the country's economy, they say, especially in the middle of a war? Others reason that it is foolish for Horthy and Hitler to deplete their military defenses by removing all the Jewish soldiers and workers. Why eliminate a large portion of a military ally with the Russian army closing in from the east? So, basically, most of us were left in a wait-and-see attitude."

"What is your personal opinion?" Carl asked.

"I don't like to wait and see," Benjamin answered, "but I don't know what to do right now. I hate to pull up stakes and make a run to who knows where, especially since Hitler may do nothing and leave us alone. Still, there is no doubt that Hitler is a psychopath when it comes to the Jewish religion. He calls Jews the enemy. Maybe he won't make a move today, but I have no doubt that he will when it suits him. If we wait until that time and do nothing, we've lost any advantage we have to prepare for an escape."

"What do you mean by that, Apa? What can we do to prepare ourselves?" said Theresa. "Getting our people out of Hungary is the only answer that occurs to me."

Benjamin shrugged. "Preparation is the key, and we need to prepare, but at this point, I have no answers. How do a million people escape? Who will lead them, and where would they go?"

"It's late," said Carl. "Why don't we all sleep on it and meet again tomorrow?"

CHAPTER TWENTY-FOUR

JULIA AND THERESA awakened early and decided to take a walk. The March air was brisk. On their way, they passed two different groups of German soldiers marching down the sidewalk in formation, their boots hitting the sidewalk like a single pile driver. The girls had to jump to the side to get out of their way, which made the soldiers laugh. It was jump or be steamrolled. For the soldiers, it was the morning's amusement.

"I guess we weren't showing the proper deference," Theresa said.

Julia agreed. "Is your father coming to the meeting this morning?" she asked.

"He is, and he's bringing two other men, Rabbi Levy and a board member who is reputedly 'very old, very wise, and very cranky.' So says my father. Apparently, he is the synagogue's resident conscience. His name is Solomon, naturally."

Julia and Theresa were the first to arrive in room 217, even before Carl. Soon, Benjamin walked into the meeting, accompanied by Rabbi Levy and a much older man with a snow-white beard. "This is Solomon Cushman," the rabbi said. "He is a very learned man and very well respected. He is the synagogue's historian, a walking library of the Jewish Empire in this area, going back to the Roman legions."

"The Roman legions?" Theresa said. "That would be almost two thousand years ago."

The rabbi nodded. "This area, all of Central Europe, was at one time part of the Holy Roman Empire."

"And afterward, it became the Habsburg Empire," Theresa said, "but I never heard of the Jewish Empire."

That comment brought a smile to Solomon's lips. "In comparison to the other religious sects, we were small, but we were mighty. At one time, our Jewish Empire topped twelve million."

The rabbi hung his head. "As you know, as a people, we have recently suffered devastating losses. Hungary, with its nine hundred thousand, is the last bastion on the continent."

There was a knock on the door, and Carl Lutz arrived.

"I'm afraid I have very disturbing news—" Carl began.

Rabbi Levy interrupted. "Is it about the groups of German soldiers? We think they were sent here in the chance that Hitler and Horthy could not come to an agreement. But now we understand that Regent Horthy is returning home to Budapest today, so maybe that fear was unfounded. Maybe Hitler and Horthy have made peace and the German soldiers will turn around and march right back to Germany. Those of us at the synagogue expect the situation to stabilize, and things to return to just as they were before Horthy left. Isn't that your thinking as well, Mr. Lutz?"

"Will you please let Mr. Lutz finish telling us his news?" said Benjamin.

"As I mentioned, I have received some news that couldn't be more disturbing," Carl said. "An unidentified German officer arrived in Budapest this morning. He was accompanied by his staff and five hundred members of the SS, including Nazi intelligence and police divisions, the SD and the SiPo. They have taken up residence in the German compound. I'm afraid they are not just soldiers passing through. They are high ranking and far more dangerous. I recommend that you all think about your security here in Budapest."

"What is that supposed to mean?" said the rabbi. "I always think about my security. Just because some officer brings in five hundred more Germans doesn't change anything, does it?"

"Oh yes, it does," said Julia in a shaky voice. "Don't you see what they are planning to do? They are bringing in sufficient Nazi soldiers and SS, enough to turn Hungary into another conquered state, like the

Netherlands. If they are following their pattern, they are going to set up machinery to round up Jews, wherever they are, and send them to their death in German prison camps. I have seen the death marches. Something must be done and quickly!"

"Settle down. We don't know that for certain," Rabbi Levy said. "Nothing has been done here yet. The wrong thing for us to do is to run like a pack of scared dogs. The Jews are powerful here in Budapest. As Solomon told you, the history of the Jewish people reaches back to the Holy Roman Empire. We are a respected and solid minority. Besides, nine hundred thousand is a lot more than five hundred."

"Oh, you want to go to war? Then you haven't been listening, because Hungary is surrounded by a million Axis troops standing on our borders," Julia countered with a degree of annoyance. "And these five hundred are troops, soldiers, not housewives and children and businessmen."

Carl held up his hand. "I think it might matter who this individual German officer is," he said. "I have asked Paul to find out. He should be reporting to me soon."

Solomon shook his head. "Unless it's Hitler himself, it doesn't matter to me. I'm not going to take my family and run because some officer shows up with five hundred soldiers. You people speak from fright, from panic. What do you propose we do? Shall I go to Chaim Sternhauf, the butcher, tell him to close his store and take his wife and children and everything he owns and pile into his jalopy and leave Budapest? And what about those who don't have a car? Do they take their horse and wagon? If I did go to him, Chaim would simply look out onto the streets and see business as usual, and he would think his rabbi is a frightened child. And where would Chaim go anyway? Romania? Slovakia? Austria? Like you just said, Hungary is presently surrounded by Axis armies standing on the border. But even with all those armies, nothing has changed, has it? Germany is taking a beating in Russia, and it can't afford to lose any of its Axis soldiers, which include a few hundred thousand Budapest men. Believe me, nothing is going to change."

Benjamin felt it was time to take a stand. "Rabbi, I know you are a proud man, but you are not opening your eyes. Things are not the same.

We are overrun. We wouldn't be running like scared dogs, we would be evaluating the facts and making preparations."

There was a knock on the door, and Lutz's secretary poked her head in. "Mr. Lutz, there is a phone call for you."

Lutz left the room.

"Do you suppose it's about the mysterious Nazi officer?" Julia said.

"It doesn't matter," the rabbi said, standing up. "I'm going back to the synagogue. Come on, Solomon, let's go."

They started to leave, but Carl returned and closed the door behind him. He sadly shook his head. "This is indeed bad news. The man of mystery who came into town with the German contingent is none other than Obersturmbannführer Adolf Eichmann."

"Oh no!" exclaimed Julia. Her face was flushed. "I know about him. Eichmann is called 'the Angel of Death.'"

Solomon shook his head. "Ach, he is no angel; he is nothing but a man. A corrupt, evil man. The concept of a wicked angel of death is not even taught in the Bible."

"Oh, then he is the Demon of Death," Julia said, standing firm. "Actually, his title is the 'grand inquisitor of the Jews of Europe.' When I was in Amsterdam, Eichmann was brought there to organize the arrest, concentration, and deportation of the Dutch Jews. Deportation to Westerbork and then to German death camps. Think of it—all those Dutch families who never hurt a soul, and Eichmann didn't give a damn." She paused. "And the children—so many children." Julia broke into tears and turned away.

Solomon shook his head slowly. "I don't know Eichmann. To me, he's just another German. But I do know that my family and their parents and grandparents have been in these hills since the third century. No one has been able to force us out, and no one ever will. But if you're right, then whatever happens will happen. And maybe they will bury me with my forefathers. Either way, I am not leaving."

Julia looked at the rabbi. "And what about your family? Are you going to stay and subject your children and your grandchildren to that danger? Are you going to leave it to Hitler or Eichmann or Seyss-Inquart to march you all into boxcars and ship you to concentration camps? Does it make sense to leave your family and the fate of the Jewish community to the will of the Nazi killers?"

Now Solomon snarled and stuck out his chest. "My family? My family? You dare to speak to me about the safety of my family? Don't you worry about my family. I can take care of my family."

"Good! That is what I want to hear," Julia said. "Now go home and pack your bags."

Carl stood up and raised his hands. "All right, all right, that's enough. Let's settle down. Solomon has a point; his community has been here for a thousand years, and they have a vested interest in the land. While we don't know anything for certain, it is a very bad sign that Eichmann has arrived with a large contingent—of that there is no doubt. I have heard of Eichmann, but I confess, I don't know why he was sent here at this time. Neither do my sources."

The rabbi shook his head. "Creating a panic by telling people to drop everything and flee Hungary at this time is not the answer. Solomon has just told you that Jews have been living and working in Hungary since the Roman times. It is their land too. Maybe there is a way to negotiate a solution. Maybe through the leader of some other country. Does Hitler really want to come into one of his Axis partners and kill a million of its citizens, especially those productive ones that are part of the country's economic foundation? There's got to be another way."

"Rabbi has a point," Carl said. "We have to know more about this and how to approach the situation. Panic is rarely the answer, and maybe there is no single answer. Maybe there are multiple answers. Let's put our collective brains to work and exchange information at least once a day."

With that, Carl stood to leave, and everyone else followed. Out in the hallway, Carl pulled Julia aside. "Julia, you are in contact with John Pehle from time to time, are you not?"

"Every day."

"It's time to confer with the WRB," he said quietly. "An influx of German soldiers, the absence of Regent Horthy, and the addition of Adolf Eichmann are a bad combination. To me, these are signs that tyranny is sitting on the doorstep. Let's find out what John thinks. He may know more about Eichmann and why he was sent here. If indeed it smacks of racial persecution and deportation, what does John think the War Refugee Board can do? After all, isn't that why it was created? To help refugees? And let's face it—we may soon have a country full of refugees."

Julia looked at her watch. It was noon, which meant it was six AM in Washington. Pehle wouldn't be awake yet, but she could send a cablegram to him that he would read when he got to the office. Maybe the WRB had information about Eichmann and why he had come to Budapest.

CHAPTER TWENTY-FIVE

JULIA PREPARED TO send a cablegram to John Pehle. She did her best to convey the circumstances in Budapest, no hyperbole, just facts. And those were bad enough. She couldn't imagine them to be any worse.

Along with Carl Lutz, Theresa, and the influential men of the Budapest Jewish community, Julia now faced a Hungarian government on the brink of collapse. With its regent lured out of the country and absent for four days, it was ripe for a takeover. She warmed up the cable machinery and prepared to relay what she knew about the current situation: the Kállay peace feelers, and Horthy's immediate, unscheduled, and unexpected trip to meet with Hitler at his castle in Schloss Klessheim in Austria.

John:
It is midday here in Budapest, and I have very troubling news to report. Regent Horthy has been gone for four days, and no one has heard from him. During his absence, hundreds, if not thousands, of Nazi soldiers have moved into Hungary. Nothing is being done about it because Hungary's commander in chief is AWOL. There are Nazi soldiers and SS personnel everywhere you look, but so far, there has been no military activity. The general opinion is that Hitler has lost confidence in Horthy, his former trusted ally, and it may only be a matter of time until he replaces him and assigns a new leader. It is likely that Hungary will become another Nazi puppet state like Czechoslovakia, Austria, or Holland.

Even more disturbing, Adolf Eichmann arrived here yesterday along with a large Nazi contingent. He has taken up residence at the German compound near Castle Hill. People in the know feel that Eichmann's appearance may be in preparation for racial cleansing. I personally witnessed the wickedness of his work when he engineered the evacuation of innocent Jewish families from Holland. Now he has been sent here to Budapest, and it is only logical that he will be called upon to engineer a similar fate for the million Hungarian Jews. Carl Lutz suggested that I contact you for any help the WRB can provide. He knows that if there is a mass exodus, it will need organization, funding, and personnel. Any information about Eichmann, or explanation of the reasons that he is now in Budapest, would be appreciated.

Yours truly,
Julia Powers

It didn't take long for Julia to receive a return cablegram: "Call me at 10 AM EST," followed by a series of numbers. At the requested time, Julia's call went first to an operator at the Swiss communications center, then to London, and then by the underseas cable to Washington.

"Eichmann in Budapest is indeed a very bad omen," Pehle said, "and I'm glad that you contacted me right away. Wherever he goes, death follows. He is Hitler's master engineer of roundup and deportations. Your information on his arrival in Budapest will give the WRB a head start. This is bound to be a refugee crisis. As far as Eichmann is concerned, I can't tell you much more than you already know. I do know that he was with Heydrich and the others at the Wannsee Conference when they pledged their allegiance to the Final Solution. His recent actions have confirmed his commitment to effectuating a *Judenfrei* Europe and the so-called Final Solution. Why Eichmann has been assigned to Budapest now, after five years of war, is a mystery to me, though it would seem to be related to Horthy's disappearance. We will begin formulating plans for rescue and evacuation of refugees in order to be prepared if Eichmann moves ahead. Believe me, we will work to help save as many as we can. I have to believe that Carl told you to contact me for that purpose. Tell him we'll try hard not to let him down."

"Thank you for your response," Julia said, "and I will pass the word.

Please be aware that things are happening fast. German troops are moving in, Horthy is no longer in control, and we hear that Kállay is out. They will appoint another prime minister."

JULIA MET WITH Carl and told him of her exchange with John. "When and if it is necessary, the WRB has the resources to fund relief organizations and rescue activities," she said. "Tell me, Carl, what is your opinion on why they sent Eichmann and his legion of killers to Budapest at this time? If not to plan the eradication of the Jewish community, then what? That is what Eichmann does. He's an expert, a cold-blooded expert. John said he was with Heydrich at the Wannsee Conference when they devised their Final Solution to the so-called Jewish problem. Now he is in Budapest to carry out what he is trained to do. John also told me that the WRB has no further information than we already know."

Carl answered with a long, serious look. "The people must be informed as soon as possible, but in a way that doesn't create mass panic. It must come down through leadership. They must devise an organized plan for the people to avoid capture and escape to someplace safe. That won't be easy, because we have seen that the leaders are not convinced. Sooner or later, they will be, but we can't wait that long. By then, it would be too late."

Julia stood. "Please listen to me, I beg you," she said gravely. "The Nazis have yet to begin their operation, but they will. First, they'll assemble them in ghettos, then round them up and load them onto trains bound for death camps. Once the process starts, it's over. There's no getting away. If we wait until they start, it will be too late for too many. You want to know what we should do to prepare? Our job is to save as many as we can. Bear in mind we cannot win. It is only a question of how many we can save. We need to lead as many as we can to escape routes. Do you agree with me?"

"I do," said Carl. "We can't do it on our own; it has to be a combined effort from within. Theresa, we need to enlist your father, the rabbi, and the other Jewish community leaders to talk to their fellow congregants. They must be alerted, and they must be convinced. They have an obligation to talk sense to their people. In the meantime, there are steps that John Pehle and I can take to set the groundwork. We can reach out to neutral countries like Switzerland, Sweden, and Turkey and any other humanitarian sources to sponsor a way out. You and Theresa have the relationships with the community's leaders, so let's use them."

"That won't be easy," answered Julia. "You heard Solomon and the rabbi each talk about their ancestors living and dying here since the Roman times." Julia shook her head.

"Then you must open their eyes," Carl said. "This time, they won't be buried with their ancestors in the Hungarian hills; their bodies will be taken to camps in Poland, and their ashes will be buried in pits."

"I am aware of that, Carl," Julia said. "So, tell me, how do I get through to the people? How do I open their eyes? How do I convince them to save themselves? Why would they listen to me, a girl from Detroit? Even Theresa. She's from here, but she's been living in America and she's younger than they are. How do we talk sense to the community's leaders when we don't have credibility?"

"I have also thought about that, and I have come up with an idea," Carl said. "I know a man who will have credibility. He is a former German legislator. He now does business in Budapest. I've known him for years. He is a humanitarian, and I'm sure he cares deeply about the senseless murder of innocent civilians. He is a decent man. When he speaks, people listen."

"If Theresa and I can arrange it, would he talk to the community leaders in a private meeting?"

"I'll talk to him. If he is in town, I'm sure he would help."

TWO DAYS LATER, Julia received a call from Carl. He had spoken with his contact, the German informant, and the man was agreeable to a meeting with community leaders, providing that the identities and the talk itself remained strictly confidential. He was still employed in Berlin and serving as a legislator. If his cooperation was discovered, he would be killed.

"I will tell you this," Carl said, "the thought of persecuting nine hundred thousand innocent Hungarian Jews is so abhorrent, he is willing to share what he knows about Eichmann and the German program in the hopes that it might make a difference."

"Okay. How do we go about accomplishing this?" asked Julia.

"He will meet us in the dark of night in a warehouse on György Street. He will dress in black to hide his identity, and you are advised to hide your identity as well. No names will be exchanged for your benefit as well as his. Because he does business here in Budapest, he speaks rudimentary Hungarian, if that will work. You may ask him whatever you wish about the Nazis' current plans, and he will share his knowledge, if indeed he knows. Please, no personal questions. Is that agreeable?"

"It is," answered Julia, "and we are so appreciative of his help. He doesn't need to worry about his rudimentary Hungarian; both Theresa and I speak German. When is he available to meet?"

"Soon. In order for the meeting to have the greatest impact on the welfare of the community, you and Theresa should include influential community leaders. Request some of them to come with you, but they must understand this is not an adversarial situation. It is not a debate. They may not argue with him. We have all been in meetings where stubborn men express opposite opinions and are prepared to argue the night away. This man is doing the Jewish community a great favor to come and give them the facts. He is available tomorrow night or the night after. After that, he is returning to Germany, probably to stay. There are several reasons for him to leave Budapest as soon as possible. You may draw your own conclusions as to why. Talk among yourselves and decide what time is best for you and your group. Let me know, and I will attend the meeting with you. He will not speak to you without my being present."

CHAPTER TWENTY-SIX

IN AN INDUSTRIAL section of Budapest, anchored by the clothing and garment industries, a group of people stood outside the door of a redbrick, two-story warehouse. *Mardenawitz Finom Szövetek* (Mardenowitz Fine Fabrics) was painted on the side. "Are you sure this is the correct building?" Benjamin said.

"That is the address he gave us—254 Dózsa György," Carl said.

"Then we should knock on the door, no?" said Rabbi Levy. He shrugged, stepped forward, and knocked. A moment later, a young man, no more than twenty, opened the door and said, "Is this the group from the Swiss embassy?"

"Yes, it is. I'm Carl Lutz," he answered, showing his ID.

Julia looked at the messenger and said to Theresa, "He looks very young, and he speaks Hungarian."

"Come this way, please," the young man said. He took them down the hall and into a large room filled with folded fabrics, benches, cutting tables, and large spools of thread.

Sitting in a darkened corner, behind one of the tables, was an older man. He wore a wide-brimmed black fedora pulled down low across his forehead. His dark blue wool coat was pulled up at the collar. He wore sunglasses. The lights in the corner had been dimmed. The visitors would have little ability to later recognize this man, even if they were to meet him on the street corner. If they were later asked by someone for a description, they could only respond, "An older man, thin, of medium height with a gray beard."

"If it is quite all right," the man said in German, "we shall try to keep our identities as covert as possible."

"We respect your wishes," said Theresa. "We also desire to protect our identities. One never knows who is doing the questioning. To begin with, we wish to express our gratitude that you have agreed to meet with our group. We are a small representative group of the Jewish community in Budapest. We understand that you may possess information about Germany's immediate intentions concerning Hungary and, of course, the Jewish community. We also understand that you may have information about Adolf Eichmann and the reasons that he has been sent to Budapest with a contingent of soldiers at this time."

The man tipped the black fedora and slowly nodded in agreement. "It is true. I do know some things that others may not. Since you are affiliated with the Budapest Jewish community, I will tell you this: There is great cause to be alarmed. Mr. Lutz was wise to seek me out. He requested that I furnish information that will help you and your community make decisions on what should be done. He told me that some of you may consider leaving the country and others will resist that idea. That is understandable. Mr. Lutz also told me that some of you have deep roots in the Budapest community, and you find it difficult, if not intolerable, to consider relocation. Is that not also true?"

"That is correct, sir," Solomon said. "My family can trace its roots in these soils for hundreds of years. That is true for many members of our community, and we want to protect our homeland and our right to live and work here."

The black fedora nodded again. He raised his head and said, "While I can understand the emotional ties you have to this land, you would be better served by listening to reason rather than emotion."

"But this is our home," said Solomon. "Wise or not, we would like to know what we can do to prevent enemies from trying to take it from us. We don't want to give up without a fight. How do we stop them?"

The informant nodded, shrugged, and stood up. "I can't help you. I am sorry, that is not why I came here today. I can't counsel you on how to fight. That's foolishness. You have no ability to stop the Nazis from advancing or even slow them down if they decide to move ahead." He turned and started walking toward the door.

"Wait!" Julia said. "That man spoke out of turn. We don't want fighting lessons. We are not looking for military defense measures. We want to know what is best for our community at this time. We understand that you are privy to closely held information regarding the German objectives in Hungary. We'd like to know what they are. What is it that they are planning to do with the city, with the government, with the people? What do they want to accomplish? When do they want to start? You were asked to share your knowledge about Adolf Eichmann and the current state of affairs as you know them. All we are seeking is information. We would appreciate anything you can tell us about Germany's plans concerning Hungary and how Adolf Eichmann fits into those plans. Anything you can tell us is more than we know now, and it will help us make intelligent decisions on what steps we should take with our families."

The man nodded, turned around, and sat down on the stool. "You ask how Adolf Eichmann fits in? Let me tell you about the man, and you can draw your own conclusions."

"That would be most helpful," Theresa said. "We are generally aware of what Eichmann has done in other European countries. We know that when Germany militarily conquered a country, like Romania or Holland, Eichmann was sent in to organize the arrest and deportation of the Jewish citizens."

The man nodded. "It wasn't because the Jews were enemy soldiers or that they even posed a danger," he said. "Indeed, of all the sectors of society, they were probably the most docile and well behaved. Yet because of Hitler's hatred of Jews, he would order his officers, like Eichmann, to follow his military into the country, gather all the Jews, and send them to concentration camps in Poland or Germany. He called that making the country *Judenfrei*."

Rabbi Levy spoke. "Tell us, if you know, how and why does a man like Eichmann ever become so cold and bitter? Is there a chance of reaching a compassionate side of him? After all, he is a human being. There must be some sense of feeling when he realizes that he is responsible for sending innocent people—women, children—to their deaths."

"He is governed by ambition, not feeling. He wants to move up in the ranks of the Nazi Party, and executing Hitler's wishes is the way to do so."

"As we know," said Carl, "Miklós Horthy was ordered by Hitler to attend a meeting at Klessheim. What do you know about that meeting?"

"Prime Minister Kállay was removed," said the man in the black hat, "because he sent the second of the secret peace messages, but Horthy was spared. He was given instructions going forward and was sent back to Budapest."

"What were the instructions?" asked Julia.

The man shrugged. "I don't know the details, but I do know that Horthy is returning to Budapest later today."

"Then Horthy will now become a Hitler puppet. Is that right?"

The man shrugged again. "You ask about the future. Who can tell?"

Rabbi Levy stepped forward. "Have you finished telling us about Eichmann?"

"There is much to tell, but you are impatient, and I will shorten the rest."

"No, please," said Theresa. "This is valuable information, and I implore you to continue."

The man took a deep breath and exhaled through his nose.

"In 1942, Eichmann and his men organized the deportation of Jews from Slovakia." Then he pointed at Julia. "As the woman here has mentioned, he organized deportations from the Netherlands. He did the same in France and Belgium. In 1943, and earlier this year, he deported the Jews from Greece and northern Italy, and now he is here in Hungary. You may draw your own conclusions. But his time in Slovakia should be very important to you. It may predict what he will do here."

Solomon raised his ancient body and stood before the group. "Look, sir, whatever your name is, I don't really care what he did in Slovakia. I live in Hungary. I can agree with you that Adolf Eichmann is a very bad man. He may have been responsible for the deportation of thousands of Jews from France or Belgium or Holland, but those countries were enemies of the Reich. They were at war with Hitler. Hungary is not. We are partners, members of the Axis powers. We fight beside them in Axis battles. We were with them on the battlefields of Russia. Because of that relationship, our citizens have never been subject to the same mistreatment as have citizens of enemy nations. While the Jews of those other nations were sent away, or taken away, our Jews have been left alone to manage their own lives in peace, and that is how I expect it to remain. Why would the appearance of Adolf Eichmann change anything?"

The man in the black fedora leaned back. He obviously wasn't getting through to all the attendees. He shook his head and emitted a quiet snicker. "Pardon me, sir, but you are a fool, and a poor representative of your community. Eichmann was at the Wannsee Conference with Reinhard Heydrich. He swore commitment to the Final Solution, remember? He even recorded minutes of that meeting, and I have seen those minutes. He noted that Heydrich spoke for an hour and continually demanded the eradication of the Jews. During their conversation, they minced no words about it at all. They spoke about methods of killing, about liquidation, about extermination, after which they broke for a glass of cognac. Do you understand, sir, mass killing is Eichmann's purpose? He lives for that. That is his raison d'être, his reason for being. He first went to Poland and visited Auschwitz in 1941, and by then, he had already begun to organize mass deportations of Jews from Germany and Bohemia. For the last several years, Eichmann's office has been *the* headquarters for the implementation of the Final Solution. And now, sir, he is here in Budapest, and why the hell do you think he is here? For the food?"

With that, the old man stood, humphed, and pulled up his coat collars to hide his face. He walked quickly out of the room without a second glance.

THE WAREHOUSE ROOM was perfectly still for a few minutes while everyone gathered their thoughts. Finally, Solomon rose, brushed himself off, and said, "You can't believe everything you hear, especially from a German. He speaks of Armageddon. He says, 'Take my word for it or perish.' Well, I don't. Take a walk outside. Go down Dohány Street.

What do you see? You see men and women and children all going about their lives. Eichmann may be here, but nothing has changed. It is still our lovely community. Speaking for me and my family, we're not panicking." With that, Solomon left the room.

Rabbi Levy raised his hand. "Don't blame old Solomon. He has lived here for eighty years, he is a true patriot, and he is set in his ways. He cannot envision anything else. I agree with him in many respects. We all need to put on our thinking caps. We don't know for a fact what Eichmann's plans are. Right now, he is staying in a room in the German compound. Nothing else. I am inclined to agree with Solomon, not to jump to conclusions, pull up stakes, and run."

"So we should wait and sit on our hands until it is too late?" Julia said. "I can't believe what I am hearing. Do you want to wait until all the troops are in place and Eichmann decides the time is right to order them to round up the Jews and put them into cattle cars? Don't you get it? It's too late then. We need to act now!"

"I agree with my sister in arms," said Theresa. "We originally wanted to come here from America to check on my parents. An opportunity opened up, and we were able to travel here. If it was as we feared, then we wanted to take my parents out of Hungary and help them immigrate someplace safe to save their lives. In many ways, our responsibilities have broadened; they are no longer limited to the Weissbach family. We are now embracing the entire Budapest Jewish community in our thoughts and plans. A month ago, it may only have been worries or fears, but now, they are realities. We must accept the fact that Eichmann is going to engineer a mass deportation to extermination camps. Why else would he be here with a military contingent? We cannot sit still while he works his evil."

"I, for one, would like to know what happened when Eichmann was in Slovakia," Julia said. "Why did the man say it was so important for us to know?"

"I would as well," said Carl. "I will contact the man and try to find out."

"In the meantime, shouldn't we start having serious discussions on what it would take to move large numbers of people out of the country, should that become necessary?" Theresa asked. "Julia is right, we can't do that overnight. At this time, there is no limitation on our freedoms. Tomorrow, who knows? It would make sense if we made plans to send people to Palestine right away!"

The rabbi spread his arms. "Theresa, you say there are no limitations? The Hungarian borders are all closed, and there are Axis troops on all of the exits. How are families supposed to get to Palestine? Will they walk? Take a train?"

This time, it was Carl who shook his head. "Maybe, but trains are stopped at the borders, and people must have identification. I suppose, if you had the right credentials, you could make it through Romania all the way to Turkey. And if you did get that far, Ira Hirschman could help you get to Palestine, but those arrangements would have to be made in advance. Theresa is right in one regard—the arrangements would take careful planning and should be undertaken right away."

Theresa's father stepped forward and gently put his arm around her shoulder. He pulled her into his chest and hugged her. "Terri, even if you could make those arrangements, not everyone can or will leave. I don't know if I can leave, but I think you should go. Both you and Julia came to Budapest for humanitarian reasons and because you love us. But now you should leave before things get worse. We don't know what is going to happen here, so why put yourselves at risk? Julia, we aren't even your family, and you stick your neck out. Look, I trust the man in the black hat. He said to leave, and the two of you can make it. Both of you have Swiss IDs and the ability to travel back to Switzerland and then to the United States. I urge you to go."

"Then come with us," Theresa said.

Benjamin shook his head. "It's not as easy as that. Pack up an entire life and leave for unknown territories? Not many would elect to do that. In my case, it would be a hardship for your mother to make a long journey all the way to Palestine. I certainly couldn't leave and run out on my congregants. I am their president and a leader that they look to for advice. Can I leave and abandon all of them? And what about Sammy and Becca? They have respective professions and are building solid futures here in Budapest. What about your Uncle Morry and your cousins? I can't turn my back on my people. I may have to stay, but you should go." He turned to Carl. "Mr. Lutz, can you arrange it? Can you take Terri and Julia to Bern and arrange for their passage home to America? I will cover the costs, whatever they are."

"Apa, I love you," Theresa said, "but it's my decision. I came here to help you and Anya escape. We can still do that. I accepted an appointment as Carl's assistant. I should not abandon him at such a precarious moment. Julia, maybe you are the one who should consider going home."

Julia solemnly shook her head. "I came with you to watch your back, and I'm glad I did. We can stick it out together. Other than Carl, I am the WRB's only contact here. I have a Swiss ID as Carl's assistant, and that should provide a measure of safety. The Nazis will honor it."

Carl smiled and nodded. "I made a good choice in hiring you two as administrative assistants, and Julia is right, your Swiss IDs prove that you work for the government of Switzerland, and they will protect you. Right now, I want to get out of this drafty old warehouse and return to my office. I will schedule another meeting, a private meeting, with my German contact for tomorrow morning. I should learn more than he was prepared to discuss today. After that, I'd like to meet with Theresa and Julia in my office. Between now and then, I'd like you to digest everything that has happened here today and check in with John Pehle at the WRB, and tomorrow, we'll make some decisions."

CHAPTER TWENTY-SEVEN

IT TOOK SEVERAL minutes for the call to John Pehle to be routed through to him at the Treasury Department. Julia identified herself and mentioned that Theresa was by her side. She reviewed the contents of the afternoon's meeting and asked for John's reaction. What more did he know about the situation? What did he advise? What was the WRB prepared to do?

"That's a lot to digest," Pehle said. "I will run it all by our group as soon as possible and assemble our recommendations. As for what we know about Hungary's current situation, the WRB has sources, some very highly placed, and I will get their feedback. You and Theresa are even better sources. You're on the ground in Budapest, and you're privy to more current information. At the WRB, we recently learned that Adolf Eichmann has been assigned to Hungary by the Nazi hierarchy. From what you tell me, he's there now."

"He is here now," Julia answered. "He arrived three days ago and has set up headquarters in the Majestic Hotel. It's in the German compound just to the north of Castle Hill. It's scary. That's less than half a mile away from the Swiss embassy, where Theresa and I are staying. We are trying to keep track of what Eichmann is doing at the present time, but we don't have specific information on what he plans to do or when he plans to do it. Some believe that he will soon begin to assemble Jewish families and send them north to the concentration camps. That would be consistent with his historical behavior. That is what he did in Holland, France, Belgium, Slovakia, and other places. Despite his history, other people here prefer to adopt a wait-and-see attitude, believing that Regent Horthy will restore calm when he returns from his meeting with Hitler. When and if he does return, Eichmann might leave."

Pehle answered, "We have not received information that Horthy is going to return. Our sources tell us that Horthy was placed under house arrest when he arrived at Klessheim, Austria. He was informed about Hitler's Operation Margarethe, the plan that Germany will assume total control over Hungary."

"This is Theresa, John. Hundreds of German soldiers are now on our streets, and Adolf Eichmann is here as well, but nothing internal has changed. Yet."

"Our information is that Prime Minister Kállay has been removed and a Hungarian named Döme Sztójay was appointed in his stead," Pehle said. "Sztójay is fiercely loyal to the Nazi cause. Edmund Veesenmayer, a Nazi military commander, was appointed to help Sztójay govern. It seems as though Hungary is now becoming a German protectorate."

"We had a meeting earlier today," Julia said. "Carl had arranged a secret meeting with a highly placed German diplomat. We weren't told his name or anything else about him, except that he is an insider and very knowledgeable about the Nazi plans. It was all hush-hush. The man told us that Regent Horthy is on his way home."

"Hmm. We hadn't heard that," Pehle said. "There's no doubt that you have access to better information than I do. If Horthy returns, it will most likely be in a compromised state, now that Sztójay has been appointed. I think our biggest concern is what will happen to the Hungarian populace, especially the Jewish populace, now that Eichmann is in residence and the government is changing. You know as well as I that Eichmann is capable of clearing out tens of thousands of innocent people within a three- or four-month period."

"What is your advice for us, John? What should we do?"

"You and Theresa should pack your bags and leave at once. Don't even bother packing your bags. Carl Lutz should be able to arrange passage through Switzerland and back home. You have Swiss IDs—that should keep you safe until you leave. But beware—IDs are only effective as long as they are honored. In the meantime, be careful and keep your eyes and ears open."

"That's your advice, John?" Julia said. "You want us to pack up and leave? You sound like my father. You know why we came here. Isn't it too soon to leave, when we haven't accomplished anything yet? We came here to help refugees, and we haven't done that."

"I know your state of mind. If you are dead set against leaving at this time, and you want to stay to help Theresa's family and the others, at least do this: Have it be a fluid decision. Stay for the time being, but evaluate your situation as you go along. Since you are staying in Budapest for the purpose of aiding refugees, we consider you to be valuable agents of the War Refugee Board. The fact that Hungary is now the largest Jewish community in Europe places one million Jews in the refugee category and a prime focus of the WRB. We very much appreciate your service as WRB agents. Take care of yourselves."

"We will continue to contact you every day and provide information," Julia confirmed. "If you learn anything or have advice, please contact me on Carl's line."

"If and when Jews are being told to move out of their homes and into a central location, or they are herded into ghetto areas, then it's time to take action, and give me a call. People will need whatever protection we can offer. They will need escape routes and personnel to guide them. Those who can't or won't escape will need places to stay out of sight, like you were able to provide in Holland."

"When you say 'protection we can offer,' are you referring to obtaining letters of protection?" Julia asked.

"In part. Those will have to come from neutral sources, not the United States, but we can help. Diplomatic letters of protection, fake IDs, and phony birth certificates are documents that save lives. Should the situation warrant it, they would be distributed in large amounts. In Hungary alone, we're looking at almost a million Jews! Carl Lutz is your number one overseer, and you should follow his directions. He can furnish Swiss letters and IDs, but he's only one man. You will need more providers than just Carl. Work on trying to develop and enlist other agents.

Here at the WRB, we should be able to give you the identities of possible contacts, representatives of neutral governments who will agree to issue diplomatic letters of immunity. Carl will be able to help in that regard."

"Are there other countries that are willing to issue letters of diplomatic immunity that Germany will honor?" Julia asked. "Will they provide the same level of protection?"

"They have to come from governments that Germany recognizes as neutral. Even then, it's not a sure thing. Germany could change its mind. You of all people should remember that the Netherlands declared its neutrality and even entered into a neutrality pact with Germany, only to see it disregarded in 1940 when Germany overran the country. At this time, Switzerland, Sweden, Turkey, and certain South American countries are considered neutral by German standards, and immunity and diplomatic credentials are honored."

Julia was quick to respond. "You mentioned Sweden as a neutral country. I know someone in Sweden. A very, very good friend."

"It's not enough to be a Swedish citizen or even a very, very good friend. One would have to be in a position of authority or dominance in Sweden to have the right to issue and distribute Swedish letters of protection. Who are you referring to?"

"My good friend Raoul Wallenberg. He is a prominent man in Sweden. Shall I reach out to him?"

"That wouldn't be enough. He would have to be authorized by the Swedish government. If you contacted him, he in turn would have to apply to the Swedish national cabinet, the prime minister, or even King Gustav to be clothed with proper authority. If your friend is as prominent as you say, he would probably be well known at those levels, but the request should come from a diplomatic source like the US State Department."

"Can you make that happen, John? Can you have Sumner Welles make that request?"

"I can try, but it may be premature. Nothing is happening yet in Hungary to justify issuance of letters of protection for mass emigration. If steps were to be taken by Eichmann, or any of the German officers, to isolate the Jews or place them in immediate danger, the WRB would be justified in requesting, or having the State Department request, that Sweden appoint a diplomat to circulate those letters. Tell me the name of your friend again."

"Raoul Wallenberg, and he is a terrific friend," said Julia. "He's smart and comes from a very well-connected family in Stockholm. I met him at the University of Michigan. He graduated with a degree in architecture. We were very good friends in college, and I trusted him. I still do. His uncle is Jacob Wallenberg, a wealthy and responsible businessman. He got Raoul a job with Kálmán Lauer, who does business all over Europe, including Budapest. Raoul has been to Budapest on business for Lauer, but he is not here right now."

"Okay. In the event that trouble starts in Hungary, I will immediately reach out to Sweden and other countries as well," said John. "I have another thought. Someone we know here in Washington is familiar with a group called the Aid and Rescue Committee of Budapest. It was formed in 1941 by Ottó Komoly and Israel Kasztner."

"We know about them. Theresa's family is friends with the Komolys, and Theresa went to school with their daughter. They all belong to the same synagogue."

"Well, they are good people to know. The original goal of the Aid and Rescue Committee was to smuggle Jews out of Poland into Hungary. Hungary was safe for Jews, but in Poland, they were sentenced to death. The committee smuggled over one thousand Polish Jews into Hungary. Even last spring, in 1943, the committee was sending emissaries to Poland to search for any surviving Jews. Those who were found were also smuggled into Hungary, although Komoly's committee is not smuggling Jews into Hungary anymore. It's too dangerous. Komoly has made arrangements with the Jewish Agency in Palestine, and they have jointly assisted refugees to immigrate there. The committee has thus far been successful, but the WRB hasn't heard from them in some time. Presumably, they are still active. If I were you, I would try to reach out to Komoly or Israel Kasztner."

"I will talk to Carl about Raoul Wallenberg and Israel Kasztner," said Julia. "I will also ask Carl to tell us what he knows about the Aid and

Rescue Committee. Carl may know a way to put us in touch with them. He seems to know everybody."

"Very good," said Pehle. "Let me know what you find out. In the meantime, we'll make plans to send a request out to Sweden for someone who can distribute Swedish letters of protection, should they become necessary. We'll be sure to mention Raoul Wallenberg. Until then, take care of yourselves. Keep your eyes open. Hungary is a powder keg that can blow at any moment. Watch yourself! You are brave young women."

THERESA SET THE handset onto the cradle and said, "I think John is right. Eichmann has been sent here for a reason, and Hungary is a powder keg."

"Then we should be lining up contacts right now," Julia answered. "The moment Eichmann begins to make Hungary *Judenfrei*, the moment he starts going through the neighborhoods and isolating innocent people, that is the moment it is too late to start. We have to be prepared before then. Our best bet is to follow John's intuition and meet with anyone and everyone who can assist."

"Right. I agree. Who do we meet with first?"

"Obviously Carl," said Julia. "The entire defense should be coordinated through Carl. He has the power, the connections, the good sense, and the ability to save the largest number. If I know Carl, he is already thinking along the same lines."

"I want to meet with Joel Brand," Theresa said. "Sammy knows him well, and I'm sure he could arrange a meeting with him, but my brother is always so busy, and it's not easy to talk to him."

"I have an idea," Julia said with a devious smile. "What if your mother was to arrange one of her fabulous family dinners? How could Sammy turn her down? I saw him chow down last time when he brought his gorgeous girlfriend."

"Alana. Her name is Alana. It's a good idea, but there isn't any reason to have a big celebration right now. It's nobody's birthday."

"What about holidays?" Julia suggested. "Is there a holiday coming up?"

"Passover is in two weeks, but I don't like that idea," Theresa said, shaking her head. "Even though Passover is the story of the Jewish exodus away from a cruel dictator named Pharaoh, it's wrong to invite the family to a religious holiday on false pretenses. You can't ask them to come to a Pesach meal and change the subject to talk about Eichmann and escape routes. We should tell the truth. We could invite them all to a family dinner, say it's very important, and leave it at that."

"You're right. Let's be honest. It is better to talk to everyone at the same time, and a dinner would accomplish that, but your mother and father would have to be on board."

"I agree. I'll talk to Anya and make sure that she is willing to host under those circumstances. We can offer to help and take her grocery shopping. We can promise that there won't be any arguments at the table, that we just want everyone to know the present state of affairs. If she agrees, then we can go talk to Apa. If either one disagrees, then a dinner is out of the question."

CHAPTER TWENTY-EIGHT

WHILE JULIA AND Theresa were making their arrangements, Carl Lutz was flying back to Budapest from Bern, where he had traveled to discuss Hungary's current state with Swiss officials. The disappearance of Horthy, the appearance of Eichmann, and the arrival of German troops was an unmistakable sign that Hungarian independence was nearing an end. Carl had gone to Bern seeking guidance and the extent of Swiss knowledge concerning Hitler's intentions where Hungary was concerned. He also discussed what he had learned in his first and second meetings with the man he now knew as Bernhard, the man in the black fedora. Bernhard's first meeting had been the group meeting with Theresa, Julia, and the other Budapest community leaders. The second meeting, just between Carl and Bernhard, had concluded right before Carl boarded the plane to Bern. That meeting only heightened Carl's urgency.

But Carl's Swiss superiors believed that Jews were relatively unharmed in Hungary, and they had admonished Carl that it was not his job or the embassy's job to defend the enemies of the German Reich. He and the embassy must remain neutral and not take sides in the war or in territorial disputes. However, Carl believed that Swiss human values were not neutral and were well known, and most countries would expect to witness Swiss humanitarian efforts. Even Germany would not expect Switzerland to be indifferent where human lives were concerned.

After discussing this matter for a day and a half, Carl returned to Budapest. When he landed, he called Julia and Theresa as he had promised and invited them to join him at the embassy office. Each of them had something important to discuss with Carl as well.

"Before we get started," Carl said, "I want you to know what happened in Bern. I had a meeting with my superiors, and there was a mixed reaction. Some of them were proud that I was taking a humanitarian stand, but others felt that I was taking sides and getting involved where I shouldn't, in violation of Swiss neutrality policy."

Julia shook her head.

"I felt the same way," said Carl. "I cannot stand by and watch this cruel inhumanity take place and do nothing. I told them about my second, private meeting with Bernhard, the one you couldn't attend. But I only told them part of the report. The other part I kept secret because I was afraid that my superiors would give me a strict order to be silent. So I kept it to myself. Bernhard revealed to me that Chelmno, Majdanek, and Auschwitz-Birkenau were not only concentration camps but were killing centers."

"That's not news to me," Julia said. "The Dutch were sent there to die. Even the little babies. We knew that."

"But that's not the whole story. Bernhard told me that he knew that prisoners were killed by carbon monoxide fumes from a car exhaust," Carl said. "Then he told me that large internal combustion engines were built in German labs, and they were designed to pipe huge volumes of exhaust through large pipes into sealed chambers at the camps. Chelmno, on the outskirts of Łódź, Poland, was the first to incorporate these machines at its camp. It was the first of the extermination camps designed to kill as many as possible as quickly as possible. That part I kept to myself. I had asked Bernhard if there was proof, and he told me in secret that there were two escapees who were writing a report, and it would be released soon. Until then, it was better to keep quiet."

"I had heard a rumor about prisoners being killed with carbon monoxide exhaust in Lithuania, but I had never heard of the internal combustion machines piping gas into large rooms to kill hundreds," Martin said.

Carl nodded, and then his face became very serious. "At one point in our conversation, Bernhard became very quiet, and a severe expression covered his face. 'Now there is an even quicker, deadlier gas,' Bernhard told me. 'It is known only to a few outside the Chelmno, Majdanek, and Auschwitz camps. It is called Zyklon B. It was developed by German scientists, and it is quick and deadly. Thousands of Jews are killed in this way every day.' Then Bernhard said, 'But you have sworn not to publicize this information before there is objective proof, not just the word of someone such as I. Germany would find a way to deny it, and other countries in the world wouldn't believe it without proof. Anyway, it is enough for you to know that Jews are being murdered in the camps every day.' Then Bernhard told me that two escapees are preparing a report and I should wait for that. I agreed that I would not publicize his information," said Carl. "It is indeed enough to know that Jews are systematically being murdered in large groups in the camps."

"I think that governments all over the world should know about the Zyklon B gas," Julia said. "Maybe that would change the minds of those who support Nazi Germany. Public opinion, maybe even Germans, would turn against Germany. Then maybe this war would end more quickly."

"I know, and I agree with you," Carl said, "but I didn't want to discuss it at the meeting in Bern. We have to find a way to disclose the poison gas so that it will have the greatest effect, and I don't want it traceable back to Bernhard. I gave my word. He is a valuable source. He told me that a report would be issued soon, and I hope he is right."

"What else happened in Bern that you think I should know about?"

"Well, I told you that my government criticized me for taking sides, but I told my superiors that I cannot sit idly by and watch Adolf Eichmann and his henchmen carry out Operation Reinhard in Hungary." Carl was firm. "If indeed it is their plan to arrest all the Jewish citizens of Hungary and send them to killing centers, I will employ every defensive measure at my disposal to prevent that from occurring, and I will actively support the rescue of as many refugees as possible." Carl paused and cleared his throat. "I know I just said *if*, but I also believe it's only a matter of time until they try. Operation Reinhard is now taking its orders from Eichmann's headquarters in the Majestic Hotel north of Castle Hill."

"When you say 'actively support,' what did your government leaders tell you that you can do?" Julia asked. "What support can we expect?"

"Well, they warned me to use caution. They said that our first rule is to remain apolitical, a neutral nation. We must always retain our Swiss neutrality. Otherwise, our effectiveness is gone. All lines of communication with the German government, or the Axis nations, or even Hungary will be cut if Switzerland does not remain politically neutral. Our embassy itself would be at the mercy of the Nazis. There is some truth to that. It has to be handled diplomatically, but that does not mean that we should turn our backs on innocent people. Where possible, Swiss letters of protection may be freely used, but again, with caution. They must continue to be genuine documents, distributed according to Swiss law. Otherwise, they will be considered fake, and they won't be honored by Eichmann or the Germans."

"How many letters can we hope to distribute?" Theresa asked.

"There is no set cap, but each letter must be numbered, registered, and issued to a specific person. We can't do it en masse. So obviously, there is a physical limitation on how many we can create, prepare, and distribute."

"In our telephone call," Julia responded, "John Pehle acknowledged that there would be a physical limitation on how many Swiss letters of protection could be circulated, and he urged us to locate and use other neutral governments for additional letters of protection. He mentioned Sweden."

Carl nodded. "We discussed that as well, and Swiss officials are in agreement. They also want us to reach out and coordinate with other groups that are experienced in rescue operations. They talked about Ira Hirschman in Turkey. They mentioned the Aid and Rescue Committee. They mentioned the Bratislava Working Group."

"That is just what John Pehle suggested," Julia said. "The WRB is familiar with the Aid and Rescue Committee. John confirmed that Ottó Komoly was the president and Israel Kasztner was the vice president. He also said that Joel Brand and his wife, Hansi, were involved, but he wasn't sure exactly how. He knew they were active in Slovakia, but again, he didn't know the details. So, Theresa and I are in the process of trying to set up a meeting with Joel. He is a close friend of Theresa's brother."

"Now that you mention Slovakia, Bernhard brought up the subject as well. He couldn't discuss everything he wanted us to know at the public meeting with Solomon and the rabbi, but he did at the confidential meeting he had with me. Do you remember that he was about to tell us something important about Slovakia, but Solomon kept interrupting him, and soon afterward, Bernhard left?"

"I do remember," Julia said. "Bernhard became frustrated and left. That was a shame."

"At my second meeting with Bernhard," Carl said, "I found out about Eichmann and Slovakia. And surprisingly, it also involved your friend Joel Brand."

"Joel Brand in Slovakia?" Theresa said. "I heard a rumor that he was involved with another rescue committee in Slovakia. Did Bernhard tell you about that?"

Carl nodded and held his hand up for Theresa to slow down. "First of all, Bernhard finished telling me about Eichmann's early history, which is important to know. Remember, he said that Eichmann's father got him a job working for an Austrian oil company, and Adolf would roam across Austria selling oil products."

"And finding locations to set up gas stations," said Julia.

"Right. Eichmann didn't like that job, so in 1933, he quit. He left Austria for Germany to find another job. But by then, Adolf's father couldn't help him. It was the Depression, and his father wasn't doing well. Within a short time, his father lost most of his money. He was financially ruined. That embittered Adolf and left a scar that he will carry his entire life. Adolf didn't have any money or property either, so you might say that the Nazis bailed him out. Money has always been an obsession with Adolf. Because he didn't have any, he felt inferior, insecure. He always had his uniforms perfectly tailored, pressed every day, and his braided cap always sat perfectly on his head. He chose to hang around with the Nazi elite—Heydrich, Himmler, Kaltenbrunner. He volunteered to do the jobs that no one else wanted to do."

"Like organizing deportations of innocent people to concentration camps from conquered countries? That's what he did in Holland."

"Correct. One of those conquered countries was Slovakia. That is what Bernhard wanted to tell us about. In 1942, Eichmann was sent to Belgium, France, Holland, and also Slovakia. It was in Slovakia that Joel Brand came in contact with Eichmann. Do you remember we discussed that Brand had brought Slovakian Jews into Hungary?"

"Right. He smuggled his wife's family out of Slovakia. He did that while he was with the Aid and Rescue Committee," Theresa said. "Along with Ottó Komoly and Israel Kasztner."

"Correct again. But when Brand was in Slovakia, he became good friends with Gisi Fleischmann and her committee, the Bratislava Working Group. She had managed to save thousands of Slovak Jews who would otherwise have been killed. She managed to take them from Slovakia into Hungary. Hungary was safe for Jews, but Slovakia was not. Thousands of those Jews are now living in Hungary. The Bratislava Working Group, which was mostly an alliance of Zionists and ultra-Orthodox Jews, raised money to pay bribes. Then they came up with an enormous scheme they called the Europa Plan. It was presented to Eichmann's deputy. The offer was to pay $200,000 as a down payment, which would stop all the deportations to concentration camps. Then they talked back and forth about paying a ransom for the prisoners' release."

Julia was stunned. "Are you telling me that they were bribing Eichmann?"

"Yes, but not directly. He's too clever for that. They negotiated with Dieter Wisliceny, an SS captain who was Eichmann's deputy. For a certain amount of money, they could buy the right to take Jews over the border into Hungary."

"That's why Bernhard wanted us to know that information," Julia said. "Does he think that Eichmann is corruptible? Can he be bought off?"

"That's what Bernhard believes, and he knows it for a fact."

"That's crazy," Theresa said. "How much money would it take to buy the freedom of one million Jews?"

Carl spread his hands. "At one point, it was $2 million."

"Oh my God," Theresa said. "Where were they going to get that much money?"

Carl shrugged. "Supposedly from Jews in the free world who were charitable. But the money couldn't be put together, and the deal fell apart. I just think that Bernhard told us to show that Eichmann is corruptible and that Joel Brand knows it. What he does with that information is anybody's guess."

Theresa shook her head. "Amazing. I think we should talk to Joel, and I have a way to do it. My mother is holding a family dinner, and my brother, Sammy, is coming. He knows Joel very well. They have been friends for years. My family knows Ottó Komoly as well, and my father can contact him."

"I am familiar with Ottó Komoly myself," Carl said. "Ottó is a well-known personality throughout Budapest. He was a lieutenant and a decorated soldier in the Austro-Hungarian Army in the First World War. He has a nice home here in the city, and he works as an engineer. He enjoys a status level that most Hungarian Jews cannot attain. The recent antisemitic restrictions imposed by the Horthy government don't apply to him. And he is on speaking terms with most community and government leaders."

"Does he have experience in rescuing refugees?" Julia asked.

"I told you about the thousands of Jews rescued from Poland by the Aid and Rescue Committee, remember? They were brought to Hungary under Ottó's supervision," Carl said. "He not only has the knowledge of rescuing refugees, he also has the experience. He is highly respected all over Hungary. You talk about letters of protection granting immunity—Ottó's status gives immunity to him."

"We are hoping that Sammy can put us in touch with Joel Brand," Julia said. "We see that as a first step to getting close to the Aid and Rescue Committee."

"I have to go now," Carl said. "As you might imagine, there is much work to be done."

CHAPTER TWENTY-NINE

THE NIGHT OF Anya's family dinner was approaching. Julia and Theresa were looking forward to connecting with Sammy, and through him, Joel Brand. At first, Sammy had declined his dinner invitation. He was very busy. Officials at the telephone company had been summoned to Acting Regent Döme Sztójay's office. Sztójay and two Nazi officers wanted to know how quickly telephone communications could be shut off, especially to designated sectors of society. They didn't say Jewish households, but that was well understood. After they were told that it would be very difficult and take a long time, one of the officers pulled out his handgun. He stood there fingering it and then said, "That would be very disappointing. Let me ask you this: What if a person doesn't pay his bill? How long does it take the telephone company to turn off his telephone?"

The response was obvious. "The phone could be confiscated and service shut off, but if you are talking about large numbers of people, that would take many months."

"Really? And what if nine hundred thousand people don't pay their bills?" the German asked of Sammy. "Are you going to let them use the phone for free? Couldn't you turn off all of their phones if you had to?"

Sammy said that, in theory, it could be done, but it would take time.

The German shook his head. "It had better not," he replied.

After that meeting, Sammy didn't feel like accepting an invitation to a big family dinner at his parents' house. It would be a joyful gathering, and he was sick to his stomach. After all, he could be called back to the company at any time. But Anya practically begged him to come, and she could be persuasive. Especially when she told him she was preparing his favorite: Hungarian brisket with honey and smoked paprika. He couldn't say no to that.

Julia and Theresa had taken Anya shopping the day before, and they had spent the entire day cooking and setting up for the dinner. Benjamin, Becca, Sammy, his girlfriend, Alana, Anya's sister Aunt Pearl, Julia, and Theresa were all seated around the extended dining room table. Sammy brought the wine, Pearl an appetizer. The plan was to keep the conversation light, at least until after the dinner was cleared. Anya said, "Unless you have knowledge of something really important that you have to tell everyone right away, let's avoid talking about the war, or the Germans, or any of their rules during the dinner. After dinner, my husband, my daughter, and her American friend Julia have something they want to talk about." Everyone agreed to be bound by Anya's rules.

During the dinner, the table talk was irrelevant and light, such as Pearl's ordeal with the dentist and Anya's recent triumph at the group's canasta game, but it was obvious that everyone was waiting for the second shoe to fall. It was as though they were growing tired of the charade and wanted to say, "Okay, tell us what's going on." But they all played along and abided by the rules. Finally, the dinner plates were cleared, and it became very quiet. Who would speak first? Surprisingly, it was Becca.

"I know something I think is new and important," she said modestly. "I heard it at the hospital. It's not pleasant, but it is important."

"Is this something we need to know at this time?" Benjamin asked.

Becca nodded sadly. "I think we do. Especially Aunt Pearl. She lives outside of the city."

"Okay," Benjamin said. "What is the news?"

"I met a girl at the hospital yesterday, a young woman named Marta Gross. She was visiting her father, who was recovering from serious injuries he received from a beating by a Nazi soldier. Marta and her family live out in the country on a farm. The other day, Nazis drove by in Wehrmacht armored vehicles, posting signs that read, 'For your safety! All citizens in this area must immediately move into shelters in the city of Csongrád.' They drove these vehicles through the neighborhood, blasting that same message on loudspeakers. A German soldier stopped and told Marta's family to move into the city right away! Marta was dumbfounded. Her family didn't know what this was all about; they and had no intention of moving. Besides, where would they go? What about the animals on her farm? What about her pets? The man gave Marta the location of an area in Csongrád where the Jews would all be staying. He told them if they didn't move, they would be forcibly taken there anyway. He repeated that it was for their safety. Marta said that two neighboring families were told the same thing. Her father, Vasyl Gross, came out and told the soldier they were not going to move, they didn't have to move, it was their house and they owned it. He argued with the soldier, who then struck him down with a club and beat him. Then the soldier said to Marta, 'Don't let me see you here again or you will be next.' And he drove away."

"You know what this is about, don't you?" Julia said. "They're marshaling Jewish families into collective areas."

"I thank Becca for sharing what the young lady told you," said Benjamin. "It is indeed important information. The question is whether or not this was a singular occurrence, or was it a precursor to a broader operation? I haven't seen anything like that happening in our neighborhood or anywhere in Budapest, and I haven't heard of it occurring in the neighboring areas, but that doesn't mean it isn't happening in Hungary. Do we know if it is happening anywhere else, or is it only in Marta's area? It could be that the Nazis wanted that specific rural area for some reason, maybe to construct a storage facility or a base."

Julia and Theresa looked at each other, groaned, and shook their heads. "You are denying reality, Apa," Julia said. "Moving Jews from the countryside into the city is step one. There is no doubt that Operation Reinhard has now commenced in Hungary. Look out on the streets. What do you see? I see Nazi soldiers everywhere I look. There are more and more of them every day. We can no longer consider ourselves safe."

Theresa pushed back her chair, stood, and addressed the group. "If you want to know the real reason why I came to Budapest from Michigan, it wasn't just to pay a nice, friendly visit to Anya and Apa. It was because I feared that which is occurring right now. I wanted to see for myself whether my family was safe and secure. If you were not, then it was my plan to help you leave. I hadn't heard from Anya or Apa in a long time, and I knew something was up. Previously, I was able to talk to you on the telephone. I was aware that the situation was deteriorating in all of the countries surrounding Hungary. We read reports of the Russian army advancing on Hungary's eastern border. We heard that Germany was overthrowing the governments of the European countries that border Hungary. There was no doubt in my mind that Hungary could be the next to fall, like in a row of dominoes. I talked to Julia, and through her contacts in the US government, she helped me travel here. If the Jewish population was in trouble, I wanted to come help you immigrate to someplace safe."

"Terri," Anya said, "we appreciate—"

"Wait, Anya, please. Let me finish. I know that no one wants to move, especially under these circumstances, but good sense tells us not to wait. We must take advantage of any opportunity still open to us. We all need to go to a place of safety. Julia and I have connections with the US and the Swiss government officials. They are monitoring the situation. They have their sources, some high up in Germany's government, and they have concluded that Hungary is no longer a safe country for Jews. You know that Hungary is the last Jewish community left in Central Europe. Germany has succeeded in removing all the Jews from the countries they have conquered, and they have sent them away to be tortured or killed. I won't go into the details on how or where the people were taken; it is too tragic. Julia has seen it, she is a witness. We need to face facts. We are in imminent danger here. I beg you to believe me, please."

"I believe you," Alana said, holding her hand on her abdomen. "I want my baby to be born and grow up in a safe, free country. Can you help us?"

Anya's eyes widened, and she quickly covered her mouth with her right hand. "Oh my God, Alana, you're pregnant! God bless you. When is the baby due?"

"September," she said demurely.

"Congratulations," Benjamin said.

Julia smiled and whispered to Theresa, "I told you."

"Alana," Theresa said, "first of all, mazel tov. Secondly, we're going to do everything we can to make sure that your baby's health and safety are protected. Your baby and all the other little babies are the reason Julia and I have come here. We want to protect you and your baby, and we have help. We've been in constant contact with the Swiss consulate and the War Refugee Board in Washington. Julia talks to them almost every day, and we get information and advice."

"What advice did they give you?" Becca asked.

"Their advice at this time is to leave Hungary before it's too late."

"Where will the people go?" Alana asked.

"There are settlements in Palestine and Turkey and other countries," said Theresa. "It's the passageways that are difficult to traverse. Many of them are closed."

"If we decide to follow advice, as we should," Alana said, throwing a stern look in Sammy's direction, "how will the people be informed?"

"There are those who have the authority, the influence, and the ability to bring people out of Hungary in large numbers. There are rescue groups. We are working on forming connections with those rescue groups right now. We have been given names, and we will be in touch with them."

"Benjamin, you are familiar with Carl Lutz. He's one of them," Julia added. "He has the authority of the Swiss government to issue Swiss letters of protection now that there is evidence that Operation Reinhard is commencing. They provide immunity from arrest and deportation. Each one of you must carry such a letter at all times. Theresa and I will get one for each of you as soon as possible. Then, if you are stopped by SS or Gestapo, the letters should protect you."

"One of the reasons we asked Anya to hold this dinner," said Theresa, "was to talk to all of you, and especially Sammy, the proud papa-to-be. It was also to ask Sammy how to get in touch with Joel Brand, who has some experience in rescue operations. Can you arrange a meeting, Sammy?"

Sammy was sitting with his arm around Alana's shoulders. He was still blushing. He didn't expect Alana's news to come out so soon and so bluntly. After all, they weren't even married yet. The wedding was supposed to occur in June. He answered, "You want a meeting with Joel? If he's in town, I'm sure I can do it. What should I tell him?"

"You may pass along the news we have shared tonight, and tell him we would like to meet with the Aid and Rescue Committee," Theresa said. "Our contacts in the US and Switzerland would like to work with them. Can you set up an appointment?"

Sammy nodded. "I'll try to contact him first thing tomorrow."

"Thank you," Theresa said. "Do any of you have any questions of Julia or me?"

"Well, I do," Benjamin said. "How certain are you, Carl, and the War Refugee Board that this Nazi operation is truly going to happen in Budapest? I haven't seen any arrests or other restrictive measures. Not any new ones anyway."

"Apa!" Theresa snapped. "Stop it. You are denying what's in front of your face. You sound like Solomon. You are waiting for evidence that your neighborhood is under siege. When that evidence comes, it will be too late. You will be taken. We need to do something before that happens."

"All we are asking is that you prepare," said Julia. "Get ready to leave on a moment's notice, and when the time is right, when we get the rescue agencies lined up, you will be ready to join them. It won't happen tomorrow, but soon."

"I have a question," said Aunt Pearl. "I live in the country, four miles from the city of Orztov. Just like this Marta Gross woman that Becca told us about. You said people from the countryside are being moved to the city, and from there, who knows? Do you think it is safe for me to go home?"

"Aunt Pearl," Benjamin said, "I'm sure that you—"

"Benjamin!" Pearl snapped. "I'm not asking you. I'm talking to your daughter. Theresa, is it safe for me to go home?"

"The truth is, I don't know," Theresa said. "I don't know where the SS squads are operating at this time or where they are going next."

"If what happened to Marta Gross's family is now happening in other rural areas all at once, like it did in Holland, then you are not safe," said Julia. "In that case, you should not go home."

Pearl closed her eyes, and tears began to fall. "What am I to do?"

"You can stay right here," Greta said, "and move into the extra bedroom."

"Greta, I appreciate your offer, but how can I do that? All my clothes are at home, my medicine, my makeup. What about Althea? She's in my house right now. What happens if I don't come home? I love that dog. I can't leave her."

"I'll drive you home, Pearl," said Benjamin. "We can pick up all your clothes and medicine and bring them back here."

Pearl said, "What about Althea?"

Benjamin had a question in his eyes, and he wavered back and forth. He turned to his wife, who returned a look with a firm nod and said, "You'd better get her too."

"Hold on a minute," Julia said. "That's awfully sweet of you, Apa, but if it's not safe for Aunt Pearl, then it's not safe for you either. If they're herding Jews from the countryside into the cities at this time, then it's just as dangerous for you to go there. You don't have a Swiss letter of protection. But I do. I'll go to Aunt Pearl's and pick up her things. And Althea too. Just give me a list and the keys to the car and front door and I'm on my way."

"Nope," said Theresa firmly. "That won't work. You don't know your way around Hungary. How are you going to find her house? And if you were stopped by some SS guard who shouted at you, would you understand him? Could you offer a reasonable excuse why you were in the country and not in Budapest? Nope, nope, and nope. I will go instead."

"And if you're going alone, who's going to collect all the clothes and things, and who's going to watch Althea?" said Julia. "You'd have to do it all by yourself."

"We'll go together," Theresa agreed. "It will be quicker."

CHAPTER THIRTY

JULIA AND THERESA decided that it would be best to leave Budapest during the dark of night and load the car at Pearl's house and return as soon as possible. She lived eighty-five kilometers away in a scenic area beside a lake. The drive would take a little over one hour. The nearest city to her was Gyöngyös. Theresa reasoned that it was more likely that the Operation Reinhard SS squads would take their prisoners during the light of day when they could see them. That turned out to be only partially correct. The SS would also approach the families at dinnertime or bedtime, when they were bound to be at home and in one place.

Benjamin held his keys out for Theresa, and his hand shook. His car was his honey, a 1940 BMW 327 Sport Coupe that he kept polished and parked right in front of the house. He cleared his throat and said, "Please be careful."

Julia smiled and said, "Don't worry, Apa, we will be very careful. We have our letters of protection that say we're administrative personnel working for the Swiss consulate, and we will stay clear of the SS."

"What I meant to say was please be careful of my car; it doesn't have a scratch on it. I just put gas in the tank and filled the tires. And please don't let the dog chew on the upholstery."

Theresa laughed and took the keys, and the two headed out. The road to Pearl's little house in the country was curvy and hilly and went through the little towns of Mogyoród, Gödöllő, Nyúldomb, and Hatvah. Though it was the middle of the night, there were still some cars on the road. Most were headed in the opposite direction, toward Budapest, with luggage strapped to the roof and on the top of the trunk. They were obviously fleeing the countryside. In Hatvah, Theresa and Julia saw large numbers of families huddled together in the square outside the church. Was this their restricted area? Were the Jews who lived in the country outside of Hatvah forced into this city? Was this their appointed ghetto? Were they under guard? Until when?

Theresa drove down the highway and then turned the car down a little dirt road. The road wound through a wooded area and ended up at a lake. "I used to love coming here as a child," she said. "Especially in the summertime. There is a pier and a floating deck, and we would spend hours jumping into that lake. My Uncle Masi was a fisherman, and he bought this property many years ago. After he died, Aunt Pearl stayed on. Even though she didn't fish and rarely went swimming, she didn't have the heart to leave. All her memories are here."

They unlocked the door and went inside the house. They were immediately greeted by Althea. She was a brown-and-white pointer, very friendly, and not much of a watchdog. Pearl had given them a list, and they went through the house gathering the items. They found a leash for Althea, a bag of her food, and a couple of bones, and soon, they were ready to go. Suddenly, the door burst open. There stood an older man dressed in overalls and a leather cap. He held a carbine in his hands, his finger on the trigger.

"Don't move," he said. "What the hell you doing in Pearl's house? You looking to arrest her? Are you Nazis? Do they have women working for the Gestapo now? Hands up!"

Althea growled, lunged forward, yanking on the leash, almost pulling Julia over. The man leveled his rifle and looked at the dog. "Let that dog loose," he said. "Come on over here, Althea, you bloodhound. That's Pearl's dog, and you'd better not hurt her."

Theresa shouted, "Stop! Do I look like a Nazi? We're not Nazis. Pearl is my aunt, and I am picking up her things for her. My name is Theresa Weissbach."

"Prove it."

She took out her wallet and showed the man her letter. "Are you satisfied?"

The man lowered the rifle and stepped back. "Sorry," he said softly. "There have been so many Nazis in this area over the last three days that you can never be too careful. I thought they were breaking in here to arrest Pearl. If she had been here, they would have forced her into their truck and taken her away. I wasn't going to let them do that."

"Where would they have taken her?"

"I don't know. Some say to a brickyard in Hatvah. You can see they are clearing out the countryside. Drive up and down the road and you won't see nobody. They want us all off our farms. Maybe they want to own the farms, but if they do, then who's going to be the farmers? The Nazis? Ha!"

"They don't want the farms," Theresa said. "They want all of the Jewish people who live in the countryside to move into the cities. They have their names and addresses. Ultimately, they want to take the Jews away to a prison."

"And because Pearl Weissbach is a Jew, that's the reason they want to take her to a prison?"

"Right. Are you Jewish?" Theresa asked. "If so, you'd better stay out of sight."

"I'm not a Jew, but I'm no Nazi either. Pearl is my friend, Jew or no Jew. That is why I pulled my gun on you." He stuck out his hand. "My name is Ansgrat. Thom Ansgrat. If Pearl is your aunt, then you must be Jewish too. If I was you, I'd watch my backside, if you know what I mean."

"I do, Thom. I appreciate the warning, but I think we should be going now."

Thom stepped aside, and Julia, Theresa, and Althea walked outside, locked the door behind them, and climbed into the BMW for the trip home.

Julia breathed a sigh of relief as Theresa fired up the car and they pulled back onto the road. The trip back was uneventful until they were fifteen kilometers outside of Budapest. They came down the hill and around a curve and were confronted by a blockade. Wooden barricades stretched across the highway. Armed Nazi guards stood to the side, stopping and searching each of the cars. They questioned the occupants and on occasion pulled them out of the car, handcuffed them, and held them captive on the side of the road. Theresa wanted to make a U-turn and drive away, but with cars in the front of her and to the rear, it was impossible. The only hope was that the Swiss IDs would do their job.

"They're looking at lists and comparing them to the occupants," Julia said. "They must have the names and addresses of Jewish residents in this area. I wonder where they got that?"

"Do you think they have the names and addresses of nine hundred thousand Jews?" said Theresa. "It would take a library to hold that list."

"Thom said they had the names of the Jewish people who lived in the country. Maybe that's why they haven't come into Budapest yet," said Julia.

"It wouldn't be hard to get that information," Theresa answered. "The synagogues would have the names and addresses of their members. There are birth certificates and registrations at the city halls. They can't go everywhere in the country at once, but they can go from section to section, and ultimately, it can be done. It's just a matter of where and when they concentrate their searches next."

Finally, Theresa's car moved to the front, and the SS guard walked up and rapped on the window. "Identifications," he said. He looked at the dog and smiled. "I wouldn't mind taking this one home," he said to his companion. Then he turned his attention back to Theresa. "Identification, now!"

Theresa pulled out her Swiss ID and showed it to the guard. "We're Swiss embassy officials," she said. He curled his fingers, instructing her to hand the paper to him. She hesitated. It could be a mistake to give her ID to the guard. She might never get it back. "We are Swiss government employees, and we have an assignment in this area," she said. "We have authority to travel these roads without interference. We are returning to the Swiss embassy in Budapest."

"Get out of the car," the guard ordered. "I'll decide who has authority. Right now, it's me! I'm going to search you two and the contents of this car. That is my authority."

Theresa stuck out her chin. "You have no right to search Swiss vehicles. You are committing a violation of German law by disrespecting Swiss immunity. I will report you. What is your name and rank?"

Julia sat silently, amazed at the boldness displayed by her friend. She held Althea, who must have recognized the confrontation and buried her head.

"*Raus!*" the man shouted and waved his gun. Again he gestured for the ID. "*Das Dokument. Steig sofort aus dem Auto aus! Mach schnell!*"

Theresa stayed firm and didn't move. The guard leveled his rifle, pointing it at Theresa's head. With his finger on the trigger, he pointed it first at Theresa, then at Julia, and then at Althea. "*Raus!*"

Theresa opened the door and got out of the car. As she did, the guard grabbed her ID. He looked it over as though he didn't understand it and tore it in half. With his rifle, he gestured for Theresa and Julia to follow him. They were walking in the direction of a group of people in handcuffs, prisoners standing by the side of the road. Theresa loudly stated, "*Immunität der Schweizer Regierung!*" and repeated it loudly.

They passed a guard with a billed cap, obviously of a higher rank, perhaps an officer. He heard Theresa's shouts and walked over. He gestured for the SS guard to talk to him in private. They had a quiet discussion, during which the guard kept shrugging and the officer shook his head. As they returned, Theresa shouted again that she was a Swiss embassy administrative assistant. The officer stated, "*Beseise es mir,*" which Theresa understood to mean, "Prove it to me." The officer repeated, "Let me see your Swiss identification."

Theresa replied, "I can't. He took it and tore it up. It's on the ground somewhere."

The officer had a questioning look on his face. Maybe Theresa was lying. She couldn't prove what she was saying. At that moment, Julia stepped up and held out her ID. "Here, look at this. A Swiss ID. Hers is just the same!"

The officer reached for it, but Julia withdrew it. She didn't want to hand it to him; she might never see it again. If they were arrested and taken somewhere, at least she would still have her ID to prove they were covered under Swiss diplomatic immunity. The officer nodded and bent over to read the ID that Julia held. He nodded again, and then faced the guard with an annoyed look on his face. "Let them pass," he said, and he walked away.

The other guards pulled back the barricade, and the BMW was finally on its way home.

As the blockade faded away in the rearview mirror and the car was speeding down the road, Theresa said, "Can I breathe now?"

Julia petted Althea and said, "Some watchdog you are."

CHAPTER THIRTY-ONE

IT WAS MIDMORNING when the BMW parked in front of the Weissbach home. Everyone was overjoyed at the reunion, and no one more so than Althea, who ran up to Pearl, tail wagging.

"I'm glad to see you back safe and sound," Benjamin said. "All these rumors are going around that the Nazis are everywhere and stopping cars at random. They aren't doing anything in Budapest, but reports come in from outside the city. People out there are being arrested and taken into holding centers in the towns. We were worried about you. To hear some people tell it, it's a full-scale German invasion."

Julia and Theresa looked at each other with an expression that said, "If he only knew."

"It's not just rumors, Apa," Theresa said. "They have invaded, there is no doubt about it, and they are everywhere. If it hadn't been for Julia's Swiss ID, we would now be in custody, probably awaiting transit to some prison camp. Mine was ripped up by a Nazi guard. I need a new one. We saw groups being gathered and held in small towns. The SS are searching for Jews in country homes, on farms, in the lake houses, and, as we know, on the road. We were stopped at a Nazi roadblock. There is no telling when they will move into Budapest, but you can be assured they're coming. Their interest isn't limited to country Jews. They'll arrest us all if they can. Hitler considers Jews to be the enemy, and his officers will follow his lead."

"Aunt Pearl, do you know a man named Thom Ansgrat?" Julia said. "He sure knows you."

"I do," said Pearl. "He's an eccentric old fellow, lives down the road. He mostly keeps to himself, but he's harmless. Once in a while, he comes by for a cup of coffee, and we chat."

Julia nodded. "We met him. He came by while we were packing up your things. He had his carbine ready to protect you."

Pearl smiled. "Sounds like old Thom."

Theresa told the family all about their road trip, including the occasion when they were confronted by the SS guards. "Apa, there is absolutely no question that the Nazi operation is progressing. Hungary has been overrun by the Germans, and they are moving ahead with their Operation Reinhard. You need to accept that fact. Stop denying it and plan for your defense."

Benjamin nodded. "I do accept it. The question is, what do we do about it? How do we plan for a defense? We have no military. Help will have to come from outside our community. Speaking of which, Carl Lutz called this morning. He wanted to talk to either of you. When I told him where you had gone, he sighed and said, 'Oh no. When they get back, God willing, please tell them to come see me at the embassy.'"

"I will talk to him, and then I need to call John Pehle," Julia said. "They both need an update on the situation as we observed it. This is essential information for the WRB. There are now over nine hundred thousand refugees needing help, whether they know it or not. We will go back to the embassy now."

"Have you heard from Sammy?" Theresa asked. "He was going to set up a meeting with Joel Brand and the Aid and Rescue Committee."

"He hasn't called," Benjamin said, "but maybe Sammy doesn't know the urgency or the desperate situations you observed. I will reach out to Sammy again. Don't worry, I will see to it that he arranges a meeting."

Back at the embassy, Julia fired up the cablegram. After being informed, John Pehle said, "In addition to your report, we are receiving a smattering of other reports on Hungary. I'm glad you contacted me, because your report is reliable and firsthand. It will carry a lot of weight with the committee. We heard that Jews are being picked up all over the country and held all in compressed areas. Is that true?"

Julia confirmed. "That's accurate, I'm sorry to say. Jewish families in the countryside are being moved into designated cities and held in close quarters they call *ghettos*. I'm sure you know what I think about that, given my experience in Holland. It is step one, and step two is transfer to a prison camp."

"As far as we know, governmental letters of immunity are still being honored," John asked. "Is that not so?"

"The SS honored our Swiss IDs, thank God," Julia responded. "Theresa and I were stopped at a Nazi barricade and were able to avoid arrest only by showing those IDs."

"That's good to know. Here at the WRB, we have been contacting governments considered by Germany to be neutral, and we have asked for their cooperation. We sent requests to Central and South American governments, asking if they would agree to give protection. If a person were to possess a document claiming citizenship of their country, would they confirm it was genuine and be willing to confer immunity? For example, if a person in Hungary had identification from one of those South American countries, would they agree to inform Germany through diplomatic channels that the holder was in fact a citizen? Those IDs are being prepared by some of the countries and should be forwarded to Carl in Bern."

"Perfect," said Julia. "We get dispatches from Bern in diplomatic pouches almost every day."

"We are also putting in requests to Treasury for funds to be transferred to Switzerland to be used in rescue operations," John said. "Please keep me advised of any changes as they occur, especially if, or when, Jews are being deported out of Hungary."

"I definitely will. Thankfully, we haven't seen that yet, but you know I feel that deportation is step two. We have to do everything in our power or hundreds of thousands of innocents will be murdered."

"I know, and we're doing everything we can."

Julia concluded by saying, "I will be meeting with Carl later today. If there is anything you should know, I will pass it on."

* * *

AT THE MEETING with Carl, Julia and Theresa related the details of their trip to Aunt Pearl's. They expressed their opinion that Operation Reinhard was occurring at lightning speed. "There are SS squads all over the country," Julia said. "They are in the little towns, they are on the road, and now we see them in large groups on the streets of Budapest. There are armed Germans everywhere you look, but as of the present time, we haven't seen mass arrests take place in Budapest. They are only happening in the countryside."

"If their orders are to move people from the countryside into the cities, there would be no reason to arrest Jews in Budapest; they're already in the city," Carl said. "I would be concerned if they started moving Jews from their homes in Budapest to central holding areas, especially near train stations, because that would be a sure sign that deportations are next. It hasn't happened yet, but I have seen an influx of people from the countryside coming into Budapest and looking for shelter."

"Where are they going to stay?" asked Theresa. "Do you have any ideas?"

"I'm afraid not. They should stay with friends, relatives, or wherever they can find housing. My wife, Gertrud, has real estate experience, and she may have a better idea of the real estate market in Budapest. If WRB has the funds, it may be possible to acquire temporary housing, even if it is only on a short-term-rental basis. You might mention that to John."

"We will," Theresa said. "It is a real shame. People who have lived peacefully in their houses for years, for generations, are now forced to look for an emergency place to stay so they won't be arrested. How is that just?"

"It's not," Carl said, "but there is one more thing. I heard this on the grapevine. Apparently, Eichmann has created a council and appointed Jews to fill it. It is supposedly a Jewish leadership council that is formed to communicate between the Nazi rulers and the Jewish community. The council will convey instructions to the Jews by posters, flyers, meetings at the synagogues, and the like. That way, Eichmann can speak directly to the Jewish people and it will have authority because it comes from a Jewish council. It is called a *Judenrat*."

"Oh no!" Julia cried. "That is the tool that the Nazis use. They make up a committee and appoint respected Jews to fill it. The Jews have no choice.

While people won't listen to instructions coming directly from the Nazis, they would more likely comply if they came from a Jewish council."

"That's the idea," Carl said. "The Judenrat will encourage compliance. People respect the Judenrat leaders."

"That's right," said Julia. "I've seen it operate. They did the same thing in Amsterdam three years ago, in 1941. Seyss-Inquart appointed two respected Jewish men, David Cohen and Abraham Asscher, as leaders of the Judenrat, although in Dutch it was called the *Joodse Raad*. The Joodse Raad was supposed to protect people from the evil Nazis and their antisemitism by opening a channel of communication. It was just the opposite. The Joodse Raad urged the people to comply with the Nazi orders, as explained to them by Cohen and Asscher, no matter how horrible, so that they would be obedient to the Nazis' unjust laws and ultimately in their orders for mass deportation. The Joodse Raad would publish that week's orders and advise the people to comply or there would be trouble for everyone. 'Don't let your fellow man down,' they said. The orders eventually told Jews to report at certain locations. I'm sure you know what happened next. When the Jews obeyed and followed those orders, they were arrested, taken to the train station, and deported. Cohen and Asscher, following Eichmann's orders, talked politely while leading the Jews to slaughter. They did that until September 1943, when there weren't any more Jews left in Amsterdam at all."

Carl nodded. "The word on the street is that a man named Samu Stern was appointed to head up the Budapest Judenrat and that he will be speaking to Jewish groups. Your father may know of him, Theresa."

"I've heard the name, but I don't know him," she said. "I'll follow up with my father."

"I DO KNOW Samu Stern," Benjamin said when presented with the information. "He has been active in the community and at the synagogue for many years. He is a scholar, and many people look up to him. He's at least five years older than I am. Maybe he's seventy? Although he still spends quite a bit of time at the Great Synagogue, I believe he is

Orthodox. I can't imagine him playing ball with Eichmann and going against his people, but you never know. He's either deceived into believing Eichmann, or he has made a deal for his own safety. I do believe that he is scheduled to speak at the Great Synagogue tomorrow following morning prayer service. Do you want to attend?"

"You bet I do," Julia said. "I'd like to debate him on the stage. He accepted a position to deceive his countrymen. I want to tell the people the truth, expose the Judenrat for the fraud that it is."

Benjamin smiled. "People can be told the truth in more courteous ways. We will attend and be polite, okay?"

CHAPTER THIRTY-TWO

THE GREAT SYNAGOGUE on Dohány Street was packed. Standing room only. Word circulated quickly that Samu Stern, head of the newly formed Budapest Judenrat, would be addressing the congregation. Supposedly, he was given detailed inside information concerning the rumors of a German takeover. Benjamin, Theresa, and Julia arrived early. Benjamin, because of his status at the synagogue, not to mention his charitable efforts, had permanently assigned seating in a forward row. After a few opening remarks by the temple president, Rabbi Levy was introduced, and he stepped up on the bimah.

"Fellow congregants, these are uncertain times," the rabbi said. "In the middle of a worldwide war, one in which Hungary finds itself, though it had no aggressive aspirations, we now face peril from within our own borders, our very homeland. The peril comes not from the Russians, whose armies threaten us on our eastern border, but from our Axis partners, who encircle us and border us on all sides. And why do we face such peril? It is because there are some who condemn us for following our faith. Simply put, we are deprecated because we are Jewish. We do not threaten others, but apparently others feel threatened."

A number of attendees voiced their agreement: "Why don't they leave us alone?" "Why don't the Germans get the hell out of Hungary!" Rejoinders came from numerous congregants, and they filled the room with angry tones.

Rabbi Levy held his hand up for quiet. "It is no secret that the German leadership has come into our country to regulate and control our social order and the privileges that we are entitled to enjoy as Hungarian citizens."

Shouts agreeing with the rabbi's description and expressing displeasure with the Germans filled the sanctuary.

Rabbi Levy held his hand up again. "You have all seen the flood of German soldiers on the streets of our town. Now, just recently, a very highly placed German officer, Obergruppenführer Adolf Eichmann, has arrived in Hungary to manage the flood of Germans. It is no one's wish to let the situation spin out of control. For that reason, Herr Eichmann has appointed a council that will act as a buffer—a middleman, if you will—to reason with and communicate between the Nazi leaders and our Jewish community. Herr Eichmann has appointed members of our community to sit on the council. Our own Samu Stern has been appointed as president of this council, which Eichmann calls the *Judenrat*."

"Why do we need a council?" someone shouted. "We do not have any difficulty governing ourselves. In fact, the Dohány Synagogue has resolved many a controversy between congregants."

The rabbi nodded. "Times are different," he replied. "The synagogue has never been asked to resolve controversies with German leaders. I understand that is one of the functions of the newly formed Judenrat. Mr. Stern has asked that we come together today so that he can explain his role as president of the Judenrat, and he will explain its function. No matter whether you approve or disapprove of the creation of such a council, Mr. Stern's intentions are to further peace. Please give him your kind attention."

Samu Stern walked up to the platform to polite applause, as he was an elder of the congregation. There were a few grumbles of "Nazi puppet," "Betrayer," and "Nazi mouthpiece." Stern waited for the sanctuary to calm down. Indeed, he was an older man, probably seventy as Benjamin had thought. He was thin, well dressed in a dark suit with a white shirt and black tie. He had sunken dark eyes and thick black eyebrows. He comported himself with dignity. He exuded confidence as he stood and looked over the crowd.

"Why would he accept this position?" Theresa said quietly. "If he wanted a position of authority in the synagogue, I'm sure he would have been considered."

Stern began, "I thank you all for coming here today and giving me the opportunity to explain the purpose of the newly formed council, known as the Judenrat. I know that many of you are critical of the role of the Judenrat. It has a German name and serves a German purpose. Many of you see it as a tool of the occupiers to control our community. I have heard some describe it as 'playing ball with the Germans.'"

The remark brought on loud grumbles of "Yeah, that's right. So why are you doing it? Playing ball with Eichmann the killer."

Julia nodded to Theresa. "That's exactly what he's doing."

"I can assure you that it is really quite the opposite," Stern said. "On the one hand, it is a vehicle for making our needs known to Regent Horthy and also to the German leaders. On the other hand, it is a forum for the respective governments to converse and make known their rules and regulations concerning our community. That way, we won't run afoul of those regulations and end up in trouble. And in the same manner, we can make our needs or displeasures known to the rulers. Think of it as a balancing act. In this way, instead of posting bulletins on trees and signboards, the leaders' rules and regulations can be explained to the Judenrat, and we can then pass them on to our community in a commonsense and logical way."

"Common sense? Who are you kidding? Logical way? Nazi collaborator," barked many in the crowd.

Stern raised his hands and continued, "I was skeptical myself when I was approached by Obergruppenführer Eichmann, but I knew that opening the lines of communication is always necessary to prevent unjust treatment. I thought, *What kind of a man would I be if I turned my back and let my people down right now when leadership is most needed? I must accept the burden of president of the council.* I was promised a free hand on choosing members of the council. I chose Erno Peto and Karoly Wilhelm, whom many of you know. In fact, Karoly has a close personal connection to Regent Horthy, and he speaks to him often. I ask you, is that a bad thing?"

Many positive utterances were voiced, and an equal number of negative comments answered his rhetorical question.

"Following my appointment, I was privileged to meet with Obersturmbannführer Hermann Krumey," Stern said. "As you can see, I am being given free access to the German hierarchy. Herr Krumey told me that there will be new restrictions on the Jewish community from time to time but that there will be no need to fear deportation if there is a centralized Jewish leadership council guiding the community. So, I am sure you will all agree that there is a need for a Jewish council to protect us and save us from deportation, as has happened to Jewish communities in other countries."

Julia leaned over and whispered to Benjamin, "They had a Judenrat in Poland and in the Netherlands. Those councils helped load Jews into boxcars to be taken to die. Don't listen to him or a word he says."

"Shh," Benjamin said, but others heard her.

Loud gripes arose from the congregants. "What kind of restrictions?" a man yelled. "Why should we be restricted in our own country by a bunch of foreign Germans?"

Stern gently waved his hand for quiet. "Discrimination is present in almost every society. Restrictions are common in every government, and there have been restrictions on the Jewish community in Hungary for centuries. Anyone who knows the history of the Habsburg Empire knows there have been periods of very strict rules and restrictions on the Jewish community."

"Oh, no," said Theresa, standing up to speak. "That's wrong. The Habsburgs lifted the restrictions on Jewish society. The Habsburgs were fair and treated us equally. Did you know that Habsburg law prohibited antisemitism? Well, it did. That law stayed in effect until the First World War, when the Habsburgs fell out of power in 1918. History teaches us that it was the rulers that came after the Habsburgs who imposed cruel religious restrictions."

"Then I stand corrected," said Stern modestly. "I am sorry. I meant to say that in history, there have been many rulers who have imposed unfair restrictions on the Jews. I suppose you might say that Jews have been subject to restrictions since the time of Moses." He shrugged.

"Moses?" said Julia loudly. "He split the Red Sea and led his people to freedom, fleeing a violent dictator. Maybe that's what we need. Someone to split the Black Sea and lead us to Palestine."

People around her clapped and shouted, "Right!"

"We don't need any more restrictions," another man said. "We want freedom."

People started to chant, "We want freedom!"

Stern took a deep breath. He was losing the crowd. Time to come to a conclusion.

"I am afraid we will not have a choice in this regard," he said with an austere expression. "As many of you know, Döme Sztójay has been appointed by the Nazi leaders as Hungary's new prime minister to replace Miklós Kállay. He will govern alongside Regent Miklós Horthy, who has returned from his meeting with Herr Hitler. Sztójay's new government has already passed a number of decrees restricting Jews. They are the new laws, and we are required to obey them or be subject to punishment."

As he suspected, his last comment riled up the crowd. "What new laws?" several people shouted.

"I don't have them all with me today, nor do I know them all yet, but I can tell you that according to recent decrees, all Jews living outside Budapest, regardless of gender and age, have to travel or be transported to a designated city. They will not be permitted to live in undisciplined rural surroundings, out of the view and earshot of the rulers. They will be gathered and reside in groups or developments, which we refer to as *ghettos*. I am told that in that way, it is far easier for the Nazi government to govern us and to keep track of our activities and control the Jewish population in these uncertain times of war."

"We are not the enemy," said many, including Julia and Theresa. Some dared to say, "The Nazis are our enemy."

Stern shook his head. "I am afraid that talk like that will not help the situation; it will only bring about stricter laws. Talk like that reinforces the Germans' belief that Jews are untrustworthy, and it reinforces their intent to corral us as dissidents."

With that last remark, several stood and began to leave. Theresa and Julia stood as well, but Benjamin put his hand on Theresa's shoulder and said, "Don't be rude. Our family is well mannered. Let him finish, and then we will leave."

Stern continued amid the dissension. "I am informed that new restrictions have already been enacted or will be enacted soon, restricting Jewish use of public transportation. I have no doubt that there will be restrictions on the use of your automobiles. I wouldn't be surprised if telephone service was curtailed at specific hours, or entirely. Finally, I believe, though it hasn't happened yet, that an evening curfew will be imposed on Jewish citizens."

That brought about the loudest rejoinders. To which Stern replied, "I am not the one responsible for these decrees, nor is the Judenrat. Don't blame the messenger. These are restrictions that will be imposed by our new rulers. It is important that we keep the lines of communication open so that we can request that the restrictions be lifted. That is why we have a Judenrat. Face it—there is a war going on, and we must follow the rules of our new rulers or we will be punished."

"Are you going to punish us?" shouted one person.

"Are you going to report us for breaking the rules?" said another. "How do they know who is breaking the rules?"

Stern shook his head. "How will they know? I can tell you this: Starting next Friday and every day thereafter, all persons defined as 'Jews' are obligated to wear a yellow star on their outer clothing. That covers anyone with Jewish blood: meaning at least one parent or grandparent, even if they don't practice. Those who have converted from Judaism to Christianity, or those who profess Christianity, are required to wear the star but are permitted to add a small white cross under the star."

With that last comment, the entire synagogue rose and started to clear out. The comments were loud and angry. Out of respect for Benjamin,

Theresa and Julia did not walk out until Samu Stern had walked down from the bimah. On his way out, Stern was heard to say, "I am not to blame for the German rules. I did not make them. Just be mindful that disobedience could result in harsh punishment."

CHAPTER THIRTY-THREE

DAYS PASSED WHILE Theresa and Julia waited for appointments to be scheduled. Carl was in Switzerland and had been there for two weeks. He cabled that he had important information in several matters and wanted to meet with them as soon as he returned. He was aware that Hungarian citizens were being rounded up and taken to ghettos in the small country towns, with the ultimate purpose of taking them to prison camps in Poland. He didn't know whether the transfers had begun yet, but there were unconfirmed rumors that trains had left northern Hungary. They were also waiting for Sammy to set an appointment with Joel Brand and Israel Kasztner, but that had not happened yet either.

Julia had made it a routine to appear at the Weissbachs' home each morning to take Althea for a walk while Theresa had coffee with Anya. When Julia returned from her walks, she usually commented on the increasing number of ordinary people she would see on the sidewalks, with no apparent place to go. Sometimes they walked in groups, sometimes carrying suitcases or their belongings. Sometimes they walked holding the hands of children.

"I don't know where they are going or where they are staying," Theresa said as she sadly shook her head, "but it is very upsetting. There are so many little children. Last night, it was cold. I don't know where they went."

"Apa said that Rabbi Levy had opened the doors to the Great Synagogue for homeless refugees at night," Julia said. "The sanctuary is very large and can shelter a great many people, but the number is increasing every day."

"That is very kind of the rabbi, but it is not a solution; it's only a temporary stopgap. These families can't go home or they'll be arrested. They left everything. Maybe the king of the Judenrat can help them," Theresa said. "He can talk to his friend Adolf."

"No, his friend is Miklós Horthy, remember? I'm sure that Eichmann is calling the shots for the Judenrat, however, and Stern is doing what he is told to do without argument."

"By leaving their country homes and moving into Budapest, aren't the families doing what the Nazis are telling them to do?" Theresa said with a shrug. "The people are following the rules to come out of the country and move into the city, aren't they?"

Julia shook her head. "No, not at all. The Nazis want them rounded up and put under guard. That is what they have done in the smaller towns. From there, they will be shipped to detention camps, just like the Nazis did in Holland. You've seen Carl's messages. The prison trains have started to roll. If the families escape and come to Budapest, they are avoiding being taken to Poland. They are staying out of Auschwitz and Majdanek prisons. For the time being."

In the middle of their conversation, Sammy entered the room and immediately asked if there was any coffee left for him.

"For my handsome boy, I'll make a fresh pot," Anya said.

"Thank you, Anya." He turned to Theresa. "I was finally able to talk to Joel."

"He is so hard to reach. How did you make that happen?" Theresa asked.

"I work at the telephone company, remember? Contacting people is my job."

"Very funny. What did Joel say? Will he meet with Julia and me?"

"Right now, Joel is in Aleppo, Syria. He said we would meet when he returns next week. He suggested Monday evening."

"That would be great," Julia said. "We have a few meetings at the end of this week, but we can meet with Joel then. Will any of the other members of the Aid and Rescue Committee be present? I'm talking about Israel Kasztner or even Ottó Komoly."

"I don't think Ottó will be there, but Joel said he would try to bring Israel Kasztner. Sometimes he's called Rezső Kasztner. He goes by both names." Then Sammy looked out of the window and said, "Have you seen all these people walking around the city? There must be thousands of them. Entire families!"

Theresa nodded. "We were just discussing that when you walked in. They come from the countryside, almost all of them are Jews, and most of them are Orthodox. They are here because they are running away from Eichmann and the SS. If they didn't leave their homes in the countryside, odds are they would have been taken into custody. Out in the country, Jews are being herded like cattle into the towns and held there. I think that's so the SS will have an easier time watching over them. Julia is convinced that sooner or later, probably sooner, they will be put into trains and shipped to prison camps in Poland."

"That's right," Julia said. "I think these people on the street know what's going on. Word travels fast. Many of them have friends or relatives in other European countries, and they have heard about *Judenfrei* and what happens when the SS takes Jews into custody. They're afraid that will happen here, and that is why they are fleeing."

"We have a meeting later this week with Carl Lutz and his wife, Gertrud," said Theresa. "She is an impressive woman. She went to business school in Bern, and then, at age eighteen, she immigrated to the US to look for a job. For three years, she worked for the Swiss consulate in St. Louis, and that's where she met Carl. In 1935, Gertrud Fankhauser married Carl Lutz in a fancy wedding in Bern. She told me all about it," Theresa said with a smile. "I wish I had been invited. Anyway, the reason I bring her up is that she has a background in real estate and has been in contact with some of the agencies here in Budapest. She is assembling lists of properties that may be used for housing some of the refugees."

"Right now, there are refugees sleeping on the benches in the Great Synagogue, or in their cars or wagons, or wherever they can find shelter," Julia said. "Hotel rooms are expensive, and they are not readily available."

Theresa agreed. "Even if the Jewish refugees have the money, the hotels don't want to rent to them. They don't want the SS storming through the hotels looking for Jews. Most of the hotels, especially the quiet, fancier ones, don't want homeless refugee families. So they put out No Vacancy signs."

"Where are these families supposed to get the money to buy or rent property for as long as they'll need it, which could be forever?" Sammy said.

"Julia is working on that," Theresa pointed out. "She has been talking to John Pehle at the WRB about funding from the Treasury Department to be used for the families' housing expenses."

"I am," said Julia, "but it is a struggle. Conservative US congressmen don't want US funds spent overseas, especially for aid to Hungarian refugees. John and his staff are fighting that battle."

"You know, this isn't the first time that Jewish refugees have been smuggled into Hungary," Sammy said. "They have come into our country before without money and were able to find shelters and jobs and raise families. And they are now successful members of Budapest society."

"Are you talking about a century ago? The Habsburg Empire era?" Theresa said. "Are you trying to compare the two?"

"Refugees who came to Hungary a couple of years ago had been hunted in their native country. They made it to Hungary, which was considered safe for Jews. Jewish refugees were welcomed when they arrived from Poland and Slovakia, but now, because of Eichmann and the Germans, they are no longer welcome and are being hunted again," Julia said.

"CARL AND GERTRUD will be returning from Bern, and they are bringing tools to help us in our humanitarian efforts," Theresa said. "He cabled us that he couldn't reveal the details over the wires, but I think that the Swiss government has approved plans for aiding the Jewish families."

"What plans?" asked Sammy.

"We'll see."

CHAPTER THIRTY-FOUR

JULIA AND THERESA arrived early for their scheduled meeting with Carl and Gertrud. To start the day off on the right foot, they brought a bag of Esterházy tortes with a thermos of hot chocolate. "I'm anxious to see what plans the Swiss have approved," Theresa said. "Carl said they have tools. I wonder what that means."

"I'm anxious to talk to Gertrud and learn what she has in mind for housing the refugees," Julia said.

They didn't have long to wait. Carl and his assistants, Paul and Martin, all joined them and took a seat around the conference table. "Uh-oh," Julia said. "We may be short on hot chocolate. I only brought four cups. Thankfully, I did buy a dozen tortes."

Carl poured himself a cup of hot chocolate and took a pastry. Then he looked at Theresa and said, "Just as a reminder, when we're done here, Gertrud would like to talk to you about Budapest real estate."

Carl set a box on the table and opened it. Inside was a sheaf of papers. The papers were an off-white color. Each page had a Swiss seal on the top and the Swiss stamp of authority on the bottom. Theresa took one out and examined it. It was titled *Die Schweizerische Gesandt—The Swiss Ambassador*. The page had two columns of writing. The one on the left was in German, the official language of Switzerland.

Theresa read it out loud for Julia. "'Department of Foreign Interests. Emigration Collective Passport. This valid passport is registered in Switzerland therefore he (she) considered to be the relevant owner.'" Theresa shrugged one shoulder. "That is a bit confusing, but translating

German to English is a little clumsy. Sorry. I think what it means is that the named person is the owner of an official Swiss emigration passport and therefore would be immune from German legal process. He or she is entitled to protection by the government of Switzerland. There is a space in the middle of the page for the individual holder's name. Did I translate it correctly?" she asked.

Carl smiled. "Yes, you did. You are holding a Swiss letter of protection, which should keep the named holder immune from German arrest. There are a thousand of those letters in this box. The section for the holder is left blank."

Julia picked one up and examined it. "This is different from the documents Theresa and I have," she said.

Carl answered, "That is because your identification is that of a Swiss administrative assistant to the Swiss embassy in Budapest."

Julia patted the box. "These are marvelous, but how do you plan on distributing them? Who should get one?"

"That is a good question," Carl said. "We only have a thousand right here. I believe that the Swiss government has authorized more, but we don't have them yet. They should arrive soon, but there will only be a few thousand more, far short of the nine hundred thousand needed to protect the entire Jewish population in Hungary. My superiors feel that if we indiscriminately flood Hungary with a million Swiss protection letters, the Germans will consider them a form only, and they will lose their effectiveness. That won't work at all. The function of these letters is to protect a Swiss citizen, or a person who is designated to be under Swiss protection, who has immigrated into a foreign land. It is a notification that the holder remains under the protection of the Swiss government. Other countries in the world, including Germany, will respect and abide by Swiss declaration of protection and will recognize their immunity from local restrictions. Accordingly, German citizens are also immune if they were to travel to Switzerland with a German letter of protection."

"Excuse me," Theresa said, "but how can one thousand people in Hungary be Swiss immigrants entitled to protection?"

"Good question," Carl responded. "But the SS squads that are roaming through the countryside don't know who is and who is not under Swiss protection. They don't know who is here on an emigration visa. If they see a person's name on an official Swiss letter of protection, they will let them pass. This should work just fine for a thousand people. Five thousand could work too."

"So who gets the magic letter?" Paul asked. "What I mean is, to whom do we distribute these letters?"

"The better question might be: Where will the SS squads be arresting people?" said Martin. "That's where we need to pass out the letters. We should try to get there first. The SS isn't here in Budapest. Why don't I drive out into the country and learn where the SS is operating and arresting people, or where they are taking them? If they move people from the countryside into a town, in what part of town are the people staying? We can pass out letters there and they will be immune from transfer, won't they?"

Carl shrugged. "Maybe, if they are not held in a guarded lockup. If they are staying in parts of town all huddled up in a ghetto, then I think it would be impossible to pass out the letters."

Julia spoke up. "Well, we know for a fact that the SS is in the town of Gyöngyös, the one near Aunt Pearl. The SS is definitely in that section and arresting people. That is where they stopped our car. Couldn't we pass the letters out to people that live there?"

Carl shook his head. "I'm afraid it's too late for that area. The SS went through there, conducted their sweep, arrested Jewish families, and has now put them on a train. Those families are gone. They are now on their way to Poland. Trains have been taking prisoners north for days now. At the rate of a thousand or more each day."

Julia and Theresa were shocked. "How do you know this?"

"We have sources."

"So in the past ten days, over ten thousand people have been sent to the death camps?"

"I'm afraid so. Probably more."

Theresa's mouth was wide open. "Ten thousand innocent people will now be gassed to death."

Carl closed his eyes and nodded. "Remember, the public doesn't know that yet. We don't have independent proof."

"Then how will we know where to pass out the letters? Who is at risk? How do you know who is Jewish and subject to being taken? The SS has the official Hungarian register, but we don't. There are very few Orthodox temples in the outlying districts. I wouldn't know where to begin to seek them out. We can't just drive down the street handing them out blindly, without knowing who the recipients are."

"We know that there are at least a thousand Jews who have already fled the countryside and are now roaming the streets in Budapest," Carl said. "Half the Jews in Hungary live outside of Budapest. I would have to believe that a thousand more are fleeing every day. A lot of them come to the Great Synagogue to sleep. We could pass out letters at the synagogue."

"That's not a bad idea," said Theresa, "but the ones at the synagogue are mostly family groups—like a father, a mother, and their little ones. If you approach a family of five, are you going to prepare and pass out five letters of protection?"

"Why not?" said Paul.

"Because it makes no sense," Julia said, "and believe me, I know about immigration visas. They are not issued to babies. Are you going to say that the Swiss Department of Foreign Interests has interviewed this three-year-old, issued a valid immigration passport to her, registered it in Switzerland, and that the child is now the certified passport owner, immune from arrest?"

"We could."

"But we only have a thousand letters. They'll be gone by tomorrow morning," Julia argued. "Carl just said we're not going to get nine hundred thousand letters from Switzerland. They would become ineffective."

"I have a better idea," Carl said. "In the space in the middle of the page where the passport holder's name is to be inserted, what if we wrote the family name? What if we issue the letter of protection to the family as a whole? Families travel together, don't they? For example, the registered owner could be the Strauss family."

"I don't believe they issue those letters to groups or families," Paul said. "I've never seen it. Maybe Bern wouldn't verify the letter."

"How do you know?" Carl said. "Has the matter ever come before the Swiss authorities?"

"I've never seen one," Paul said, "but then, I haven't seen letters like this at all. I never needed one. I have a Swiss birth certificate."

Carl held up his index finger. "Suppose we issue one to the Strauss family and we list the names of the mother, father, and each of the children right on the face of the letter? Wouldn't that work? If they call here to the Swiss embassy to check, we would be sure to let them know that the family visa is valid."

"I like that idea," Julia said, "but I have a question. What about the family's uncles and aunts? Like Aunt Pearl. Maybe she's traveling with them. Could she be included too? And her children, the cousins too? Would that work?"

"Why not?" Paul said. "If it's good enough for the children, then a family letter should cover the whole family. Do we think some SS Scharführer is going to take the chance of overstepping his bounds and arresting someone with a Swiss family passport in violation of German law?"

Carl smiled. "Then right now, in front of us, we have a thousand letters in this box. Conceivably, that could cover a thousand families, which means several thousand individuals. I have been promised eight thousand letters by the Swiss government."

"Fabulous," Theresa said. "Who knows how many that could protect? We could take them to the Great Synagogue and cover everyone in there. I don't think there are more than fifty families."

"Okay," Carl said, "That's a great start. Theresa and Julia, will you take a pack of letters to the synagogue tonight? Theresa, have your father talk to Rabbi Levy and tell him what we are doing. When and if the time comes, he can help distribute to Budapest families. Right now, the SS is not operating in Budapest."

"I will talk to Apa as soon as I get home. How do you want us to proceed with letters at the synagogue?"

"I think we should involve the rabbi. Invite each of the families, one at a time, into a private room and fill out the letter. Make sure that the letter is handed only to the head of the family. Tell him that he must keep it guarded and confidential. I'm sure he won't argue about that. Don't do it in the middle of the hall or in front of other people; you never know who will be listening or who might report that it wasn't issued by the embassy."

"But we are administrative assistants of the embassy. Aren't we authorized to do this?" asked Theresa.

"You are, but let's do it privately."

"Carl is right," Julia said. "What if Samu Stern is at the synagogue and he turns around and tells his buddy Eichmann? Eichmann could then tell all the SS guards to disregard the letters."

"Samu Stern is not welcome at the synagogue anymore," Theresa said. "Speaking of Stern, he said that shortly all Jews would be required to wear yellow stars on their outer clothing. If I have a Swiss letter of protection, am I required to wear a yellow star?"

"That's a good question," Carl said. "It has philosophical overtones. I suppose if you're proud to be Jewish and you want to stand with your brethren, then you should wear the star. If you trust the effectiveness of the letter of protection, you could wear the star and still be immune. After all, there are Jews in Switzerland too. I think that would be up to the wearer."

Julia curled her lip. "I don't think I would wear a star if I didn't have to. The Nazis consider it a sign of discrimination. It invites an SS to stop and question you. Besides, a Swiss letter of protection should make the holder immune from local discriminatory laws."

"I bet my father would wear one just to show solidarity," said Theresa.

"All right, then let's take a stack and pass them out tonight," Carl said. "Now we have something else important to do today. Let me go and get Gertrud, and we will talk about real estate."

AFTER A BREAK, Carl and Gertrud returned to room 217. Julia, who had never met Gertrud, walked over and introduced herself. She immediately conveyed how honored she was to be working with her. Gertrud was an impressive woman. She was graceful and well dressed, and she projected a confident image. There was an aura about her, a certain stateliness, that commanded respect. Julia thought that upon seeing Carl and Gertrud together, one could easily mistake Gertrud for the vice consul.

Gertrud shook Julia's hand. "I am honored to meet you, Julia. Carl has told me so much about you. To use his words, such a courageous, noble lady. I see you as one who is willing to put her life at risk and travel to the other side of the world to come to the aid of a tyrannized community."

"You're making me blush," Julia said, "but I can say the same thing about you, for you are a Swiss lady and you are here in Hungary as well."

Gertrud smiled. "Oh, I'm just the wife of a vice consul who tags along with her husband wherever he goes." With that, Julia and Gertrud burst into laughter.

"It's nice to see you again, Gertrud," said Theresa. "I am so happy that we will be working together. I understand that you have been talking to real estate agencies about available properties."

Gertrud opened her leather briefcase and took out a notebook. "This page has addresses of properties known to be on the market for sale, and on this page, these are vacant rentals."

Theresa read the sheets and nodded. "I know where these listings are. Some are in pricey neighborhoods, and some are in industrial areas. From the listing, it appears that some are furnished. I would love to accompany you whenever you are available to go check them out."

Gertrud smiled. "I have a car. If you are available, let's go."

"One question I have for you and Carl," Julia asked. "How are the down payments or the first two months' rental to be funded? I doubt very much if the refugees in the synagogue and on the streets of Budapest have brought very much money with them."

"The embassy has an account, though it is limited. We are hoping that other sympathetic countries might be charitable. I know that Carl has a call into London."

"That's exactly why I asked," Julia said. "As you may know, Theresa and I are the appointed representatives of the US War Refugee Board. It is in the charter of the organization to aid refugees, especially in Europe.

Perhaps your husband has alerted you to the WRB and the fact that it is associated with the US Treasury Department."

Gertrud smiled. "He has."

"Funding housing for homeless refugees fits right into the WRB purpose clause," Julia continued. "I will contact John Pehle as soon as I can. I will impress upon him the necessity for funds to acquire housing. Please let me know how much money is needed, and I will convey that to John. I talk to him every day."

"It sounds like we have a plan," Carl said. "Gertrud and Theresa can go out to locate properties. And, Theresa, if you wouldn't mind, can you contact your father to make arrangements to visit with Rabbi Levy? In addition to involving him in the distribution of the letters, he may have an idea about the extent of the current housing needs. Depending on what the rabbi says, my staff and I can start preparing letters tomorrow. Gertrud will be drafting leases. We'll meet back here at five o'clock tonight. Martin can go with Julia. He has the use of an embassy car."

With that last remark, Theresa looked over at Julia, who was smiling. Theresa whispered, "Uh-oh."

CHAPTER THIRTY-FIVE

GERTRUD AND THERESA arrived at the embassy meeting room shortly after five o'clock. Carl was notified and quickly joined them. Gertrud opened her briefcase and pulled out a folder full of documents. "We have six signed leases and four pending leases," she said.

"How are they signed?" Carl asked.

"As you instructed me. The lessee is listed as *Schweizerische Gesandtschaft—The Swiss Embassy*, and it is signed by Gertrud, its authorized representative. Three of the leases are for whole-floor apartments in brownstone buildings, a total of nine units, and three are for single-family homes. Four more apartment leases are pending. One is on the first floor, and two are on the second floor."

"Good work," Carl said with a smile. "So that means that the apartment is leased directly to the government of Switzerland, and the government is the authorized tenant. How many people do you envision can occupy these leased apartments?"

"We discussed that," said Theresa. "Right now, there are homeless refugees living in the sanctuary of the Great Synagogue. They share the two bathrooms, they sleep on benches, and there are no kitchens or living areas. I trust you can envision how difficult it is for people with babies and young children, but they have no choice. These are not vagabonds or derelicts by any means. They are good people who have fled their comfortable lives to protect their families from the SS. Gertrud and I have concluded that they wouldn't mind sharing an apartment."

"That's correct," Gertrud said. "Take a look at 512 Juharfa. It has two bedrooms, a sitting room, and a small reading room. What did we say, Theresa? Three families or four families? Of course, it would depend on the size of the families, but we used a family of four as the model."

"The apartment at 1032 Folyokep is on the third floor, and it is a studio, but it's a good-size studio. Two families can live there easily," Theresa said. "And 96 György is an empty two-story building with large three-bedroom apartments on each floor. We figured between seven and eight families could live there, depending on the size of the family. It would be tight, but there is room."

"We saw one apartment building that we think has potential. It looked empty. There was a broken window. I don't know how much more work it needs, but I think it could hold four families. It wasn't one of the properties on my list, so there wasn't any way to contact the owner today. I just left a note on the door."

Gertrud poured herself a cup of coffee and became wistful. "You know, Carl and I have been here for a couple of years now. As more-or-less outside observers, we've seen what has been happening to the Jewish community. Some restrictions have been imposed, some limitations, decidedly unfair, but they have been minor. Throughout the years of this terrible war, the Budapest Jewish community has remained strong and safe. We never observed soldiers coming to arrest or discipline the Jewish residents in any way. So, why did everything suddenly change in 1944? The war started five years ago. It isn't like the Jews took up arms or revolted. Why did the Nazis suddenly pick this time to attack the Jews?"

"Maybe it was because of Miklós Kállay," Theresa said. "He sent those letters to Germany's enemies seeking to negotiate peace agreements. Hitler found out about them and concluded that Hungary was untrustworthy. There is no doubt that those messages precipitated the takeover."

Gertrud shook her head. "But Kállay isn't Jewish. Nothing in his treasonous letters even mentions the Jews. The Jews didn't commit treason. In fact, Jewish soldiers and workers supported the Hungarian army fighting alongside Germany in Russia. Making the country *Judenfrei* won't make Germany any safer. So, why now?"

"I think I know," said Julia, entering the room. "Kállay's treason was just an excuse to conquer Hungary. As long as Hungary was loyal, Hitler left it alone, even though it had a significant Jewish population. Once there was a sign of treason, a German takeover was inevitable."

"But why take it out on the Jews?"

"Because Hitler does that wherever he goes. First, he conquers a country, then he orders the elimination of all Jews. He makes it *Judenfrei*. And he does it by annihilation."

"Julia's right," Carl said. "Once Germany takes over a country, it is only a matter of time until the imposition of antisemitic laws that mirror what is already in effect in Germany and its occupied countries. Hitler's extreme hatred of the Jews causes banishment of all from German-controlled territories."

"You could accomplish banishment by putting them on a train and sending them somewhere else—like Turkey or Palestine. You could remove them without killing them," Gertrud said. "It would be no more work. They wouldn't need prisons or concentration camps. The Jews wouldn't resist, and it would be a lot cheaper."

"My wife, you are engaging in rational thinking," Carl said. "Hitler is a psychotic sociopath. Rational thinking does not apply."

Gertrud nodded and looked at Julia. "How did it go at the Great Synagogue? Did the rabbi cooperate?"

Julia smiled and turned to Martin. "Tell them, Marty. Did Rabbi Levy cooperate?"

Theresa closed her eyes. She heard Julia say *Marty* and thought, *Uh-oh*.

"He cooperated one hundred percent," Martin said. "The rabbi is totally on board."

"Tell us what happened," Carl said.

"Because of the influx of refugees at the synagogue, the rabbi is no longer in a wait-and-see state of mind. He is counseling the families the best he can, but he is overwhelmed. They tell him about their travails and their anguishes, and it's all pretty much the same. They were living a peaceful life in the country or in a small town, and the Nazi soldiers marched in from out of nowhere and started loading them into trucks. They drove them to the nearest town and put them in a confined area—a ghetto."

"How did the families get away? Did they escape from the town?"

"Not any of the ones we talked to," Martin said. "Once you've been taken into a town and put into a ghetto, you are held under guard as a group until they send you away. The ones in the synagogue found out about the arrests because rumors spread quickly, and these families didn't wait for the SS to get there. They dropped everything and left on their own as fast as they could. They all made their way to Budapest, to the heart of the Jewish community, figuring that there was safety in numbers."

"Theresa's father, Benjamin, took us into the synagogue," Julia said. "Benjamin is a well-respected man there. He used to be the president, and he is still a member of the board of directors. I have heard Theresa say that he thinks of the congregation as family. In the same way, the congregation looks up to him and regards him as a leader. When we talked about the Swiss letters of protection, the rabbi was totally unaware that they existed. He was surprised that the Nazis would honor anything. 'That is a gift from heaven,' he said. 'How are we going to pass them out and to whom?' Benjamin volunteered. He said that he and the rabbi could meet with the families, one at a time, in private, and take down the information for the letters. Then they could bring that information to Carl so that he could prepare the letters for them."

"That's an extra step," Carl said. "Why doesn't the rabbi fill out the letters himself?"

"He is not authorized," Martin said. "He might make a mistake."

"How can he make a mistake?" Carl asked. "All he needs to do is type in the family names in the empty spaces on the forms we give to him, and bingo! Now it's authorized. What about the housing? Did you talk to the rabbi about assigning people to available housing?"

Martin shook his head. "As of this morning, we didn't know whether we would have any available housing or what kind of housing it would be. Second, we weren't sure how to approach that issue. Are we going to let the rabbi decide who gets to move into the housing? Is it going to be a lottery, or is he going to choose the people?"

"Why does that matter?" asked Carl. "Whatever he wants should be okay. Let's get the refugees out of the synagogue and into safe housing."

"I understand what Marty is saying," said Julia. "Picking families and giving them housing puts the rabbi in an awkward position. He has to stay independent, detached, neutral, like Switzerland, and not play favorites. The families that don't get chosen will resent him and the synagogue and may cause trouble. Maybe pull the names out of a hat."

"No. Not a good idea. These are official documents created by the Swiss government for a specific recipient. If the Nazis learned they were drawn out by luck, they would be worthless. Benjamin and the rabbi will have to interview families, decide which ones are appropriate for the available housing, and make the assignment. And it has to be confidential."

"What is next on your calendar?" Gertrud asked Theresa.

"I don't know whether you are familiar with my brother, Samuel Weissbach," said Theresa. "Everyone calls him Sammy. He's an executive at the telephone company. He is also a good friend of Joel Brand, who helped form the Aid and Rescue Committee. As Carl knows, I have been trying to set a meeting with the Aid and Rescue Committee for some time. We were referred there by John Pehle at the WRB as an organization that might help families escape from Europe. We are hoping to have a meeting with them on Monday night, but I'm not sure; it hasn't been confirmed. I asked Sammy to come over here tonight if he was available."

There was a knock on the door, and Theresa said, "My goodness, that was quick. Maybe Sammy heard us talking?"

Martin went to answer the door and said, "Even better. It's a delivery."

"It's our dinner," Carl said. "I hope you all are hungry."

While the group was enjoying a dinner of Hungarian meatballs, Gertrud said, "Do any of you know anything about the glass factory at 29 Vadasz Street? It's a huge building, not far from Saint Stephen's Basilica." After no one responded, Gertrud added, "It looks vacant to me. Terri and I took a walk around it. Terri looked in the windows. We didn't see any people or materials. It's not on the list of vacant properties that I was given, but we decided to investigate and see if it was for rent. It could house a lot of people. Multiple families."

Once again, there was a knock on the door, and this time it was Sammy.

"We have some meatballs left over," Theresa said.

Sammy shrugged, nodded, and filled his plate.

"Do you know anything about setting a meeting with the Aid and Rescue Committee?" Theresa asked.

"Tomorrow night," he said, "and Joel's bringing Rezső Kasztner."

"Wow," said Theresa, "that is very accommodating of him."

"He's not doing it to be accommodating. Joel has his own agenda. He has a matter he wants to discuss with both you and Carl."

"Do you know what it's about?" asked Carl.

"I have a hunch. I think it's about money. The WRB has it, Switzerland has it, and Joel has a history of using money to fund rescue operations."

"What other rescue operations?" asked Gertrud.

"I'm not real sure," Sammy said.

"Carl can tell you about the Bratislava Working Group," Theresa said. "It's another rescue group located in Slovakia and run by a woman named Gisi Fleischmann. The man in the black fedora, the man named Bernhard, had a meeting with Carl, my father, the rabbi, Solomon Cushman, Julia, and me recently. He told us a lot of confidential information, including all about the Slovakian working group. Then he broke off in the middle of his discussion because Solomon was a bit rude."

"Not just a bit," said Julia.

"True, but Carl just told us that he and Bernhard had a second, private meeting. At that meeting, Bernhard told a story about Joel Brand and the Slovakian working group."

"That's right," Carl said, "but it is still all confidential. It doesn't go outside this room, at least for the present time. I have a hunch that something is going to happen soon and that the whole thing will become public knowledge. But not now."

"What does that mean, the 'present time'?" Gertrud asked.

"It means that soon the public will learn what happens when the Nazis take Jewish prisoners into the concentration camps, but I gave my word to Bernhard not to say anything right now. Bernhard also told me about Eichmann's assignment a few years ago when he was sent to Slovakia as the grand inquisitor. He did the same things he is now doing in Hungary—that is, to capture all the Jews and ship them to concentration camps. From what happened in Slovakia, Bernhard is certain that Eichmann can be manipulated. He is corrupt. He can be bought."

Eyebrows were raised, and Carl continued, "Gisi Fleischmann and an Orthodox rabbi named Michael Dov Weissmandl formed the Bratislava Working Group. It was a group within the Slovakian Jewish Council. In 1942, Eichmann was sent to Bratislava, Slovakia, to arrest Jews and send them to camps in Poland. Gisi raised money and bribed Eichmann's deputy, Dieter Wisliceny, to suspend the deportations of Jews from Slovakia to Poland. She also bribed him to allow Jews to escape to Hungary. Gisi paid a $50,000 bribe to Wisliceny to have Eichmann stop the mandatory transports out of Slovakia. It was successful for a time, and only two transports left for Poland after Wisliceny was paid. Joel Brand was present in Slovakia at that time. Both the Working Group and Brand believed that their bribes had succeeded.

"In 1943, tens of thousands of refugees made their way into Hungary from Slovakia, so much so that Hungarian authorities decided it was excessive. On Horthy's orders, the border guards began to deny entrance. They turned the refugees around and sent them east to Ukraine. Hansi Brand's relatives were in the group that was expelled from Hungary, and then they were trapped in Ukraine. That was a disaster, because Germany was in control of Ukraine. Joel couldn't let his wife's relatives be victimized by the Nazis, and he devised a plan to rescue them. He paid a hefty bribe to bring those relatives back to Hungary. After that, Joel became a strong believer in the power of bribes."

"We plan to meet with that committee tomorrow night," Theresa said. "But I don't know yet where we are meeting. Are you planning on coming with us?"

"I don't think I can," said Carl. "So that you are better prepared, let me finish telling you what I know about them. In 1943, Joel and Hansi joined with Rezső Kasztner to form a rescue organization. Rezső is a lawyer and journalist from Transylvania, which became a part of Hungary a few years ago. Anyway, Joel, Rezső, and Ottó Komoly jointly set up the rescue organization they called the Aid and Rescue Committee."

"I have heard it called *Va'adat Ha-Ezrah ve'Hatzalah*, or *Va'ada* for short," said Sammy. "I know that Ottó Komoly was and is its chairman. I don't know if you are aware of this, Carl, but Gisi was also active in the Aid and Rescue Committee at one time. I have met her, and she is an amazing woman. I don't think I have ever met a woman quite like her. She is brilliant and powerful and dedicated to social needs."

"Absolutely true," Carl said. "Bernhard told me that after her brother was killed, Gisi took both of her daughters down to Palestine. That was in 1939. She didn't stay with them. She returned to Bratislava to run the Working Group. She couldn't walk out on her people. Her daughters were safe in Palestine. She hoped to join them after the war was over."

Carl paused for a moment to let a memory play out in his mind. "She was totally selfless," he said. "Joel Brand witnessed how Gisi used bribes to save tens of thousands of Slovakians. He knew that Eichmann and all of his underlings were corrupt and susceptible to bribes. In the fall of 1943, a man named Oskar Schindler visited Budapest and met with the Aid and Rescue Committee. Schindler himself has rescued, and continues to rescue, Jews by employing them in his factories in Poland. I'm not sure of the reason why Schindler came to Budapest at that time, but I know that he and Brand and Kasztner discussed rescue operations. At that meeting, Joel learned that Schindler had been bribing Nazi officers to let him bring Jewish refugees into his factory in Kraków. This encouraged Joel and the committee on the use of bribes to further their rescue operations. Brand and the Aid and Rescue Committee negotiated with the Nazis on that basis."

Carl took a breath. "That's really all I have on the Aid and Rescue Committee. Make sure you let me know whatever I can do to help. I will ask, but I'm skeptical about whether Swiss authorities will secretly furnish money to fund bribes of German officials. If that were to become known by the Nazi hierarchy, they would certainly consider that as taking sides and violating our neutrality policy."

"Switzerland has helped us in many ways," said Julia. "Maybe we can get the funds from the WRB. We will keep you informed of what happens at the meeting."

"I hope it takes place," said Carl. "I am very anxious to learn what they have to say. In fact, I will be here working late Monday night. If the meeting actually occurs, and if it isn't too late when it finishes, please stop by and tell me about it."

CHAPTER THIRTY-SIX

IT WAS ALMOST midnight on Monday when Julia and Theresa returned to the Swiss embassy. Just as he promised, Carl was still working in room 217.

"Well," he said, "I'm assuming the meeting occurred. You're here, and it's late. Fill me in."

"The negotiations with Eichmann started a few months ago. Dieter Wisliceny, Eichmann's second-in-command, approached the Aid and Rescue Committee. Wisliceny said that Eichmann was willing to talk. He told them that for the payment of money, Eichmann was prepared to moderate or suspend the anti-Jewish measures. Kasztner took Joel to meet with Wisliceny and told him they were in a position to continue with Gisi Fleischmann's offer, the one she called the Europa Plan."

"Was that the one where they were to exchange the lives of all of Europe's Jews for $2 million?"

"Generally, that was discussed. There was other talk about a $50,000 down payment and then a $200,000 down payment. Wisliceny finally agreed that for $2 million payable over time and a $200,000 down payment, one million Jews would be released. Gisi went to the Allies and pleaded for the money. They didn't even give her an answer. She couldn't get the deal funded, and it fell apart. Some said that it wasn't the amount of money that was the roadblock but the refusal of the Allies to do business with Nazi Germany or to send that much money to Europe."

Carl shook his head. "Now the Aid and Rescue Committee wants to restart that plan. How are they going to change minds in Washington and London?"

"Joel thinks that they can. He says he won't have any trouble raising the $2 million. So they presented it to Wisliceny, who said they were interested. Joel demanded that there be no deportations, mass executions, or antisemitic programs in Hungary while they were negotiating. He didn't want countryside families arrested and taken into the cities, no herding people into ghettos or camps, and that Jews who held immigration certificates for Palestine, issued by the British mandatory government, be allowed to emigrate without being stopped. Wisliceny said he thought that could be arranged, but he would have to check with Eichmann. He said he would meet with them in a week and give them an answer."

"We've heard this story before," Carl said. "That is what Gisi Fleischmann offered, but she couldn't get the deal funded, and so it died."

"I know, but Joel said that this time they had the money, and they were more confident. I don't know where he was getting the money, but he said he could do it. Two weeks after their meeting with Wisliceny, Joel received a message that Eichmann wanted to meet with him. Joel was told to wait in the Opera Café. He went there, and he was driven by the SS to Eichmann's headquarters."

"At the Majestic Hotel on Castle Hill?"

"Right. When he arrived at the hotel, he met Eichmann and Kurt Becher, an emissary of Reichsführer Heinrich Himmler."

"Himmler?" said Carl with raised eyebrows. "This went right to the top."

"You should have heard Joel describe Eichmann," Theresa said. "Joel said that Eichmann wore a sharp, tailored uniform, and his eyes were steely blue, hard, and sharp. When he looked at you, his eyes seemed to bore holes through you. Joel kept on describing him like he was describing some unearthly creature. He said, 'It was only later that I noticed his small face with its thin lips and sharp nose.' He mentioned that Eichmann's speech was like 'the clatter of a machine gun.' But the bottom line was that Eichmann was ready to talk about negotiating a deal."

"Which deal?" Carl asked. "Was it the same as the Europa Plan or a different deal?"

"If it's real," Theresa said, "it is earthshaking, but probably impossible. According to Joel and Kasztner, Eichmann proposed that Joel broker a deal between the SS and the United States or Britain—he didn't care which one. The Nazis would exchange one million Jews for ten thousand trucks for the Eastern Front, and large quantities of tea and other goods. Eichmann called it *Blut gegen Waren*, which means 'Blood for Goods.'"

"Are you serious?" Carl said. "He was exchanging blood for goods?"

"Right. Isn't that awful? Joel quoted Eichmann, who reportedly said, 'I have already made investigations about you and your people, and I have verified your ability to make a deal. Now then, I am prepared to sell you one million Jews. *Blut gegen Waren*. Blood for goods.' Eichmann said that Joel could take the one million Jews from any place or country he could find them. Eichmann mentioned Hungary, Poland, and Austria. Or he said that Joel could take them out of Nazi detention camps. 'Theresienstadt, Auschwitz, or wherever you like.'" Theresa looked at Carl. "It makes me sick to my stomach, but that's what Joel said."

"This can't be real," Carl said. "How could he offer to take them from concentration camps? I thought they were killing centers."

"Joel said the same thing to Eichmann. Eichmann shook his head. 'Auschwitz is a prison camp. Many perform work there. It is a false rumor that Jews are taken there to die, though some do die: sickness, age, whatever. Thousands and thousands of prisoners are sleeping in huts.'"

"Joel believed him?"

"I don't know, but he told us that's what Eichmann said. He also said he would take the proposal back with him to Berlin and discuss it, and he was confident it would be approved. In the meantime, Joel was to do the same thing. He was to present the proposal to the US representatives and the British representatives and determine what kinds of goods they were in a position to offer. Eichmann even arranged a permit for Joel to travel to America and to England to discuss it."

"Did Berlin approve of the deal? I can't believe this," Carl said.

"Eichmann came back a couple of weeks later and told Joel that Berlin would go along with it. In the meantime, while they were talking, no mass deportations would take place. He asked Joel what the leaders in

London and Washington had to say. Joel had no answer. He wasn't going to propose anything to the Allies until he knew that the deal would be acceptable to Berlin and they would go through with it. At that point, Eichmann said that Berlin would approve of exchanging one million Jews for ten thousand new trucks for the Waffen-SS to use only on the Eastern Front or for civilian purposes, not to fight against US or British. And in addition, Eichmann wanted two hundred tons of tea, eight hundred tons of coffee, two million cases of soap, and a quantity of tungsten and other materials. If the Allies agreed to do the deal, and if Joel could return with proof in the way of a partial payment, Eichmann said he would immediately release ten percent, or one hundred thousand Jews, for every one thousand trucks."

"Is that where the negotiation stands at this time?" Carl asked.

Julia nodded. "Joel said he is already approaching the US and Britain through his contacts. I promised to convey the details of the plan to John at the WRB. I'm going to call him in a few minutes. Afterward, I'm scheduled to meet up with Theresa and her father at the synagogue. We are supposed to take him a dozen letters of protection. As you know, he is interviewing families who have escaped capture by Nazi squads in the countryside."

"Gertrud was going to go with you, but she has two apartment inspections tonight. She and Martin are going after dinner. How many letters did you want?"

"Benjamin said a dozen," Julia said. "That will cover twelve families, or maybe forty-eight people. That was a brilliant idea of yours, the family plan. Right now, I'm going to call John Pehle. I don't look forward to this call. How do I tell him about the blood-for-goods proposal and the need for ten thousand trucks? If this goes through, I will be the most shocked girl on earth."

JOHN PEHLE'S RESPONSE conveyed incredulity. "What?" he said in a voice raised three octaves. "He wants *what*? And he calls it *Blood for Goods*? Eichmann has the unconscionable nerve to call the release of innocent human beings *blood*. That is so crass and inhuman, it is beyond belief."

"Basically, he proposes to release a million humans for ten thousand trucks, and tea and coffee, and other things," Julia said. "Joel Brand thinks that Eichmann will do it. Joel is going to his contacts in Washington and London to see if he can get it funded."

"I can't imagine where he is going to get those vehicles and materials. Churchill won't go for this. Can you imagine taking trucks away from your own armed forces and your industries and sending them to your enemy? Churchill won't do business with Hitler. I can take this up to Morgenthau at Treasury, but it's going nowhere. From there, it would need either presidential or congressional approval. I know you can't see me right now, but I'm shaking my head as hard as I can. It's not happening."

"John," Julia pleaded, "these are a million human lives that otherwise will be put to death. We can take them right out of the concentration camps, and Eichmann has promised to halt deportations from Hungary while we are negotiating."

"And you believe him? Do you think Eichmann will keep his word? He's just playing us."

"I don't know. What does he have to gain by playing us? Joel said that Eichmann has paused transports from Hungary to camps in Poland."

There was a brief hesitation on the phone, and finally, John said, "What does Carl think about this offer?"

"Same as you. Very pessimistic. He said it can't be real," Julia said. "He doesn't believe Eichmann."

"Exactly. Why would we take the word of a mass murderer? He is a callous, soulless fiend," John said. "Why would we trust anything he had to say? Besides, he would earn Hitler's wrath. Hitler wants to eradicate Jews more than he wants to receive trucks."

In her mind, Julia could see John's face, his lips tight in an angry sneer. "I know it sounds crazy," Julia answered. "I am just doing what I'm told."

"Let me discuss this with the rest of the WRB, and we'll get back to you. Let's plan on touching base on Tuesday. Call me at ten o'clock Eastern time."

CHAPTER THIRTY-SEVEN

JULIA AND THERESA were at the embassy gathering the morning's supply of letters of protection when Carl's secretary came in. "There is a Samuel Weissbach here to see you," she said. "Shall I let him in?"

"Absolutely," Theresa said. "He's my brother."

Sammy came into the room, said, "*Jó reggelt*," and hugged Theresa.

"Good morning to you as well," she responded. "What brings you over here this early?"

Sammy's face was serious. "I need to talk to you. It's very important and very private." He looked at Julia and said, "I would like you to listen as well, if you wouldn't mind. I need advice."

They took Sammy into a private office and shut the door. "What's wrong?" said Theresa. "Is everyone okay?"

Sammy nodded. "We're fine. As you predicted, neither the British nor the Americans would accept Eichmann's offer to negotiate for the release of a million Jews."

"That's not a surprise. I read it in an editorial in the *Times* of London and saw Winston Churchill's furious remarks."

Sammy nodded. "That's true. The transports that were paused are due to start rolling again from the smaller country towns. Do you remember meeting Rezső Kasztner?"

Julia and Theresa nodded.

"I believe that it was Rezső and Joel Brand who began the negotiating process with Eichmann back in Slovakia. They were notified by his assistant, who said Eichmann was amenable to negotiating for money and material items," Theresa said. "I think it was also Eichmann's deputy who approached Gisi Fleischmann at the Bratislava Working Group."

"You have a good memory, Terri. It was Wisliceny who communicated the blood-for-goods offer."

"But you believe that it has failed. So what brings you here?"

"Because there is another deal in the works. Rezső approached Wisliceny and proposed a deal to allow Rezső to take a number of Jews out of Hungary on a train. The train would go through Austria to Switzerland. For that, Rezső is offering to pay money and jewelry. I understand that Eichmann considered the deal and set a price. For that set amount, Rezső will be allowed to take seventeen hundred Jews."

"Who are the seventeen hundred Jews? Where are they supposed to come from?" asked Julia. "Will they be released from concentration camps?"

Sammy shook his head. "No, this is a personal, cash deal. Rezső and his friends drew up a list of people, mostly Rezső's family, friends, and other wealthy Jews. They would agree to pay Eichmann's price to escape going into concentration camps."

"You've seen the list?" Theresa asked. "Do you know the people on the list?"

"Many of them, not all, but don't criticize him. It's not only wealthy friends. There are two hundred fifty children, many of them orphans."

"Who chose the passengers to go on Rezső's train?"

"Hansi Brand, for one. You may have heard that Joel is currently under arrest, being held by the British in Egypt for trying to make the blood-for-goods deal. When Joel left for Palestine, Hansi stayed behind to help Rezső. Ottó Komoly and others from the Aid and Rescue Committee chose the rest of the list. Some are calling it 'Noah's ark,' because the list is a cross section of the Jewish community, including people who worked in public service. I've seen the list. There are 972 females and 712 males in all; the oldest being eighty-two, and the youngest just a few days old. There are housewives, farmers, industrialists, bankers, journalists, teachers, and nurses."

"And those people will escape the death camps? Good for Rezső," Julia said. "He is a champion rescuer. The fact that he paid money, and his family and friends are going to safety, is an accomplishment. I know some will criticize him for doing business with murderers, paying a ransom to the devil, but he is looking to save lives."

Sammy looked at Theresa. "Terri, do you feel that way, too?"

"I guess so. It does turn my stomach to pay a ransom to a bastard like Eichmann, but if it rescues seventeen hundred innocents, then it was a smart move." Theresa suddenly stopped. Her eyes were wide open. "Sammy! Are you going on the Kasztner train?"

"I've been a friend of Rezső for a long time, and when he started putting together his list, he offered a seat for both Alana and me. Alana is now five months pregnant. If escapes require long journeys on foot or over rough terrain, Alana can't do it. So this is what I came to talk to you about. Do you think I should go, or would I be making a deal with the devil?"

"Are you nuts?" said Julia. "You put your butt and that pretty, pregnant girlfriend of yours on that train without a second thought. You and Alana have your baby in a safe, free land, not here in Nazi-occupied Hungary."

"I agree," said Theresa. "My niece should be born in Switzerland. If you need Carl's help in any way, you let me know. When is the Kasztner train leaving?"

"As soon as we can get our money together and our things packed. Each person is allowed to take two changes of clothing, six sets of underwear, and food for ten days."

"Is this costing you money, Sammy? How much do you have to pay?"

Sammy swallowed. "Five thousand Reichsmarks—twenty-five hundred apiece. Apa is helping me with the money."

Julia whistled. "Wow! That's a lot of money, over a thousand American dollars apiece. But it's well worth it if it saves a life."

Sammy looked at his sister with a tear in his eye and said, "Rezső is taking nurses, and I suggested that Becca go along, and Rezső said it would be all right, but Becca doesn't want to leave her post at the hospital—not now, during the war, when so many need her. If you think you can change her mind, the train leaves pretty soon."

Theresa smiled. "I respect my sister for making that decision. She is a dedicated girl."

"I know, but anyone who stays risks being captured and transported to Auschwitz to die. Who knows when the SS will start rounding up Jews in Budapest? Who knows if they will all be taken? We don't know for certain what happens when the trains take prisoners to those camps."

"The man in the black hat said they will die," Julia said.

"That doesn't make sense," Theresa said. "Joel was negotiating with Eichmann for release of a million Jews out of Auschwitz, Majdanek, and Chelmno. How could he make the exchange of blood for goods if they're all dead? He said Auschwitz is only a prison. It is hard to believe that twelve thousand people are being taken and murdered every day. Maybe it is just a prison."

"Terri, I don't want to take that chance, and neither should you," said Sammy. "I might be able to get you on the train. You're family. I talked to Rezső about it, and he said there would probably be room. If not, you can have my seat."

Theresa broke into tears. "Sammy, I love you so much, but you need to be with Alana and your baby when it's born. I came here on my own to rescue my family, and I will be okay. I have a Swiss ID. Don't worry about me. What about Anya? Take her on the train."

"I suggested it, but Anya said no. She is staying behind with her husband in the only country she has ever known."

"That's my Anya," Theresa said.

Sammy smiled at his sister, gave her a strong hug, and said, "When you get the chance, you come visit us in Switzerland."

CHAPTER THIRTY-EIGHT

AS HAD RECENTLY become their habit, Julia and Martin met Benjamin at the Great Synagogue in the morning, and Theresa went with Gertrud to find vacant housing. A stack of Swiss letters of protection and the addresses of six more apartment buildings were brought to the synagogue to be distributed by Benjamin. The process seemed to be working. Benjamin and the rabbi would meet with homeless families who had been practically living in the synagogue. They would discuss the letters of protection and how they were to be used. They would ascertain the families' housing needs, and if they had available space in an apartment, they would have the fathers sign a special lease agreement with the Swiss embassy. The agreement would describe the apartment and the conditions and responsibilities of their occupancy. Often, the apartment was "shared," and the lease agreement would be between two or three families who all agreed in advance to the terms. They agreed to respect the rights of the other families in the use of the available beds, the kitchen, and the bathrooms, and especially the quiet times.

"You look tired this morning, Apa," said Julia. "Did you get enough sleep last night?"

Benjamin shrugged. "What is enough? I slept a few hours. I was here at the synagogue until very late."

"Was it a service, or were you having another of those stormy sessions?" Julia asked with a smile.

Benjamin shook his head. "Neither one. It was sick children. It started with the Rosen girl. She had a fever and trouble breathing. I examined her and discovered that she had a case of the croup. I called Goszin, who agreed to open the pharmacy. The girl's father ran to get the medicine. But we had to quarantine the girl as best we could. She is in a classroom on the second floor."

"I'm proud of you, Apa. How many times are you tending to children at this synagogue?"

"Too often. I don't count how many. And it's not just children. Some of them are new mothers, and they need help. They are out of their comfort zone, miles away from their families and their community, and they feel lost."

While Julia and Benjamin were talking, Samu Stern came into the building. He was met with grumbles. Many considered him a Nazi agent. "You know I am here on behalf of the Judenrat," he said. "Think what you will; I am your friend. I have some important news to discuss with you, and I ask that you pass it along to the members of the congregation."

"Is it good news, or does it come from your German friends?" one of the congregants asked. "Is it news, or is it more demands?"

Benjamin reached over to the member and tapped him on the shoulder. "Let's not be impolite. Mr. Stern is the president of a Jewish organization formed to communicate with the Germans. He is an honest man and deserves respect."

"Thank you, Benjamin," Samu said. "I came here this morning to tell you about new regulations that are going into effect starting tomorrow. It is better that you hear it from me rather than unknowingly breaking the laws and getting into trouble. As you know, Hungarian Jewish citizens outside of Budapest are being gathered into groups in the nearby towns. They are staying in closed housing units until they can be transported to camps outside of Hungary where they will live with other Jews."

"Do you mean like Auschwitz and Majdanek? People tell us that Jews are taken there to be killed. Who's going to tell us the truth?"

Stern said in an irritated tone, "I am. No one told me that anyone is to be killed. That is a vicious rumor. They are being held in a prison camp until the war is over. You don't have any proof they are being killed."

"We have met with people who tell us that, and they have been there. Have you been there?" Julia asked with her chin out.

Benjamin raised his hand. "Let him speak, Julia. Samu has a thankless job. It's not easy or pleasant. Let him finish." He looked at Stern. "Tell us, Samu, did the transportations start again? We understood that there was a pause during negotiations."

Stern nodded. "There was a short pause while Obergruppenführer Eichmann was talking with the Aid and Rescue Committee," he said, "but that is over now. The Allied countries are unwilling to be reasonable and meet Eichmann's terms."

"You mean that Churchill and Roosevelt are refusing to be 'reasonable' and supply trucks to the German army in exchange for the blood of Jewish families, right? Isn't that true?" Julia said angrily. "Wasn't that the response of the Allied countries?"

Stern took a deep breath. "The British press learned of the offer and published it in their papers. They called it a 'monstrous offer' and 'blackmail.' They said it was a trick. The Russians were against it because the trucks were to be used in the attacks on their territory. Then British and US immigration departments wanted to know where the million Jews were supposed to go. The US Congress wouldn't raise the money or consider the deal. Joel Brand traveled to Palestine to promote the deal, but he was arrested by the British. He is still under arrest. The trains have resumed transporting Jews from the Hungarian small towns directly to the camps. They are poised to transfer twelve thousand Jews per day."

"Oh my God," Benjamin said. "Per day? What about Budapest? Are the German troops coming here?"

Stern shut his eyes and nodded. "I'm sure they will when they are finished in the smaller towns. All of Hungary is to be *Judenfrei*."

"Is that what you came to tell us?" the rabbi asked. "Is that your news?"

"Partially. There are new regulations enacted by the Gestapo. They also go into effect immediately."

"What are they planning on doing now?" Julia said.

"Don't blame me," Stern said, "I'm just the messenger. Each Jewish person over the age of five is to be identified as a Jew when he or she goes outside the home. To do that, he or she must wear a ten-by-ten-centimeter yellow star that reads 'JUDE.' We have been given a supply of yellow Jewish badges. They are to be worn on the outside of the clothing, in the stomach area. Failure to wear the star would mean arrest, or worse."

"Where are we to obtain these yellow badges of sin?" the rabbi said.

Stern bit his lip. He bowed his head and again shook it back and forth. "You may obtain them at the office of the Judenrat at 6508 Planjacz."

"Well," Benjamin said, "thank you for bringing us this miserable report. We understand it is not your fault, but you may leave now."

"That's not all," Stern said. "The SS is planning on collecting all telephones from Jewish households. In that way, they are cutting off communication with the outside world."

Stern could see the bitterness in the eyes of the listeners. "Do you want to hear the rest? You should, because you could be arrested for violations."

"Yes," said the rabbi, "tell us the rest."

"As of next Monday, Jews are forbidden from owning a car and must declare the value of their property on a disclosure form that, once again, may be obtained at the Judenrat. I'm not privileged; I have to do the same thing myself."

"Why are they taking away our cars?" the rabbi said.

"You know the answer, Rabbi," Julia said. "They want to make sure that you can't go anywhere when they come to herd all the Jews into areas near the train station. They did the same thing in Holland."

Stern stood to leave. "Rabbi, and you too, Benjamin, I would ask that you spread the word. Let the people know what the new laws are. If your fellow congregants don't follow the laws, they will be punished. That is the reason I came here. Now I have to go to the other synagogues. I wish you well." Stern turned and left the building.

For a moment, everyone was silent and looked from face to face. Finally, Benjamin said, "We must make plans to pass out as many letters of protection as we can. Those with letters will be diplomatically immune from the new laws. They may still keep their phones and their cars. Those families with letters can try to emigrate out of Hungary while there is still time."

"Then that is the answer," said Julia firmly. "All Jews must make their way out of Hungary, one way or another, before being arrested by the Nazis, and we must help them do that. It is as clear as the lies on Mr. Stern's lips. All Hungarian Jews are going to be arrested and put on trains for Auschwitz. It is not a place where they will live with other Jews; it is a place where they will die with other Jews. We had better believe that, and pass the word."

"We have to inform Carl about everything that Mr. Stern had to say," Martin said. "If I know Carl, he will be very upset. I know that Benjamin believes that letters are the answer and that they should be given to every Jew in Hungary, but I don't know how many more letters we will receive from Bern."

"Will the letters work forever," Julia said, "or will there come a time when the Nazis ignore them? I don't trust them. Let's go straight to the embassy and talk to Carl. Maybe he will have other ideas."

Martin winced. "We can't go this afternoon. Carl is at a very hush-hush meeting at the embassy. I don't know how long it will last."

"What is it about?" Julia asked.

"Even I don't know the details. There are two men meeting with Carl behind closed doors. They've been there since early this morning." Martin leaned forward. "You can't say anything to anyone else, but Carl is meeting with two men who escaped from the Auschwitz prison camp and have written a report. They are supposed to deliver it to Carl under certain conditions."

"What conditions?"

Martin shrugged. "I don't know. Just don't say anything. Carl will tell us when he is ready."

WHEN THE CONFIDENTIAL meeting was finally over, Julia met with Carl and conveyed the content of the morning's meeting with Samu Stern. Carl was shocked. "I have been here for over two years, and this is a total turnaround. The Jews of Hungary have always been good, loyal citizens. They are undeserving of these punitive restrictions. Theresa's father is right. Emigration is the only way. We must secure as many Swiss letters as we can and pass them out to families. Then we need to make plans for mass emigrations."

"Families need to emigrate out of Hungary on pilgrimages to safe lands," Theresa said. "Like Moses in the biblical times. History is full of pilgrimages. We need to lead our people out of tyranny to freedom in safe countries."

"To Jaffa?" Julia said. "That is what Ira Hirschman does. He is in Turkey now, and he would help us get to Palestine, maybe Jerusalem. We just need to get to Ira. It's a pilgrimage to the holy land."

"It sounds like a fairy tale," Theresa said. "How are we going to do that?"

"It's not a joke. It can be done," Julia insisted. "We just need to get emigration groups to Turkey. Businessmen and people with diplomatic immunity travel on trains to and from Hungary every day. Trains still deliver manufactured goods, farm produce, machinery, and businessmen every day. We just need to get on one of those trains with proper credentials."

"Right. We need to pass out as many Swiss letters as we can," Theresa said. "Then the holders will have diplomatic immunity. Can we get one hundred thousand?"

Carl shook his head. "We are promised eight thousand, and that is the limit. Remember, we increased the number from eight thousand individuals to eight thousand families. I can try to convince Bern to print more, but I doubt they will. We may need to manufacture more certificates, passports, and letters ourselves, in our own print shop."

"Seriously," Julia said. "You sound like me."

Carl shrugged. "I will keep requesting them from Bern, but we need other neutral governments to step up."

"Then what about Sweden? Sweden is a neutral country," Theresa said, "and the Swedish do business in and out of Hungary all the time. I know that Raoul Wallenberg's boss, Kálmán Lauer, is a Hungarian Jew. He was born here. He has traveled to Budapest with Raoul many times on business. Of course, Mr. Lauer is a Swedish citizen now, so he enjoys immunity. Sometimes he takes a plane, but more often, he and

Raoul take the train. What if Mr. Lauer could bring us letters of protection from Stockholm?"

"What if he brings us Rudy?" Julia said. "We need to contact him right away."

"He won't be able to do it on his own," Carl said. "Letters have to be sponsored by the Swedish government. Somehow, we have to convince the Swedish government to help out. Maybe your friend Rudy has influence. I know I can't ask Bern to make the request of Sweden; they would consider it a violation of their duty to remain impartial."

"What if the US were to request it?" Julia said. "I mean confidentially, behind the scenes. I'm thinking of the War Refugee Board."

"That is a possibility, I suppose. What influence does the WRB have in Stockholm?"

"I don't know," Julia said. "I am scheduled to place a call to John Pehle at four o'clock this afternoon. Maybe John can forward a request through diplomatic channels. Knowing the WRB, that's why it was chartered."

"That would be good to hear. Ask John and let me know. Right now, however, I have to travel to Geneva," Carl said. "I may be gone for a few days. It has to do with the meeting I just concluded. I'll tell you all about it when I return."

AT FOUR PM Budapest time, ten AM Washington time, Julia and Theresa placed a call to John Pehle.

"Twelve thousand people in one day?" John said incredulously. "How can they possibly do that?"

"There are trains running day and night," Julia said. "I am told that two hundred thousand Jews have already been taken from southern Hungary and are on their way to camps in Poland. The SS hasn't come into Budapest yet, but it won't be long."

"What is Carl doing?" he asked.

"Right now, he's traveling to Switzerland. Geneva, I think. He said he had an important report to deliver to his government, and he was sure we would find out about it soon. Until then, he couldn't discuss it. He has already supplied three thousand letters of protection indicating that the bearer is under the protection of the Swiss government, and we are promised five thousand more, but Switzerland doesn't want to go beyond that amount. They are very hesitant about getting involved or being perceived as partial. They fear they will lose their status. If they do, all of the letters will be worthless. Theresa and I believe that Sweden, also a respected neutral country, is in a position to help. Raoul Wallenberg is a very good friend. His family is prominent in Sweden, as is his boss, Kálmán Lauer. Raoul has traveled to Budapest on business with Mr. Lauer before. If the US were to make a humanitarian request, the Swedish government might authorize letters of protection for Hungarian Jews. But it would have to be done right away. Maybe the WRB could suggest such a request, you know, maybe with President Roosevelt. Hungary loses tens of thousands of Jews every day."

"One thing that troubles me," John said. "If we succeed in passing out thousands and thousands of letters of protection, at what point will Berlin see this as a ploy for making Jews untouchable? At what point will Berlin realize that all of the Jews in Hungary are not diplomats or Swiss citizens? If that happens, then all we have will be worthless pieces of paper."

"Well, for one thing, Berlin doesn't know how many letters are being distributed, nor do they know who has one," Julia said. "There are no records. No one is keeping an index of individuals holding Swiss letters. All a Nazi agent knows is that a person produces an official paper with the holder's name and a number between one and eight thousand. It's not public knowledge how many have been issued or to whom. But you have a point. Sooner or later, there may be so many Swiss letters that Berlin will conclude it is a ruse. That's why Switzerland has limited them to eight thousand, and that is why we need other sources."

"I promise that the WRB will do whatever we can to put through an official request to Sweden," John said. "Let me get off the phone and I will get to work."

CHAPTER THIRTY-NINE

A WEEK LATER, Carl returned from Geneva. He immediately called Julia, Theresa, Martin, and three staff members to room 217. He asked them to have a seat at the conference table. In front of each of them was a copy of a report running thirty-three pages. Tapping his index finger on the cover of the report, Carl said, "Before you is a report prepared by Rudolf Vrba and Alfred Wetzler. It was originally written in Slovak, but it has been translated into several languages, including Hungarian, English, and German."

Martin started to pick up the report and leaf through it, but Carl said, "Not yet, Martin. Let me tell you about it first, then all of you may examine it. I was meeting with two gentlemen three days ago when Julia stopped by, but I couldn't interrupt my meeting to talk to her. I apologize."

Julia smiled and nodded.

"It was because of this report. Believe me when I say it is momentous. It is the proof that Bernhard was seeking before he could tell the world the story about the Auschwitz-Birkenau detention camp. It is such an important story that, if told without proof, it would be pushed aside. No one would believe it. Rudolf and Alfred have written it all in such great detail, with hand-drawn sketches of the rooms, that it cannot be denied."

Carl continued to tap on the report with his finger like a hammer drill. "Rudolf Vrba and Alfred Wetzler are two Slovakian Jewish men who were taken into custody by the Nazis as they marched through Bratislava two years ago. They were transported to Auschwitz, much like Hungarian Jews are being transported today. When they arrived, they exited a train and stood in line. They waited while an SS officer went through the line, person by person, doing quick selections: those who would live and those who would die. Alfred and Rudolf were big and strong, and they were selected as laborers. They continued to survive because they were strong, were hard workers, and didn't cause trouble. They were sent throughout the camp doing construction and repairs, carrying heavy equipment, digging trenches. As such, they were able to observe the daily lives of the other prisoners, those who were selected to go to the right and those who unfortunately went to the left—those who lived and those who died."

Carl looked around the table. "Do you want to hear the rest and read this report? It isn't easy, and it's not a requirement. It takes a strong stomach, but it's the kind of report that can change the world. If you stay, I will want you to help me distribute and publicize this report as best you can."

Julia, Theresa, and Martin quietly nodded.

"The report says that in March 1943, the Nazis inaugurated the first crematorium at their concentration camp. To demonstrate its efficiency, they took eight thousand Kraków Jews and subjected them to gassing and cremation. They did this before an audience of German officers and civilians. In fact, the camp personnel drilled special peepholes in the wall so that the guests could view the gas chambers in use. The events of that day are described on page 13 of the report. You will also see a sketch of the gas chamber and people inside."

At that moment, Theresa gagged and ran out of the room.

"I'm so sorry," Carl said. "We can stop here, if you wish. The report contains more descriptions like that."

"I'll stay and hear the finish," Martin said. "I want to know what is in the report and what kind of people we're facing."

"I want to know what the rest of the world will find out," Julia said. "If I have to be the one to tell them, I will. The world needs to know what kind of people the Nazis are."

Carl nodded. "Yes, they do, and they will all know soon. This report is presently being sent through diplomatic channels around the world, but you are certainly welcome to tell anyone you choose. The Vrba-

Wetzler report relates in gruesome detail what happened to those who were selected to die, or who had outlived their usefulness. On page 18: 'When everybody is inside, the heavy doors are closed. Then there is a short pause, presumably to allow the room temperature to rise to a certain level, after which SS men with gas masks climb on the roof, open the traps, and shake down a preparation in powder from out of tin cans labeled "CYKLON: For use against vermin," which is manufactured by a Hamburg concern.'"

Hearing that, Julia and Martin sat with faces frozen in shock.

"'People clawed at the walls with their fingernails, they screamed, and they charged against the door.' We are talking about men, women, and even children. All ages. When the screaming stopped and the room was silent, and after a time had passed for the gas to disperse, the bodies were carted out."

Julia and Martin both stood. Now they had heard enough.

"I'm sorry again," Carl said, "but I want you both to know what we are going to do with this report. Before we discuss it, Julia, why don't you go out and see how Theresa is? If she's up to it, I would like her to be included in the balance of our discussion. We will need the cooperation and assistance of her father."

A few minutes later, Julia returned with Theresa. Theresa's eyes were red, and she carried a handkerchief. She was embarrassed and she apologized, but Carl waved it off.

"I felt the same way when I first read this report," he said. "I cried, and it stayed with me all night."

Theresa nodded.

"György Mandl, also called George Mantello in Switzerland, is presently serving as the first secretary to El Salvador's embassy in Geneva. I know him well. Maybe Benjamin Weissbach knows him too, for he comes from Budapest and is an Orthodox Jew. George has a close friend, a diplomat from Romania, Florian Manoliu, who lives here in Budapest."

Carl pointed to the report. "Florian was the person who initially received the report from Vrba and Wetzler. After reading the report, Florian wanted the world to know. He met with Vrba and Wetzler, and then he met with me. He showed me the report. He wanted me to deliver it to his good friend George Mantello when I returned to Geneva. That was the secret meeting I had a week ago. Florian asked me if I could help get the report published. They knew that it would have to be published from Switzerland to be believed. It would be considered factually unbiased, and the world would soon read about it. So, I took it back with me to Geneva and gave it to George. Three days ago, it was published, and it has lit a fire. The world is reading it, officially and through the underground. There are protests all over Switzerland: street protests, sermons in Protestant churches, a huge press campaign has started and spread all over the world with over four hundred glaring headlines. They call it Europe's twentieth-century Dark Age and barbarism. By the way, publishing this report was contrary to Swiss rules, but it happened anyway."

"Sermons in the Protestant churches?" asked Martin. "I'm Protestant. What church, and what did they say?"

"Do you know Pastor Paul Vogt?" Carl asked.

Martin nodded enthusiastically, responding, "Yes. I do. Very well."

"Pastor Vogt arranged for thousands of copies of the report to be made and distributed. Literally thousands. He preached a series of sermons, which then appeared in the world press. Pastor Vogt laid the blame squarely on German and Hungarian governments for being complicit in the murder of Jews in the Nazi camps."

Carl took out a folded section from the Sunday Geneva newspaper. On the pages, the headline was GENESIS 4:9–10. "This section was repeated in several newspapers across Switzerland, and then elsewhere. It repeated Pastor Vogt's sermon. Want to see?" Carl unrolled the newspaper section.

Then the Lord said to Cain, "Where is your brother Abel?"
"I don't know," he replied. "Am I my brother's keeper?"

The Lord said, "What hast thou done? Behold! Your brother's blood cries out to me from the earth." Today, God's scrutinizing and inquiring eyes are focused upon us Christians. And He demands of us, Where, where, where! Where is your brother, the homeless Jew? . . . Where are the homeless Jewish children today?

"Winston Churchill himself read the article and responded with a letter to the press. This is what was written."

There is no doubt that this persecution of Jews in Hungary and their expulsion from enemy territory is probably the greatest and most horrible crime ever committed in the whole history of the world.

Theresa clapped. "The whole world will now condemn Hitler and Germany, but more importantly, maybe the Hungarian people will now rise up and treat their brothers and sisters humanely. Maybe they will force Horthy to leave."

"You're right, Terri. President Roosevelt called for the German and Hungarian officials, including Regent Horthy, to be tried as war criminals when the war is over. The president called for the WRB to find a solution to the genocide being perpetrated by Germany and Hungary. When you talk to John Pehle this afternoon, no doubt he will tell you."

"IT'S TRUE," SAID John to Julia and Theresa when they called. "The president responded to the growing furor over the Vrba-Wetzler report. I suppose FDR had to. After all, Churchill wrote that blasting opinion in the *Times*. Just last night, the president reached out to us at the WRB. We had a meeting and appointed Iver C. Olsen as the War Refugee Board representative in Stockholm, Sweden. In addition to his duties with the WRB, Olsen is also confidentially employed as the chief of currency operations for the Stockholm station of the Office of Strategic Services. He will provide US funds when and where needed for rescue operations."

"You mean if someone like Raoul Wallenberg needs money to run a rescue operation, Mr. Olsen will fund it with WRB money?"

"That's exactly what I mean. Given the Vrba-Wetzler report, Congress is loosening its tight grip on money for refugee rescues. And you will be happy to know that because of you and Theresa, and your suggestions regarding Raoul Wallenberg, the WRB is reaching out to the Swedish foreign ministry. We are asking that a Swede be appointed to lead a mission to rescue the Jews of Budapest. In addition to you two, Wallenberg is recommended by his former manager, Kálmán Lauer, who says that Wallenberg is the right man for the job and possesses all the qualities needed."

"Oh, you have no idea," Julia said. "All the qualities and then some. Do you want us to reach out to him and tell him that a formal request is coming?"

"It wouldn't hurt. I understand he is a part owner of the Central European Trading Company. Until recently, they did quite a bit of business here in Budapest, but since March, when the Nazis invaded, the activities have stopped."

"That is understandable," Theresa said. "Mr. Lauer is Jewish, though I don't know why Raoul would stop coming here. And now he is being contacted by the WRB?"

Carl nodded. "I am scheduled to have a telephone conversation with him later this afternoon. Do either of you care to be present? You may be able to influence him to accept the appointment."

"I care to be present," said Julia enthusiastically. "What time?"

Carl smiled. "Four o'clock. See you then. In the meantime, I suggest that both you and Theresa meet with Theresa's father and the rabbi of the Great Synagogue and bring him up to date on the present state of affairs."

Theresa held up a copy of the report. "May I take a copy with me? I think the rabbi and my father should be informed. I don't know what they will do or tell their congregants, but I don't want to keep it secret."

CHAPTER FORTY

THE GREAT SYNAGOGUE seemed a bit less crowded than it had the last time Theresa visited. Maybe homeless families had moved into some of the seventy-six safe houses that Gertrud had leased. Now owned by Switzerland and identified with Swiss markings, they were beyond the reach of the Hungarian or German authorities. The most recent acquisition was Arthur Weiss's Glass House. It was a well-known glass manufacturing facility that was shut down by the Nazis. Arthur had since disappeared. Gertrud acquired it, and now it housed over two thousand residents at any given time. It was busy. Still, even as of this date, there were many families living in the sanctuary of the synagogue. Almost all of them wore yellow stars with the word *Jude*. In fact, walking through the neighborhood, one might encounter dozens of pedestrians with the same star.

"Your father is in the clinic," Rabbi Wise said, gesturing to the back corner of the room.

Theresa's forehead wrinkled. "The clinic? Here? What clinic?"

"That would be the room formerly used as the assistant rabbi's office. Now there is an examining bed and medical supplies. Your sister, Becca, takes leave from her nursing duties at Semmelweis University Hospital now and then to help your father out. There are a lot of sick kids."

"We just came from a very important meeting at the Swiss embassy and we were advised to come here to talk to you and Apa," Theresa said. "Did you hear about the Vrba-Wetzler report?"

The rabbi shrugged. "I know who Alfred Wetzler is. He's not a member here, and I don't know anything about his report."

"Is my father available?" Theresa asked. "Can he take a break from his clinic? Can he join us? I'd prefer not to relay this story in pieces."

"I'll bring him to the study as soon as he is free," Rabbi said.

THIRTY MINUTES LATER, a weary Benjamin Weissbach, wearing a stained doctor's gown, came into the study with Rabbi Wise. He hugged his daughter and told her how much he missed spending time with her and how he wished the times were different. "Still, it is heartwarming to see you, and you too, Julia. Rabbi tells me that you have something important to discuss."

Theresa laid a copy of the Vrba-Wetzler report on the table. "You know that the Nazis have been gathering all of the Jewish citizens in the Hungarian countryside and putting them into trains to be shipped to the Auschwitz camp, don't you?"

Both the rabbi and Benjamin nodded. "Samu has been telling us about it," Rabbi Levy said. "Most of the families living south of Budapest have been taken into custody and shipped north. The Nazis haven't moved their operation into Budapest, and we are hopeful that they never will. We don't know why they are concentrating on the farmland. Maybe it is just because they don't trust Jews, and they can't keep an eye on them when they are so spread out. At least that is what Samu thinks. He warns us that it may happen here in Budapest soon, and if it does, just cooperate. We're on the lookout for the Nazis, you'd better believe it."

"You know it isn't just the Nazis," Julia said. "They couldn't do this on their own. They couldn't herd a hundred thousand Jews into small towns and hold them until the trains take them north. They need the help of the Hungarian soldiers. And the Nazis don't drive the trains. The Hungarians do. This deadly operation couldn't happen without the cooperation of the Hungarian leadership."

"I suppose that is correct," Benjamin said. "Even so, Samu says that if we don't cooperate, things will go very badly. If we do cooperate, then they won't harm us."

"He's a liar," Theresa said vehemently. "Over three hundred thousand Jews have been transported from Hungarian small towns to ghettos and then to the Auschwitz camp. What happens there is beyond your imagination. The prisoners are taken off the train, and . . . and . . . I'm sorry. I can't continue. It's all in the report. Read it and then we'll discuss it."

BENJAMIN AND RABBI Wise sat turning the pages in the report. They were silent, but tears filled their eyes. "Who has seen this report?" Benjamin asked. "Is it valid?"

"The whole world has seen it. The whole damn world except the Nazi-occupied countries, although I'm sure that sooner or later it will find its way in. I just hope there are Jews still alive when it does, and that steps are taken to save them. Both Germany and Hungary have been condemned by Churchill, Roosevelt, the pope, religious leaders, and other government officials all over the world."

"Three hundred thousand Jews?" said the rabbi with a choke in his throat. "Lovely innocent people whom I have married, and celebrated their bat and bar mitzvas. They have come to services, I have seen them smile and dance." He shook his head. "Why? Why are they now being put to death in the most inhumane way possible?"

"What do your authorities recommend?" Benjamin asked Julia. "What are we to do?"

"That is the same question we asked in the Netherlands," Julia said, "and the answer was to save as many lives as you can. We can't save them all. We have already lost three hundred thousand, but maybe we can save the little boy you just doctored, and his family, and the families in this hall. Their lives are all precious, and we must fight to save them."

"I understand. That has been my life's profession. I have dedicated my life to saving people one at a time. How do I do that now?"

Theresa answered, "Number one: Encourage everyone to get a letter of protection. They are still being prepared, and they are being honored.

Make sure they understand that they must declare themselves to be under the protection of Switzerland and exempt from Hungarian restrictions. The Nazis won't question the validity."

"We've run out of Swiss letters of protection," Benjamin said. "We passed them all out to families. We had six hundred, and they were given to six hundred families, which covered about twenty-eight hundred people."

"That's good. Then maybe we have saved twenty-eight hundred lives. We will soon have more letters," Theresa said. "We hope to get them from Sweden and even El Salvador, and then we can save more."

Tears rolled down Theresa's cheeks. Benjamin went over and put his arms around her. He hugged her and told her how much he loved her and what a wonderful girl she was.

"But every day, twelve thousand more Hungarians are taken and put into a gas chamber because they're Jewish. Why, Apa? How can one human do this to another? I know that the Nazis are cruel, soulless people, but why are Hungarians stepping up and joining them? Why is Hungary turning against its own people, the ones they knew, the ones they grew up with and played with in the schoolyard? Why is Miklós Horthy telling his military to help round up the people and transport them by trains? I can't understand why my fellow Hungarians want to kill me and my sister and my mother and . . ." Theresa couldn't finish.

The rabbi asked, "When we talked about what your superiors are suggesting for us, you said number one was the letters of protection issued by neutral countries. What is number two?"

Julia stepped forward. "Number two is to get out of Hungary whenever you get the chance. Everyone won't get a letter. There just won't be enough to go around, and who knows how long those letters will be honored? You need to get out of this godforsaken country."

"That's why you came here in the first place last winter, isn't it, Terri? You came to take Anya and me out of Hungary before it reached this level. Isn't that right?" Benjamin said. "But we didn't listen."

"Don't blame yourself; it wasn't like this six months ago. When Julia and I arrived, we were surprised at how calm Budapest was and how safe the community was. We were all fooled, just like you."

"How are we supposed to get out of Hungary?" said the rabbi. "The borders are closed. Hungary is surrounded by Axis countries, none of which have many Jewish residents left. Our people are probably thinking the same thing."

"You must believe there is a way. There are people that care about you—brilliant, honest, righteous people with goodness in their hearts. They are working on finding ways to save as many lives as they can." Theresa counted them off on her fingers. "Carl Lutz, his staff at the Swiss embassy, John Pehle and the War Refugee Board in Washington, Gisi Fleischmann and the Bratislava Working Group in Slovakia, the Jewish Council, Ira Hirschman, Ottó Komoly and the Aid and Rescue Committee, and so many more. Their combined efforts have saved and will save hundreds of thousands of people."

"Ira Hirschman led eight thousand Jews out of Hungary, through Romania, down to Turkey, and then to Palestine. He did it because he sought and obtained permission from those countries. And don't forget about Sweden. We are reaching out to Raoul, and he is a good man," said Julia.

"I know that good people will come forward," said the rabbi. "We just have to pray that it happens sooner rather than later for so many."

Theresa nodded. "They will find a way."

Julia checked her watch. "Right now, we have to return to the embassy. There is a phone call from a certain Swedish man, and we have to join the call."

IN THE EMBASSY'S first-floor communications room, telephone connections had been established between Budapest and Stockholm. Julia, Theresa, Martin, and Carl stood together waiting for Raoul Wallenberg to come on the line. It had all been arranged by the WRB. In fact, they had spent considerable time explaining the situation to the Swedish foreign ministry and the representatives of King Gustav V.

"This is Raoul Wallenberg," said the voice on the line. To Julia, the sound was immediately recognizable, and her heart skipped a beat. It seemed like yesterday.

"Raoul, this is Swiss Vice Consul Carl Lutz. Thank you for placing the call this morning. We are given to understand that you have been in contact with John Pehle at the War Refugee Board in Washington."

"I have, and I have been in lengthy discussions with our government, including King Gustav. I might add that King Gustav is very upset, having read the Vrba-Wetzler report. King Gustav spoke with Sir Winston Churchill earlier today."

"All of us here in Budapest share your alarm," Carl said. "Something must be done to save the lives of the innocent people who are in harm's way through no fault of their own. As we speak, trains are leaving from Hungary carrying thousands of souls. We welcome your assistance on behalf of the Kingdom of Sweden."

"It is my honor, and I appreciate the privilege of being allowed to participate. I hope to see you soon. I am making arrangements for the manufacture of Swedish Schutz-Passes right now. They will identify the holder as a Swedish citizen."

"Wonderful. We look forward to you and your Schutz-Passes," Carl said. "By the way, there are a couple of people here who would like to say hello, if that's all right."

"Sure. Who would that be?"

"Hi, Rudy," said Julia, with a lump in her throat. "It's been a long time."

"Julie, is that you? I can't believe it. What are you doing in Budapest? The last I heard, you were in Holland, but that was a few years ago."

"I came here with Theresa to help her family. Now I am staying to help as many people as I can. We both work as administrative assistants to Carl at the Swiss embassy."

From over Julia's shoulder. a voice said, "Hi, Rudy, it's Terri Weissbach."

"Oh, my goodness, Terri. This is such a pleasant surprise. I can't wait to see you both. I wish it were under different circumstances, but we'll have a Wolverine reunion. I should get in over the weekend. I'll be staying at Kálmán's apartment. See you on the ninth."

CHAPTER FORTY-ONE

THE FIRST STEP on Raoul Wallenberg's Budapest agenda was to check in at the Swedish legation office. Then he was scheduled to spend the day with Carl Lutz at the Swiss embassy and become better acquainted with the situation in Hungary. He didn't need to familiarize himself with Budapest, as he had spent many a day in the ancient city. He had even been there, off and on, during the war, but not since the Germans had taken control. Not since there had been a *Judenfrei* operation. Carl had requested that Julia and Theresa be present as well, if that wouldn't step on Raoul's plans. "Definitely not," he answered. "I am so pleased that they are working for you."

For Julia, the reunion was a bit awkward. A hug from Raoul made her feel as if it were only yesterday. A thousand memories circled around in her head. Oh, the choices she had made, the paths she had followed. Had she done otherwise, had she stayed with Rudy, had she never met Spencer and his stupid band, life would have been so much different. They were a good couple in Michigan. Who knows what would have developed? But then, there would have been no Amsterdam, nor that part of her life when she helped to save so many children. Nor would she had experienced the times she'd spent with Teddy and Sara and the underground rescue group. The receipt of her Distinguished Service Medal would never have happened. Nonetheless, his hug brought back memories of warm nights and joyful days in Ann Arbor. She was happy to see him. He hadn't changed a bit.

I wonder if he's experiencing the same feelings I am, she thought. *They say he never married, at least not yet.* Julia looked over at Theresa, who was enjoying the reunion as well, though she had never known Rudy romantically. They were just good friends.

After a few minutes of small talk, it was time to get down to business. "I understand that trains are leaving every day from Hungary and heading straight to the Auschwitz concentration camp," Raoul said. "Twelve thousand a day, isn't that what you told me? How many have they taken and how many are left?"

"Very good questions," Carl said. "We estimate that four hundred forty thousand people have been taken, never to be heard from again. They were primarily from the countryside, outside of Budapest. It is thought that somewhere around four hundred thousand Jews are left in all of Hungary, including Budapest. Many have received letters of protection, and many are living in safe houses rented or owned by Switzerland. Those houses have identification badges on the front, showing that they are Swiss owned and occupied."

"Two days ago, the pope joined other nations' leaders, including our Swedish King Gustav, in condemning Miklós Horthy, the ruler of Hungary, for allowing his military and transportation militia to cooperate with the Nazis and transport his Jewish subjects to their deaths," said Raoul. "King Gustav also joined with Churchill, Roosevelt, and other leaders in demanding that Horthy be tried for war crimes and sentenced to a similar fate."

"That's true," said Carl, "and it had an effect. When it seemed like the whole world was coming down on him, Horthy ordered the Auschwitz transports to be paused. As of today, trains have stopped transporting Jews out of the country. It's unclear how that will sit with the Nazis, but Horthy called for his military and train personnel to cease all train transports leaving Hungary."

"Did the Nazis also stop arresting people in the countryside? I have heard that the Nazis have not, but is that true? Are they still arresting people?"

"We don't know," Carl said. "This is all happening in real time. There have been no major announcements coming from Hungarian leadership.

No one has declared that the Jews are free to leave, or that they won't be arrested, or that they can have their phones or their cars or that any restrictions have been lifted. Horthy may have the title of regent, but Hungary is still under German control. Eichmann is still in charge. His mission has always been to remove Jews from wherever they can be found and then send them north to Auschwitz. He may not have the manpower to run the trains right now, but don't fool yourselves. It's Eichmann, not Horthy, who will dictate the future of Jews in Hungary." Carl turned to Raoul and the envelope he was carrying. "It's quiet at the moment, but one cannot trust the Nazis. So it is still of the utmost importance that we pass out our letters of protection. I understand that you brought Swedish documents."

Raoul reached into the envelope and took out a stack of papers. "There are Schutz-Passes, or safe passes. I was able to convince the Ministry of Foreign Affairs to issue forty-five hundred passes to begin. Believe me, I have the full support of my government."

"You're lucky," Carl said. "Mine has set a limit, and no more letters of protection can be issued."

"And they are also sending volunteers to help me," Raoul added. "They have set aside offices here at the Swedish legation. They have authorized me to rent thirty-two safe houses for Jewish refugees. Of great importance, I am authorized to declare Jews of Hungarian origin to be Swedish citizens. My capital has made the political choice to admit these migrants as immigrants after the war, on humanitarian grounds, should they be able to make their way to Sweden."

"God bless them," Carl said. "I know of no other country willing to do that. Certainly not Switzerland."

"And not the United States either," Julia said.

Carl reached behind him and pulled out another stack of papers. "You remember George Mantello. He and his good friend Florian Manoliu were the ones who brought the Vrba-Wetzler report to me. George is the first secretary in the El Salvador consulate in Geneva." Carl held up papers. "I am holding one thousand citizenship papers formally issued by El Salvador. All that is needed is for the holder to print his name and put a picture of his face on the certificate and he is then a recognized citizen of El Salvador. Because of Salvadoran neutrality, the holder is free to come and go as he pleases. The Germans and the border police in Hungary and in Romania will honor that status. George said we will have thirteen thousand by the end of the week."

Raoul examined one of the Salvadoran passports and said, "How are these to be authenticated? If a Nazi officer was to question the validity of the Swedish Schutz-Pass, he could contact the Swedish legation. They would verify it. How is someone to authenticate a citizenship paper from El Salvador?"

"Same way. Contact the Salvadoran embassy in Geneva. They'll verify it."

Carl stood. "Okay, we all have passes. Let's get out there and distribute them. It's a beautiful day."

CHAPTER FORTY-TWO

IT WAS A few days later when Carl summoned his staff to the conference room. The staff numbered thirteen, including Julia and Theresa, of course. Raoul was present as well. "I have some disturbing news today," Carl said. "The Germans have discharged Miklós Horthy and removed him from his position as regent. He has been stripped of all his powers. In his place, the Germans have appointed the Hungarian Arrow Cross Party to run the country. Identifying itself as the Hungarian National Socialist Party, it is in fact a far-right Fascist party beholden to Eichmann and Hitler. It sides with the Germans in all things and is extremely antisemitic. Ferenc Szálasi is to be the prime minister. It didn't take but a few hours for him to issue an order to begin rounding up Jews and holding them in close quarters until he can arrange to ship them north. I'm afraid that things are going from bad to worse."

"I thought the Hungarians were the only ones capable of operating the transit system to Auschwitz," said Julia. "That's what we were told. That is why it was so effective for Horthy to order a stoppage."

"Horthy is gone," Carl said, "but the Arrow Cross Party is made up of Hungarians. I don't know how many trainloads they are planning, but I saw them leading groups of captives in single file out of town. They were heading west, toward Austria."

"So it is more important than ever to pass out the passports, the citizenship papers, and protection letters," Raoul said.

"The letters and passports are wonderful, and so far, they're working," said Julia. "When people get stopped and they produce a letter, they are detained for a moment and then released. Until the next time. But that's not the solution. Getting these people out of the country and away from the Nazi murderers is the only guarantee of safety. Ira Hirschmann took eight thousand people south through Romania to the sea, through Turkey, and then to Palestine. Now they can lead a life without fear. Ira was the WRB's representative to Romania at one time. That's why he didn't have a problem. Don't we have a contact in Romania now who could arrange for us to take refugees through?"

"If you are talking about the Romanian diplomat Florian Manoliu, he lives here in Budapest, and he is a friend," Carl said.

"Couldn't he arrange for us to lead groups through Romania? Especially if the group had Swedish or Salvadoran IDs?"

Carl nodded. "I don't know why not. You would still need someone to assemble and manage the group and a staff to lead them on that pilgrimage. I'll talk to Florian. But you are a hundred percent right when you said that the Germans, with the help of the Arrow Cross Party, want to eliminate all the Jews. The writing is on the wall. The only answer is to get them all valid IDs or, better yet, lead them out of the country. And time is not on our side. We must move quickly." He looked at Julia and Theresa. "I need you two to work on passes this afternoon. There are a number of blank Swiss letters of protection. They may not be genuine, but they are dead look-alikes. And they bear the numbers one to eight thousand, just like the originals. When viewed in the field, one at a time, who can tell the difference? They must be made to appear authentic with signatures and stamps. The markers and tools for making the letters are in the drawers."

"Yes, sir," they said.

LATER THAT AFTERNOON, while Julia and Theresa were working on the letters, Martin and Carl came into the office. "Give us all of the letters and passports you can right now," Carl said. "Give the Swiss letters to me and the Salvadoran letters to Martin. There is a line of Jewish prisoners being marched on foot toward Austria by Hungarian soldiers with rifles. It's an Arrow Cross death march. They are no doubt on their way to trucks or trains that will take them to the Mauthausen concentration camp."

Julia and Theresa packaged the letters and certificates and handed them to Carl, Martin, Paul, and another staff member. "Where are you taking these letters?" Theresa asked.

"We are going to drive out to where they are marching and pass them out to the prisoners. Paul, Martin, and I are taking our cars." He looked at Theresa. "Do you want to come? We could use the help. You can ride with us."

Theresa was shocked. "You are going to hand out letters to prisoners on a death march, even though the letters are fake and don't come from Switzerland?"

"Yes. Do you want to come? If you do, hop in the car."

The group drove out toward the west sections of Hungary. The cars had insignias plastered on the doors that identified them as owned and operated by Switzerland, and each of the staff members wore a red vest with a Swiss insignia in the middle. After forty minutes, they saw the end of the line on the trail. There were men, women, and even children being forced to walk thirty miles or more. If they fell or could not walk any farther, they were shot.

When they reached the line, they parked the cars on the side of the road in the grass, and the staff members, including Julia and Theresa, quickly exited and walked directly toward the line. They saw the guards, but ignored them as they were told to do. The guards shouted at them to leave, that they had no business interfering with Hungary's right to manage their prisoners.

Carl walked forward, sticking out his chest. "You are the ones who have no right!" he yelled. "They are diplomatically immune. They are Swiss citizens. You are violating international law, and we will report you immediately to your leader, Heinrich Himmler, Reichsführer of the Schutzstaffel, commander of the SS! It is you who will be arrested and thrown into prison if you interfere with our right to protect our Swiss citizens."

One of the guards countered with, "How are we supposed to know? They're wearing their yellow stars."

Julia, Theresa, and Carl's staff members were quickly handing out letters of protection to people in the line, to fathers and mothers, saying, "You are a Swiss citizen, and this letter proves it. It applies to your entire family. The Germans cannot order you around. Neither can the Arrow Cross. Take off that star; they must let you go free. Come with us." They passed them out until there were no letters left, gesturing for the captives to follow and walk in the opposite direction. "If the guards come over here to challenge you, wave that letter at them. The guards will know you are protected."

"You know, that doesn't always work," Martin whispered to Theresa. "The other day, Nathan Ashburg was stopped by the Arrow Cross. He pulled out his Swiss letter of protection and showed it to them. One of the Arrow Cross grabbed it and tore it into pieces, saying, 'What letter?' Then they arrested Nathan and took him away. No one has seen him since. They don't know where he is." Martin grimaced with tight lips. "I'm just saying that the letters work with the SS, but when it comes to the Arrow Cross, you can't count on them. They don't give a damn."

Some of the guards looked at the letters, talked to one another, showed them to a superior, and handed them back. Those with letters were allowed to walk with Carl's staff members back toward Budapest.

"I wish we had more letters," Theresa said.

"Then let's head back to the embassy," Julia said.

THERESA AND JULIA were busy creating more Swiss letters of protection with numbers between one and eight thousand when a staff member notified Theresa that her mother was in the vestibule. "My mother!" Theresa shrieked, jumped out of her chair, and darted to the entrance hall. There stood Greta Weissbach, and she was upset.

"Terri, Terri, the Arrow people were just at the house! They demanded to see Apa, but he wasn't there. I said he was at the synagogue, but they said no. Then he might be at the hospital, I said. They were nasty people, Terri, and one of them grabbed my arm. 'You come with us until we meet with Dr. Weissbach.' He started to pull me toward the door. Althea started barking at him, and another Arrow said, 'Take the dog instead.' Then he talked right into my face with his terrible breath and said, 'You tell your husband that he can pick up the dog at the station. If he doesn't show, we'll come back for you.' They threw a rope around Althea and left."

"Did they say what they wanted with Apa? Did they tell you the reason?"

Greta shook her head. I heard one of them say, "He's a leader of his people. If we take him, others will follow without question."

That afternoon, Carl, Martin, Julia, and Theresa walked to 60 Andrássy Avenue and requested an audience with Ferenc Szálasi, the leader of the ruling Arrow Cross Party. "Well, well, Mr. Ambassador, to what do we owe the pleasure?" Szálasi said.

"Two of your militiamen appeared at a Swiss residence today and demanded to see a resident, also covered by a Swiss letter of protection. When he was not at home, they took the family's dog. This is a flagrant disregard of Swiss diplomatic immunity. That immunity is guaranteed to us by Herr Hitler and Herr Himmler. Even Herr Eichmann respects the independence of Switzerland and those under its protection. I would hate to tell them it is being disregarded. I am due to meet with them next week."

"Oh, most honorable Swiss ambassador, I wouldn't dream of violating our sacred treaties. My men and I both understood that Dr. Weissbach has a Jude shield on his front door and he wears a Jewish star on his clothes. We saw no Swiss shields, and there is no Swiss marking on his person. You can't be both, can you?" Szálasi wrinkled his forehead to convey his state of confusion. "You'll forgive us for concluding that he is merely a Jew."

"What do you want of the doctor?" Carl asked.

"That is the private business of the Hungarian government," Szálasi said with a smile on his face. Then he sat back and tapped his chin with his index finger. "Even if he were to have Swiss identification, of which I am not convinced, there is no breach of our mutual diplomacy in asking Dr. Weissbach a few questions here at the station."

"In fact, there is," Carl said. "He is diplomatically immune from the

Hungarian legal process. We insist that you leave Dr. Weissbach and his family alone."

"We'll take that under consideration, Ambassador Lutz, and you may leave now. Oh, by the way, convey my condolences to the Weissbachs. The dog died."

CHAPTER FORTY-THREE

THE WEISSBACH FAMILY was about to sit down and have a family brunch, this time in celebration of Becca's twenty-sixth birthday. Anya had prepared a lovely breakfast, even though some of the favorite dishes were missing. For example, there were no chocolate tortes. Shopping in the Jewish quarter of town had become more difficult. Many of the shops were shuttered. Deliveries of goods and materials to Jewish stores had been curtailed. Neither the Germans nor the Arrow Cross Party had begun Auschwitz deportation activities in central Budapest, but people realized that it could happen any day. On the street, the fear on people's faces was as palpable as the star on their jacket.

A large portion of the homeless refugees had found shelter in safe houses, thanks to Gertrud and Raoul, but there were still families living in the synagogue. Benjamin had taken to operating his clinic almost every day, and the Jewish community knew it. There were lines at the synagogue starting at eight thirty each morning. He was assisted by his nurse, Becca.

As the family sat at the breakfast table and prepared to recite the berakah, the blessing before a meal, each could think of a list of prayers they thought would be more appropriate. "To me, it is more important to pray for the blessing of peace, of civility, of kindness, and an end to this horrific cruelty," said Becca, "than it is to bless the bread. In light of what is going on, a simple berakah lacks substance and meaning for me."

Benjamin shook his head. "We will continue to recite our berakah. It is important not to lose our faith and our Jewish identity. We thank the Lord for the food we are about to eat."

Suddenly, there was a loud knock on the door. Someone was rapping with their knuckles. "Dr. Weissbach! Dr. Weissbach! Please open the door!"

It was Paul, Carl's assistant, and he was frantic. "A woman has been shot," he said. "Carl rescued her and brought her to the embassy, but the poor woman is bleeding badly. He sent me to get you, Dr. Weissbach."

Benjamin jumped to his feet and headed for the door. "Becca, go to the clinic, grab my bag and essential trauma supplies. I will meet you at the Swiss embassy." With that, Benjamin, Theresa, and Julia dashed out the front door and headed down the street.

"She is in room 207," said Martin. He was shaking. "She's lying on a couch. Carl is trying to help her with a compress on the wound." He led Dr. Weissbach to the room and opened the door. Carl had his hand on her side over the wound. He looked like he had just walked in from a rainstorm, soaking wet, head to foot, still dressed in his suit and tie.

"Okay, I'll take it from here," Benjamin said. In a moment, Becca joined him, and the others left the room.

Carl went to change his clothes as Martin explained what had happened. "We were walking along the river near the base of Castle Hill, when the Arrow Cross gang led a group of women to the edge of the river. The women were all wearing those yellow stars. They lined them up on the bank of the Danube, and one by one, they started to shoot them. Carl shouted, 'No! Stop that!' and ran toward the women. Then one of the gunmen pointed his rifle to shoot Carl, but another one interfered. 'Don't shoot him; he's a politician from the Swiss embassy. We'll get into trouble.' So the man shrugged, turned to his left, and shot a woman standing right in front of Carl. Then he pushed her into the river. Without a second thought, Carl jumped into the river to save her. He dove under the water, grabbed the woman, and pulled her to the riverbank. Then we carried her here to the office."

As Julia stood in the hallway, Theresa's father was trying to save the life of a woman maliciously shot, all because she wore a yellow star. A single thought ran through Julia's mind: *The time has come to finish what we came here to do.* Seven months earlier, when she stood with Theresa in the Treasury Building, their goal was to come to Budapest and check on her parents. If necessary, and if possible, they would help her mother, father, sister, and brother leave Hungary and escape to a safe land. They were told by the WRB that the Jewish community in Hungary was still safe and unharmed. They were assured by other individuals that the Germans had not taken any measures against them. Notwithstanding, they took the opportunity to travel to Budapest so that Theresa could be reunited with her parents, even if only for a short while.

Now, half of Hungary's Jewish population had been tyrannically murdered in the cruelest way imaginable. There was no longer any deniability. The Vrba-Wetzler report provided solid proof of the murders, and the world had been informed. The world's leaders were outraged, but it didn't seem to slow the killings down. The remainder of the Jewish community was in immediate danger of being slaughtered in the same manner. Julia knew that it had happened elsewhere; to the three million in Poland, to the quarter million in Romania, to the quarter million in Czechoslovakia, to the seventy-five thousand in France, and now, to at least a half million in Hungary.

How little Julia and Theresa knew back in January when they had made their plans in Washington. They would come to Budapest with Carl Lutz, see her parents, and, if the time was right, they would help them leave. Well, the time had been right months ago, but they were still there. As far as Julia was concerned, the mission was now to save as many innocent people as she could, but how to go about it?

From what Julia had learned, it seemed as though an escape route existed going south through Romania, but they would need cooperation and support. Julia decided to contact John Pehle and ask him and the WRB to put their heads together and devise a plan to take as many as she could out of the jaws of death, to safety and freedom, far from Hungary.

* * *

"SHE IS GOING to live," said Becca, coming out of the room. "Apa did an amazing job. The woman—her name is Sylvia Katz—is fortunate that Apa is such a fine surgeon. The bullet grazed her ribs, not far from a major artery. Apa was able to stitch her up."

"Why did Arrow Cross choose those eight women and bring them to the river?" Julia said.

"They are members of the same synagogue," Becca answered. "When they came out of morning prayers, they were grabbed by those men, their hands were tied, and they were taken to the river to die. They didn't do anything other than walk out the synagogue's front door wearing their yellow stars. I have heard that women wearing yellow stars were grabbed and beaten, but this is the first time that I know of that they were lined up and shot."

"No place is safe," Julia said, "and no person is safe, especially not Apa. We need to leave Hungary."

"Easier said than done," Becca replied.

CHAPTER FORTY-FOUR

IT WAS NINE AM Washington time when Julia placed a call to John Pehle. "Good morning, John," she said in a serious tone. "Do you have a few minutes to talk to me?"

"Always. Are you all right?"

"Personally, yes, but the conditions here have deteriorated badly over the past several days, and they're getting worse by the hour."

"That's what I understand. I spoke to Carl earlier this morning. He filled me in on the recent attacks by the Arrow Cross regime. We are so proud of Carl. The man is a genuine hero. Imagine jumping into the Danube in his business suit to save a woman who had been shot by the Arrow Cross gang."

"I don't have to imagine it," Julia said. "I saw him right afterward. I'm witnessing what's happening here, and in a way, that is why I called you. I want to do more than witness. I want to make a difference. The Arrow Cross have their eyes on the rest of the Jewish community, like a hungry wolf, starting with the leaders. They came by to arrest Dr. Weissbach at his home, but fortunately, he wasn't there. Now I hear they are asking about the rabbi. They want to take away the leaders so the people have no guidance. John, I want to save lives before the Nazis and the Arrow Cross take them all away. They've already killed more than half the Jewish population here, over four hundred forty thousand."

"What do you have in mind, Julia?"

"I want to take a large number of Jews out of here, to a place they can be safe. I thought maybe the WRB could help me."

John made a whistling sound. "No one can accuse Julia Powers of lacking courage. Okay then, let me ask some basic questions. How many are you contemplating? How will they be chosen? Where are you planning to take them, and how are you going to get there? Who is going with you? Who will lead them? Do you have answers to those questions yet, or are you still in the planning stage?"

"How many? As many as I can take to a place far away. If we don't rescue them, John, they will die. They will be taken by a train to Auschwitz and poisoned, or marched to the Mauthausen camp in Austria, or murdered in cold blood in the middle of a Budapest street. If you witnessed it, if you saw it, you wouldn't believe your own eyes, that such a wicked, bloodless gang of devils would . . . would . . ." The rest was garbled. Julia was crying so hard she couldn't finish the sentence.

"Julia, I'm here for you," John said. "Calm down, if you can. We're going to make this happen. You're going to take some people out. We're going to save some lives. Let me work on it and see what I can come up with. Have you spoken to Carl or Raoul about your plan? Are Theresa and her father part of your preparation?"

"I haven't spoken to anyone yet," Julia said. "Not even Theresa. It came to me as Dr. Weissbach was doctoring that poor mother who was shot for no reason and pushed into the river. They shot her for fun, John. I cannot stand by and watch any more of this. I have to do something. Will you help me?"

"Yes, I can, and yes, I will. I will contact essential people. In the meantime, you need to provide a reasonable estimate of the size of a group that can be rescued. I need to know in order to arrange for the transports. Is it three hundred or a thousand? Or more? How soon will you have the group assembled? Then I'd like to know how many of them would have passports, letters of protection, or foreign birth certificates."

"I'll get that information to you as soon as I can. I will have to meet with Carl and Theresa."

"And Raoul Wallenberg, make sure you include him. He knows the territory, and he wields a lot of influence. And Dr. Weissbach, and maybe the rabbi. They will all help you choose and assemble the emigrants."

"Certainly. I didn't mean to leave anybody out."

"Call your meeting, but expect that there will be resistance to such a bold move. That's typical. Let them share their ideas with you. Let them know you spoke with me and that the WRB is behind it."

"I will."

"Call me whenever you can," said John. "I will work on it from my end. I'd also like to run this by Carl and Raoul, if you don't mind."

"I SHOULD HAVE expected it," Theresa said with a smile. "You want to bring a group of Jewish families out of Hungary, away from the Arrow Cross, and take them somewhere safe. But you don't know where you will be taking them yet, right? Have you talked to John Pehle about it?"

"I did, and I'm even more encouraged. We're going to take people out of Hungary before the Arrow Cross can kill them, and you know they will. It's like Holland. You can't save them all, but you can try to save as many as possible. John told me to have a meeting and invite important people like you and your father. Are you in agreement? Do you want to come with me and rescue as many as you can?"

Theresa nodded. "I sure do. It seems like a Herculean task, but I'm with you."

"Then get your father, and let's meet with him, and maybe the rabbi. John is planning on talking to Carl and Raoul. They will tell us what is possible and what is impossible."

THE GREAT SYNAGOGUE was even less crowded than the last time Julia was there. The number of families had decreased, not because they were arrested but because they were now living in the safe houses that were acquired by Gertrud and Raoul. There were over one hundred units now housing thousands of residents. They had emblems on each of the doors showing that the properties were owned by Switzerland or Sweden. They were untouchable, and so were the people who lived inside, as long as they stayed inside. Those who remained in their own homes, like Apa and Anya, were required to paste a yellow shield on the door reading *Jude*. Even though he and Anya had Swiss IDs, Apa chose to put a Jude shield on his door, and he wore a yellow star on his jacket, all to show solidarity with his community. If he was stopped, he would show his Swiss ID, but it was risky. Who knew what the Arrow Cross Party would do? Would they tell him that he couldn't be both? Would they tell him that he was a Jew and he couldn't change it?

The Arrow Cross had recently taken to breaking into houses that had *Jude* on the door. As a result, many of the residents had taken them down, even though they didn't have Swiss or Swedish IDs. That was a direct violation of Hungarian law because they were required to identify themselves. It was doubly dangerous because the Arrow Cross had an index of where the Jews lived. Many were afraid to live alone, so they were now living in the synagogue.

Theresa, Benjamin, and Rabbi Levy met with Julia in the rabbi's study. Julia told them about her plan, that she had decided to take a group out of Hungary to safety. She told them what she had discussed with John Pehle and the questions he wanted answered. She told him that she didn't know how many families would want to go. She would have to find out. She needed experienced leaders for the journey, like Rabbi Levy and Benjamin Weissbach. Wherever the group of refugees settled, wherever the WRB thought it best, they would need leaders to help establish and run a settlement. Of the greatest importance, they would need financial support. Wherever they landed, wherever they settled, they would need to make a home. They would need housing, they would need essentials.

"I applaud you for taking the initiative to rescue our endangered people," said Rabbi Levy. "And I am honored that you think I should go with you as a leader, but I cannot leave my flock. Their fate is mine, and I am here to guide them and comfort them. That is the vow I have taken."

"You would still be guiding them," Julia said, "but in a new land. A land with no Nazis or Arrow Crosses. Maybe it will be a bigger number than you lead here, or maybe not. Apa, will you go with us? And bring Anya and Becca and Aunt Pearl?"

Benjamin grimaced and shrugged. "You should certainly take Anya and

Becca, but for me, I don't know. How can I leave my fellow congregants, the ones I have led for so many years? Just like Rabbi Levy, their fate is mine."

Surprisingly, the rabbi turned to Benjamin and said, "Ben, I disagree with you. You won't be *leaving* your congregants; you will be *leading* them. As powerful and determined as these two young girls are, you can't put the entire burden of the pilgrimage on their backs. The people respect you and look up to you. They already recognize you as a leader. They will need you as they make their way on their journey and as they build their settlement in a new land."

Benjamin realized that the rabbi was right, and he nodded. "I thank you, Rabbi. I will do my best." Then he looked at Julia and Theresa. "Where is the journey going to take us, Julia, and how are we going to get there? Hungary is landlocked in the middle of Axis Europe. Are we going to Switzerland? Do you have answers to those questions? Is this a dream, or are plans actually being formed?"

"I don't have answers yet," Julia said, "but I did discuss this at some length with John, and it's not just a dream; it's going to happen. I asked him where we could take our journey. As I'm sure you are aware, there are no close destinations that are safe. I initially thought of Switzerland too, but it is a thousand-mile journey through Austria and Germany, and Carl said that Switzerland is opposed to mass immigration. Not that they don't like us, but the immigration quotas would prevent it, and it wouldn't be our permanent home. They have restrictive quotas like the US. Then I thought of Sweden and what King Gustav said after he read the Vrba-Wetzler report. He said that Sweden would welcome us and make us all citizens. But getting there is the problem. It's a two-thousand-mile journey, almost all of it through the heart of Nazi Germany. That leaves British Mandatory Palestine, and according to John, that should be our destination. It is a thirteen-hundred-mile journey through Romania and Turkey and then on to Tel Aviv."

"Do we have permission to travel through Romania?" Rabbi Levy asked.

"John is working on that, and he is confident we will have it. Ira Hirschman was an ambassador there."

"What about Palestine?" the rabbi said. "I understand the British are very strict with their immigration rules. Will they let us settle there? I remember the Balfour Declaration. We discussed it in synagogue and whether some should consider moving to Palestine. The Balfour Declaration said, 'His Majesty's Government view with favour the establishment in Palestine of a national home for the Jewish people.'"

"That was in 1917," Benjamin said. "Their attitude has changed. Because of the Arab uprising and the tensions between the British and the Arabs in Mandatory Palestine, the British Parliament issued a formal statement called the White Paper of 1939, which placed restrictions on further Jewish immigration."

"So the British ignored what they said in the Balfour Declaration?" Theresa asked.

"Not exactly, but they placed tight restrictions to appease the Arabs," Benjamin answered.

"John thinks he can get diplomatic permission for a settlement through the WRB. Remember, it was Churchill who so vehemently condemned what was revealed in the Vrba-Wetzler report and called for the Nazi leaders to be tried for war crimes."

The rabbi spread his hands. "Then who is going to lead this pilgrimage to Palestine, and who are the pilgrims?"

"Those were John's questions this morning," Julia said. "Now it is in our lap, and we must supply the answers. Which families will go with us? How should we make up this list?"

The group looked to Benjamin. "Rabbi and I will talk to families, one at a time," he said, "and determine who is prepared to make this journey and start a new life in a new land. It won't be easy, and many will choose not to go. They would rather rely on their letters of protection or just hope that the Arrow Cross doesn't come to them."

"I am scheduled to talk to John tomorrow morning," Julia said. "I will be anxious to learn who he was able to talk to and who will be involved. How long will it take him to line up the transports? How will it be financed? When he does tell us, how much time will we have to get ready? It might be very short. That means that you need to start talking to potential passengers right now."

"Be aware," Benjamin said, "that our conversations with families must be confidential. We can't afford to let the Arrow Cross know of our plans to escape. As much as they want us out of Hungary, they would take all measures to prevent it. They only want us to go north to Auschwitz."

CHAPTER FORTY-FIVE

THERESA AND JULIA spent the next two days trying to solve tricky issues. For several reasons, they decided that their convoy train should not leave from Budapest's central station. That station was full of Arrow Cross personnel or Nazi SS. They were still shipping Jews north to Auschwitz and Majdanek, although at a slower pace.

"In fact," Julia said to Theresa, "Raoul Wallenberg was at the station yesterday handing out Schutz-Passes to Jewish prisoners by pushing them through the train windows. At one point, when the SS blocked his way on the platform, he climbed up and walked on the roof of the train, leaning over and reaching the passes down to passengers' hands sticking out the windows. 'Those are Swedish subjects!' he yelled. He thought that while the Arrow Cross might disregard them and not let the holders off the train, the Germans would honor them at the camps and let them go free."

Julia decided that she and Theresa should check out the train stations on the line south of Budapest. They drove south to Cegléd. Arriving at the smaller, quieter station, Theresa said, "It makes sense to leave from here, but how do we get all our passengers out of Budapest and down to this station?"

Julia shrugged. "I am supposed to meet with Carl later today, and we will have John on the phone with us. How are your father and Rabbi Levy doing signing up families for the journey to the new settlement?"

"It's surprising, for many different reasons," she said. "Some of the families are too frightened to make such a long journey, especially with small children. Some are just the opposite. They may have small children, but they're ready to go. They're willing to brave the journey so their children can grow up in a free land. Some of the families are choosing to stay in Budapest because they have Swiss or Swedish passes, and they're confident in the protection provided. Others are afraid that when the Arrow Cross runs out of prisoners with yellow stars who have no passes, they will take anyone they can find, letters of protection or not. Many believe that Eichmann and the Arrow Cross will never stop as long as there is a single Jew left alive."

"How many are on the passenger list so far?"

"So far, Apa and Rabbi say that one hundred fifty families are signed up."

Julia smiled and nodded. "So that's about six hundred people, more or less. Terrific, but we can take more than that. Many more. Tell them to keep trying."

CARL, MARTIN, AND Raoul were waiting in the embassy communications room when Theresa and Julia arrived. "We spoke to the Cegléd station engineer, Gunther Walz, a very nice man," Julia reported. "He said that the SS hasn't been at his station for weeks. When Horthy was removed and Szálasi appointed, the Arrow Cross started transporting all the Jewish prisoners from the central station, Budapest Keleti. Gunther told us that when the SS did transport from his location, they would load prisoners either in passenger cars or boxcars or both. Passenger cars would seat anywhere between fifty and one hundred people. Boxcars more. Trains with twenty cars could carry up to three thousand people."

Then they heard John's voice over the speakerphone. "I'm here with Theodore Hartigan, who has volunteered to spend some of his off-hours working on this project. We have been in touch with Ira Hirschman in Ankara, Turkey. As you may know, Ira marshaled eight thousand people from Slovakia to Hungary and then to Palestine in a series of transports. He is very anxious to assist in bringing your group down from Hungary. He is assisted by Laurence Steinhardt, the US ambassador to

Turkey. You may know him, Julia; he was with the State Department as a senior diplomat."

"I know him," Raoul said. "He was the US first minister to Sweden in 1937, the year I returned home. He was awarded the Order of the Polar Star in 1936 by King Gustav. I believe he is Jewish."

"That is correct," John said. "He played a major role in rescuing a group of Jewish children from Romania, bringing them down to Turkey. He is a very valuable contact, and we're asking him to do the same for you. He is credited with rescuing many refugees, including American airmen who were shot down in bombing raids in southern Europe. I mention all this because we talked to Laurence, and he is anxious to help your convoy make its way from Hungary all the way to Palestine. He and Ira would like to help you establish a settlement in Palestine, not far from where Laurence and his family live. He told me that his contacts in Bulgaria should make it easier for you to travel all the way to Turkey on land without having to cross the Black Sea."

"That would be wonderful," Julia said. "When would he and Ira be ready to help us? I ask that because Gunther Walz told me that next Tuesday is a very quiet day at the Cegléd yards. There are no freight trains scheduled that he knows of, but if they came, it would be later in the day. It would be best for him to help us load our group, starting early in the morning."

"Will we be ready by then?" Theresa asked.

"I will have a Swedish train to take us south, and I should be ready by then," Raoul answered. "Naturally, I will go with you and make sure that everyone along the way knows it is an official Swedish legation train under the authority of King Gustav V. Just tell me how many cars you will need."

Julia smiled and thought, *Dependable Rudy. I always wondered how I let him get away, but the truth is, I wasn't prepared for the long haul. I needed to grow up. Maybe neither of us was ready back then. Maybe we never would be right for each other. Or maybe . . .*

Martin spoke up. "How will all the passengers get from their homes in Budapest to the train station at Cegléd? Have we made arrangements?"

"Since they are all in Budapest," Carl said, "we can provide trucks to pick them up at various stops in the city. Talk to your father, Theresa, and give me a list of people and convenient pickup spots."

"I have an idea," Julia said. "Assuming that SS and Gestapo and Arrow Cross men will be roaming the streets, like they do all day long, I propose that we leave in the middle of the night. I don't ever see them walking around at that time."

"Excellent idea," said Carl. "Let's start picking up families at three AM."

"And we'll arrange for our train to leave Cegléd first thing in the morning," Raoul said.

CHAPTER FORTY-SIX

IT WAS A clear, moonlit night in late September when a canvas-covered pickup truck stopped at the corner of Cinclolai and Kereztun. In less than a minute, three families came out of a building, stuffed pillowcases in hand, and climbed into the back of the truck. The families had been told not to make a sound. The truck's next stop was six blocks away. Ten blocks east of the Great Synagogue, a red farm delivery truck stopped in front of a large apartment building. It was quickly filled with eight families carrying their small bags of luggage. When it was fully loaded, it drove toward the Cegléd station, six miles south. The trucks unloaded their passengers, turned around, and headed back for more.

As the trucks arrived, Raoul and Julia were there to greet the families and help them step down. They led the passengers in the direction of the waiting train. The engine was belching steam. Benjamin and Theresa stood waiting on the platform, showing them their assigned cars and helping them climb the steps with their bags. Becca and Greta helped them find their seats. Sometimes it was necessary for the children to sit on their parents' laps, but it was the middle of the night, and they were sleepy anyway. When the passenger cars were full, the boxcars, with carpets and blankets on the floors, were loaded next. Altogether, there were thirty-one cars. Three thousand two hundred Jewish passengers would soon be heading south through Hungary.

At six AM, the Stockholm Express, as Julia called it, pulled out of the Cegléd station and headed for Oradea, Romania, two hundred miles to the south. Five hours later, the train pulled into the Oradea station. By then, everyone was wide awake and had made a serious dent in the boxes of food that Raoul had supplied with the train. At the Oradea station, they were met by Ira Hirschman and Laurence Steinhardt. They had secured permission for the train to travel south through Romania. Everyone was given thirty minutes to stretch their legs, get a snack, and climb aboard the train headed toward the Turkish border, five hours away.

For most of the trip, Julia and Theresa, the two best friends, sat together, so proud of what they had done. They had met up in Michigan, traveled to Washington, and flown to Budapest. They had seen it turn from a safe, prosperous town to the most dangerous place on earth. They had rescued Theresa's family, as was their mission, and were taking them to a new life and a new settlement in Palestine. Benjamin would lead his flock, find a new rabbi, and form a new synagogue. He and Becca would start a clinic and care for the group. Many would put their skills to work. Some were carpenters, some were mechanics, some were teachers, some were restaurateurs, some were shopkeepers, and thankfully, some were farmers. There were two dentists, one barber, and a woman who ran a beauty salon. Each of them would be needed.

As for Julia and Theresa, and what the future had in store for them, they were with the group. For the time being, they would be settlers. Even if they wanted to leave, there wasn't anywhere else for them to go. They were never going back to Hungary, maybe not to Europe either. They couldn't get back to the US while the war was going on. To a great extent, they were responsible for the new settlement, and they intended to throw their lot in with the rest. That was just fine. They were safe, and they were among friends.

AUTHOR'S NOTE

The Righteous is a literary work in the genre of historical fiction, which I have always thought was something of a contradiction in terms. After all, history is factual; it has occurred. Fiction is imaginary, a product of the author's creative mind. Yet they are frequently combined to tell a good story. For *The Righteous*, we have Julia Powers and Theresa Weissbach, college best friends, one from Michigan and the other from Budapest. Together, they tell a story of Hungary during the last years of World War II. As with my other novels, I have endeavored to relay the facts, the events, and the historical figures as close to reality as possible.

The story took place in and around Hungary in 1944. Prior thereto, Hungary's European neighbors had fallen victim to Nazi subjugation and the cruel decimation of their Jewish communities. Unlike those countries, Hungary was not overrun by the Germans in the first four years of the war. The Hungarian Jewish community, numbering almost a million citizens, had been relatively stable and undisturbed. Jews were not arrested or deported to concentration camps as they were in the other European countries. All that would change in 1944.

The world's response to the plight of European refugees was to change in 1944 as well. At that time, the US did not have an organization whose purpose was to aid or rescue European civilian refugees. Through the efforts of John Pehle, Josiah DuBois, Randolph Paul, and Secretary of the Treasury Henry Morgenthau, a document was drafted for the establishment of the US War Refugee Board. Its purpose was set forth in the following opening line: *"One of the greatest crimes in history, the slaughter of the Jewish people in Europe, is continuing unabated.*" On January 22, 1944, President Roosevelt signed the War Refugee Board into law, and it was funded through the Treasury Department. Our story traced the combined efforts of the War Refugee Board and its founders as they tried to save the lives of as many civilians as they could.

The book's title, *The Righteous*, refers to the individuals who came forward during those final years to aid and rescue innocent people from the Nazi terror. The term *righteous* is borrowed from Yad Vashem, Israel's official Holocaust memorial museum. Yad Vashem's memorial garden honors "the Righteous Among the Nations," specifically those non-Jewish persons who came forward to aid Jewish refugees during the war. For example, Yad Vashem honors Switzerland's Carl Lutz as righteous for the humanitarian rescues he accomplished. Similarly, Sweden's Raoul Wallenberg is honored. Both were instrumental in aiding and rescuing Hungarian Jews. The United States Holocaust Memorial Museum is located in the National Mall on a street called Raoul Wallenberg Place.

Our book expands the title *Righteous* to make it more inclusive. Within these pages, *righteous* is not limited to non-Jewish heroes; the story also follows righteous Jewish heroes, such as Ira Hirschman, Ottó Komoly, Gisi Fleischmann, Israel Kasztner, and Joel Brand. When our two fictional characters, Julia and Theresa, interact with one or more of these righteous individuals, you get to know them better. I have endeavored to portray them as accurately as possible.

Once again, this book would not have been possible without the kind assistance and contributions of others. I give my heartfelt thanks to those who made the publication and its circulation possible. They have lent their talents, encouraged me along the way, and helped me to complete this project. They have edited the manuscript in great detail and provided invaluable suggestions. No one has done that more faithfully and judiciously than my tireless wife, Monica, who reads each and every page as it comes out of the printer. My thanks go to the staff at St. Martin's Press. No author has ever had a better editor than St. Martin's Press editor in chief George Witte, who provided his valuable experience as he edited the manuscript word for word, punctuation mark for punctuation mark.

Thanks as well to the St. Martin's Press staff: Sophia Lauriello, Rivka Holler, and Hannah Dorosin, and thanks to the copy editors at ScriptAcuity Studio. Each spring, the Jewish Book Council sets the wheels in motion so that the Jewish Community Centers, the book clubs and reading groups are all introduced to the year's offerings, and my deep appreciation is given to Suzanne Swift, Evie Bernstein, Naomi Firestone Trotter, and Miri Pomerantz Dauber. Thanks to my agent, Mark Gottlieb, and Trident Media Group. And finally, thanks to my many friends and followers who want to know when my next book is coming out. With any luck, it's next September.

ABOUT THE AUTHOR

RONALD H. BALSON is an attorney, professor, and writer. His novel *The Girl from Berlin* won the National Jewish Book Award and was the Illinois Reading Council's adult fiction selection for the Illinois Reads program. He is also the author of *Eli's Promise* (a Target Book Club selection), *A Place to Hide, An Affair of Spies, Defending Britta Stein, Karolina's Twins, The Trust, Saving Sophie,* and the international bestseller *Once We Were Brothers.* He lives in Chicago.